GHOSTED

CREATED BY
JOSHUA WILLIAMSON

GHOSTED

JOSHUA WILLIAMSON
WRITER

JUAN JOSE RYP
ARTIST CHAPTER ONE

VLADIMIR KRSTIĆ LACI
ARTIST CHAPTERS TWO - FIVE

GORAN SUDZUKA
ARTIST CHAPTER FIVE

MIROSLAV MRVA
COLORIST

RUS WOOTON
LETTERER

SEAN MACKIEWICZ
EDITOR

SERIES COVERS BY
DAN PANOSIAN

COLLECTION COVER BY
MATTEO SCALERA

IMAGE COMICS, INC.
Robert Kirkman – Chief Operating Officer
Erik Larsen – Chief Financial Officer
Todd McFarlane – President
Marc Silvestri – Chief Executive Officer
Jim Valentino – Vice-President

Eric Stephenson – Publisher
Corey Murphy – Director of Sales
Jeremy Sullivan – Director of Digital Sales
Kat Salazar – Director of PR & Marketing
Emily Miller – Director of Operations
Branwyn Bigglestone – Senior Accounts Manager
Sarah Mello – Accounts Manager
Drew Gill – Art Director
Jonathan Chan – Production Manager
Meredith Wallace – Print Manager
Randy Okamura – Marketing Production Designer
David Brothers – Content Manager
Addison Duke – Production Artist
Vincent Kukua – Production Artist
Sasha Head – Production Artist
Tricia Ramos – Production Artist
Emilio Bautista – Sales Assistant
Jessica Ambriz – Administrative Assistant
IMAGECOMICS.COM

SKYBOUND

For SKYBOUND ENTERTAINMENT
Robert Kirkman - CEO
David Alpert - President
Sean Mackiewicz - Editorial Director
Shawn Kirkham - Director of Business Development
Brian Huntington - Online Editorial Director
June Alian - Publicity Director
Rachel Skidmore - Director of Media Development
Helen Leigh - Assistant Editor
Michael Williamson - Assistant Editor
Dan Petersen - Operations Manager
Sarah Effinger - Office Manager
Nick Palmer - Operations Coordinator
Lizzy Iverson - Administrative Assistant
Stephan Murillo - Administrative Assistant

International Inquiries: foreign@skybound.com
Licensing Inquiries: contact@skybound.com

WWW.SKYBOUND.COM

CHAPTER ONE

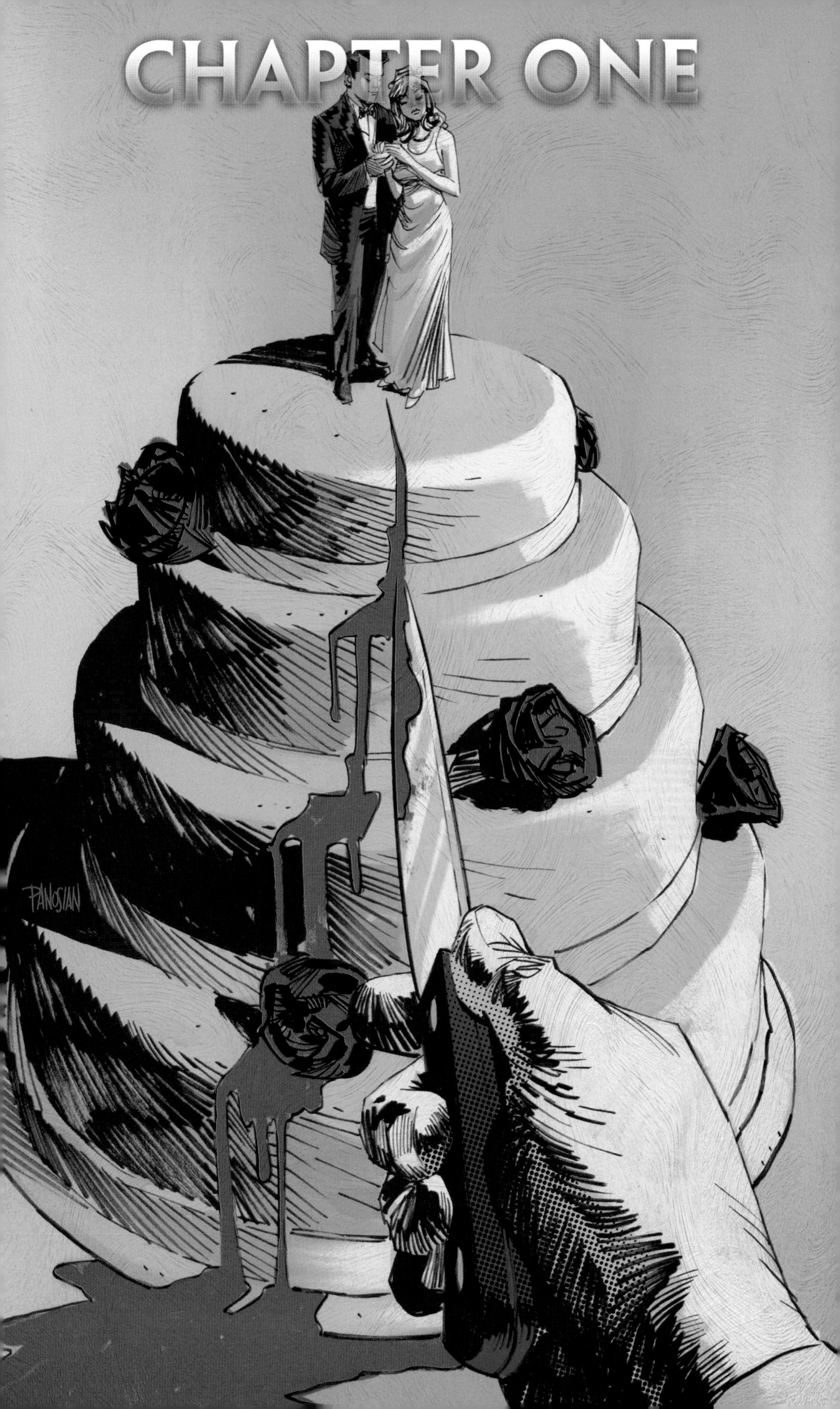
PANOSIAN

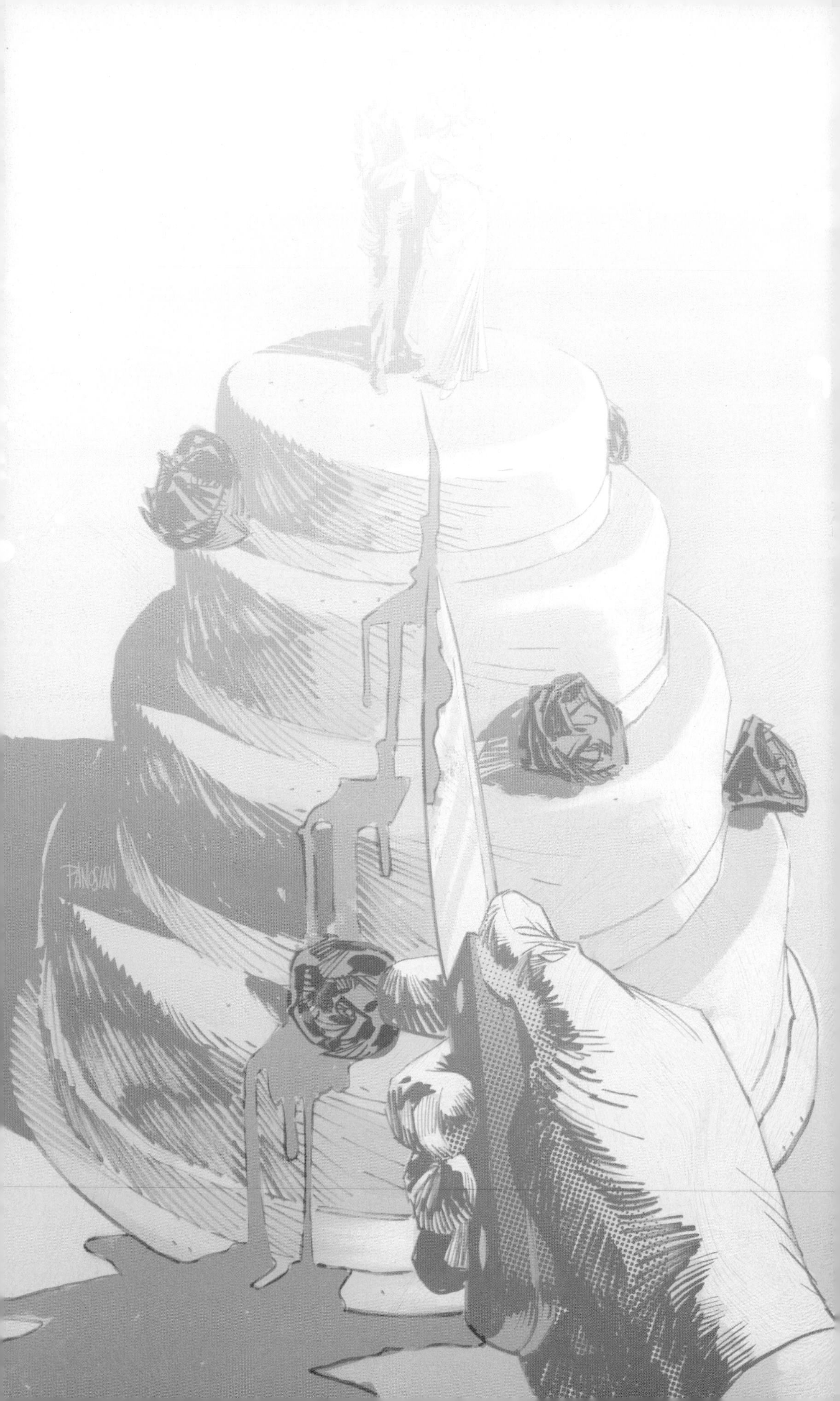
PANOSIAN

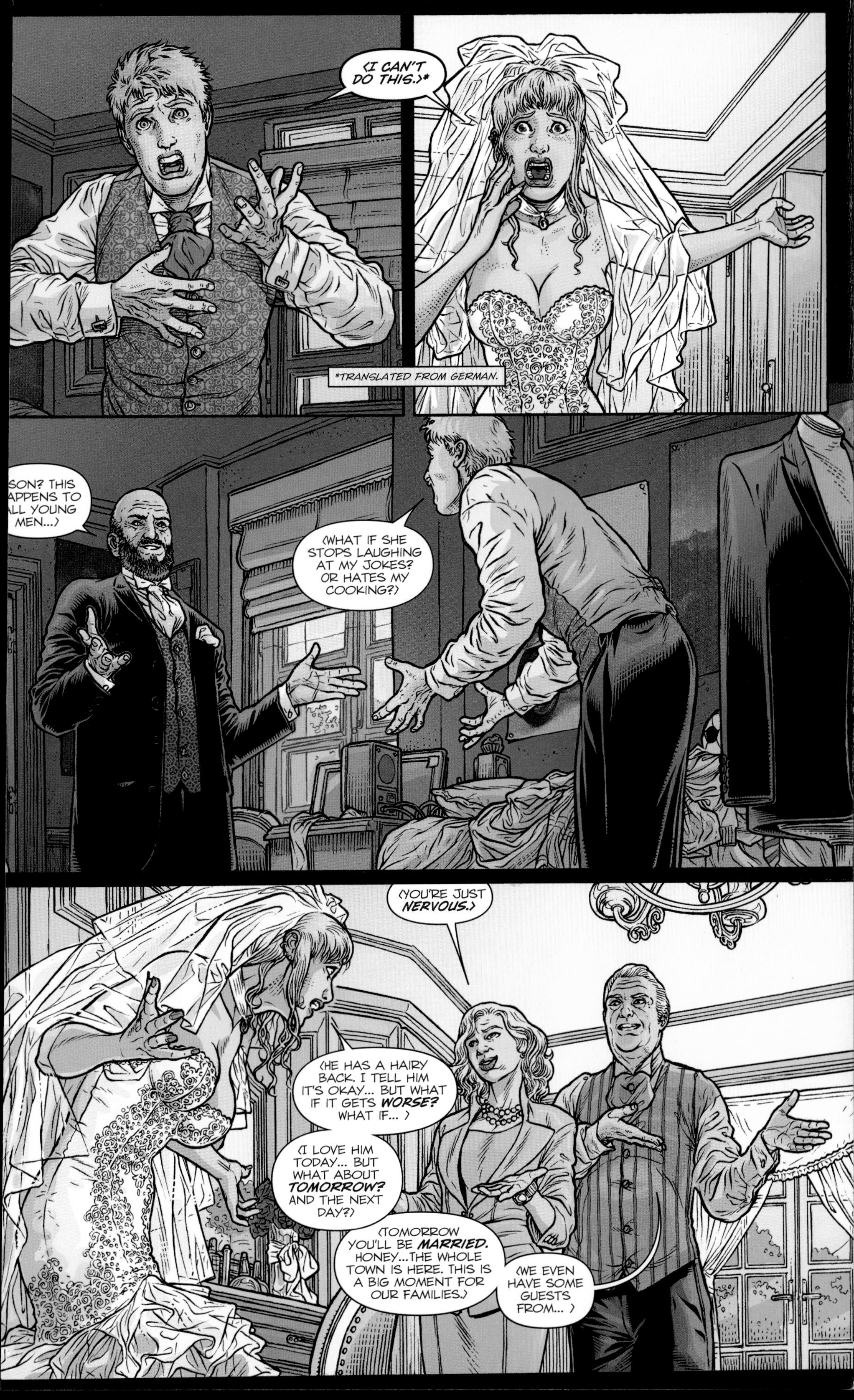

‹I CAN'T DO THIS.›*
*TRANSLATED FROM GERMAN.
SON? THIS APPENS TO ALL YOUNG MEN...›
‹WHAT IF SHE STOPS LAUGHING AT MY JOKES? OR HATES MY COOKING?›
‹YOU'RE JUST NERVOUS.›
‹HE HAS A HAIRY BACK. I TELL HIM IT'S OKAY... BUT WHAT IF IT GETS WORSE? WHAT IF... ›
‹I LOVE HIM TODAY... BUT WHAT ABOUT TOMORROW? AND THE NEXT DAY?›
‹TOMORROW YOU'LL BE MARRIED. HONEY...THE WHOLE TOWN IS HERE. THIS IS A BIG MOMENT FOR OUR FAMILIES.›
‹WE EVEN HAVE SOME GUESTS FROM... ›

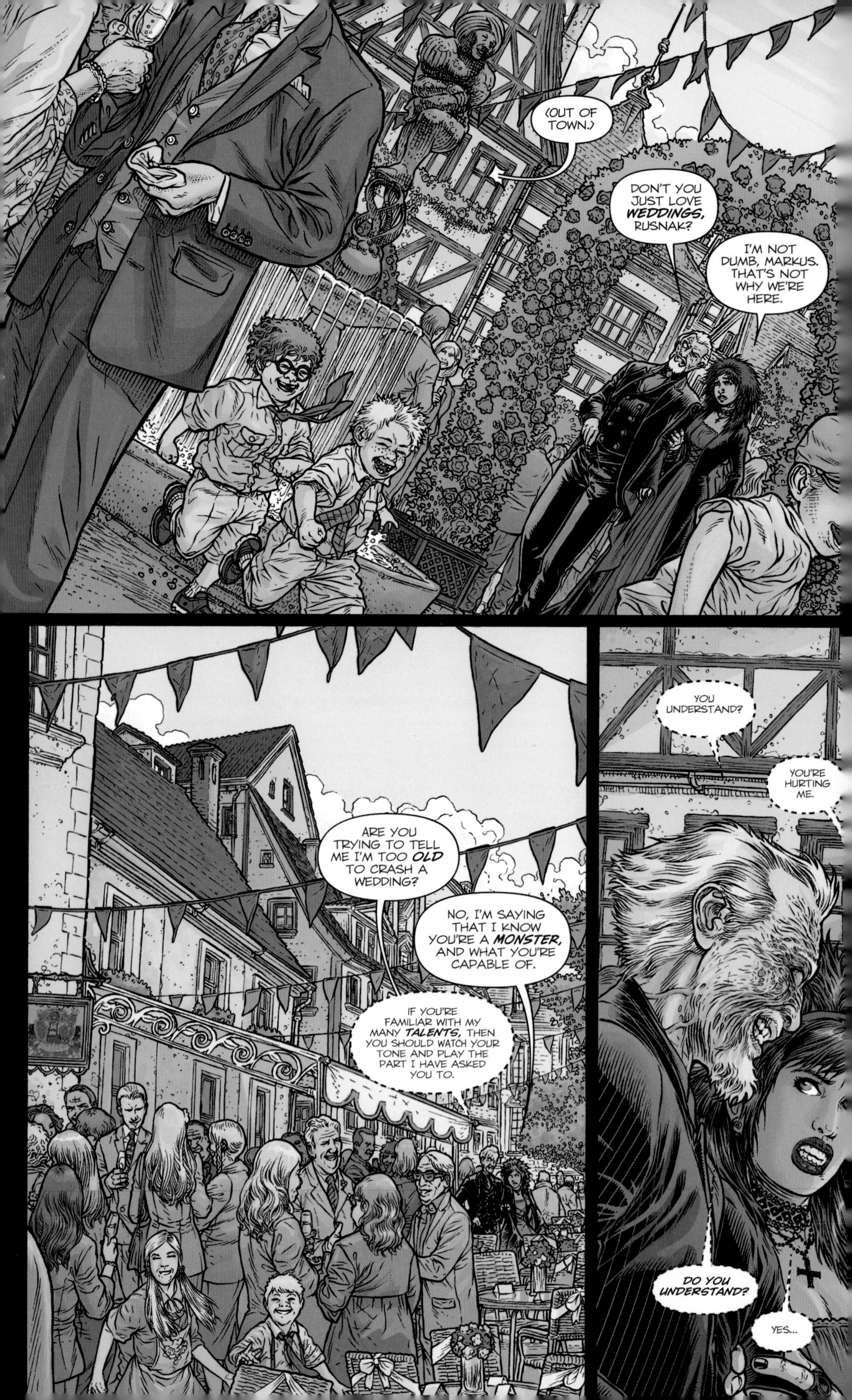
‹OUT OF TOWN.›
DON'T YOU JUST LOVE **WEDDINGS,** RUSNAK?
I'M NOT DUMB, MARKUS. THAT'S NOT WHY WE'RE HERE.
ARE YOU TRYING TO TELL ME I'M TOO **OLD** TO CRASH A WEDDING?
NO, I'M SAYING THAT I KNOW YOU'RE A **MONSTER,** AND WHAT YOU'RE CAPABLE OF.
IF YOU'RE FAMILIAR WITH MY MANY **TALENTS,** THEN YOU SHOULD WATCH YOUR TONE AND PLAY THE PART I HAVE ASKED YOU TO.
YOU UNDERSTAND?
YOU'RE HURTING ME.
DO YOU UNDERSTAND?
YES...

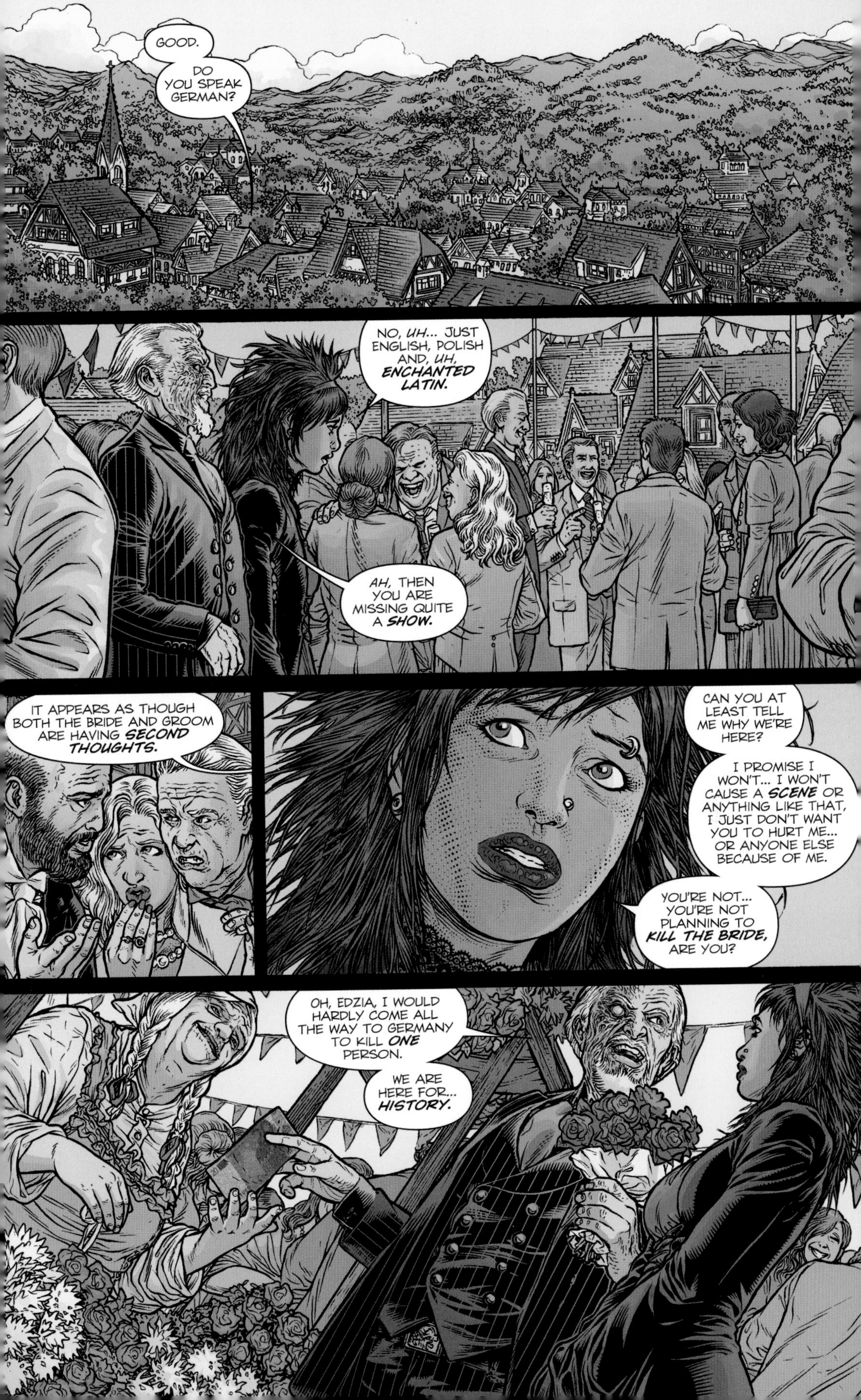
GOOD.
DO YOU SPEAK GERMAN?
NO, UH... JUST ENGLISH, POLISH AND, UH, ENCHANTED LATIN.
AH, THEN YOU ARE MISSING QUITE A SHOW.
IT APPEARS AS THOUGH BOTH THE BRIDE AND GROOM ARE HAVING SECOND THOUGHTS.
CAN YOU AT LEAST TELL ME WHY WE'RE HERE?
I PROMISE I WON'T... I WON'T CAUSE A SCENE OR ANYTHING LIKE THAT, I JUST DON'T WANT YOU TO HURT ME... OR ANYONE ELSE BECAUSE OF ME.
YOU'RE NOT... YOU'RE NOT PLANNING TO KILL THE BRIDE, ARE YOU?
OH, EDZIA, I WOULD HARDLY COME ALL THE WAY TO GERMANY TO KILL ONE PERSON.
WE ARE HERE FOR... HISTORY.

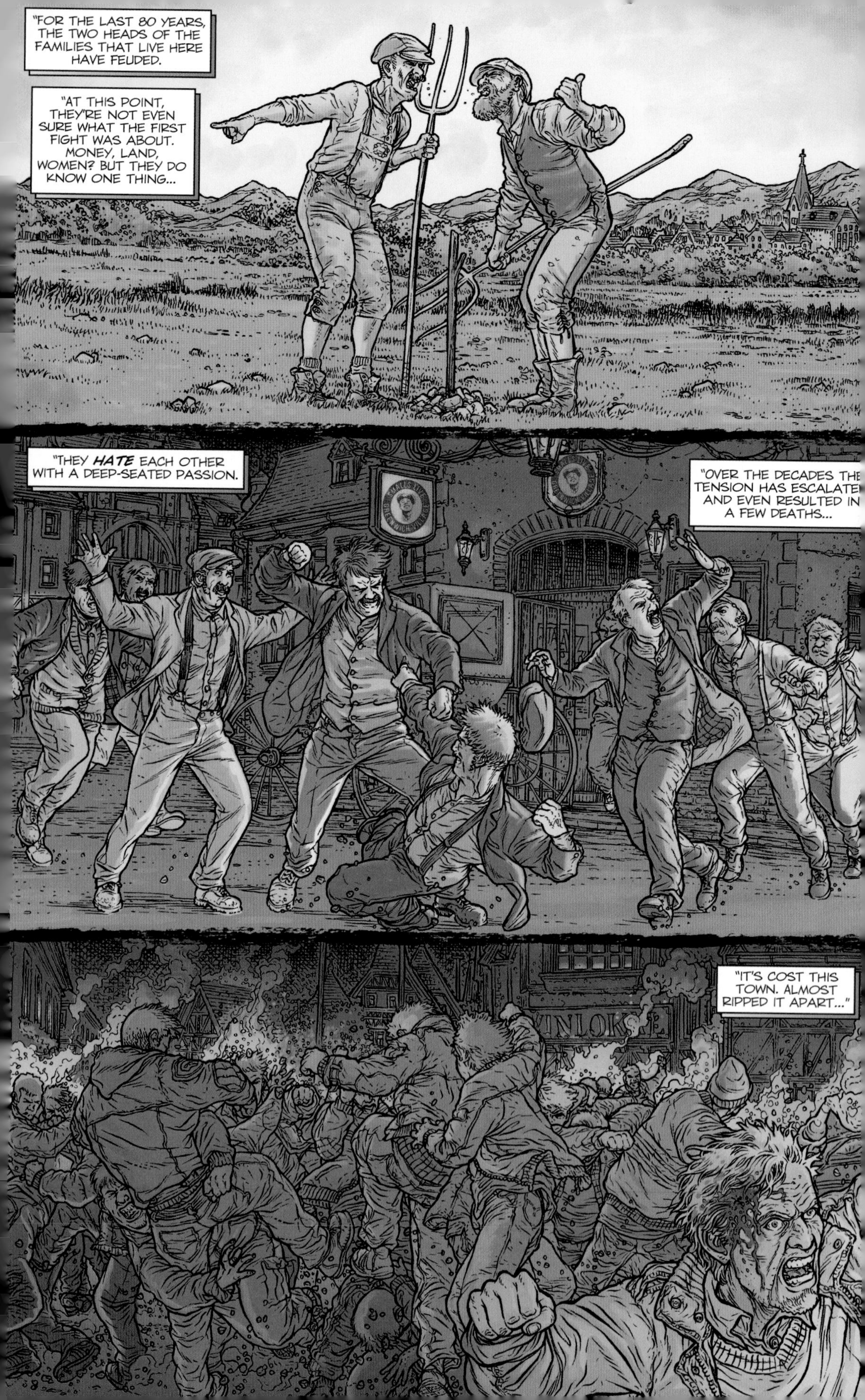
"FOR THE LAST 80 YEARS, THE TWO HEADS OF THE FAMILIES THAT LIVE HERE HAVE FEUDED.
"AT THIS POINT, THEY'RE NOT EVEN SURE WHAT THE FIRST FIGHT WAS ABOUT. MONEY, LAND, WOMEN? BUT THEY DO KNOW ONE THING...
"THEY **HATE** EACH OTHER WITH A DEEP-SEATED PASSION.
"OVER THE DECADES THE TENSION HAS ESCALATE AND EVEN RESULTED IN A FEW DEATHS...
"IT'S COST THIS TOWN. ALMOST RIPPED IT APART..."

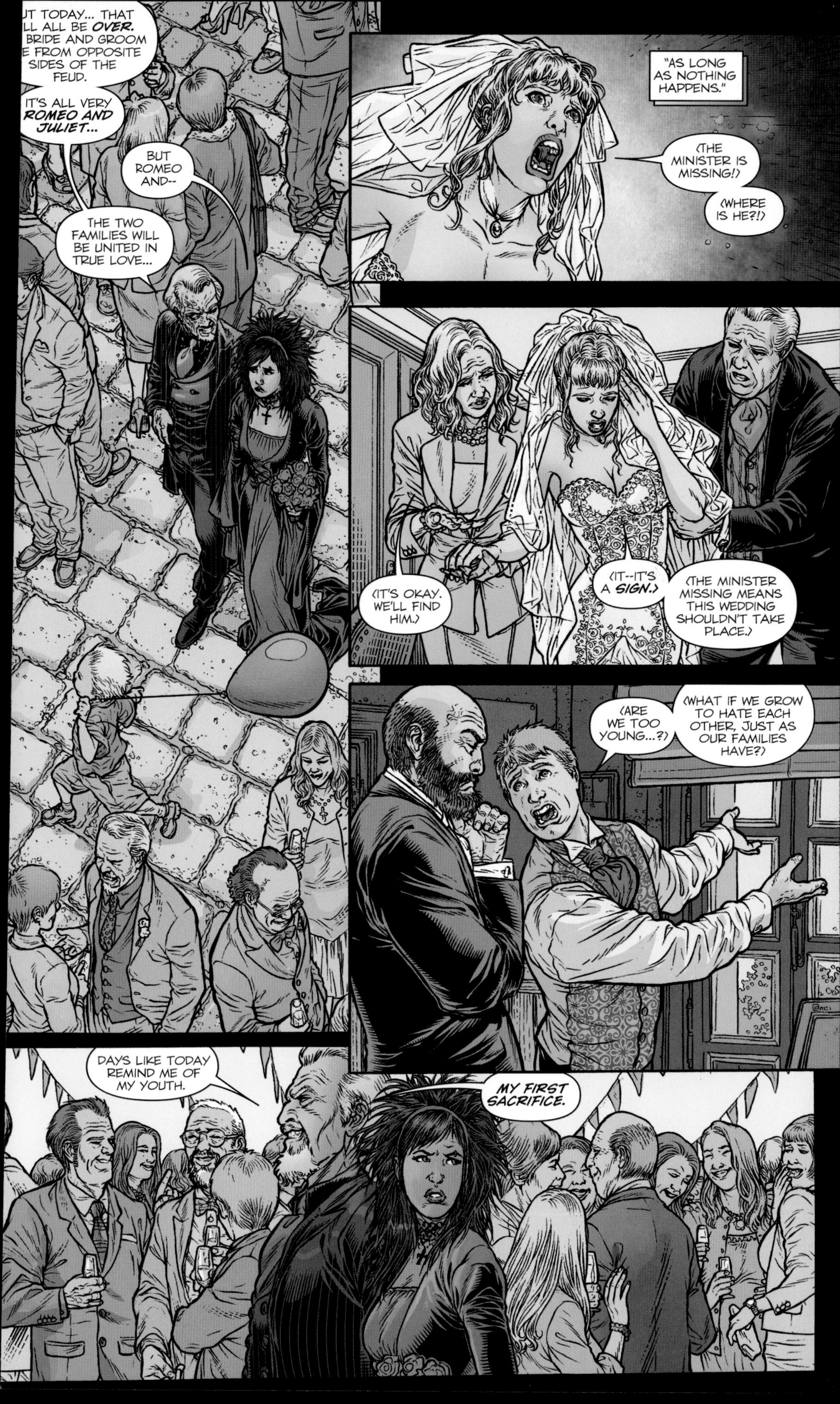

UT TODAY... THAT LL ALL BE OVER. BRIDE AND GROOM E FROM OPPOSITE SIDES OF THE FEUD.
IT'S ALL VERY ROMEO AND JULIET...
BUT ROMEO AND--
THE TWO FAMILIES WILL BE UNITED IN TRUE LOVE...
"AS LONG AS NOTHING HAPPENS."
‹THE MINISTER IS MISSING!›
‹WHERE IS HE?!›
‹IT'S OKAY. WE'LL FIND HIM.›
‹IT--IT'S A SIGN.›
‹THE MINISTER MISSING MEANS THIS WEDDING SHOULDN'T TAKE PLACE.›
‹ARE WE TOO YOUNG...?›
‹WHAT IF WE GROW TO HATE EACH OTHER, JUST AS OUR FAMILIES HAVE?›
DAYS LIKE TODAY REMIND ME OF MY YOUTH.
MY FIRST SACRIFICE.

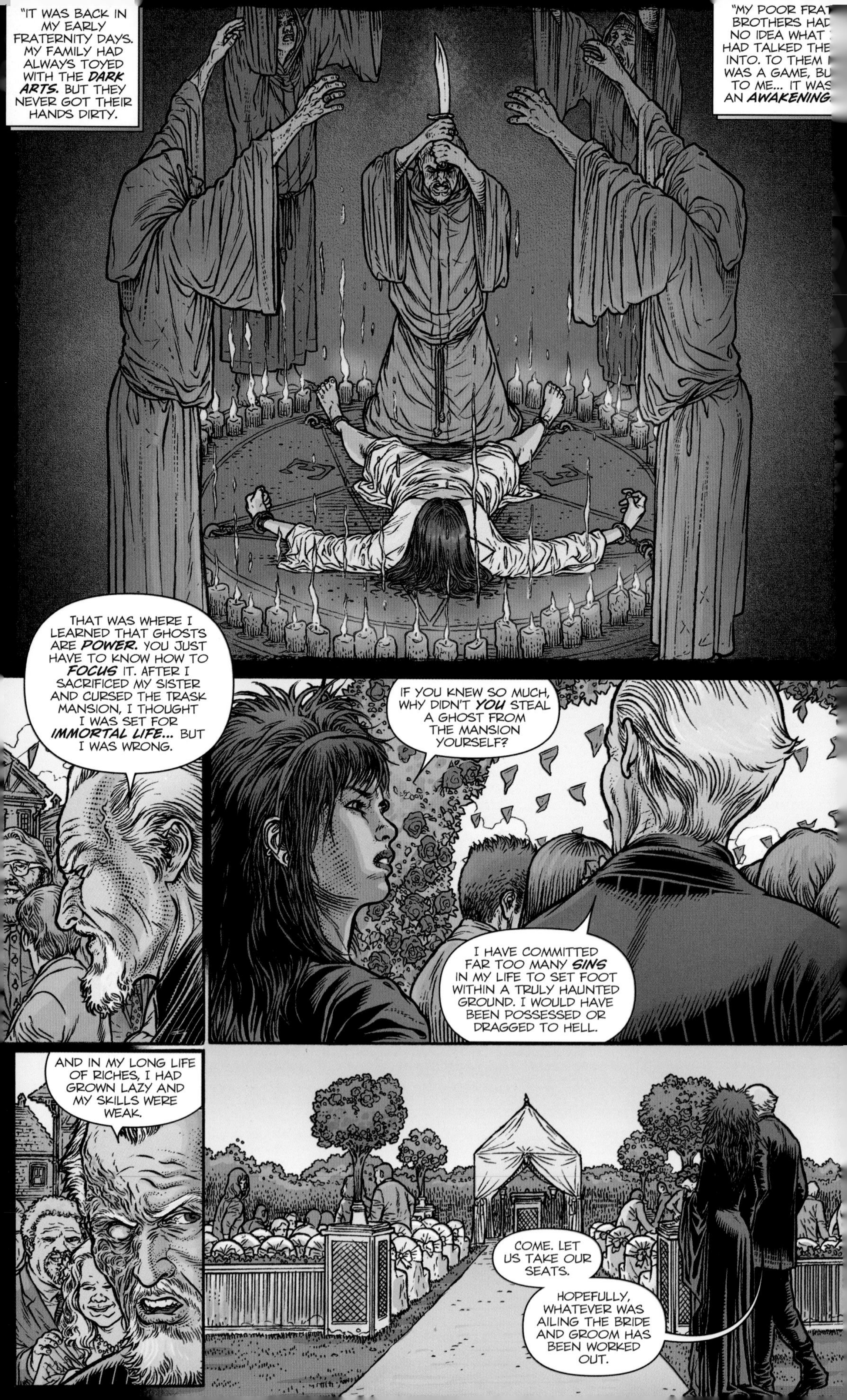
"IT WAS BACK IN MY EARLY FRATERNITY DAYS. MY FAMILY HAD ALWAYS TOYED WITH THE *DARK ARTS.* BUT THEY NEVER GOT THEIR HANDS DIRTY.
"MY POOR FRAT BROTHERS HAD NO IDEA WHAT HAD TALKED THE INTO. TO THEM WAS A GAME, BU TO ME... IT WAS AN *AWAKENING*
THAT WAS WHERE I LEARNED THAT GHOSTS ARE *POWER.* YOU JUST HAVE TO KNOW HOW TO *FOCUS* IT. AFTER I SACRIFICED MY SISTER AND CURSED THE TRASK MANSION, I THOUGHT I WAS SET FOR *IMMORTAL LIFE...* BUT I WAS WRONG.
IF YOU KNEW SO MUCH, WHY DIDN'T *YOU* STEAL A GHOST FROM THE MANSION YOURSELF?
I HAVE COMMITTED FAR TOO MANY *SINS* IN MY LIFE TO SET FOOT WITHIN A TRULY HAUNTED GROUND. I WOULD HAVE BEEN POSSESSED OR DRAGGED TO HELL.
AND IN MY LONG LIFE OF RICHES, I HAD GROWN LAZY AND MY SKILLS WERE WEAK.
COME. LET US TAKE OUR SEATS.
HOPEFULLY, WHATEVER WAS AILING THE BRIDE AND GROOM HAS BEEN WORKED OUT.

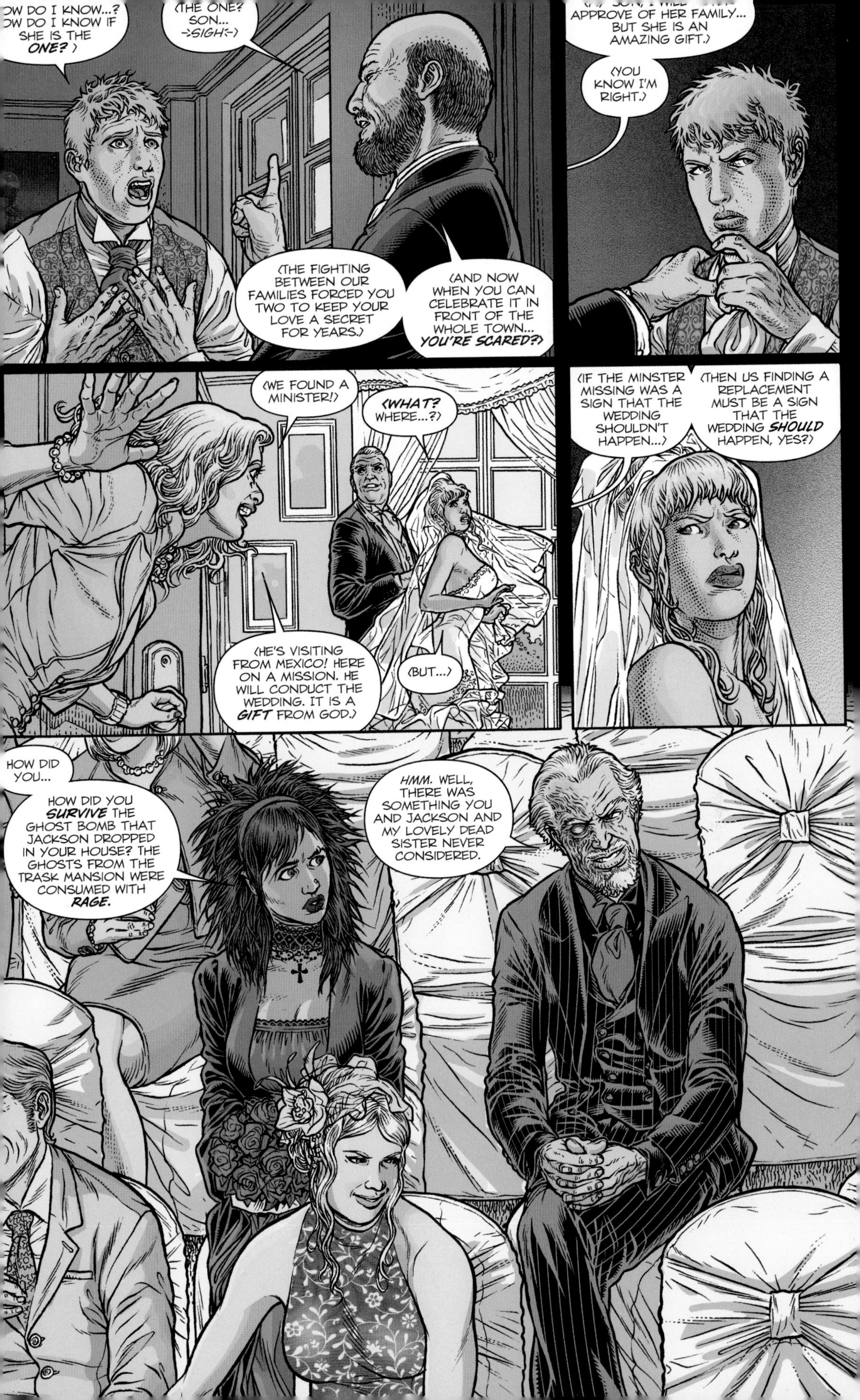
OW DO I KNOW...? OW DO I KNOW IF SHE IS THE ONE? ›
‹THE ONE? SON... ~SIGH~›
APPROVE OF HER FAMILY... BUT SHE IS AN AMAZING GIFT.›
‹YOU KNOW I'M RIGHT.›
‹THE FIGHTING BETWEEN OUR FAMILIES FORCED YOU TWO TO KEEP YOUR LOVE A SECRET FOR YEARS.›
‹AND NOW WHEN YOU CAN CELEBRATE IT IN FRONT OF THE WHOLE TOWN... YOU'RE SCARED?›
‹WE FOUND A MINISTER!›
‹WHAT? WHERE...?›
‹HE'S VISITING FROM MEXICO! HERE ON A MISSION. HE WILL CONDUCT THE WEDDING. IT IS A GIFT FROM GOD.›
‹BUT...›
‹IF THE MINSTER MISSING WAS A SIGN THAT THE WEDDING SHOULDN'T HAPPEN...›
‹THEN US FINDING A REPLACEMENT MUST BE A SIGN THAT THE WEDDING SHOULD HAPPEN, YES?›
HOW DID YOU...
HOW DID YOU SURVIVE THE GHOST BOMB THAT JACKSON DROPPED IN YOUR HOUSE? THE GHOSTS FROM THE TRASK MANSION WERE CONSUMED WITH RAGE.
HMM. WELL, THERE WAS SOMETHING YOU AND JACKSON AND MY LOVELY DEAD SISTER NEVER CONSIDERED.

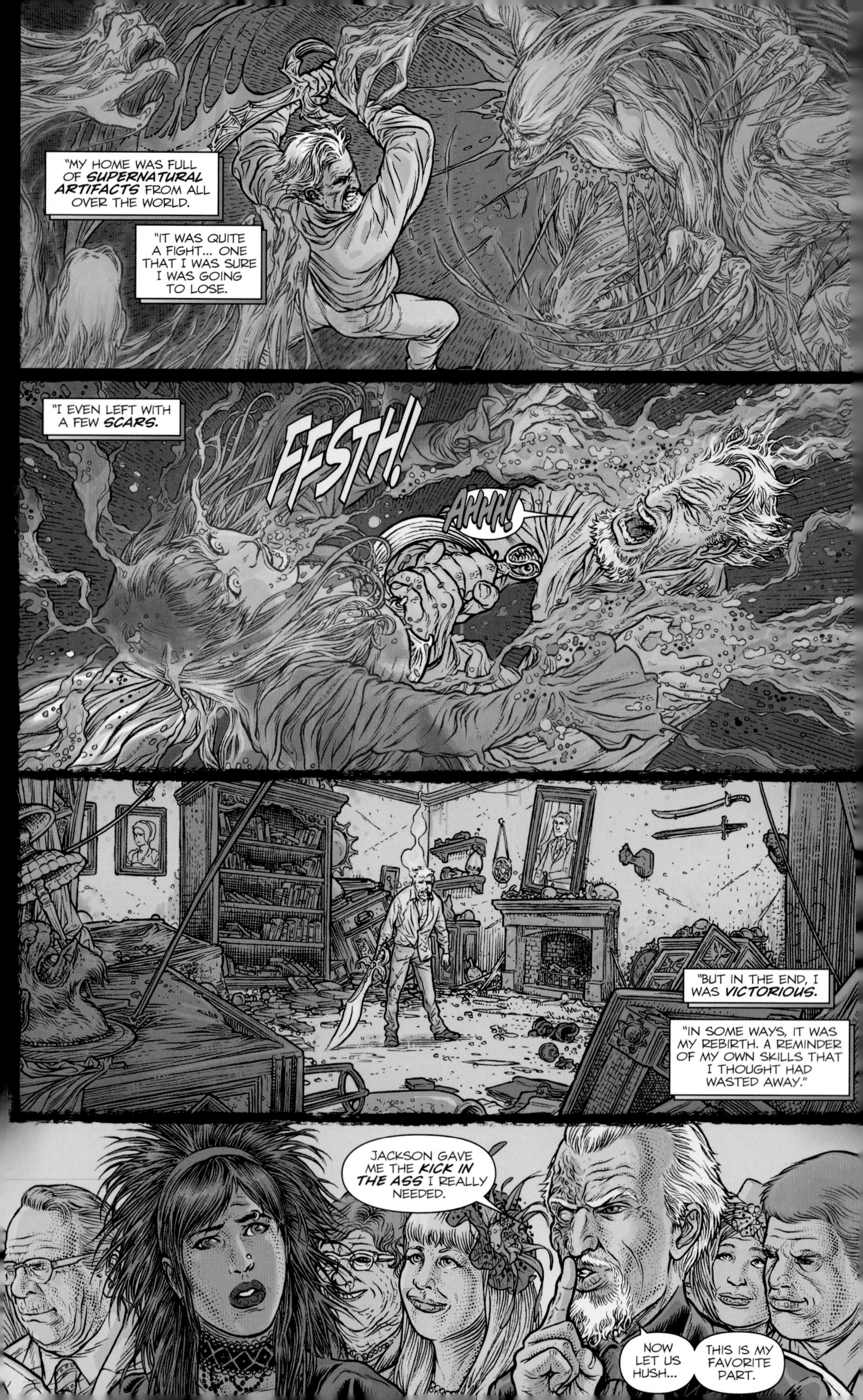

"MY HOME WAS FULL OF SUPERNATURAL ARTIFACTS FROM ALL OVER THE WORLD.
"IT WAS QUITE A FIGHT... ONE THAT I WAS SURE I WAS GOING TO LOSE.
"I EVEN LEFT WITH A FEW SCARS.
FFSTH!
AHHH!
"BUT IN THE END, I WAS VICTORIOUS.
"IN SOME WAYS, IT WAS MY REBIRTH. A REMINDER OF MY OWN SKILLS THAT I THOUGHT HAD WASTED AWAY."
JACKSON GAVE ME THE KICK IN THE ASS I REALLY NEEDED.
NOW LET US HUSH...
THIS IS MY FAVORITE PART.

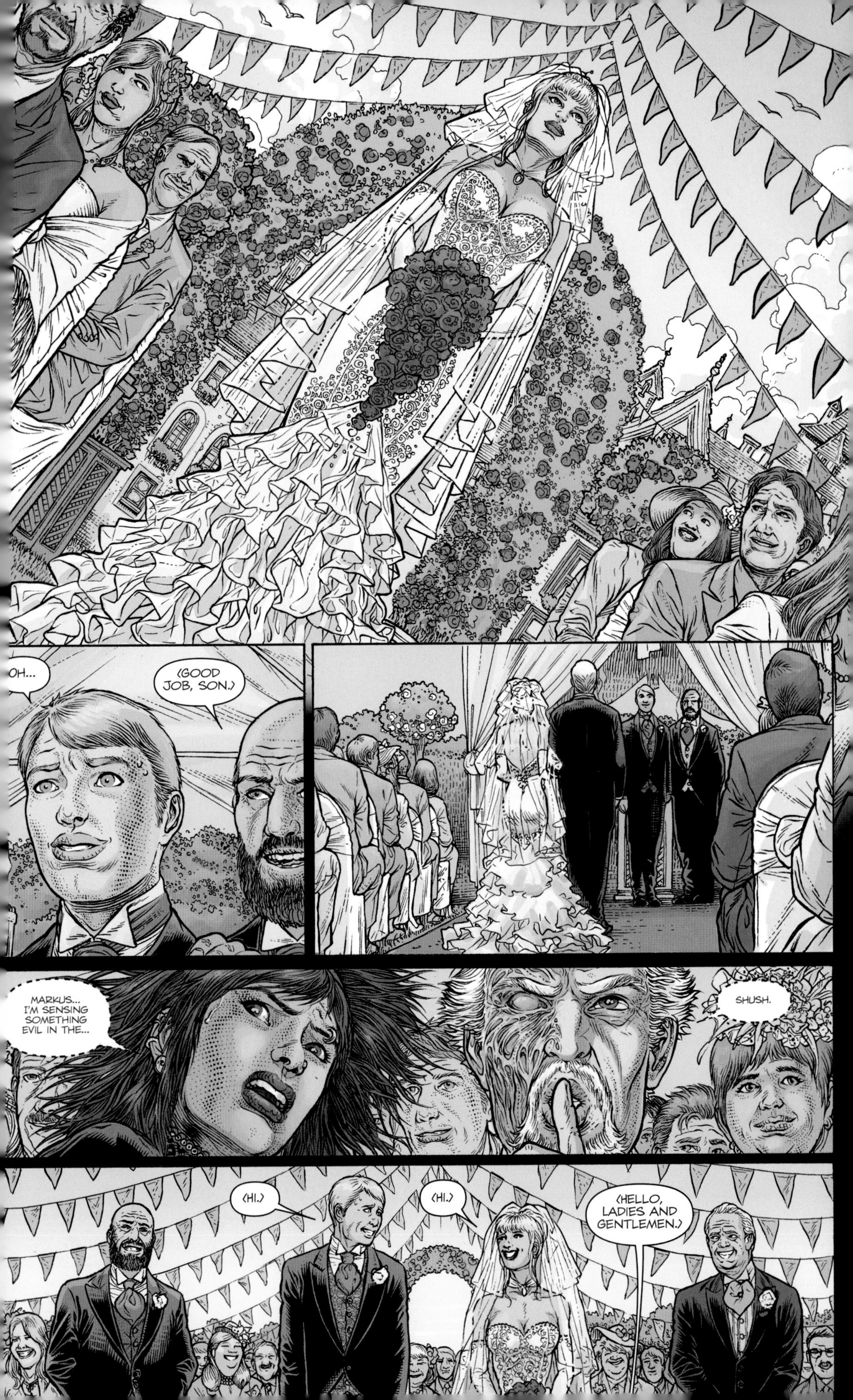
OH...
⟨GOOD JOB, SON.⟩
MARKUS... I'M SENSING SOMETHING EVIL IN THE...
SHUSH.
⟨HI.⟩
⟨HI.⟩
⟨HELLO, LADIES AND GENTLEMEN.⟩

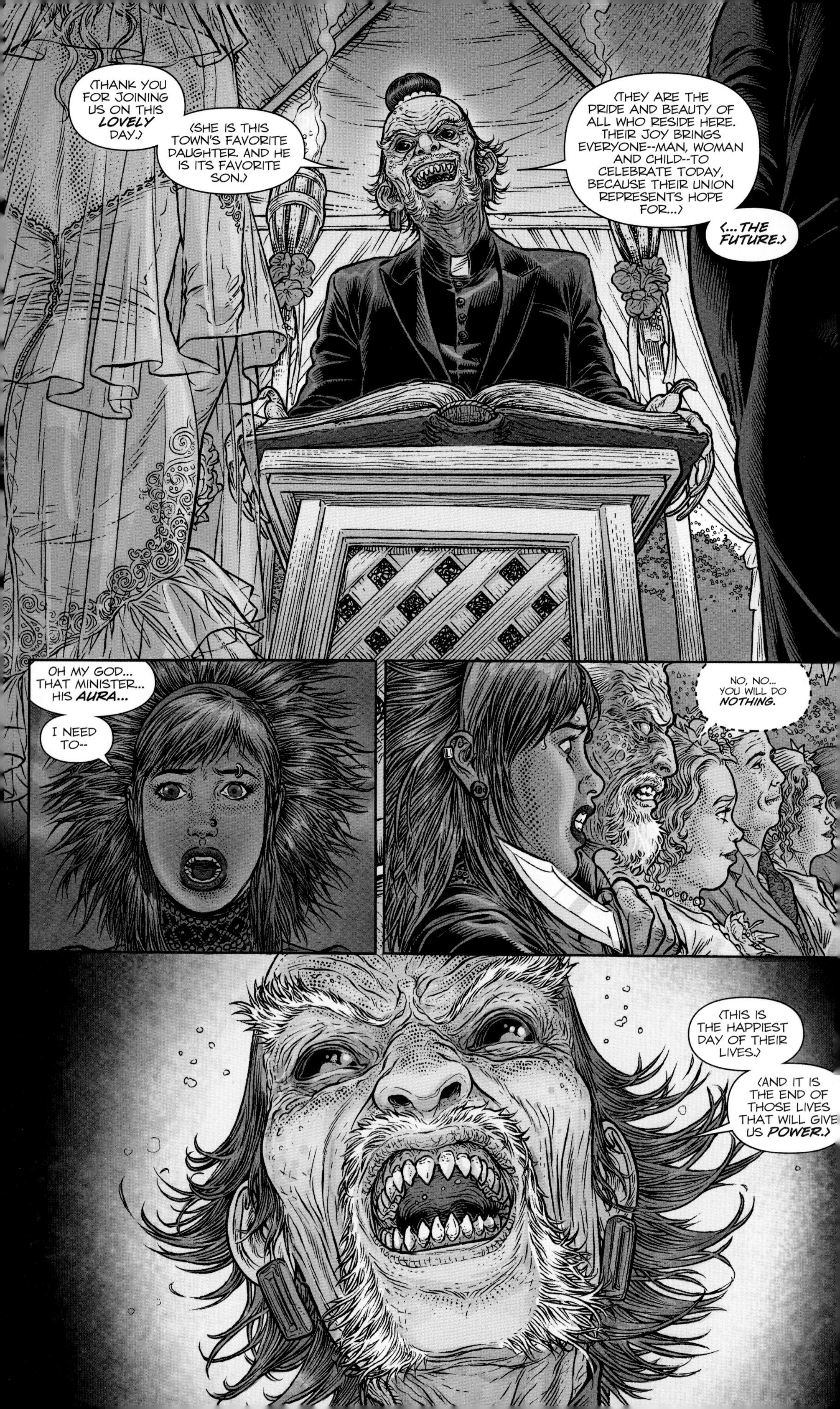

‹THANK YOU FOR JOINING US ON THIS *LOVELY* DAY.›
‹SHE IS THIS TOWN'S FAVORITE DAUGHTER. AND HE IS ITS FAVORITE SON.›
‹THEY ARE THE PRIDE AND BEAUTY OF ALL WHO RESIDE HERE. THEIR JOY BRINGS EVERYONE--MAN, WOMAN AND CHILD--TO CELEBRATE TODAY, BECAUSE THEIR UNION REPRESENTS HOPE FOR...›
‹*...THE FUTURE.*›
OH MY GOD... THAT MINISTER... HIS *AURA*...
I NEED TO--
NO, NO... YOU WILL DO *NOTHING.*
‹THIS IS THE HAPPIEST DAY OF THEIR LIVES.›
‹AND IT IS THE END OF THOSE LIVES THAT WILL GIVE US *POWER.*›

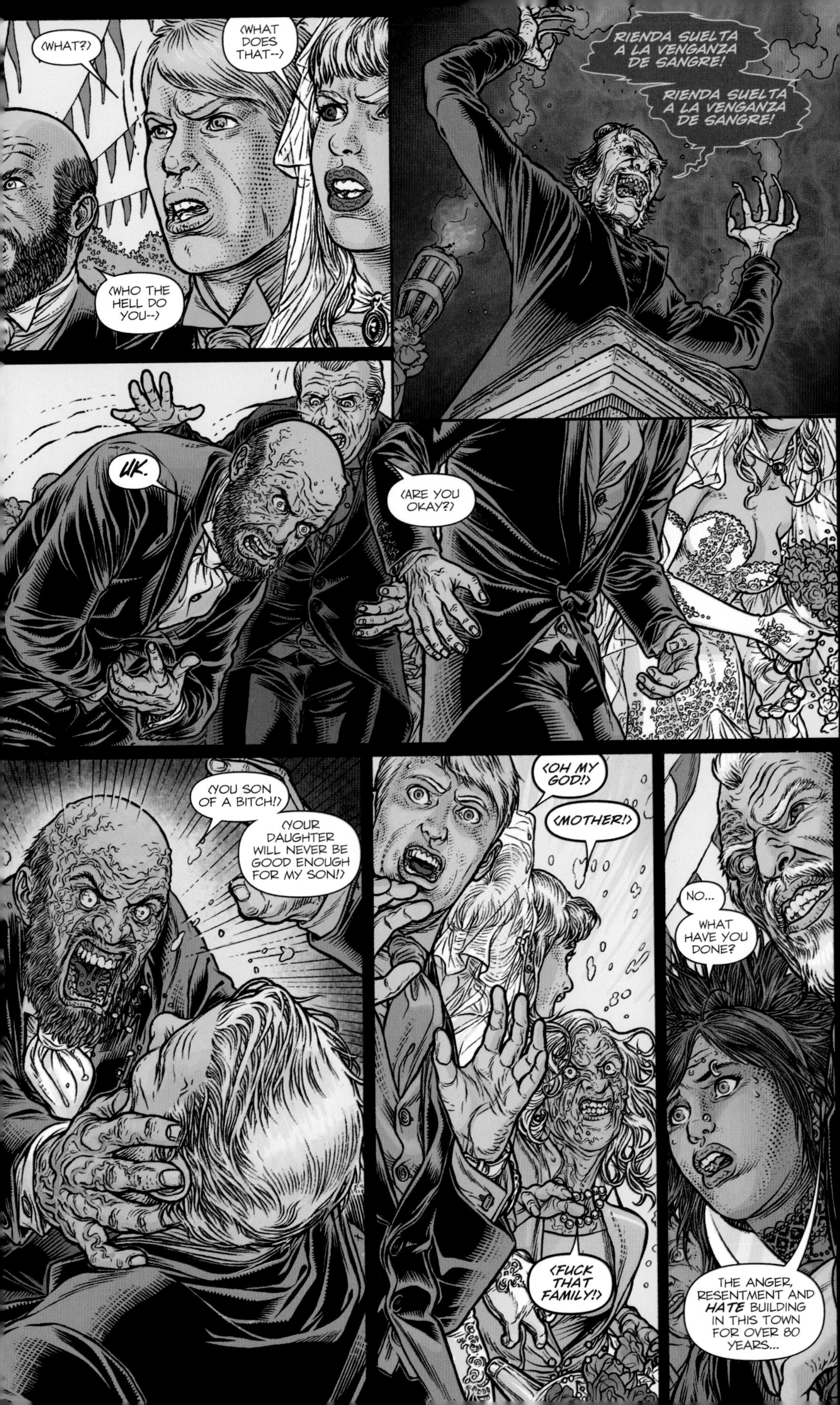

(WHAT?)
(WHAT DOES THAT--)
(WHO THE HELL DO YOU--)
RIENDA SUELTA A LA VENGANZA DE SANGRE!
RIENDA SUELTA A LA VENGANZA DE SANGRE!
UK.
(ARE YOU OKAY?)
(YOU SON OF A BITCH!)
(YOUR DAUGHTER WILL NEVER BE GOOD ENOUGH FOR MY SON!)
(OH MY GOD!)
(MOTHER!)
(FUCK THAT FAMILY!)
NO...
WHAT HAVE YOU DONE?
THE ANGER, RESENTMENT AND HATE BUILDING IN THIS TOWN FOR OVER 80 YEARS...

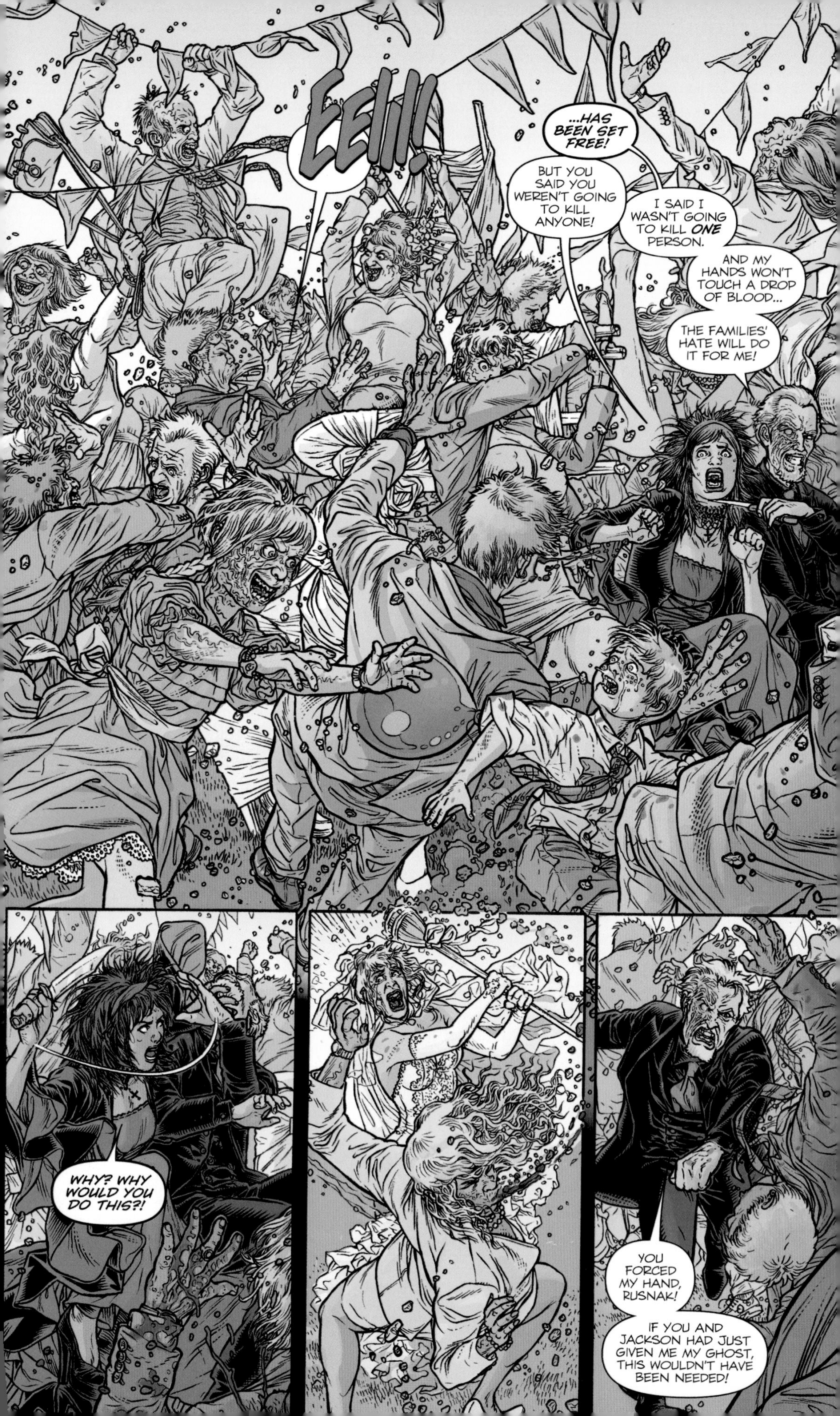
EEII!!
...HAS BEEN SET FREE!
BUT YOU SAID YOU WEREN'T GOING TO KILL ANYONE!
I SAID I WASN'T GOING TO KILL ONE PERSON.
AND MY HANDS WON'T TOUCH A DROP OF BLOOD...
THE FAMILIES' HATE WILL DO IT FOR ME!
WHY? WHY WOULD YOU DO THIS?!
YOU FORCED MY HAND, RUSNAK!
IF YOU AND JACKSON HAD JUST GIVEN ME MY GHOST, THIS WOULDN'T HAVE BEEN NEEDED!

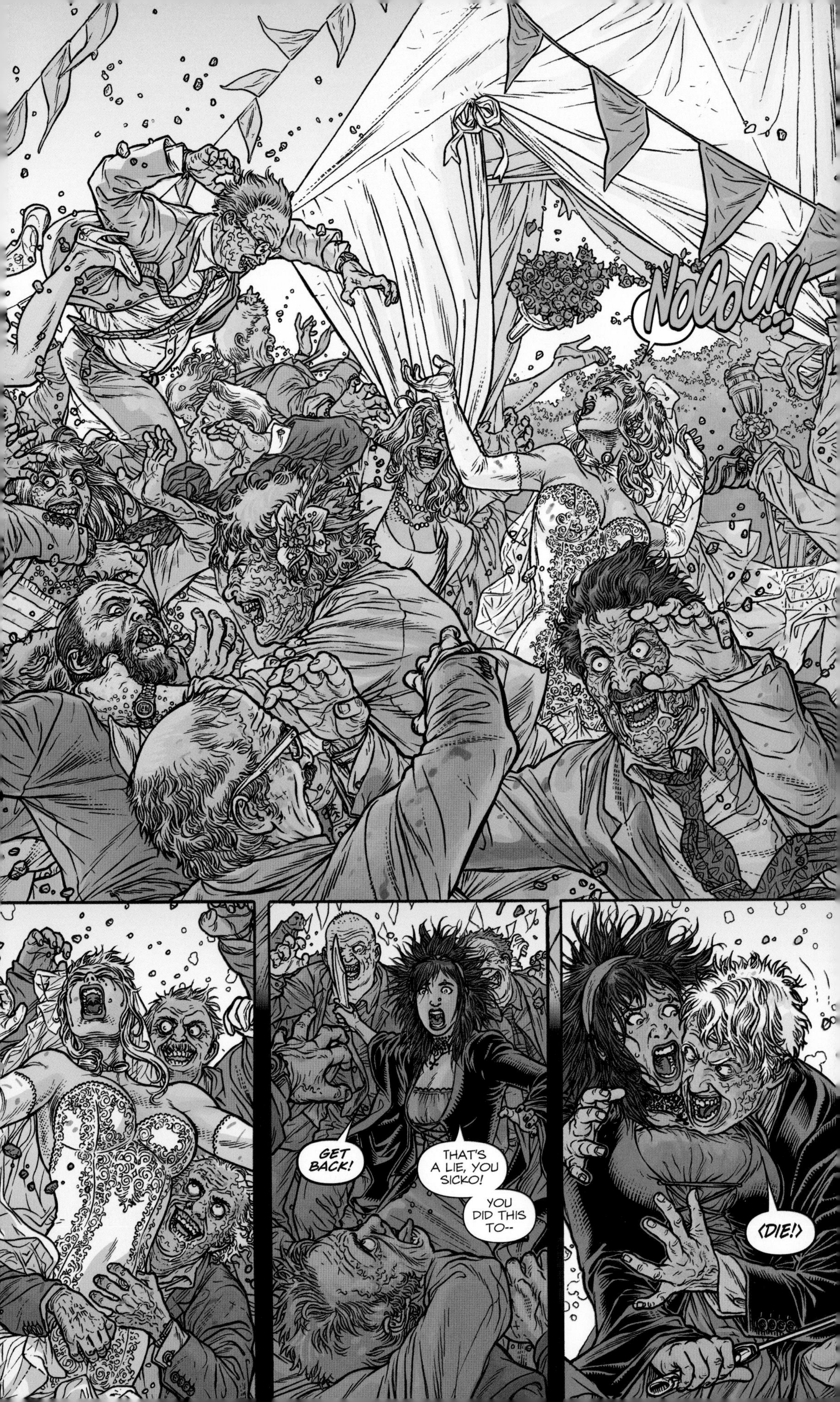
NoOoO!!!
GET BACK!
THAT'S A LIE, YOU SICKO!
YOU DID THIS TO--
<DIE!>

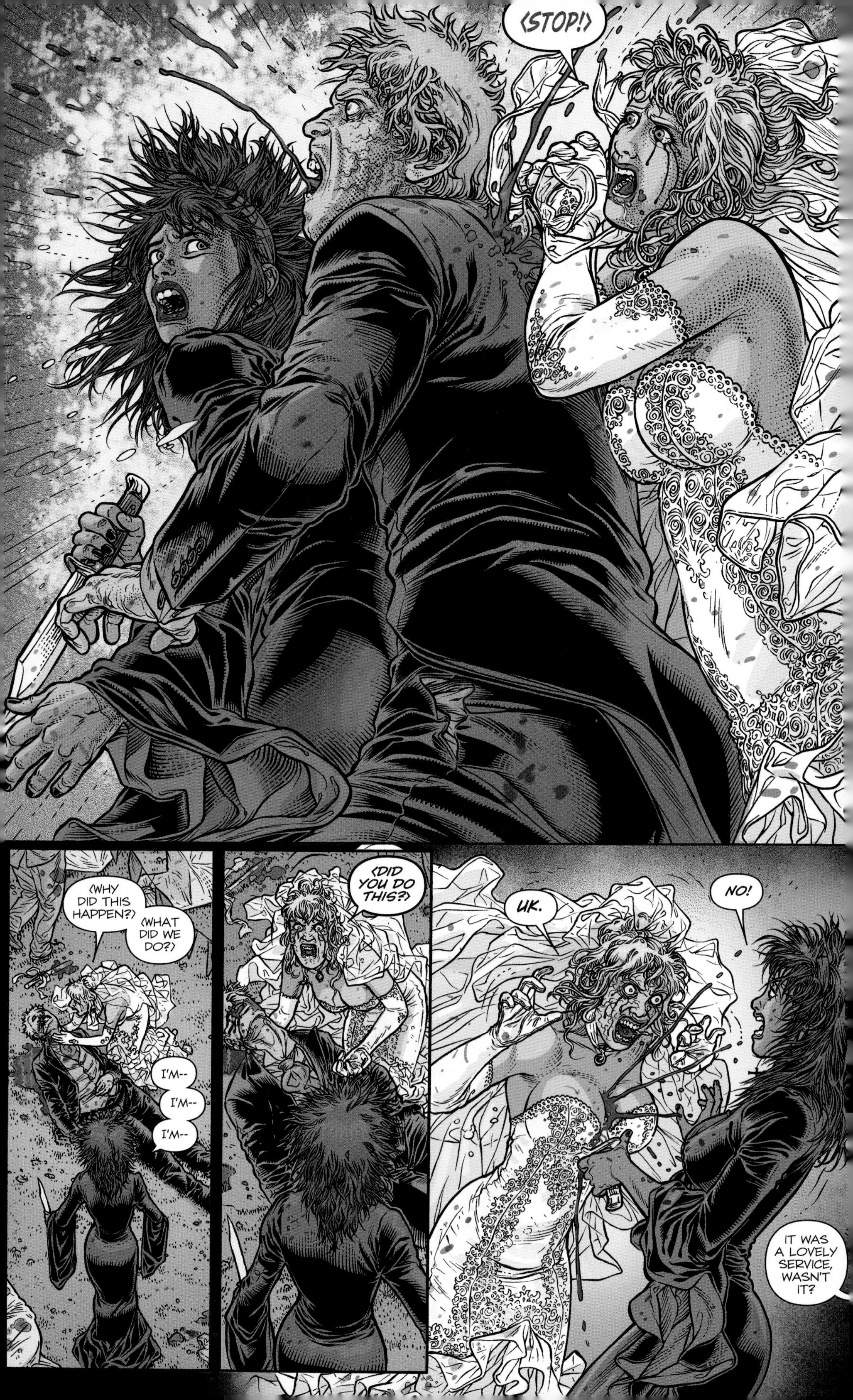

(STOP!)
(WHY DID THIS HAPPEN?)
(WHAT DID WE DO?)
I'M--
I'M--
I'M--
(DID YOU DO THIS?)
UK.
NO!
IT WAS A LOVELY SERVICE, WASN'T IT?

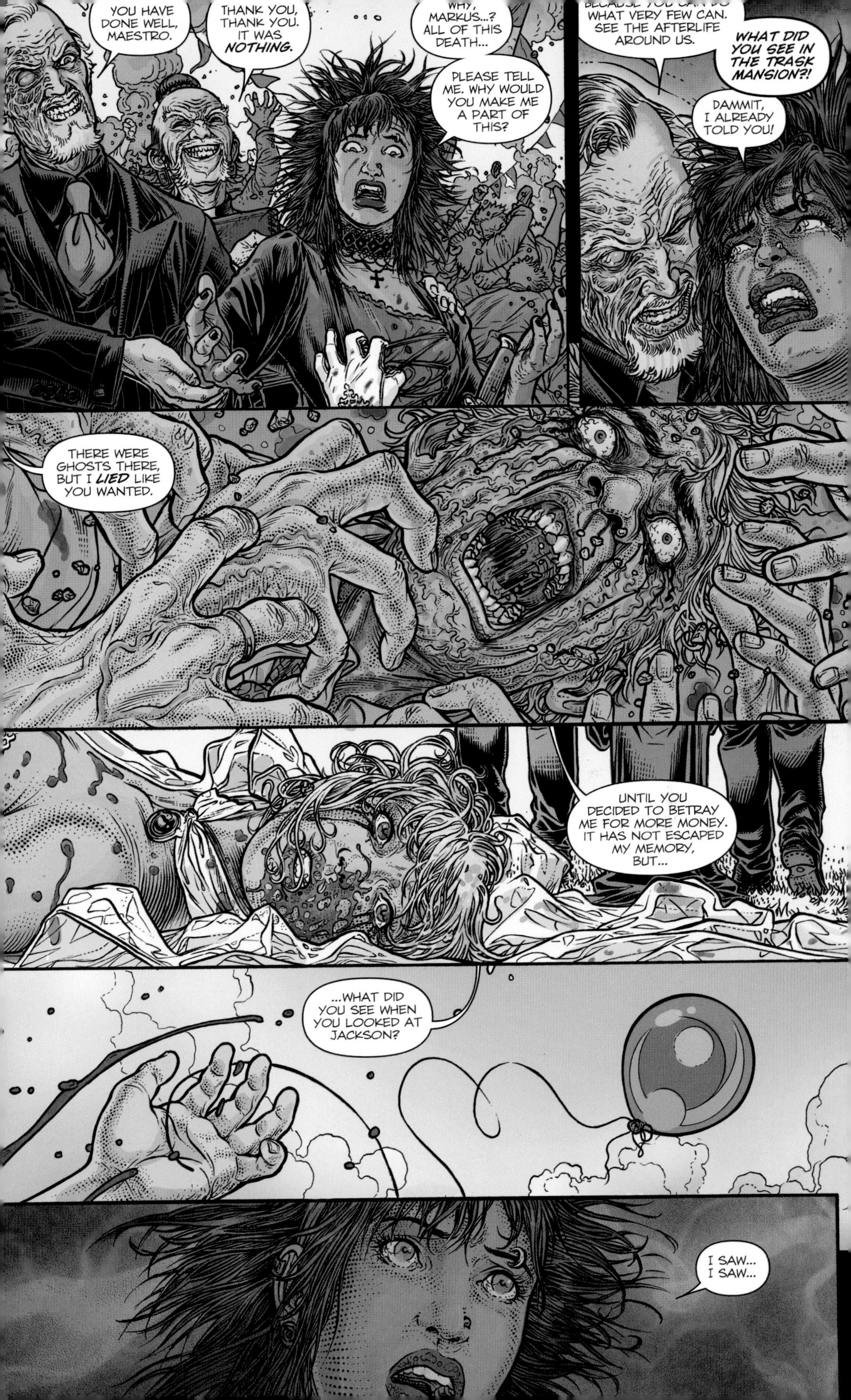
YOU HAVE DONE WELL, MAESTRO.
THANK YOU, THANK YOU. IT WAS NOTHING.
WHY, MARKUS...? ALL OF THIS DEATH...
PLEASE TELL ME. WHY WOULD YOU MAKE ME A PART OF THIS?
WHAT VERY FEW CAN. SEE THE AFTERLIFE AROUND US.
WHAT DID YOU SEE IN THE TRASK MANSION?!
DAMMIT, I ALREADY TOLD YOU!
THERE WERE GHOSTS THERE, BUT I LIED LIKE YOU WANTED.
UNTIL YOU DECIDED TO BETRAY ME FOR MORE MONEY. IT HAS NOT ESCAPED MY MEMORY, BUT...
...WHAT DID YOU SEE WHEN YOU LOOKED AT JACKSON?
I SAW... I SAW...

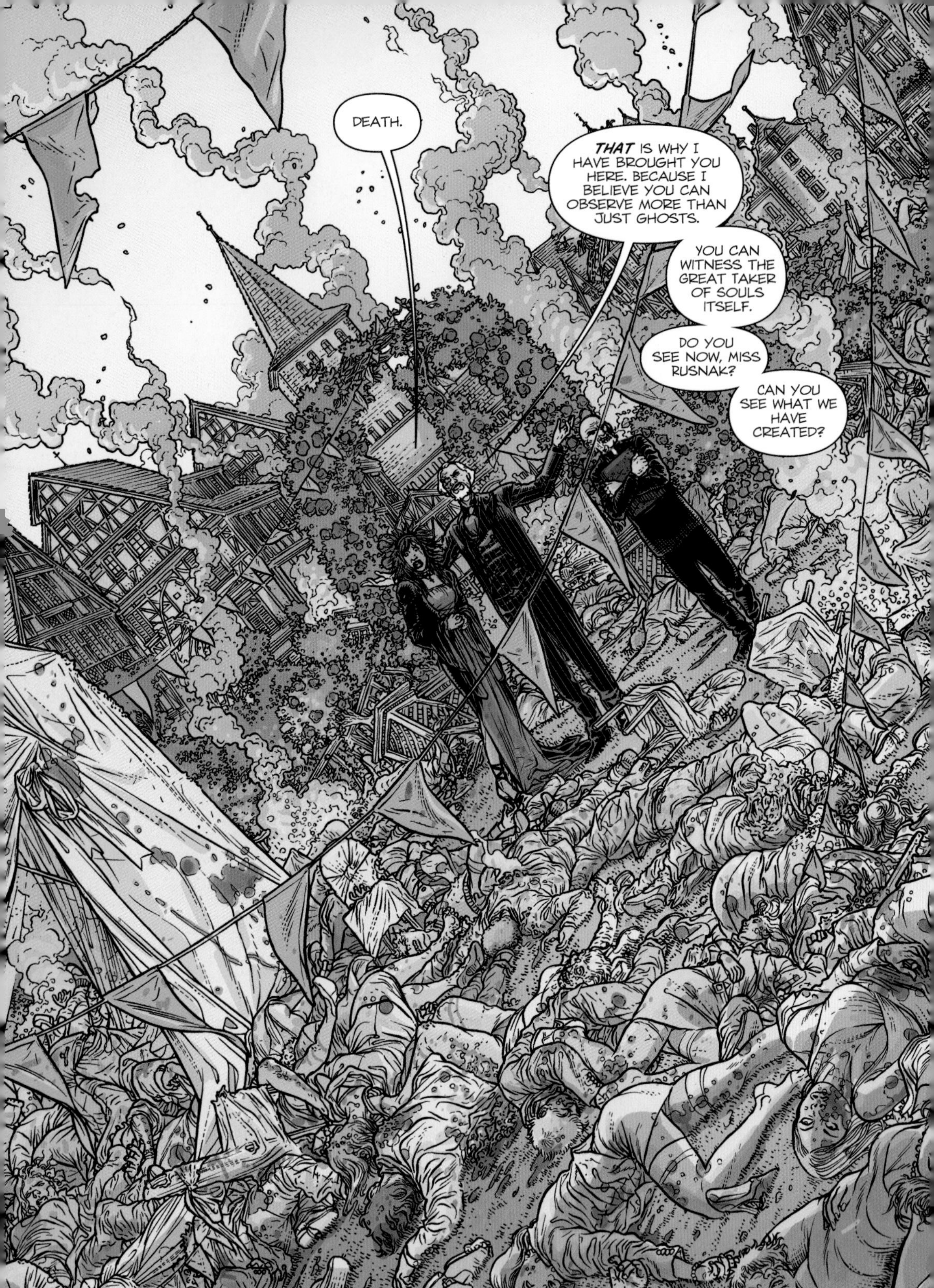
DEATH.
THAT IS WHY I HAVE BROUGHT YOU HERE. BECAUSE I BELIEVE YOU CAN OBSERVE MORE THAN JUST GHOSTS.
YOU CAN WITNESS THE GREAT TAKER OF SOULS ITSELF.
DO YOU SEE NOW, MISS RUSNAK?
CAN YOU SEE WHAT WE HAVE CREATED?

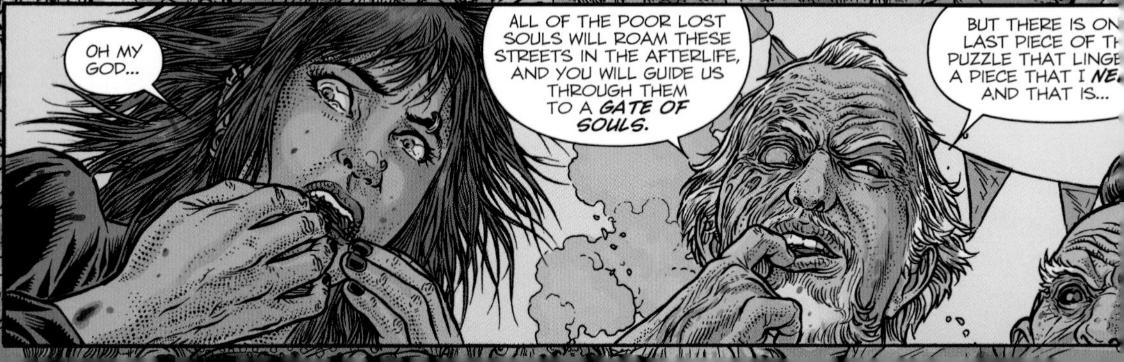
OH MY GOD...
ALL OF THE POOR LOST SOULS WILL ROAM THESE STREETS IN THE AFTERLIFE, AND YOU WILL GUIDE US THROUGH THEM TO A GATE OF SOULS.
BUT THERE IS ON LAST PIECE OF TH PUZZLE THAT LINGE A PIECE THAT I NE AND THAT IS...

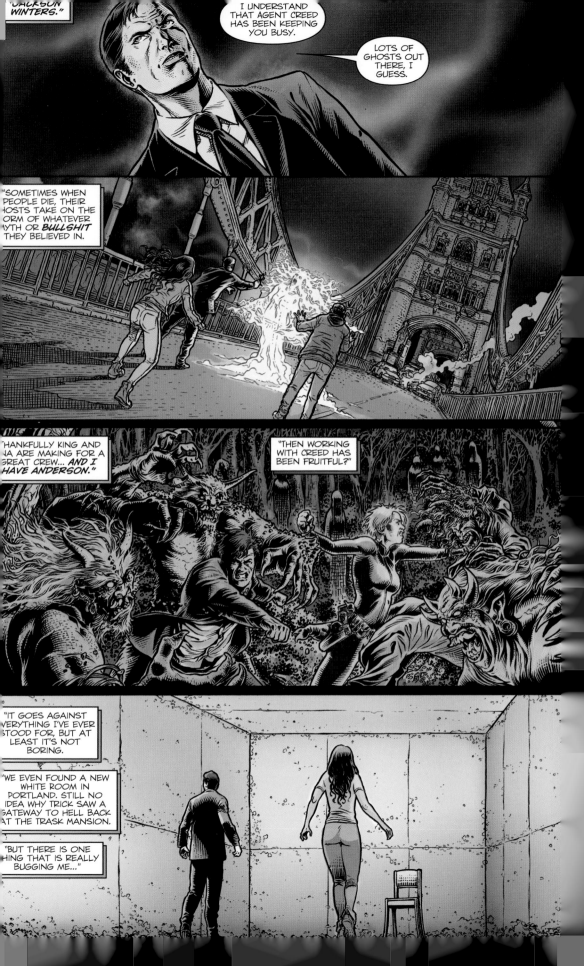

"JACKSON WINTERS."

I UNDERSTAND THAT AGENT CREED HAS BEEN KEEPING YOU BUSY.

LOTS OF GHOSTS OUT THERE, I GUESS.

"SOMETIMES WHEN PEOPLE DIE, THEIR GHOSTS TAKE ON THE FORM OF WHATEVER MYTH OR *BULLSHIT* THEY BELIEVED IN.

"THANKFULLY KING AND NA ARE MAKING FOR A GREAT CREW... *AND I HAVE ANDERSON.*"

"THEN WORKING WITH CREED HAS BEEN FRUITFUL?"

"IT GOES AGAINST EVERYTHING I'VE EVER STOOD FOR, BUT AT LEAST IT'S NOT BORING.

"WE EVEN FOUND A NEW WHITE ROOM IN PORTLAND. STILL NO IDEA WHY TRICK SAW A GATEWAY TO HELL BACK AT THE TRASK MANSION.

"BUT THERE IS ONE THING THAT IS REALLY BUGGING ME..."

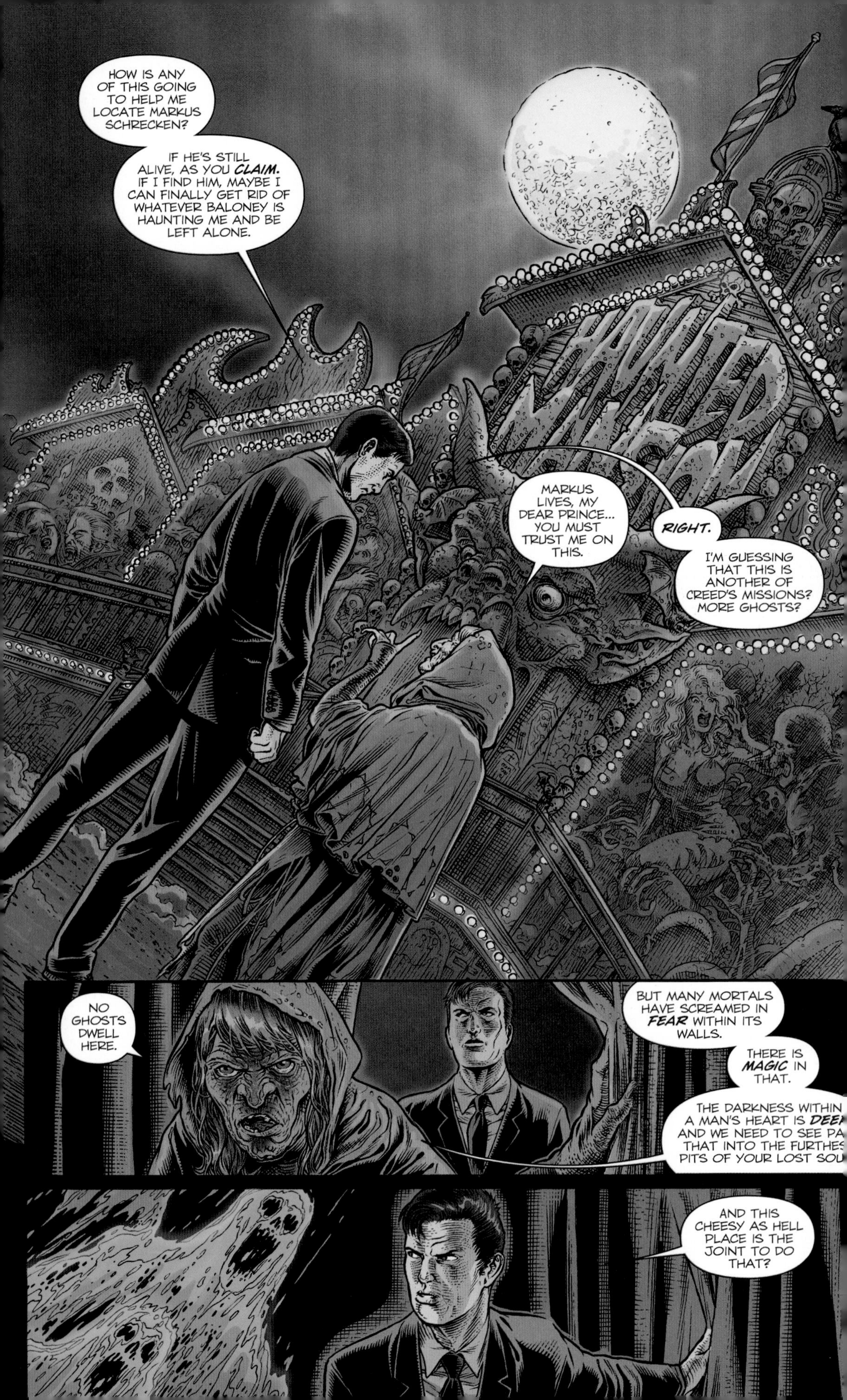
HOW IS ANY OF THIS GOING TO HELP ME LOCATE MARKUS SCHRECKEN?
IF HE'S STILL ALIVE, AS YOU CLAIM. IF I FIND HIM, MAYBE I CAN FINALLY GET RID OF WHATEVER BALONEY IS HAUNTING ME AND BE LEFT ALONE.
MARKUS LIVES, MY DEAR PRINCE... YOU MUST TRUST ME ON THIS.
RIGHT.
I'M GUESSING THAT THIS IS ANOTHER OF CREED'S MISSIONS? MORE GHOSTS?
NO GHOSTS DWELL HERE.
BUT MANY MORTALS HAVE SCREAMED IN FEAR WITHIN ITS WALLS.
THERE IS MAGIC IN THAT.
AND THIS CHEESY AS HELL PLACE IS THE JOINT TO DO THAT?

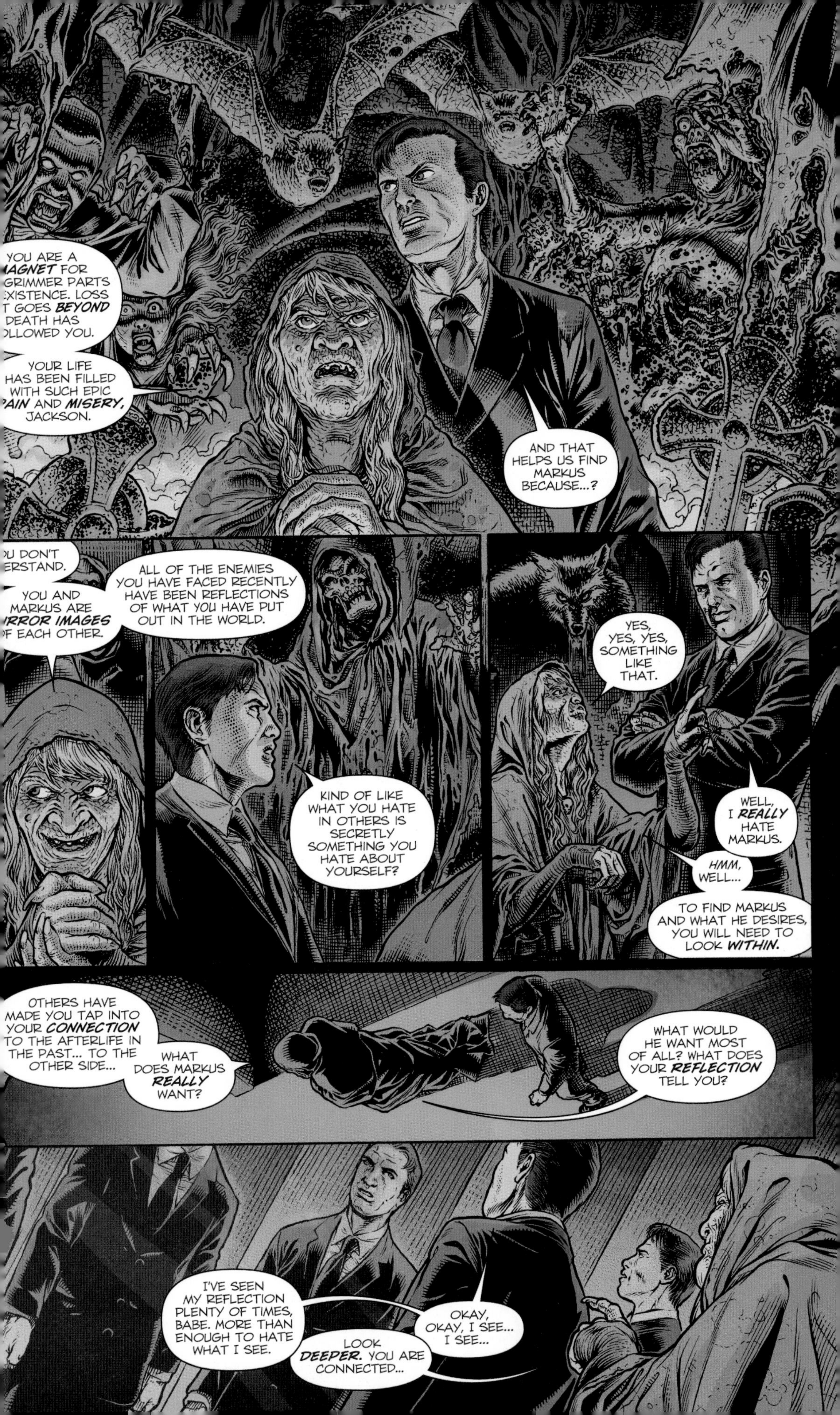
YOU ARE A
AGNET FOR
GRIMMER PARTS
EXISTENCE. LOSS
T GOES BEYOND
DEATH HAS
LLOWED YOU.
YOUR LIFE HAS BEEN FILLED WITH SUCH EPIC
AIN AND MISERY, JACKSON.
AND THAT HELPS US FIND MARKUS BECAUSE...?
U DON'T
ERSTAND.
YOU AND MARKUS ARE
RROR IMAGES
F EACH OTHER.
ALL OF THE ENEMIES YOU HAVE FACED RECENTLY HAVE BEEN REFLECTIONS OF WHAT YOU HAVE PUT OUT IN THE WORLD.
KIND OF LIKE WHAT YOU HATE IN OTHERS IS SECRETLY SOMETHING YOU HATE ABOUT YOURSELF?
YES, YES, YES, SOMETHING LIKE THAT.
WELL, I REALLY HATE MARKUS.
HMM, WELL...
TO FIND MARKUS AND WHAT HE DESIRES, YOU WILL NEED TO LOOK WITHIN.
OTHERS HAVE MADE YOU TAP INTO YOUR CONNECTION TO THE AFTERLIFE IN THE PAST... TO THE OTHER SIDE...
WHAT DOES MARKUS REALLY WANT?
WHAT WOULD HE WANT MOST OF ALL? WHAT DOES YOUR REFLECTION TELL YOU?
I'VE SEEN MY REFLECTION PLENTY OF TIMES, BABE. MORE THAN ENOUGH TO HATE WHAT I SEE.
OKAY, OKAY, I SEE... I SEE...
LOOK DEEPER. YOU ARE CONNECTED...

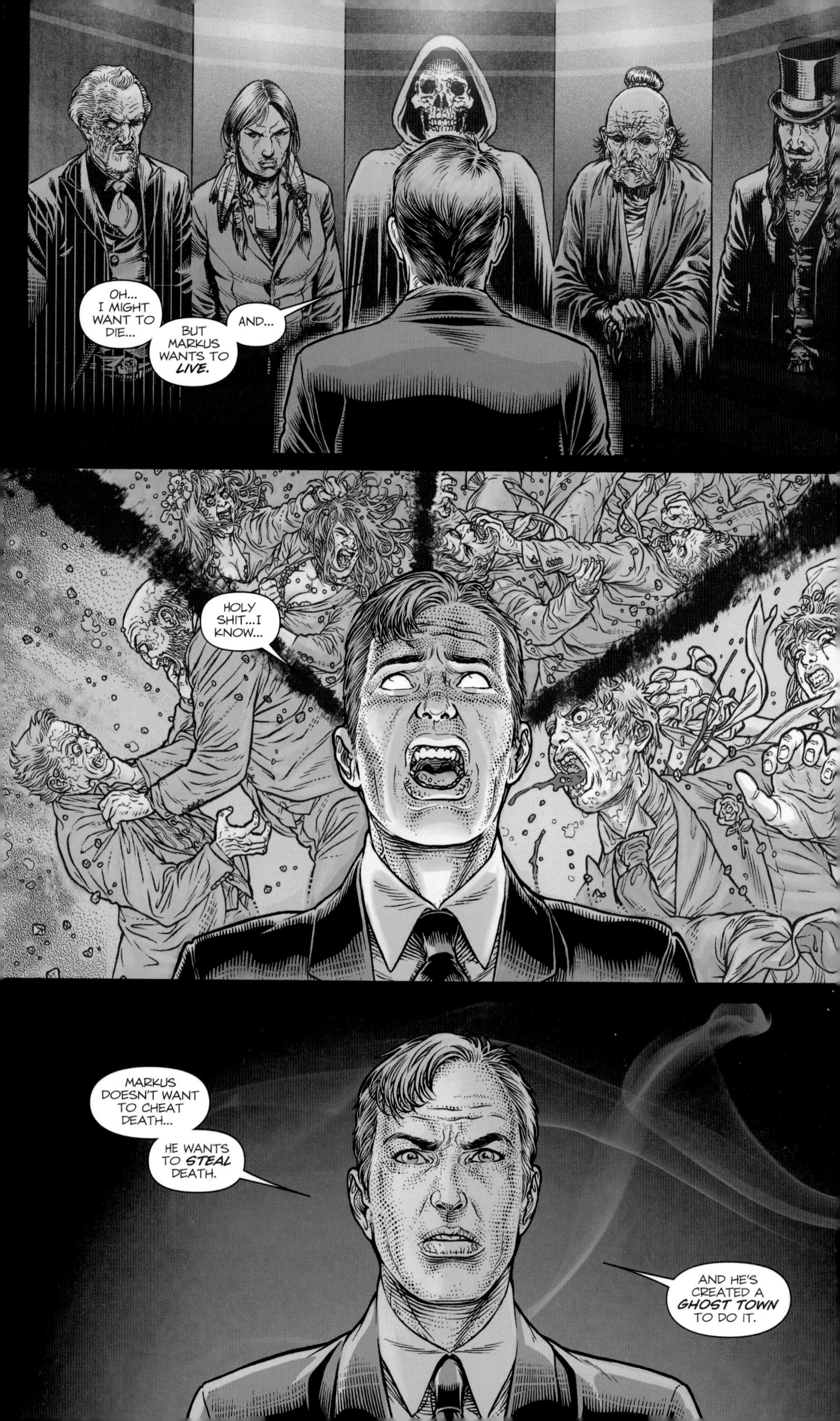
OH... I MIGHT WANT TO DIE...
BUT MARKUS WANTS TO *LIVE.*
AND...
HOLY SHIT...I KNOW...
MARKUS DOESN'T WANT TO CHEAT DEATH...
HE WANTS TO *STEAL* DEATH.
AND HE'S CREATED A *GHOST TOWN* TO DO IT.

CHAPTER TWO

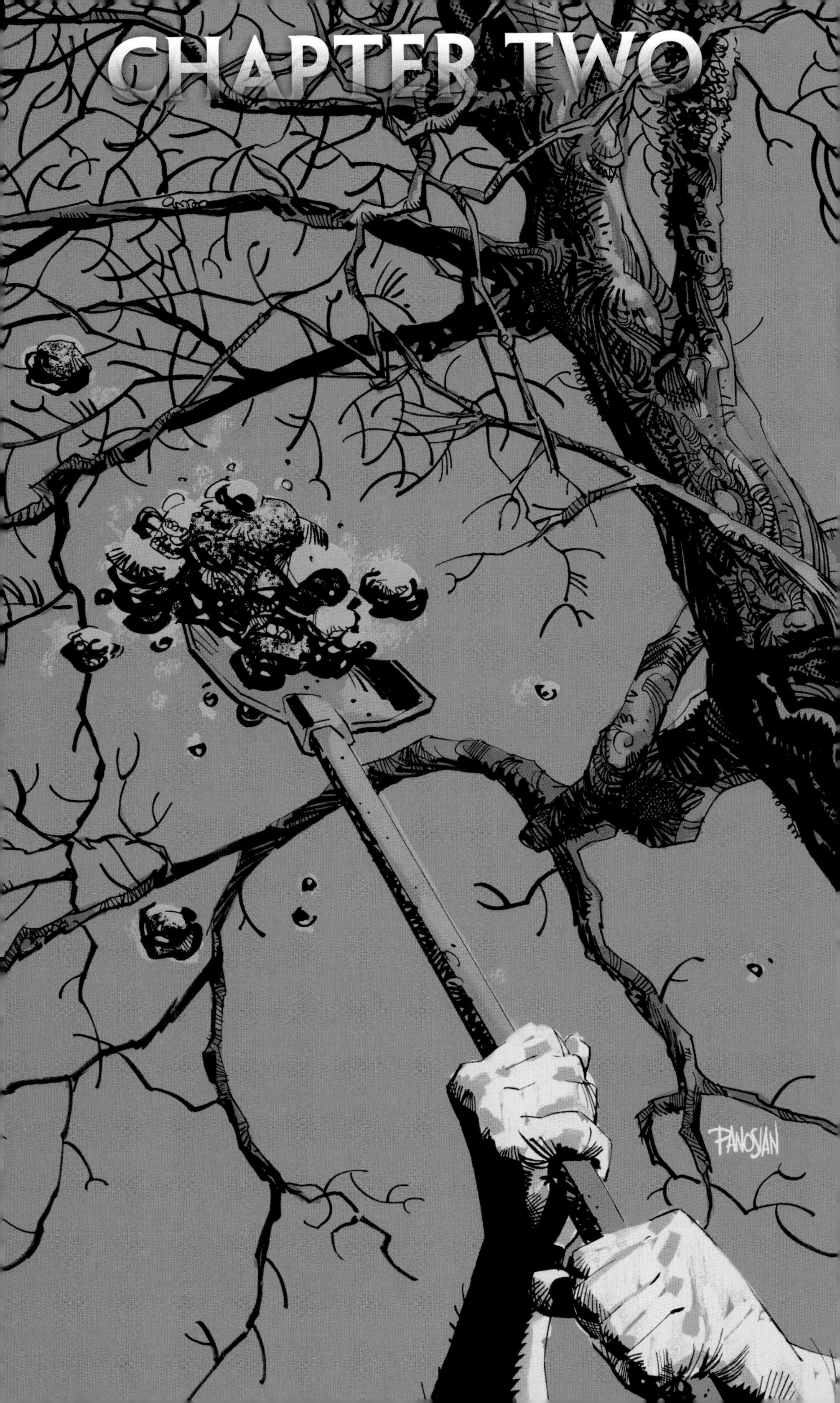
PANOSIAN

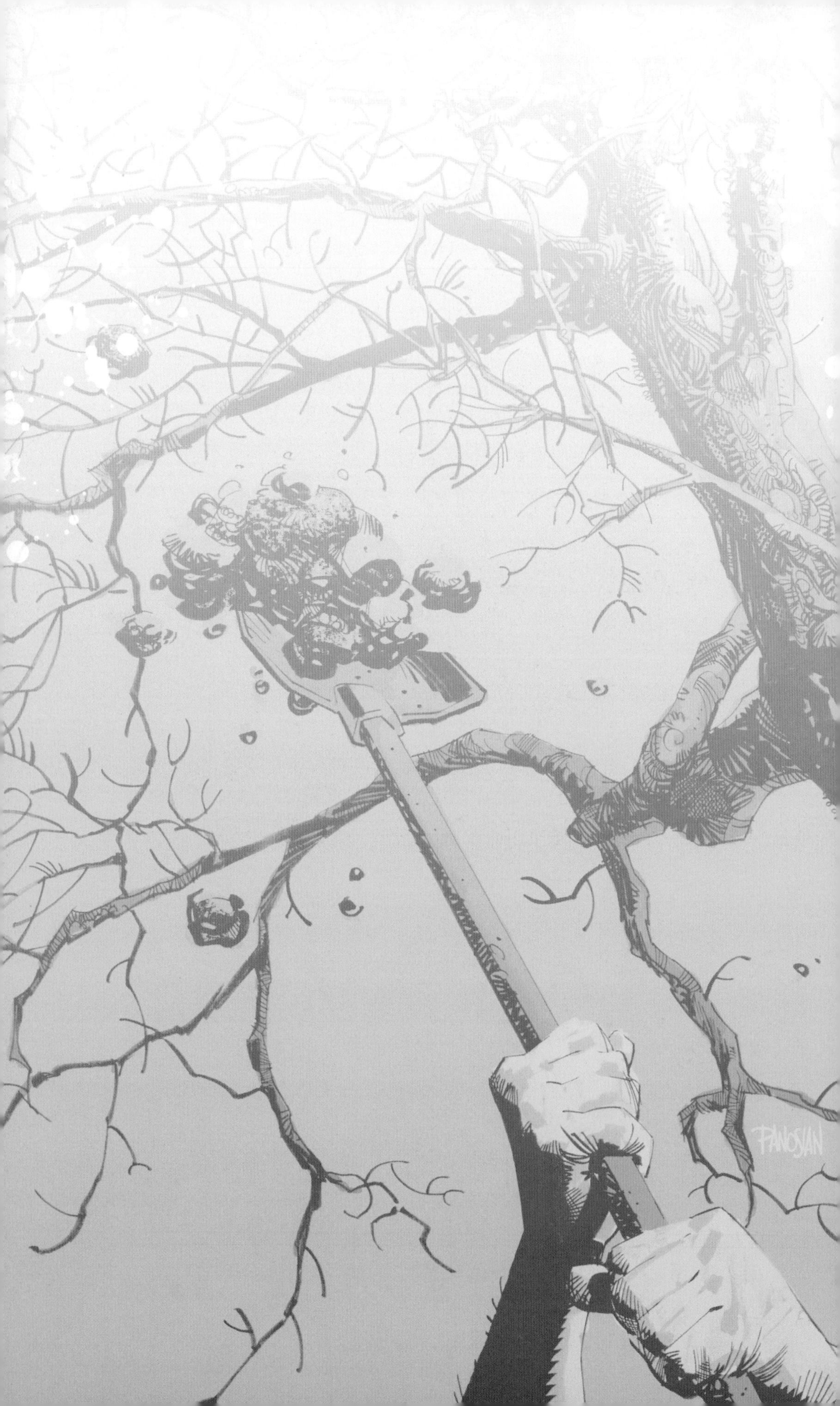
PANOSYAN

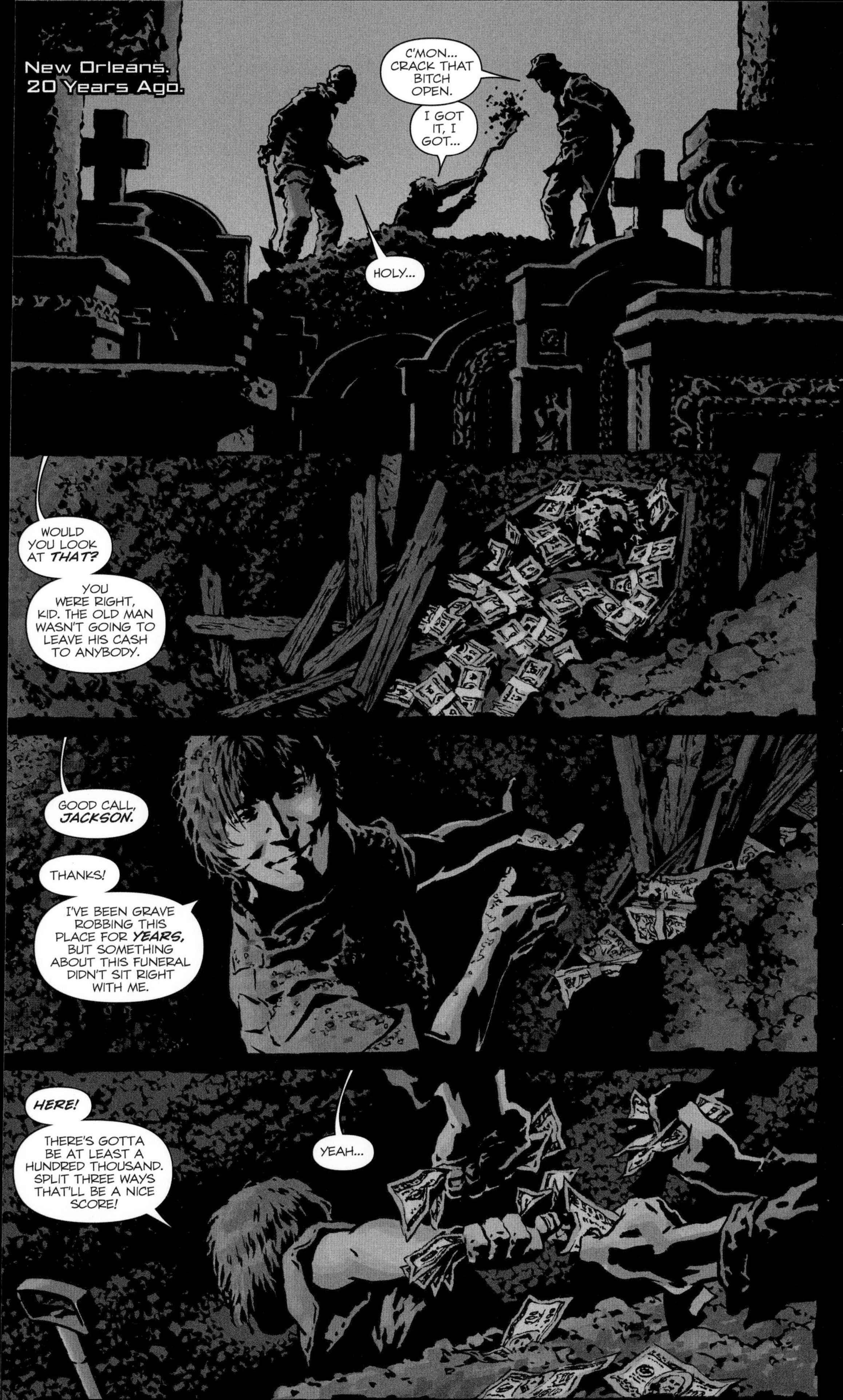
New Orleans.
20 Years Ago.
C'MON... CRACK THAT BITCH OPEN.
I GOT IT, I GOT...
HOLY...
WOULD YOU LOOK AT *THAT?*
YOU WERE RIGHT, KID. THE OLD MAN WASN'T GOING TO LEAVE HIS CASH TO ANYBODY.
GOOD CALL, *JACKSON.*
THANKS!
I'VE BEEN GRAVE ROBBING THIS PLACE FOR *YEARS,* BUT SOMETHING ABOUT THIS FUNERAL DIDN'T SIT RIGHT WITH ME.
HERE!
THERE'S GOTTA BE AT LEAST A HUNDRED THOUSAND. SPLIT THREE WAYS THAT'LL BE A NICE SCORE!
YEAH...

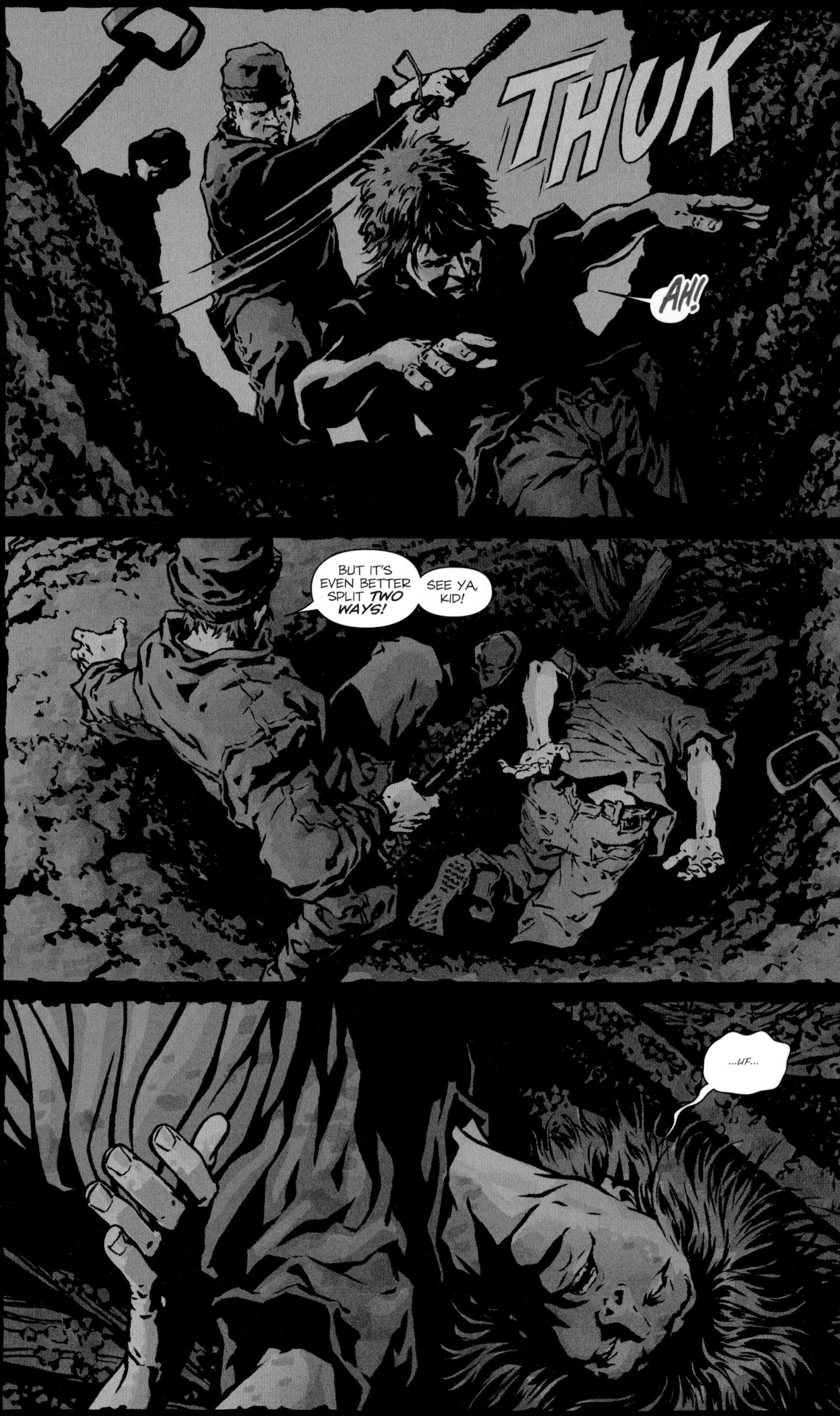
THUK
AH!
BUT IT'S EVEN BETTER SPLIT TWO WAYS!
SEE YA, KID!
...UF...

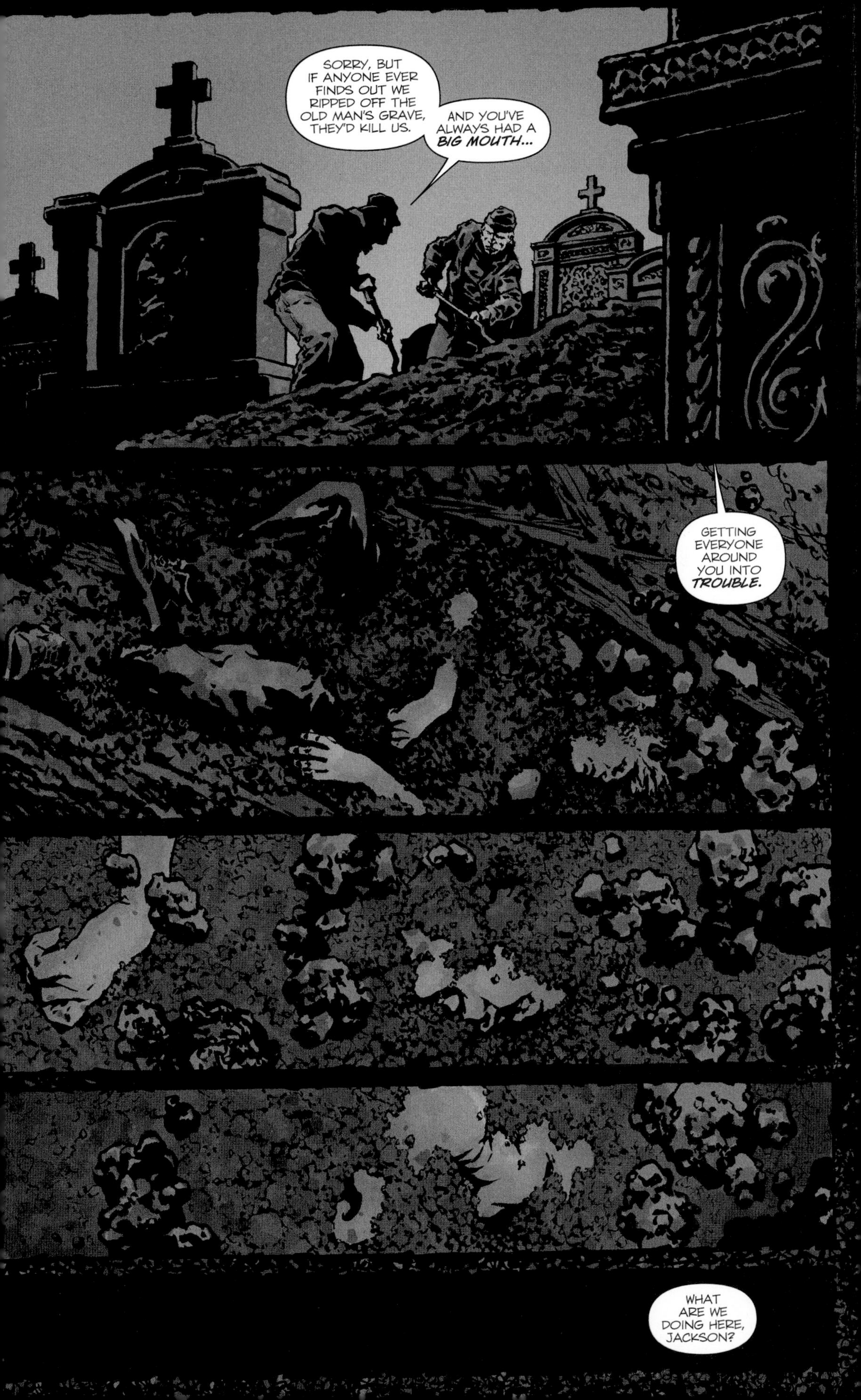
SORRY, BUT IF ANYONE EVER FINDS OUT WE RIPPED OFF THE OLD MAN'S GRAVE, THEY'D KILL US.
AND YOU'VE ALWAYS HAD A *BIG MOUTH...*
GETTING EVERYONE AROUND YOU INTO *TROUBLE.*
WHAT ARE WE DOING HERE, JACKSON?

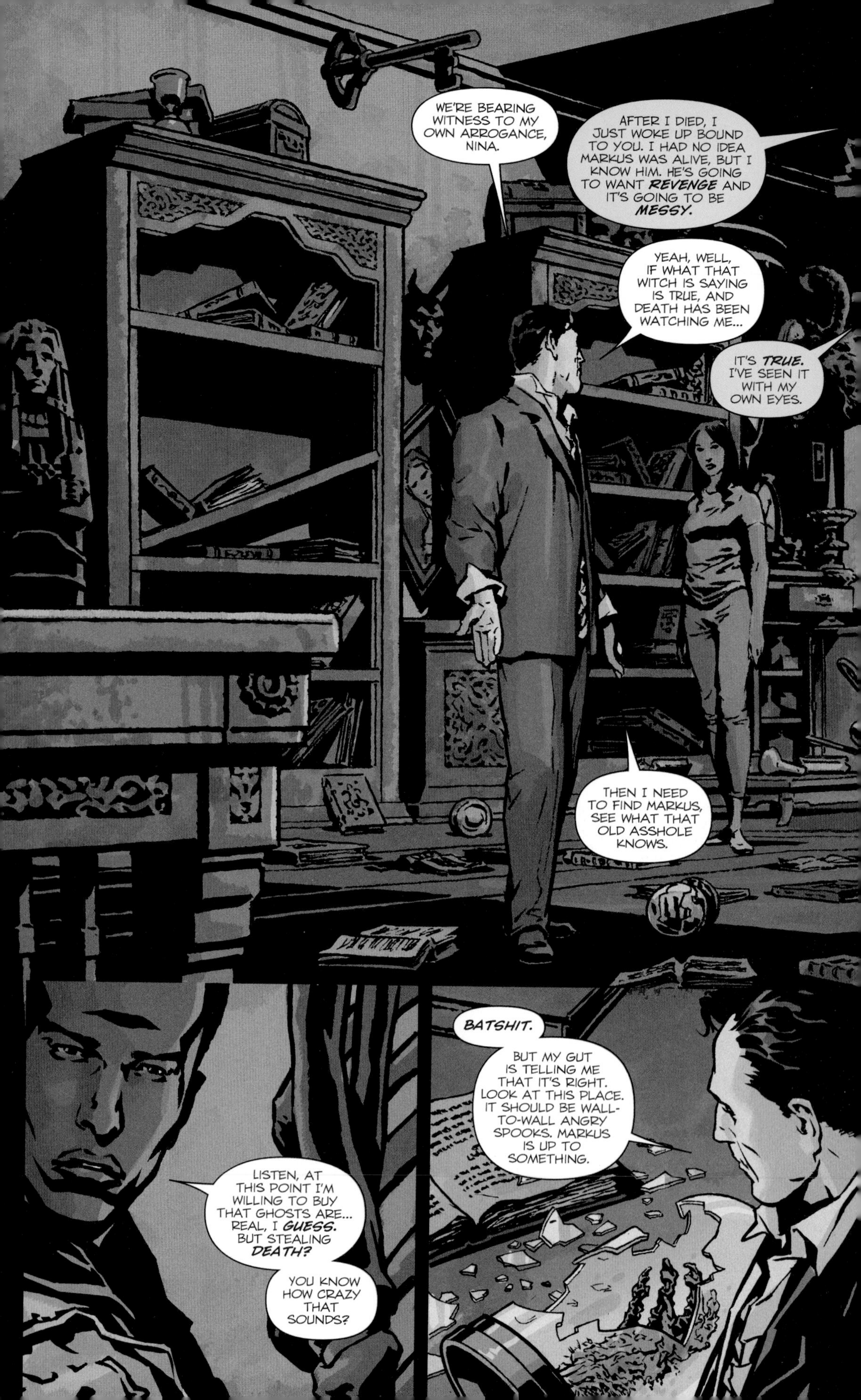
WE'RE BEARING WITNESS TO MY OWN ARROGANCE, NINA.
AFTER I DIED, I JUST WOKE UP BOUND TO YOU. I HAD NO IDEA MARKUS WAS ALIVE, BUT I KNOW HIM. HE'S GOING TO WANT REVENGE AND IT'S GOING TO BE MESSY.
YEAH, WELL, IF WHAT THAT WITCH IS SAYING IS TRUE, AND DEATH HAS BEEN WATCHING ME...
IT'S TRUE. I'VE SEEN IT WITH MY OWN EYES.
THEN I NEED TO FIND MARKUS, SEE WHAT THAT OLD ASSHOLE KNOWS.
LISTEN, AT THIS POINT I'M WILLING TO BUY THAT GHOSTS ARE... REAL, I GUESS. BUT STEALING DEATH?
YOU KNOW HOW CRAZY THAT SOUNDS?
BATSHIT.
BUT MY GUT IS TELLING ME THAT IT'S RIGHT. LOOK AT THIS PLACE. IT SHOULD BE WALL-TO-WALL ANGRY SPOOKS. MARKUS IS UP TO SOMETHING.

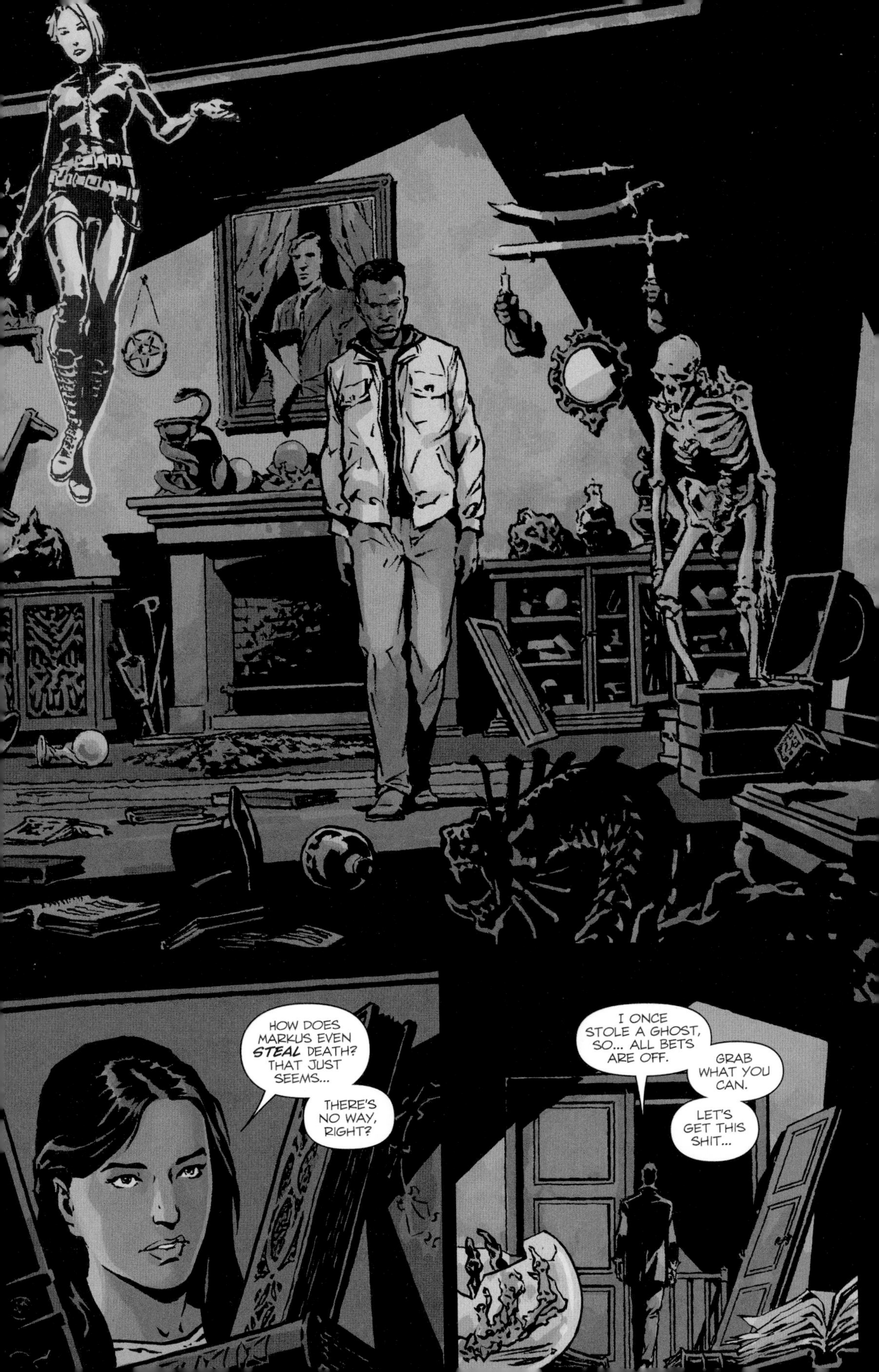
HOW DOES MARKUS EVEN STEAL DEATH? THAT JUST SEEMS...
THERE'S NO WAY, RIGHT?
I ONCE STOLE A GHOST, SO... ALL BETS ARE OFF.
GRAB WHAT YOU CAN.
LET'S GET THIS SHIT...

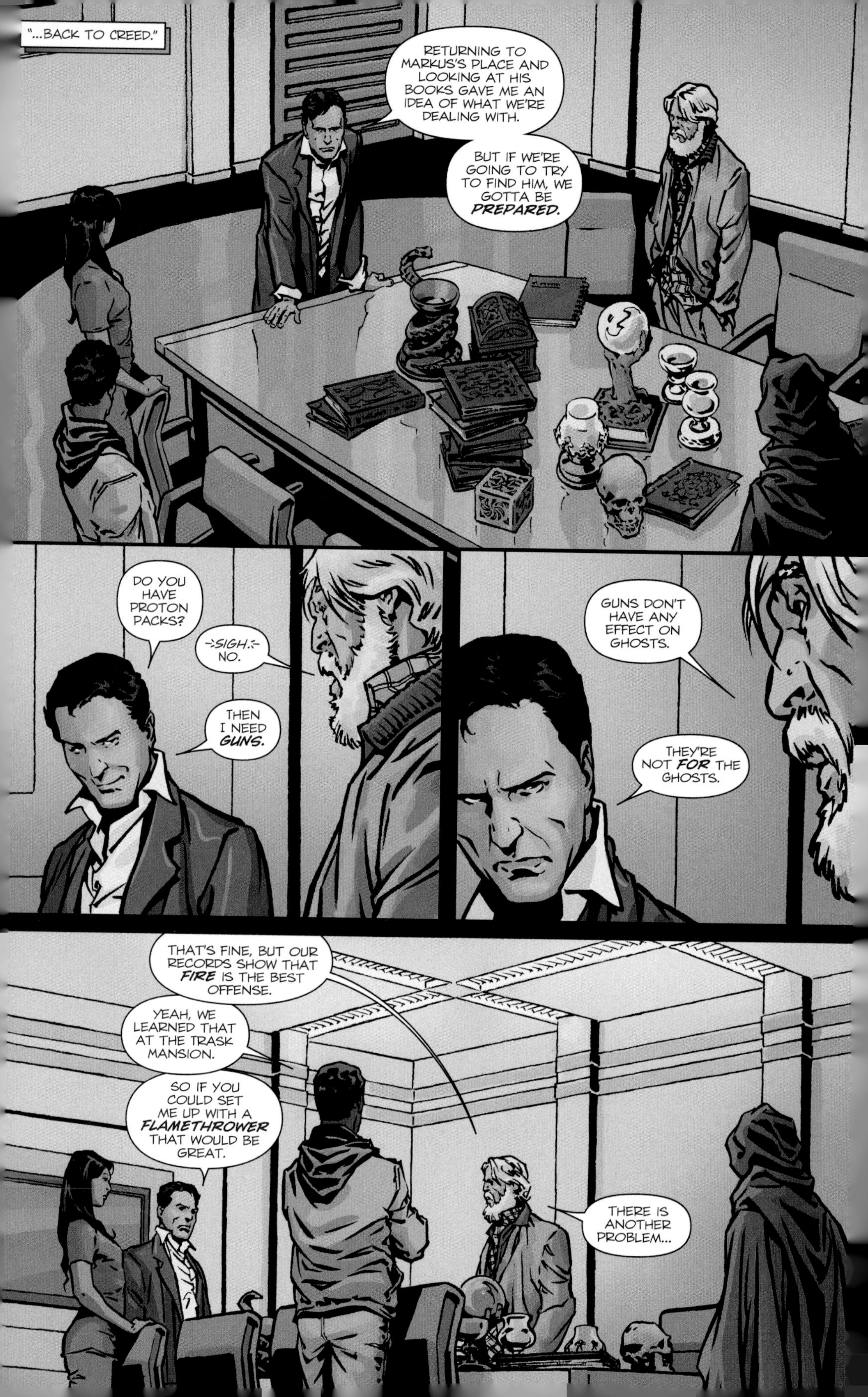
"...BACK TO CREED."
RETURNING TO MARKUS'S PLACE AND LOOKING AT HIS BOOKS GAVE ME AN IDEA OF WHAT WE'RE DEALING WITH.
BUT IF WE'RE GOING TO TRY TO FIND HIM, WE GOTTA BE *PREPARED.*
DO YOU HAVE PROTON PACKS?
-SIGH.- NO.
THEN I NEED *GUNS.*
GUNS DON'T HAVE ANY EFFECT ON GHOSTS.
THEY'RE NOT *FOR* THE GHOSTS.
THAT'S FINE, BUT OUR RECORDS SHOW THAT *FIRE* IS THE BEST OFFENSE.
YEAH, WE LEARNED THAT AT THE TRASK MANSION.
SO IF YOU COULD SET ME UP WITH A *FLAMETHROWER* THAT WOULD BE GREAT.
THERE IS ANOTHER PROBLEM...

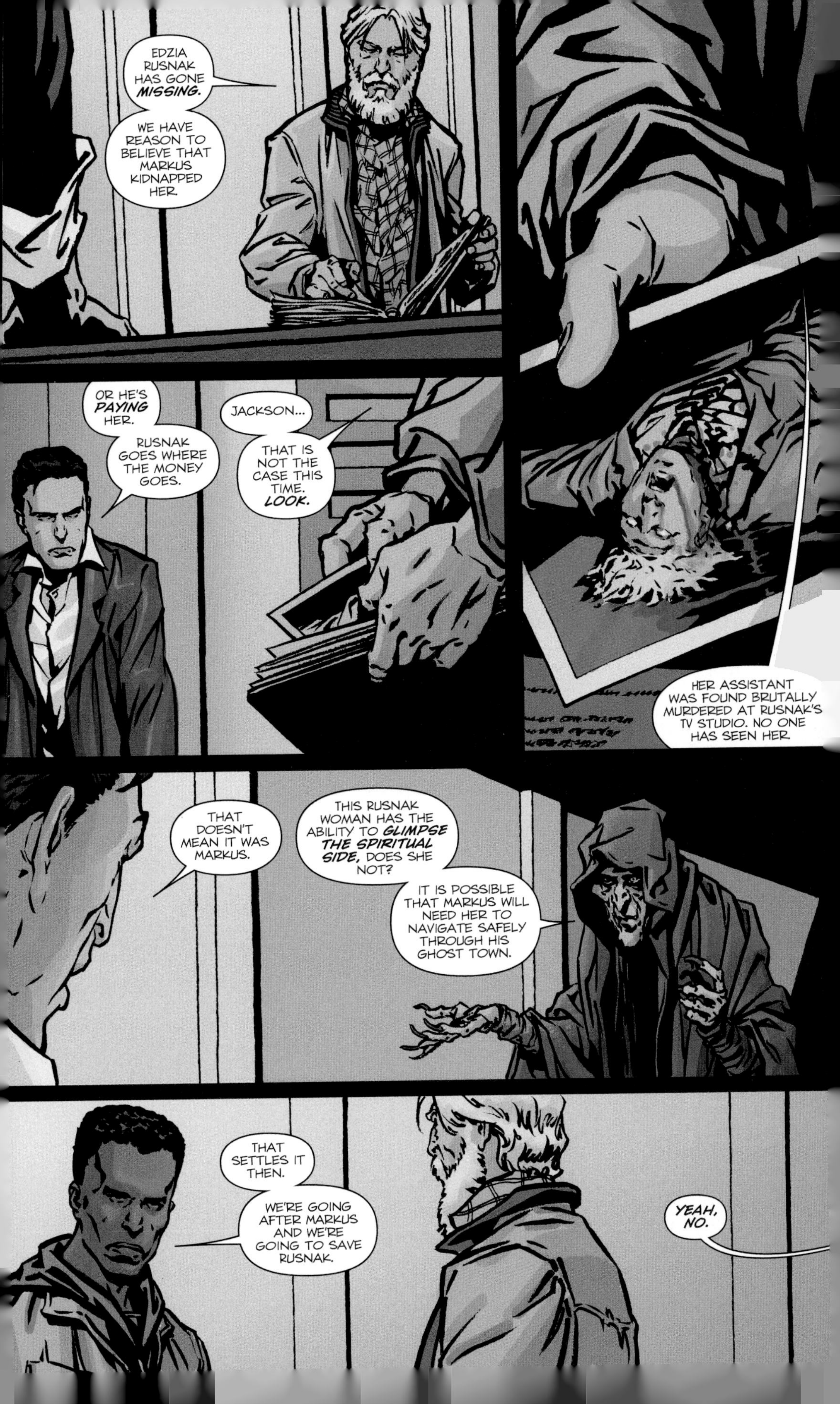
EDZIA RUSNAK HAS GONE MISSING.
WE HAVE REASON TO BELIEVE THAT MARKUS KIDNAPPED HER.
OR HE'S PAYING HER.
RUSNAK GOES WHERE THE MONEY GOES.
JACKSON...
THAT IS NOT THE CASE THIS TIME. LOOK.
HER ASSISTANT WAS FOUND BRUTALLY MURDERED AT RUSNAK'S TV STUDIO. NO ONE HAS SEEN HER.
THAT DOESN'T MEAN IT WAS MARKUS.
THIS RUSNAK WOMAN HAS THE ABILITY TO GLIMPSE THE SPIRITUAL SIDE, DOES SHE NOT?
IT IS POSSIBLE THAT MARKUS WILL NEED HER TO NAVIGATE SAFELY THROUGH HIS GHOST TOWN.
THAT SETTLES IT THEN.
WE'RE GOING AFTER MARKUS AND WE'RE GOING TO SAVE RUSNAK.
YEAH, NO.

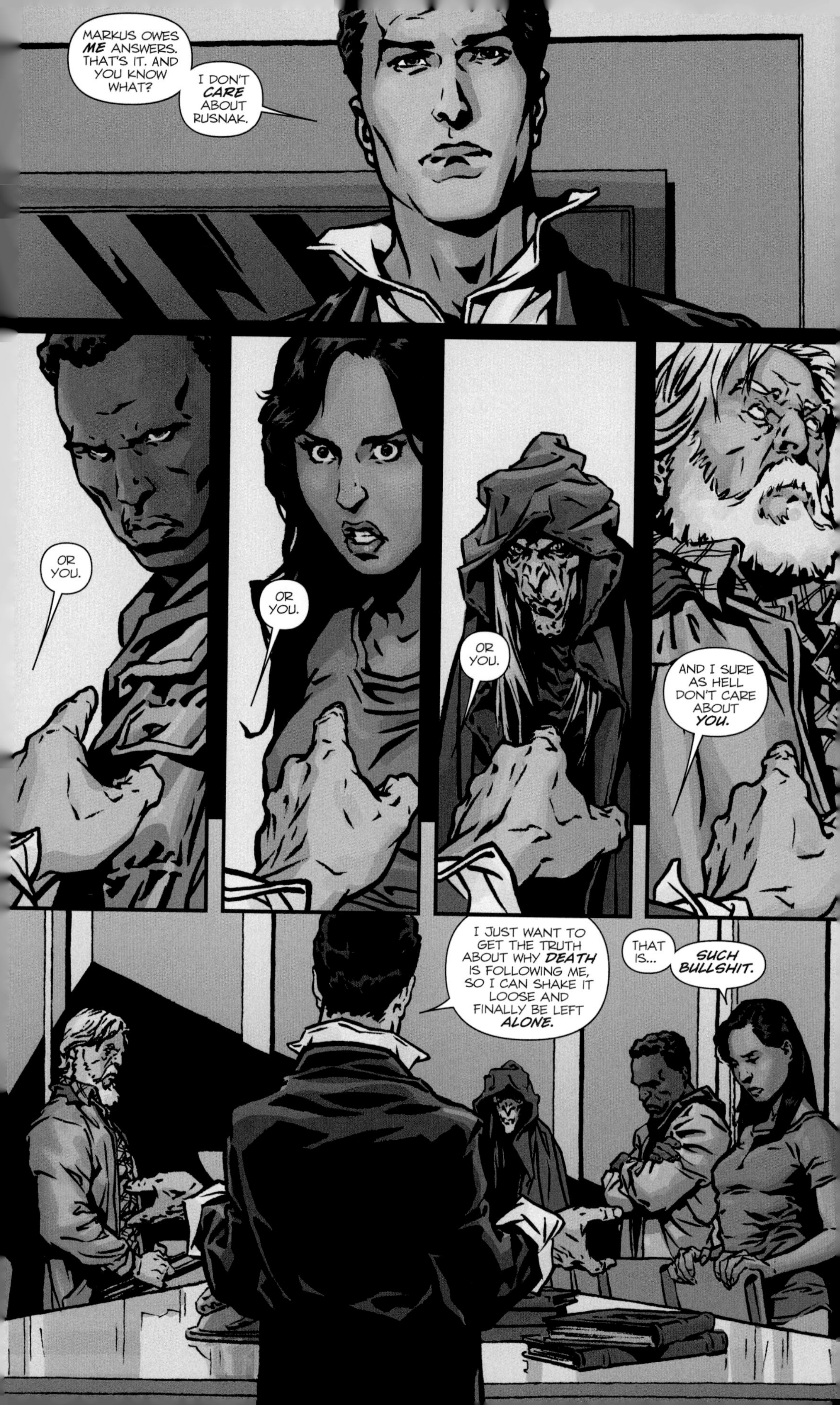
MARKUS OWES ME ANSWERS. THAT'S IT. AND YOU KNOW WHAT?
I DON'T CARE ABOUT RUSNAK.
OR YOU.
OR YOU.
OR YOU.
AND I SURE AS HELL DON'T CARE ABOUT YOU.
I JUST WANT TO GET THE TRUTH ABOUT WHY DEATH IS FOLLOWING ME, SO I CAN SHAKE IT LOOSE AND FINALLY BE LEFT ALONE.
THAT IS... SUCH BULLSHIT.

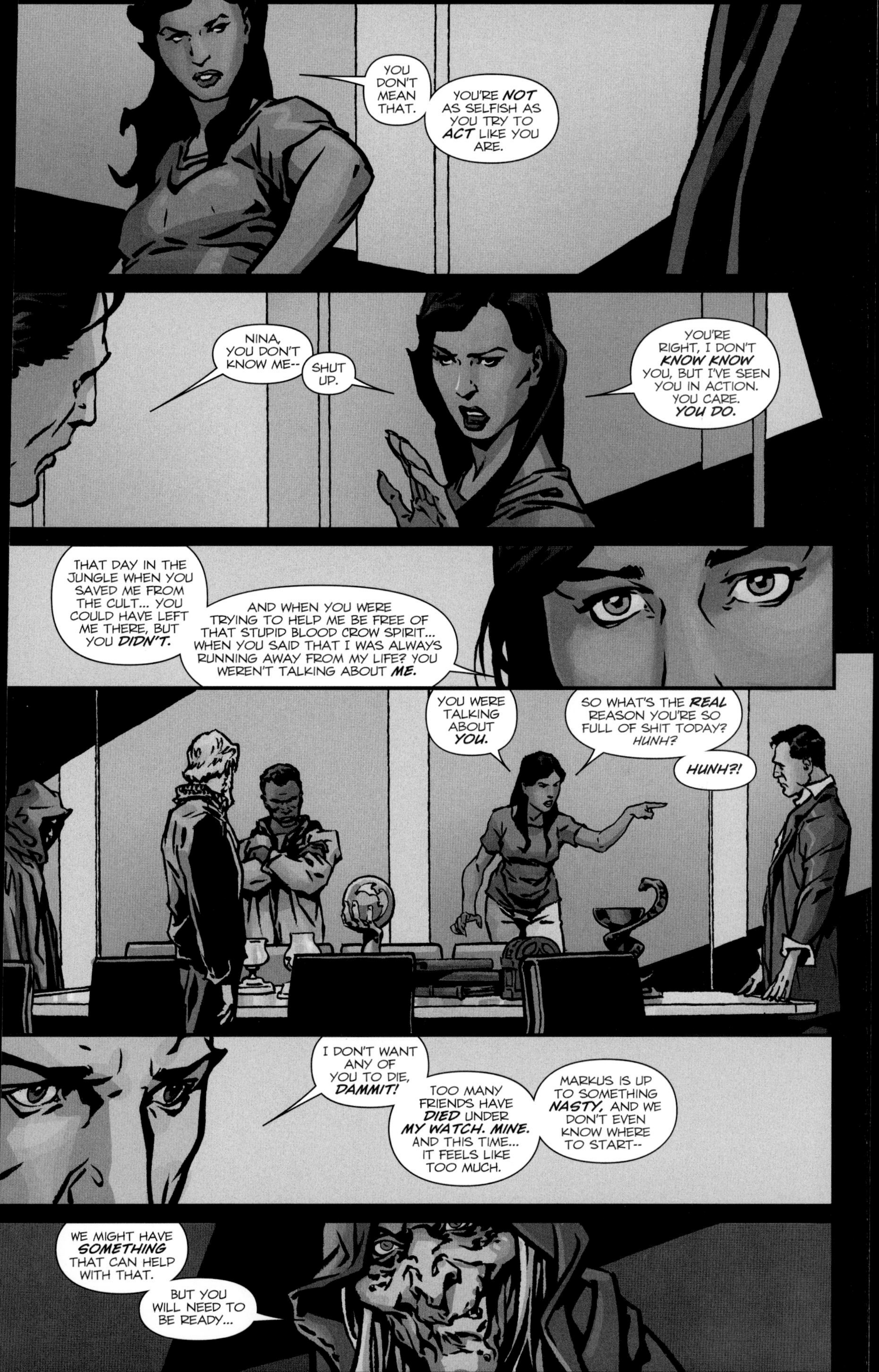
YOU DON'T MEAN THAT.
YOU'RE **NOT** AS SELFISH AS YOU TRY TO **ACT** LIKE YOU ARE.
NINA, YOU DON'T KNOW ME--
SHUT UP.
YOU'RE RIGHT, I DON'T **KNOW KNOW** YOU, BUT I'VE SEEN YOU IN ACTION. YOU CARE. **YOU DO.**
THAT DAY IN THE JUNGLE WHEN YOU SAVED ME FROM THE CULT... YOU COULD HAVE LEFT ME THERE, BUT YOU **DIDN'T.**
AND WHEN YOU WERE TRYING TO HELP ME BE FREE OF THAT STUPID BLOOD CROW SPIRIT... WHEN YOU SAID THAT I WAS ALWAYS RUNNING AWAY FROM MY LIFE? YOU WEREN'T TALKING ABOUT **ME.**
YOU WERE TALKING ABOUT **YOU.**
SO WHAT'S THE **REAL** REASON YOU'RE SO FULL OF SHIT TODAY? *HUNH?*
HUNH?!
I DON'T WANT ANY OF YOU TO DIE, **DAMMIT!**
TOO MANY FRIENDS HAVE **DIED** UNDER **MY WATCH. MINE.** AND THIS TIME... IT FEELS LIKE TOO MUCH.
MARKUS IS UP TO SOMETHING **NASTY,** AND WE DON'T EVEN KNOW WHERE TO START--
WE MIGHT HAVE **SOMETHING** THAT CAN HELP WITH THAT.
BUT YOU WILL NEED TO BE READY...

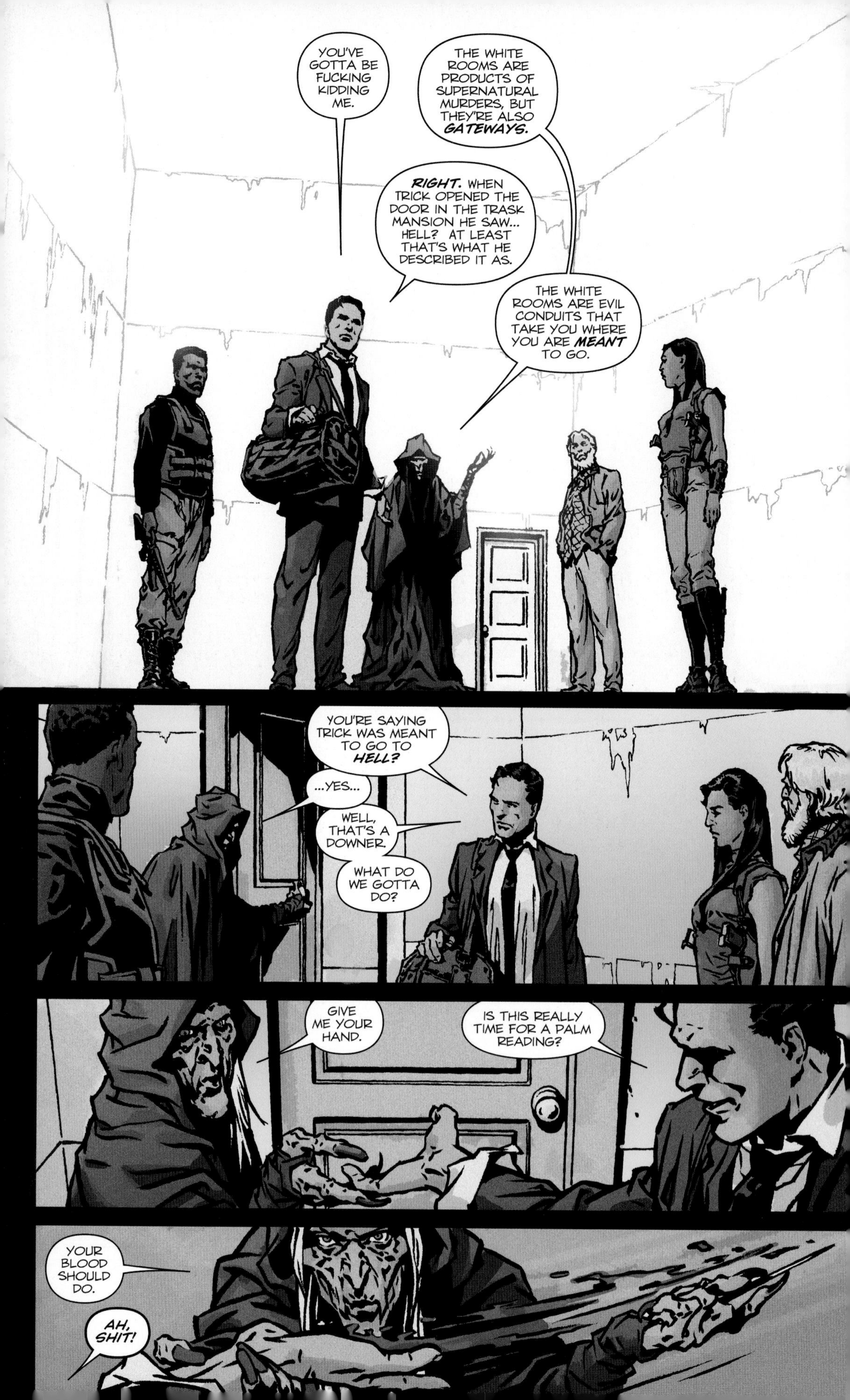

YOU'VE GOTTA BE FUCKING KIDDING ME.
THE WHITE ROOMS ARE PRODUCTS OF SUPERNATURAL MURDERS, BUT THEY'RE ALSO **GATEWAYS.**
RIGHT. WHEN TRICK OPENED THE DOOR IN THE TRASK MANSION HE SAW... HELL? AT LEAST THAT'S WHAT HE DESCRIBED IT AS.
THE WHITE ROOMS ARE EVIL CONDUITS THAT TAKE YOU WHERE YOU ARE **MEANT** TO GO.
YOU'RE SAYING TRICK WAS MEANT TO GO TO **HELL?**
...YES...
WELL, THAT'S A DOWNER.
WHAT DO WE GOTTA DO?
GIVE ME YOUR HAND.
IS THIS REALLY TIME FOR A PALM READING?
YOUR BLOOD SHOULD DO.
AH, SHIT!

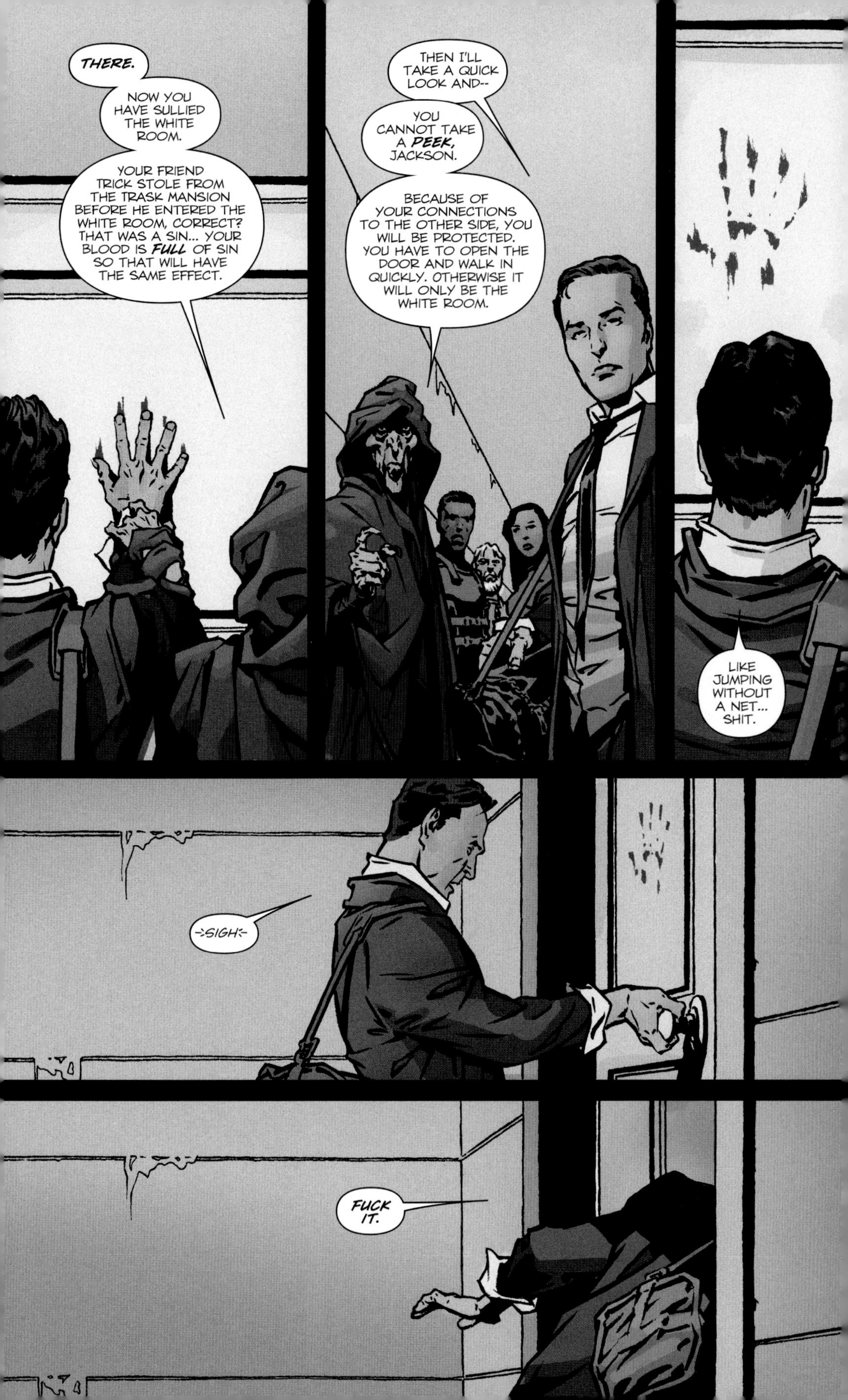
THERE.
NOW YOU HAVE SULLIED THE WHITE ROOM.
YOUR FRIEND TRICK STOLE FROM THE TRASK MANSION BEFORE HE ENTERED THE WHITE ROOM, CORRECT? THAT WAS A SIN... YOUR BLOOD IS FULL OF SIN SO THAT WILL HAVE THE SAME EFFECT.
THEN I'LL TAKE A QUICK LOOK AND--
YOU CANNOT TAKE A PEEK, JACKSON.
BECAUSE OF YOUR CONNECTIONS TO THE OTHER SIDE, YOU WILL BE PROTECTED. YOU HAVE TO OPEN THE DOOR AND WALK IN QUICKLY. OTHERWISE IT WILL ONLY BE THE WHITE ROOM.
LIKE JUMPING WITHOUT A NET... SHIT.
-SIGH-
FUCK IT.

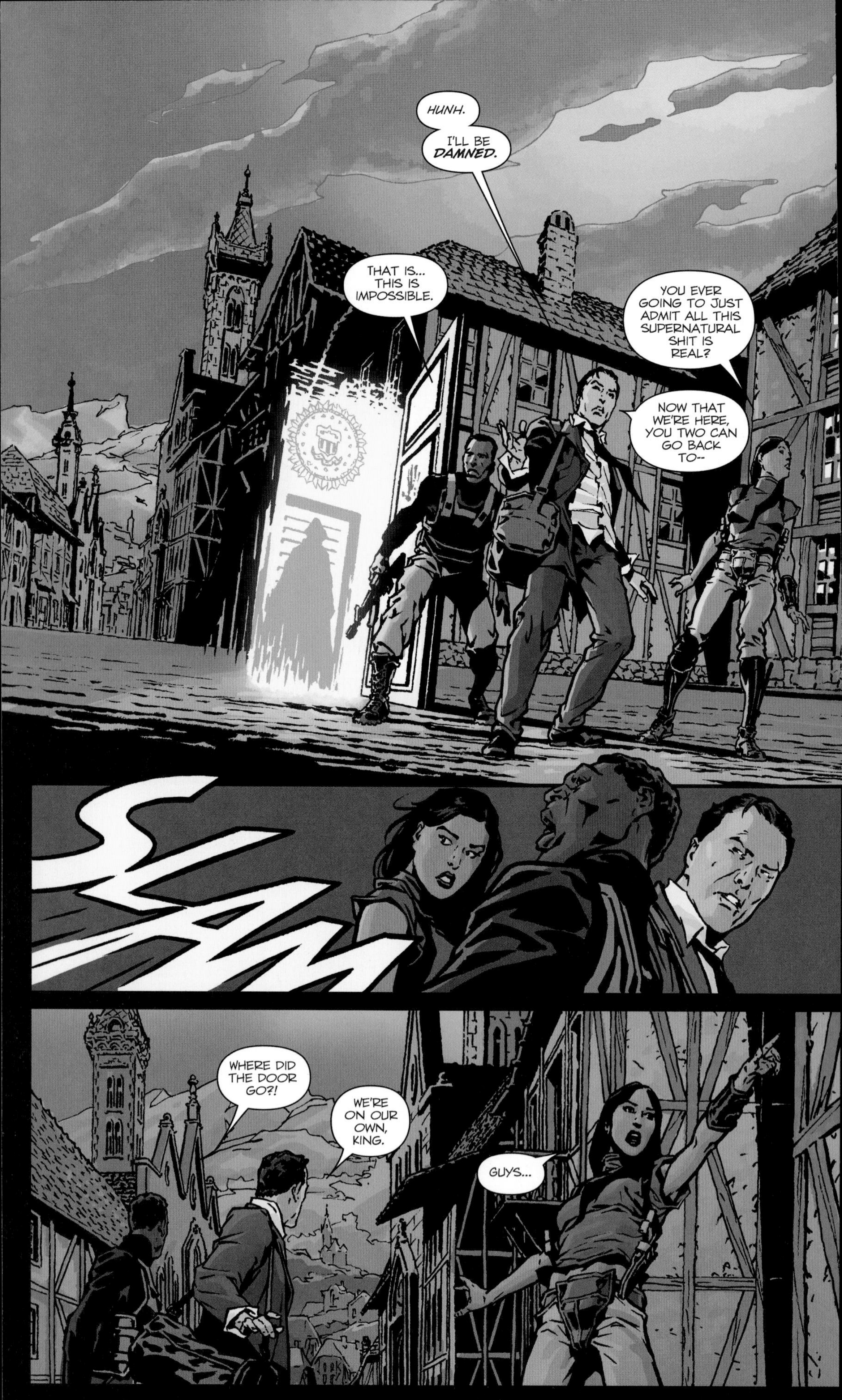
HUNH.
I'LL BE DAMNED.
THAT IS... THIS IS IMPOSSIBLE.
YOU EVER GOING TO JUST ADMIT ALL THIS SUPERNATURAL SHIT IS REAL?
NOW THAT WE'RE HERE, YOU TWO CAN GO BACK TO--
SLAM
WHERE DID THE DOOR GO?!
WE'RE ON OUR OWN, KING.
GUYS...

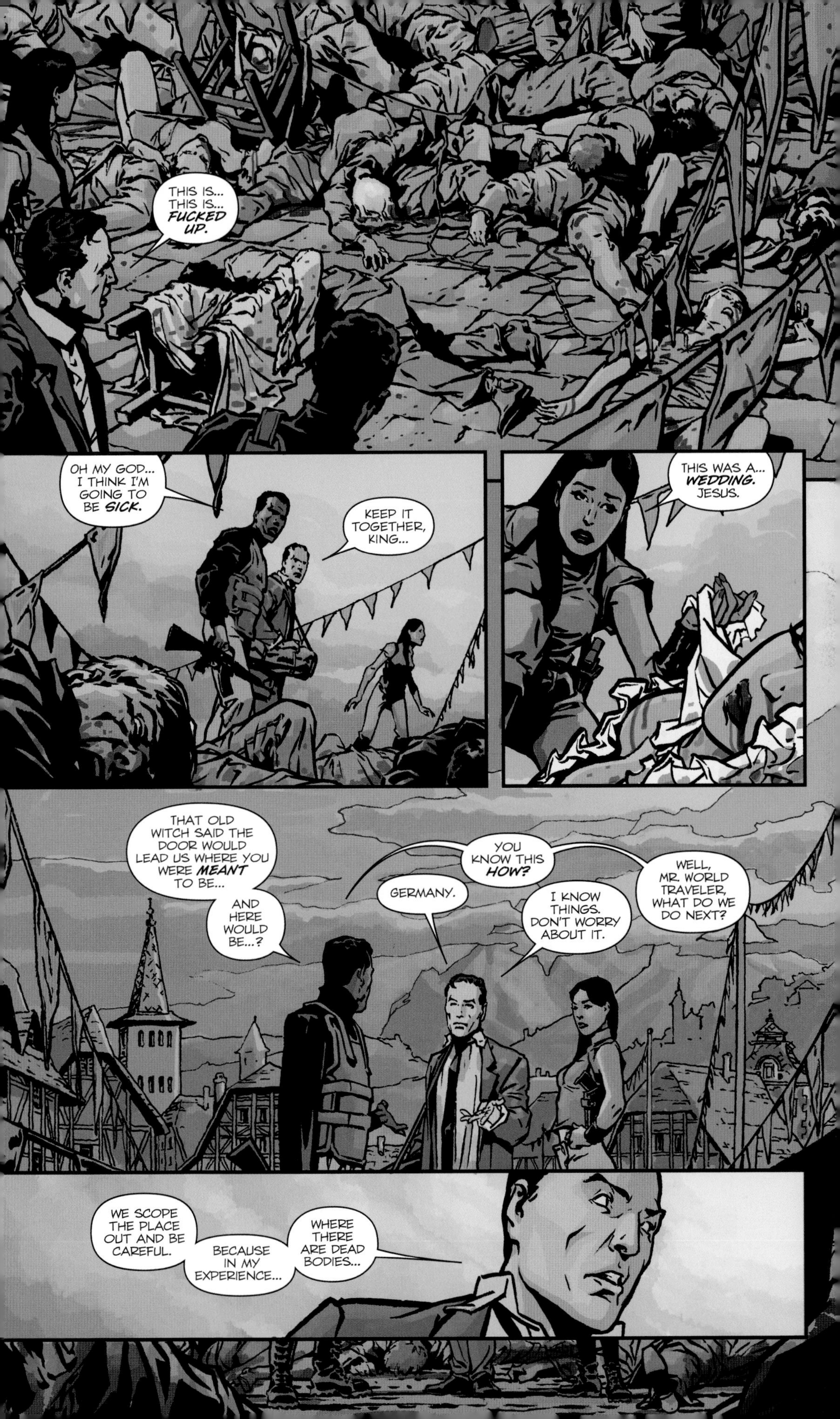
THIS IS... THIS IS... FUCKED UP.
OH MY GOD... I THINK I'M GOING TO BE SICK.
KEEP IT TOGETHER, KING...
THIS WAS A... WEDDING. JESUS.
THAT OLD WITCH SAID THE DOOR WOULD LEAD US WHERE YOU WERE MEANT TO BE...
AND HERE WOULD BE...?
GERMANY.
YOU KNOW THIS HOW?
I KNOW THINGS. DON'T WORRY ABOUT IT.
WELL, MR. WORLD TRAVELER, WHAT DO WE DO NEXT?
WE SCOPE THE PLACE OUT AND BE CAREFUL.
BECAUSE IN MY EXPERIENCE...
WHERE THERE ARE DEAD BODIES...

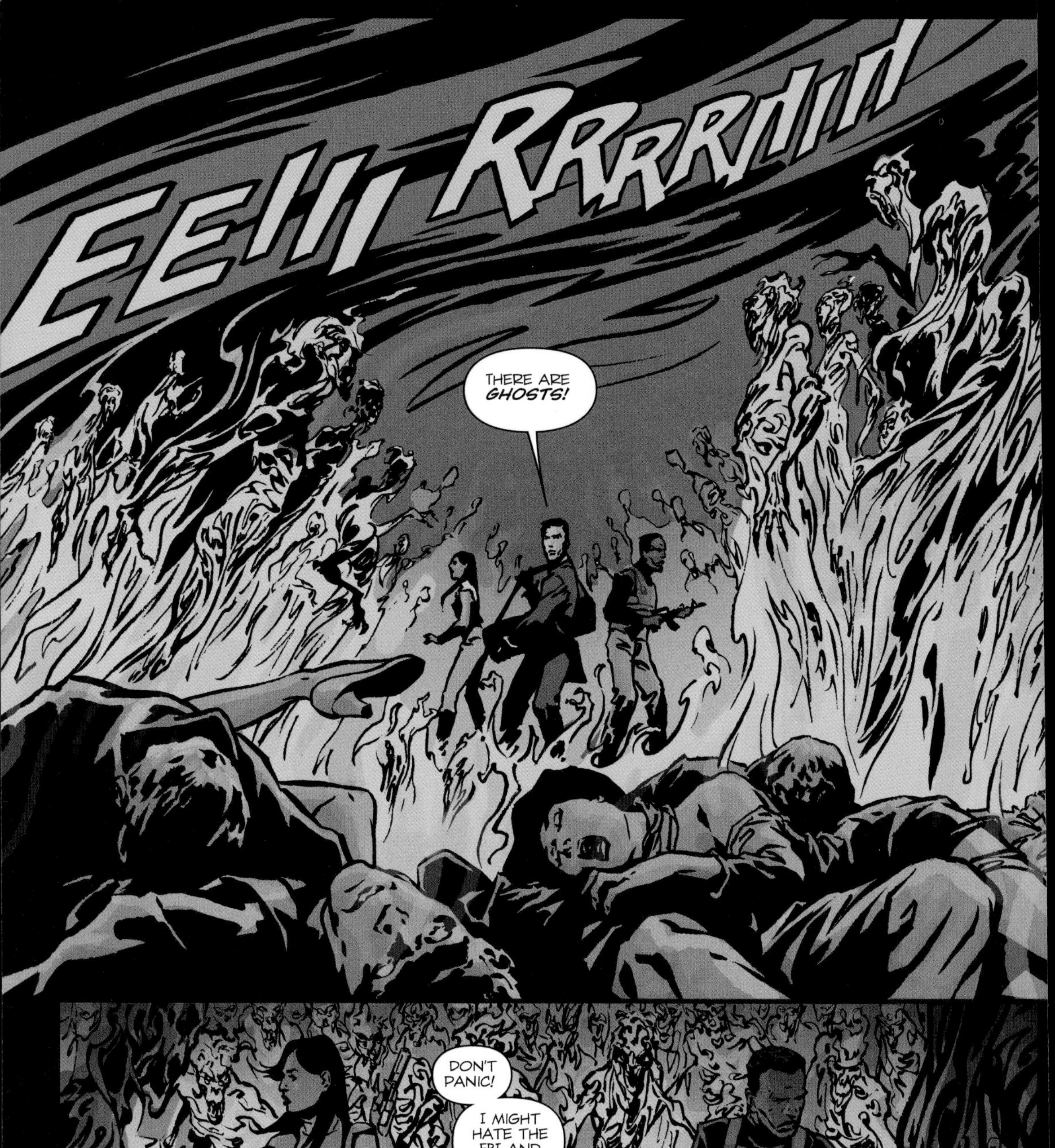
EEIII RRRRRIIII
THERE ARE *GHOSTS!*

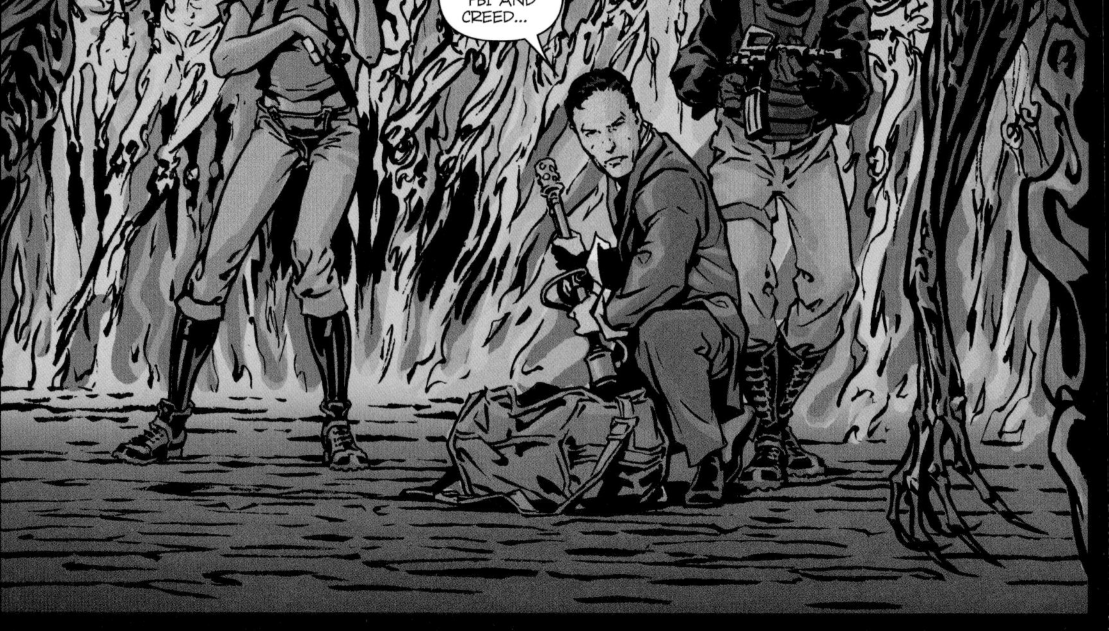
DON'T PANIC!
I MIGHT HATE THE FBI AND CREED...

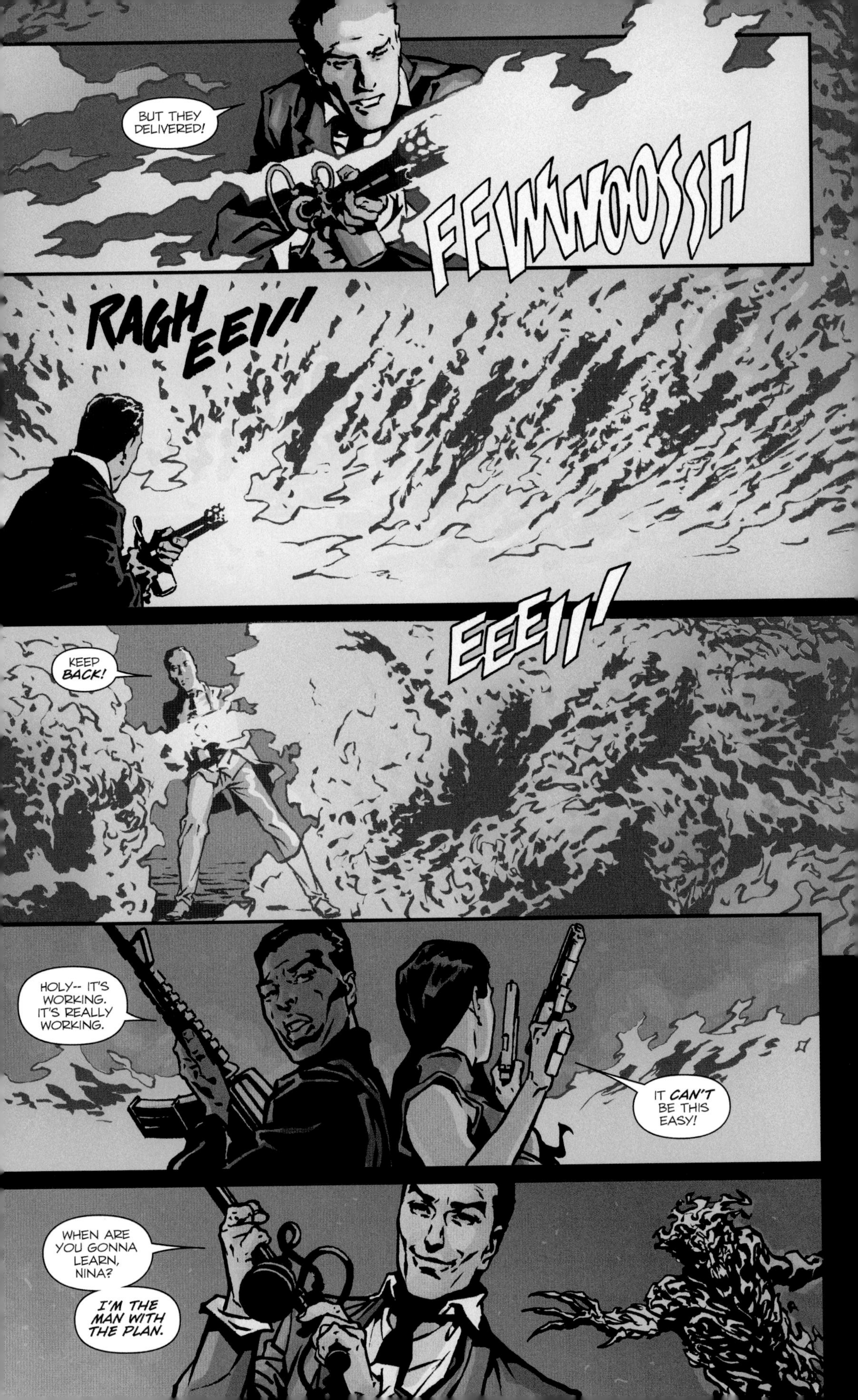

BUT THEY DELIVERED!
FFWWOOSSH
RAGH EEI!!
EEEI!!
KEEP BACK!
HOLY-- IT'S WORKING. IT'S REALLY WORKING.
IT CAN'T BE THIS EASY!
WHEN ARE YOU GONNA LEARN, NINA?
I'M THE MAN WITH THE PLAN.

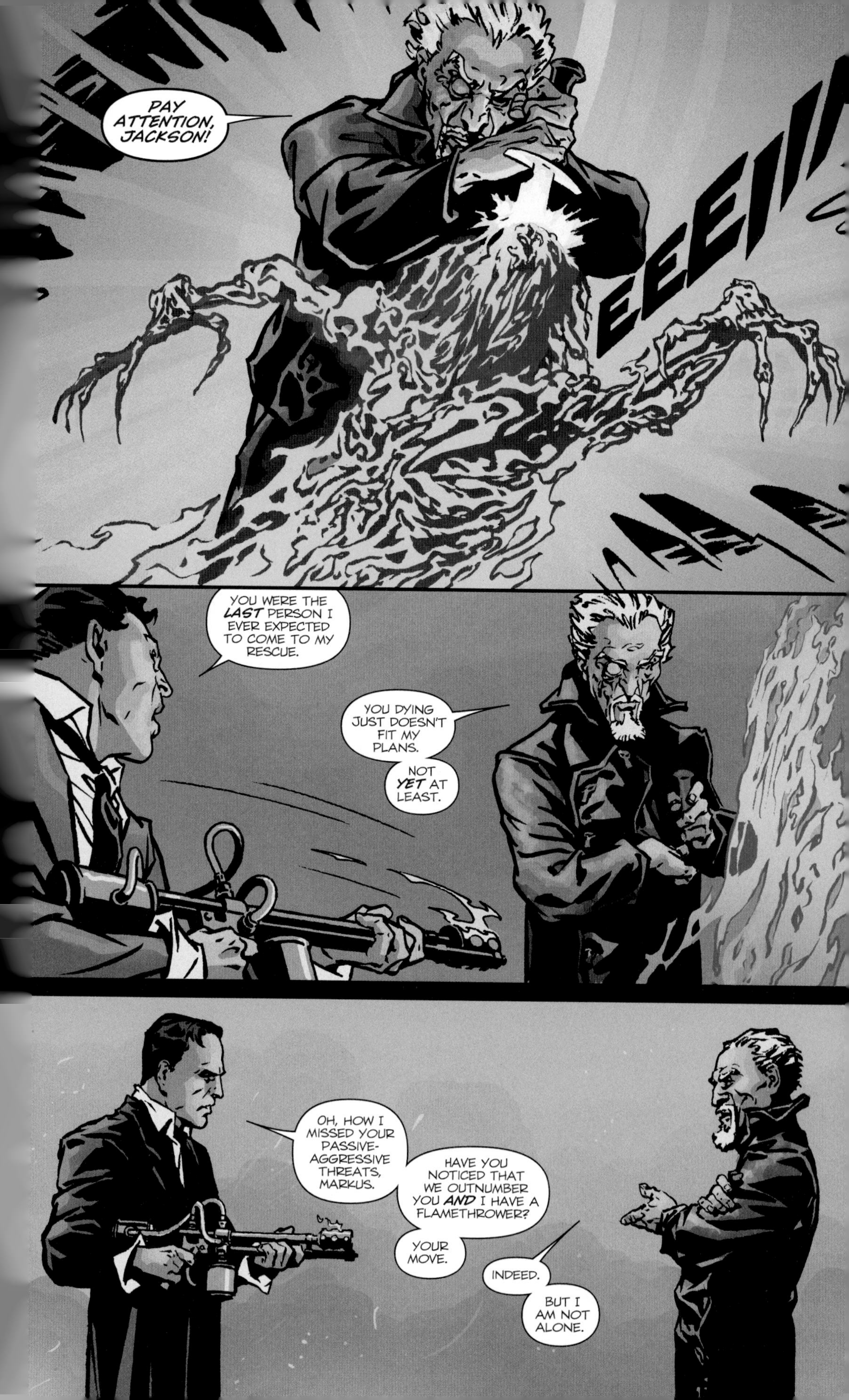
PAY ATTENTION, JACKSON!
EEEIII
YOU WERE THE LAST PERSON I EVER EXPECTED TO COME TO MY RESCUE.
YOU DYING JUST DOESN'T FIT MY PLANS.
NOT YET AT LEAST.
OH, HOW I MISSED YOUR PASSIVE-AGGRESSIVE THREATS, MARKUS.
HAVE YOU NOTICED THAT WE OUTNUMBER YOU AND I HAVE A FLAMETHROWER?
YOUR MOVE.
INDEED.
BUT I AM NOT ALONE.

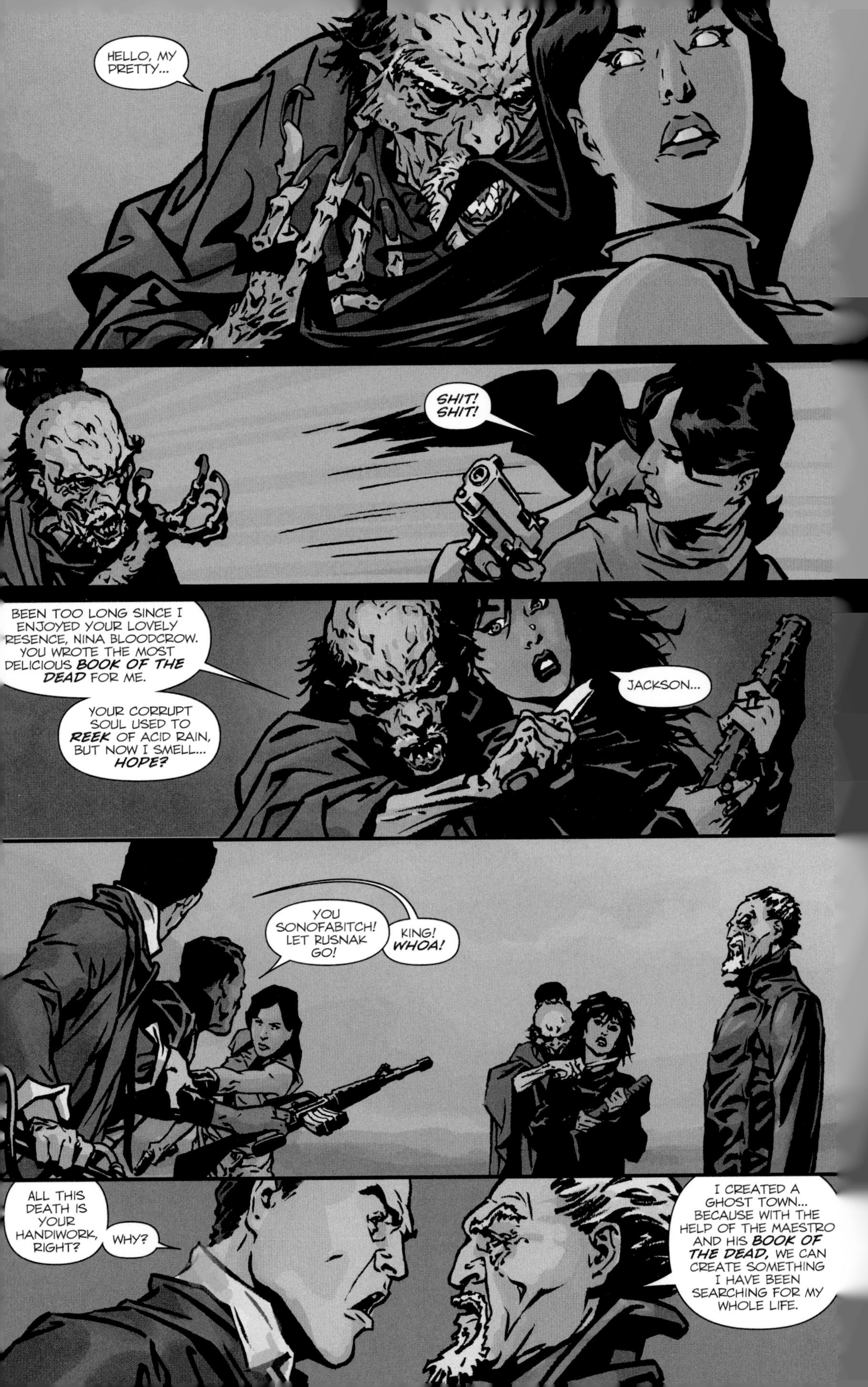
HELLO, MY PRETTY...
SHIT! SHIT!
BEEN TOO LONG SINCE I ENJOYED YOUR LOVELY RESENCE, NINA BLOODCROW. YOU WROTE THE MOST DELICIOUS BOOK OF THE DEAD FOR ME.
YOUR CORRUPT SOUL USED TO REEK OF ACID RAIN, BUT NOW I SMELL... HOPE?
JACKSON...
YOU SONOFABITCH! LET RUSNAK GO!
KING! WHOA!
ALL THIS DEATH IS YOUR HANDIWORK, RIGHT?
WHY?
I CREATED A GHOST TOWN... BECAUSE WITH THE HELP OF THE MAESTRO AND HIS BOOK OF THE DEAD, WE CAN CREATE SOMETHING I HAVE BEEN SEARCHING FOR MY WHOLE LIFE.

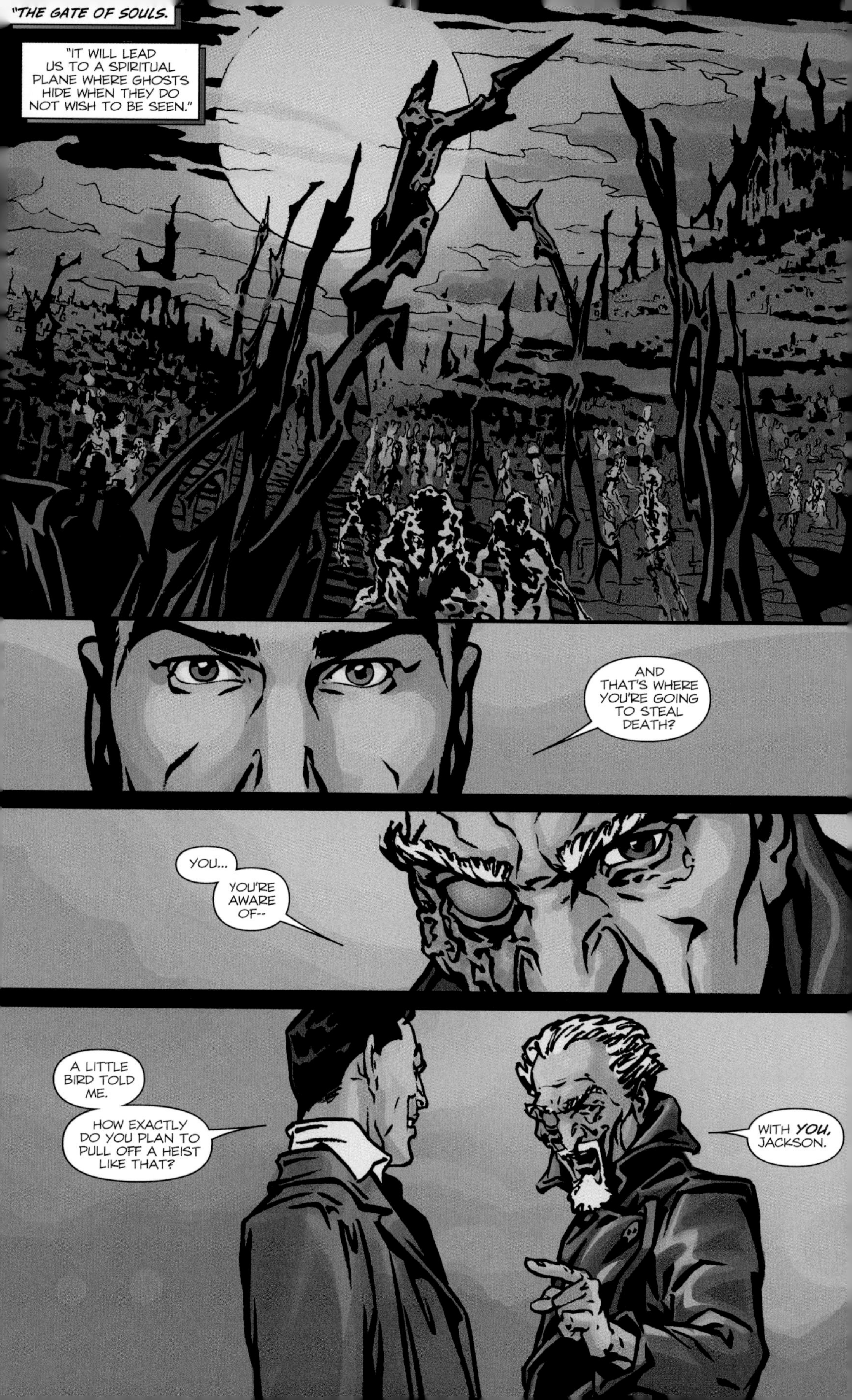
"THE GATE OF SOULS.
"IT WILL LEAD US TO A SPIRITUAL PLANE WHERE GHOSTS HIDE WHEN THEY DO NOT WISH TO BE SEEN."
AND THAT'S WHERE YOU'RE GOING TO STEAL DEATH?
YOU...
YOU'RE AWARE OF--
A LITTLE BIRD TOLD ME.
HOW EXACTLY DO YOU PLAN TO PULL OFF A HEIST LIKE THAT?
WITH *YOU,* JACKSON.

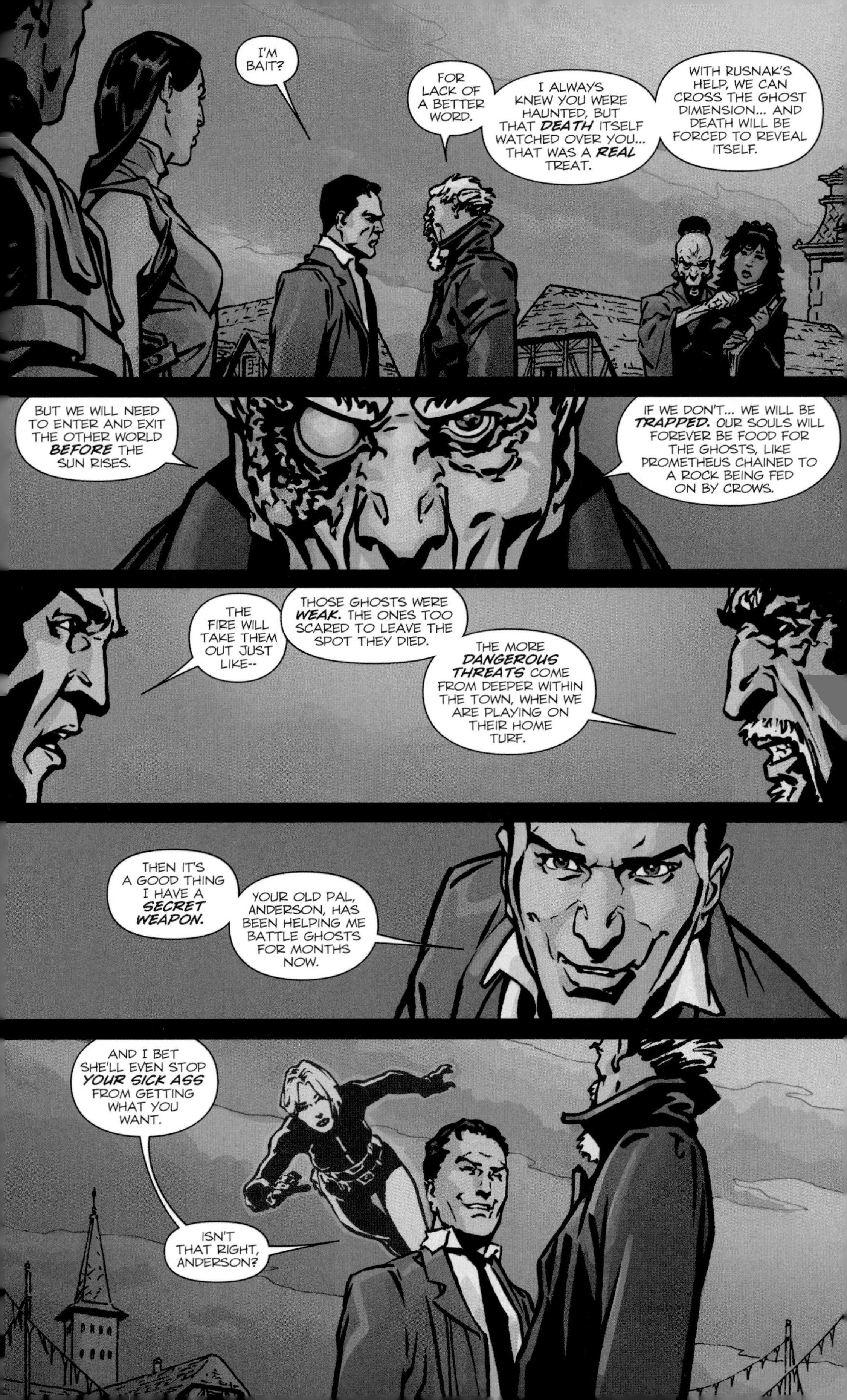
I'M BAIT?
FOR LACK OF A BETTER WORD.
I ALWAYS KNEW YOU WERE HAUNTED, BUT THAT DEATH ITSELF WATCHED OVER YOU... THAT WAS A REAL TREAT.
WITH RUSNAK'S HELP, WE CAN CROSS THE GHOST DIMENSION... AND DEATH WILL BE FORCED TO REVEAL ITSELF.
BUT WE WILL NEED TO ENTER AND EXIT THE OTHER WORLD BEFORE THE SUN RISES.
IF WE DON'T... WE WILL BE TRAPPED. OUR SOULS WILL FOREVER BE FOOD FOR THE GHOSTS, LIKE PROMETHEUS CHAINED TO A ROCK BEING FED ON BY CROWS.
THE FIRE WILL TAKE THEM OUT JUST LIKE--
THOSE GHOSTS WERE WEAK. THE ONES TOO SCARED TO LEAVE THE SPOT THEY DIED.
THE MORE DANGEROUS THREATS COME FROM DEEPER WITHIN THE TOWN, WHEN WE ARE PLAYING ON THEIR HOME TURF.
THEN IT'S A GOOD THING I HAVE A SECRET WEAPON.
YOUR OLD PAL, ANDERSON, HAS BEEN HELPING ME BATTLE GHOSTS FOR MONTHS NOW.
AND I BET SHE'LL EVEN STOP YOUR SICK ASS FROM GETTING WHAT YOU WANT.
ISN'T THAT RIGHT, ANDERSON?

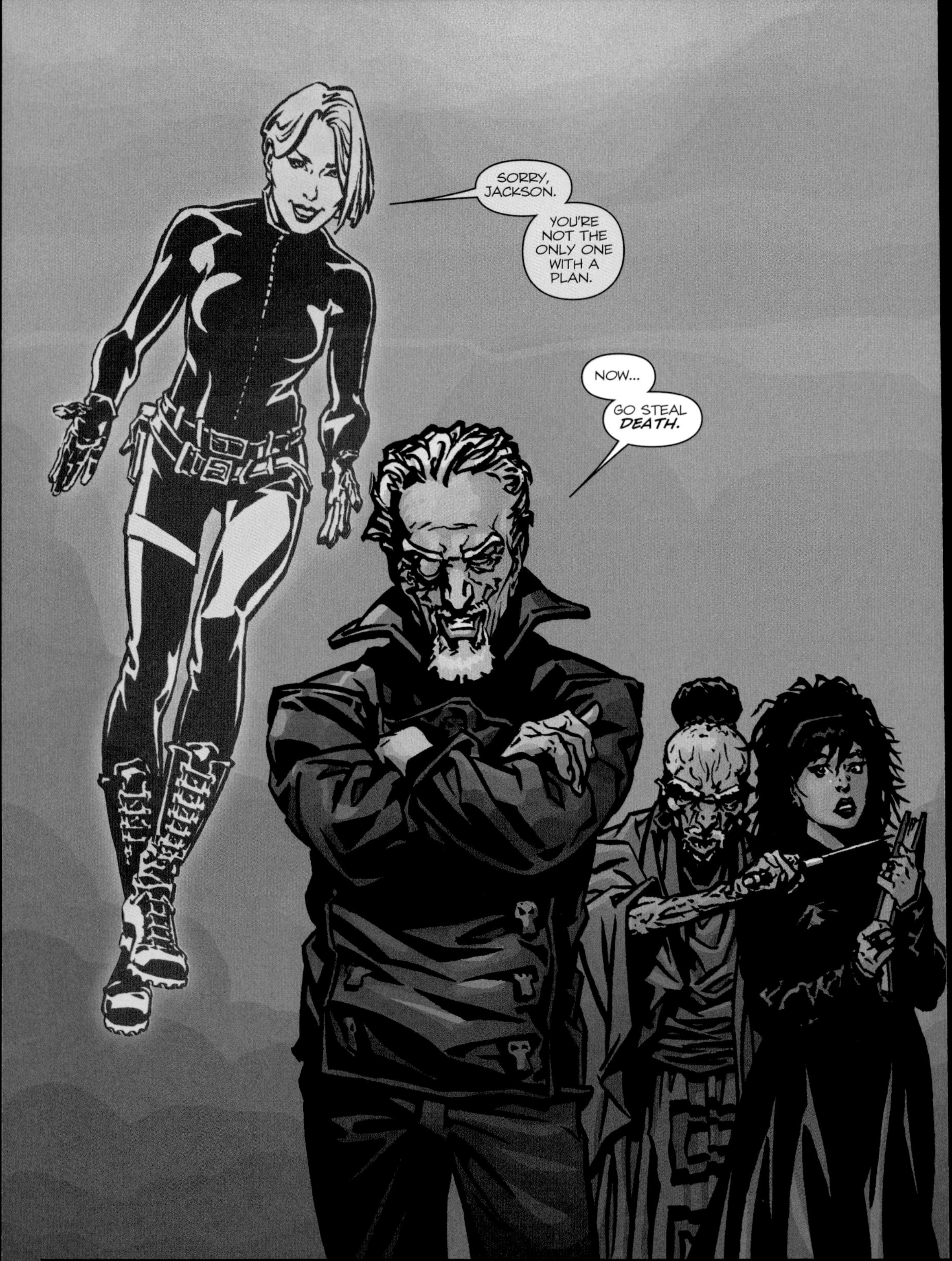
SORRY, JACKSON.
YOU'RE NOT THE ONLY ONE WITH A PLAN.
NOW...
GO STEAL *DEATH*.

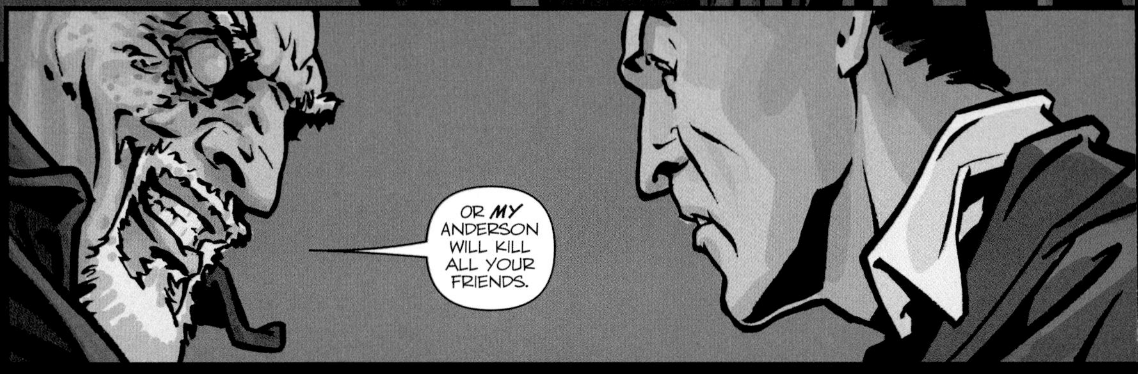
OR *MY* ANDERSON WILL KILL ALL YOUR FRIENDS.

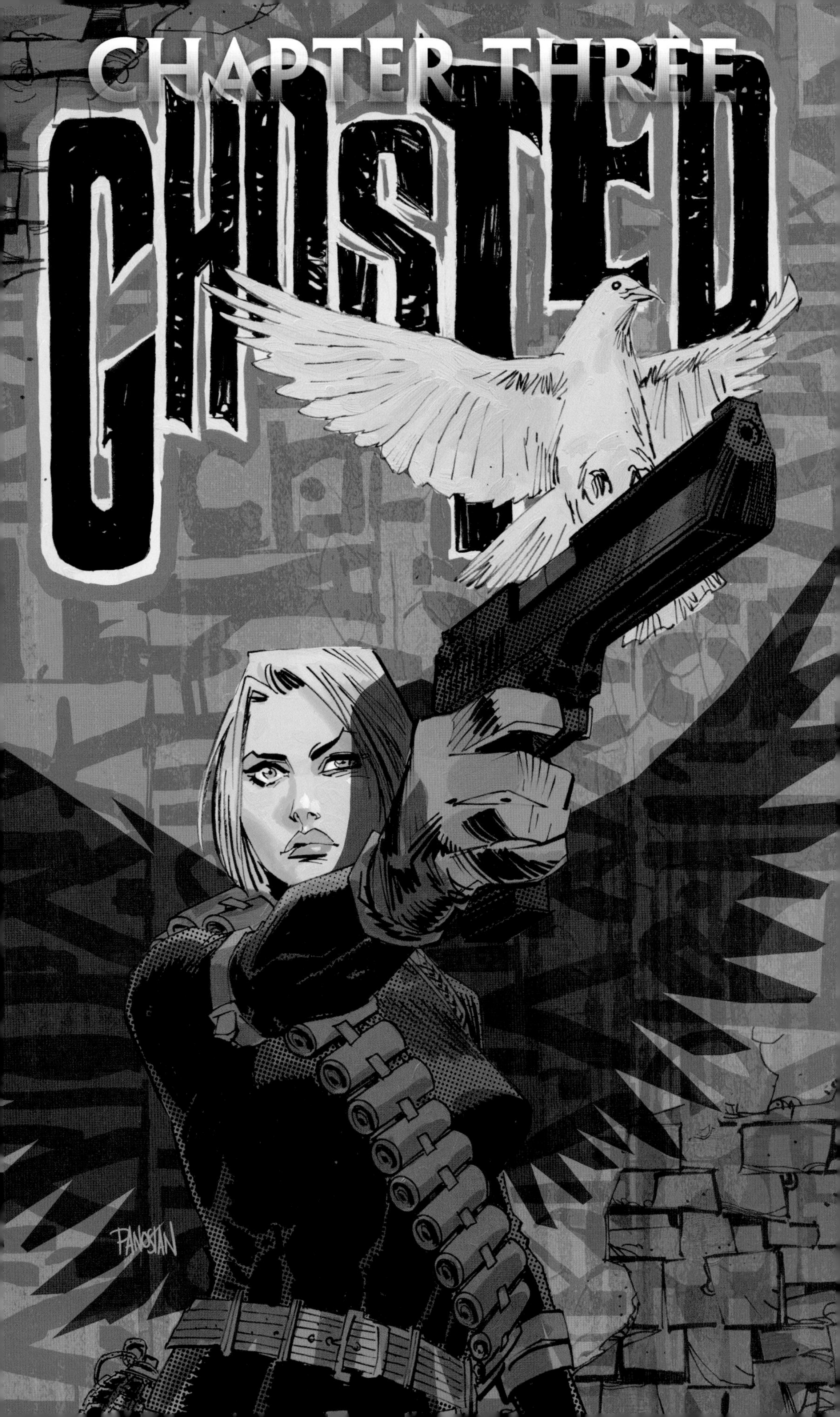
CHAPTER THREE
GHOSTED
PANOSIAN

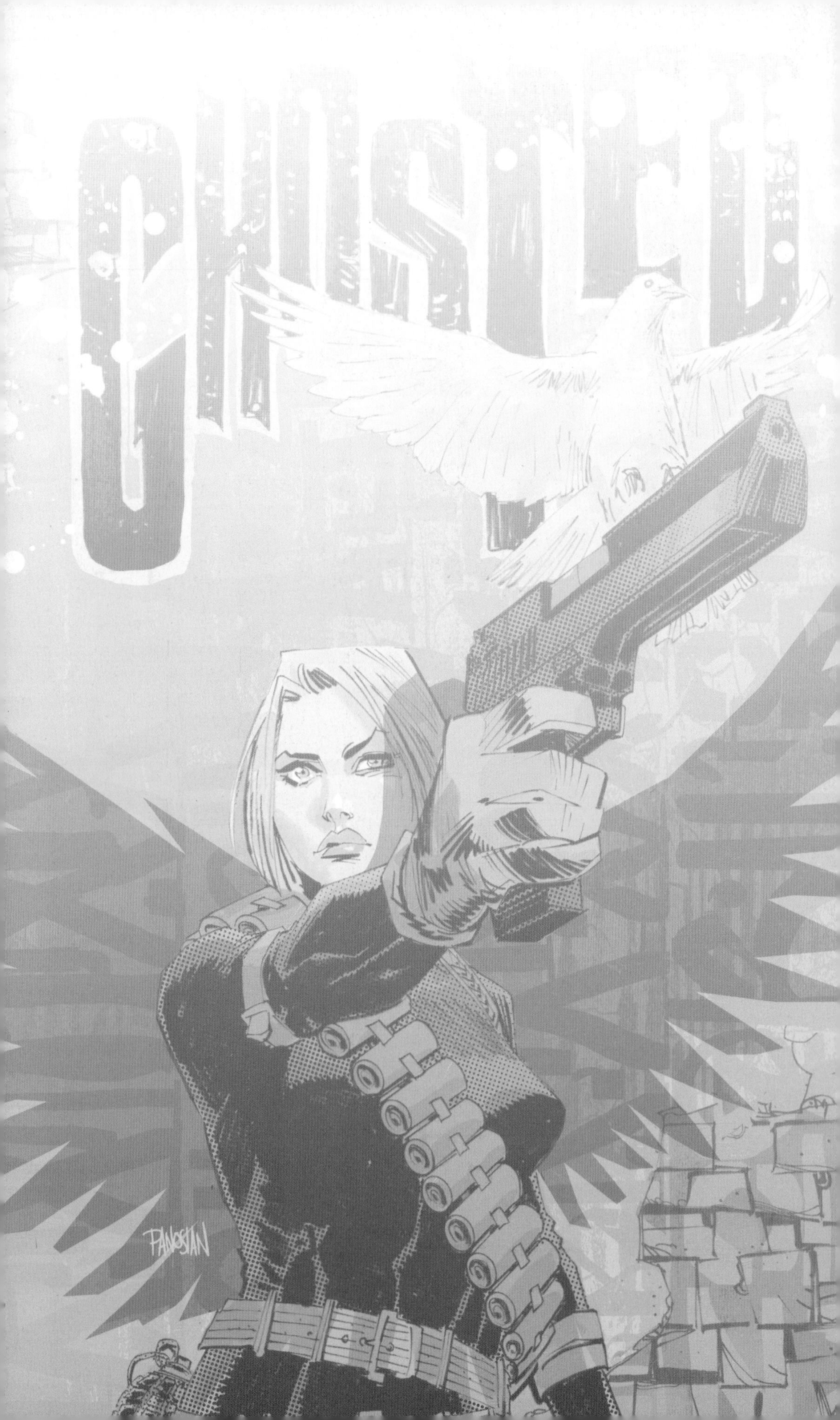
PANOSIAN

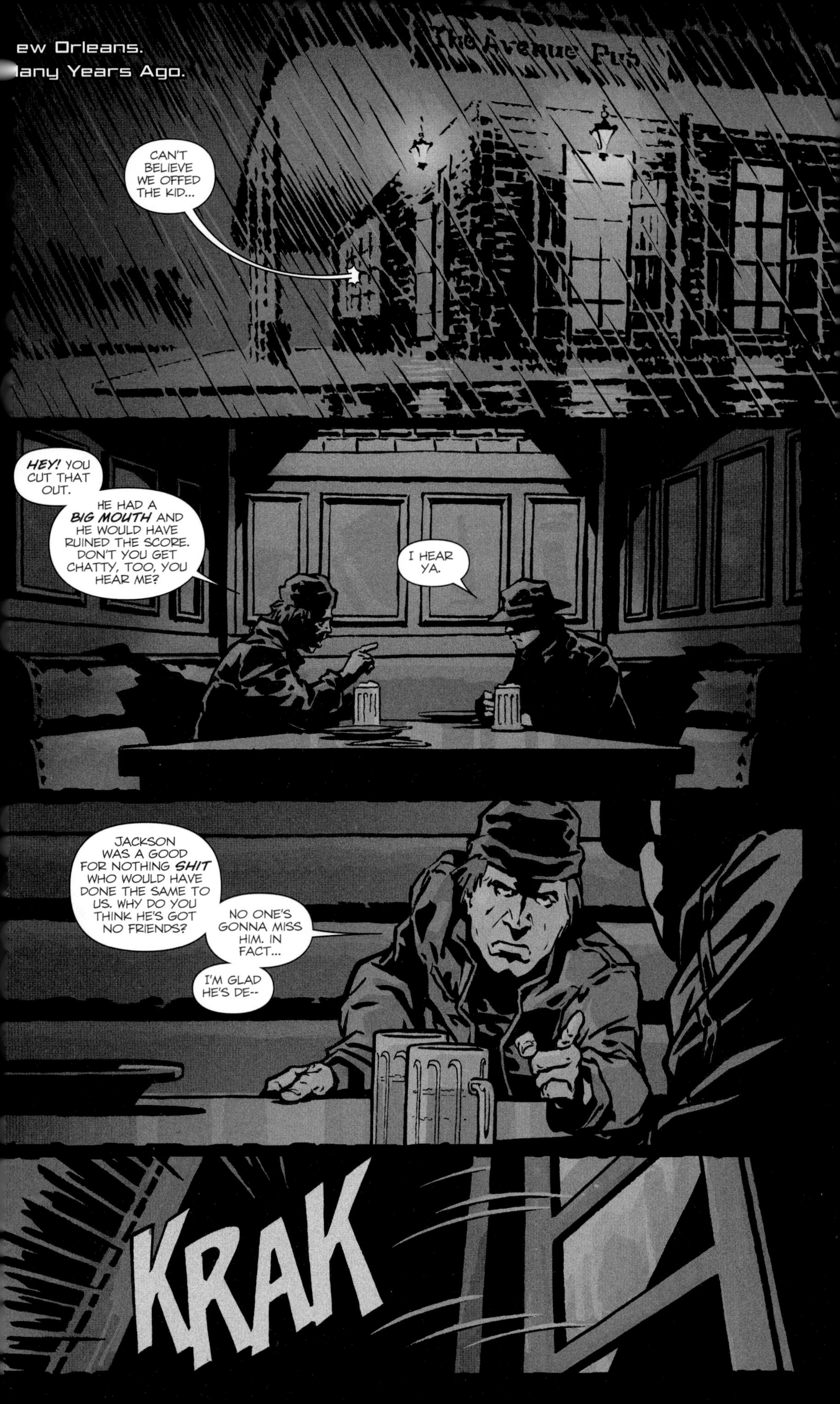
ew Orleans.
lany Years Ago.
The Avenue Pub
CAN'T BELIEVE WE OFFED THE KID...
HEY! YOU CUT THAT OUT.
HE HAD A BIG MOUTH AND HE WOULD HAVE RUINED THE SCORE. DON'T YOU GET CHATTY, TOO, YOU HEAR ME?
I HEAR YA.
JACKSON WAS A GOOD FOR NOTHING SHIT WHO WOULD HAVE DONE THE SAME TO US. WHY DO YOU THINK HE'S GOT NO FRIENDS?
NO ONE'S GONNA MISS HIM. IN FACT...
I'M GLAD HE'S DE--
KRAK

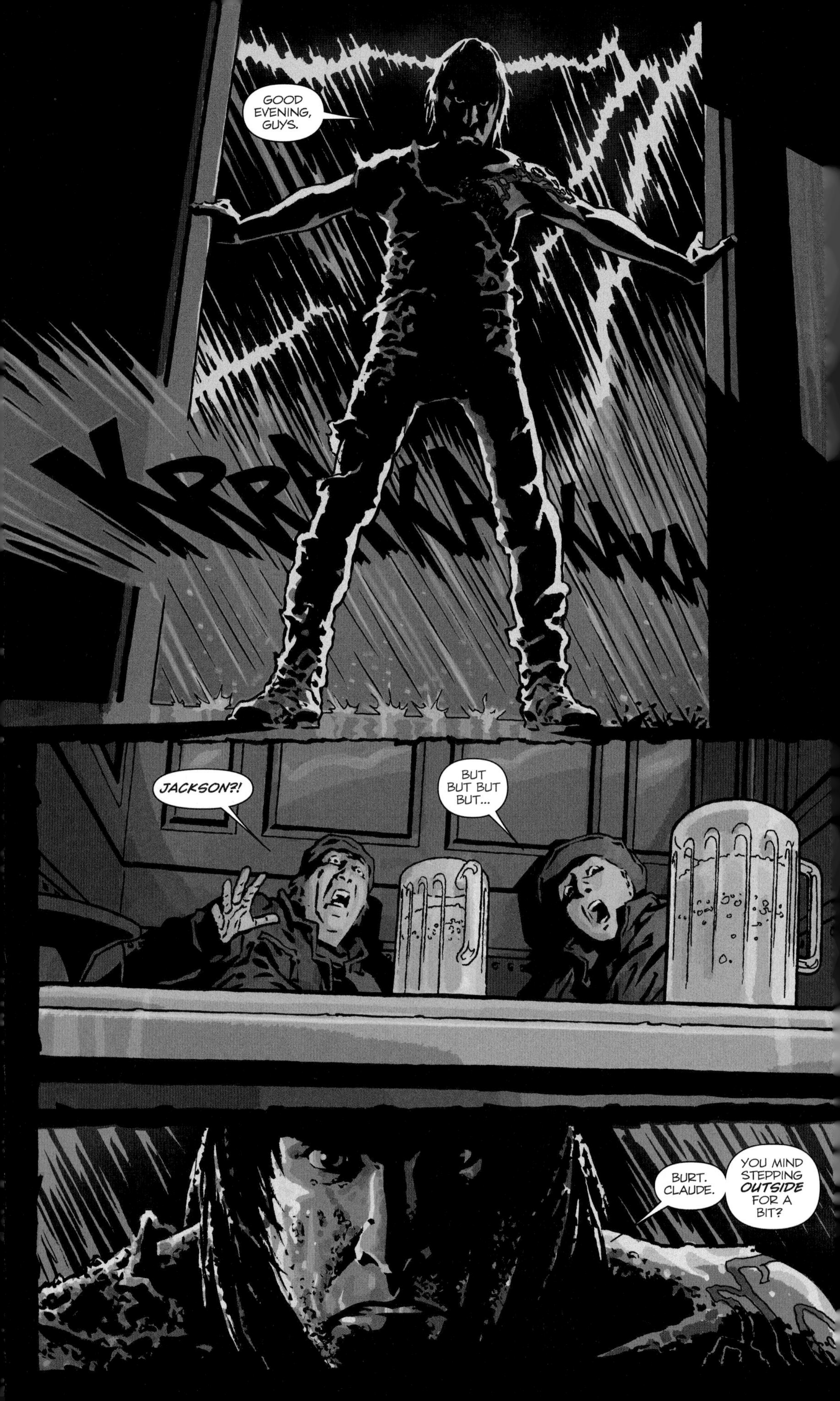
GOOD EVENING, GUYS.
JACKSON?!
BUT BUT BUT BUT...
BURT. CLAUDE.
YOU MIND STEPPING **OUTSIDE** FOR A BIT?

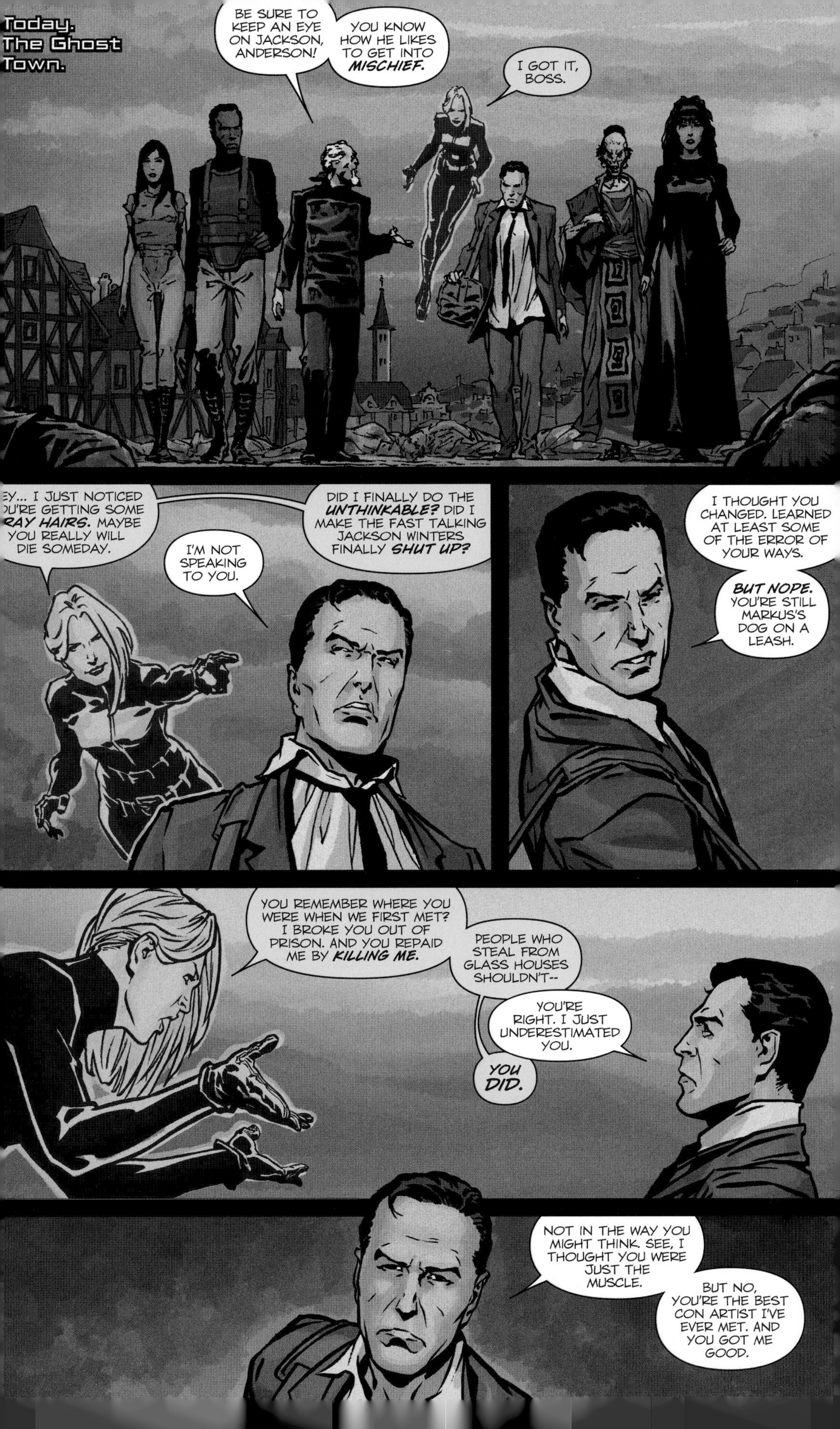
Today. The Ghost Town.
BE SURE TO KEEP AN EYE ON JACKSON, ANDERSON!
YOU KNOW HOW HE LIKES TO GET INTO MISCHIEF.
I GOT IT, BOSS.
EY... I JUST NOTICED OU'RE GETTING SOME RAY HAIRS. MAYBE YOU REALLY WILL DIE SOMEDAY.
DID I FINALLY DO THE UNTHINKABLE? DID I MAKE THE FAST TALKING JACKSON WINTERS FINALLY SHUT UP?
I'M NOT SPEAKING TO YOU.
I THOUGHT YOU CHANGED. LEARNED AT LEAST SOME OF THE ERROR OF YOUR WAYS.
BUT NOPE. YOU'RE STILL MARKUS'S DOG ON A LEASH.
YOU REMEMBER WHERE YOU WERE WHEN WE FIRST MET? I BROKE YOU OUT OF PRISON. AND YOU REPAID ME BY KILLING ME.
PEOPLE WHO STEAL FROM GLASS HOUSES SHOULDN'T--
YOU DID.
YOU'RE RIGHT. I JUST UNDERESTIMATED YOU.
NOT IN THE WAY YOU MIGHT THINK. SEE, I THOUGHT YOU WERE JUST THE MUSCLE.
BUT NO, YOU'RE THE BEST CON ARTIST I'VE EVER MET. AND YOU GOT ME GOOD.

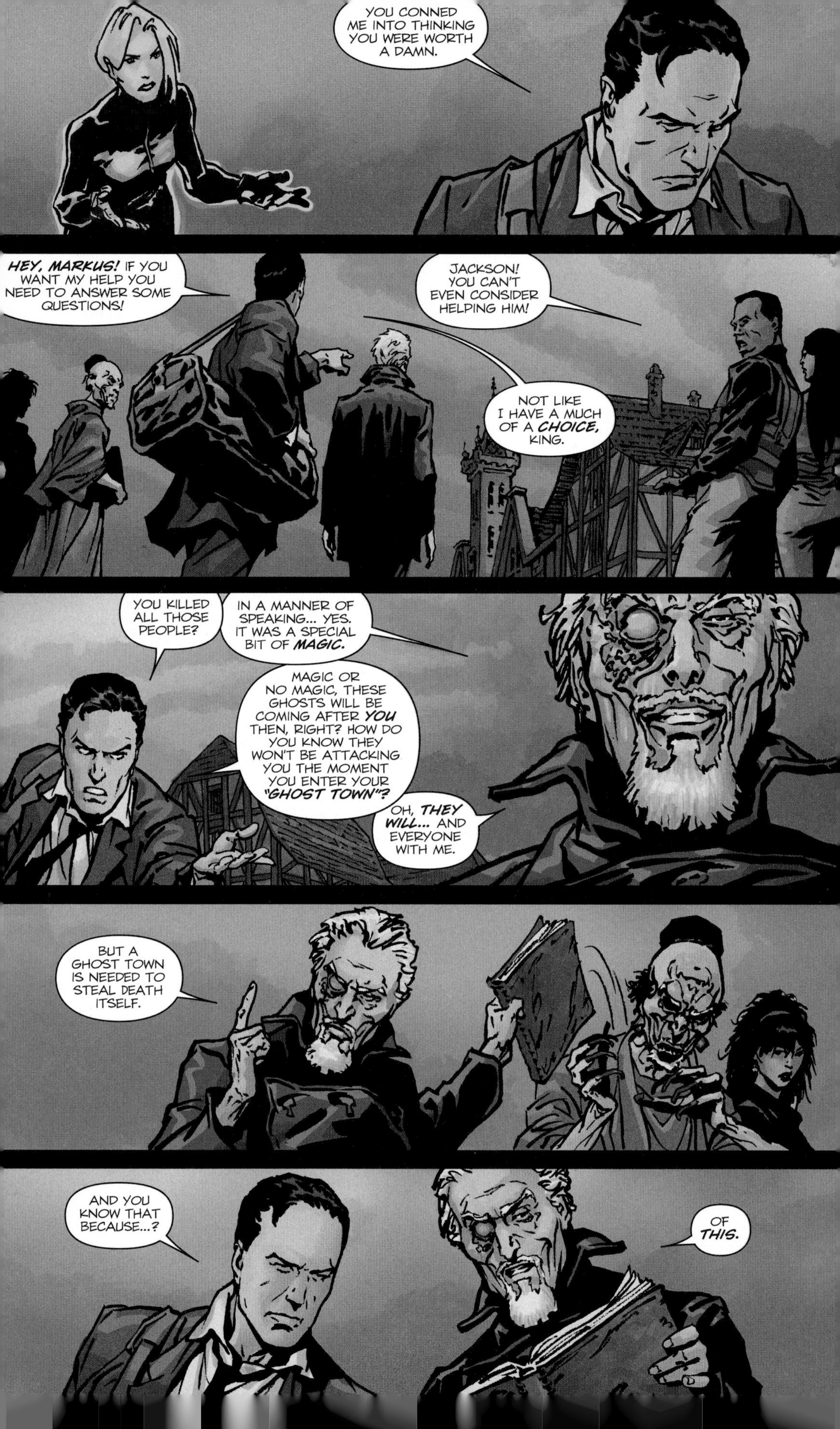
YOU CONNED ME INTO THINKING YOU WERE WORTH A DAMN.
HEY, MARKUS! IF YOU WANT MY HELP YOU NEED TO ANSWER SOME QUESTIONS!
JACKSON! YOU CAN'T EVEN CONSIDER HELPING HIM!
NOT LIKE I HAVE A MUCH OF A CHOICE, KING.
YOU KILLED ALL THOSE PEOPLE?
IN A MANNER OF SPEAKING... YES. IT WAS A SPECIAL BIT OF MAGIC.
MAGIC OR NO MAGIC, THESE GHOSTS WILL BE COMING AFTER YOU THEN, RIGHT? HOW DO YOU KNOW THEY WON'T BE ATTACKING YOU THE MOMENT YOU ENTER YOUR "GHOST TOWN"?
OH, THEY WILL... AND EVERYONE WITH ME.
BUT A GHOST TOWN IS NEEDED TO STEAL DEATH ITSELF.
AND YOU KNOW THAT BECAUSE...?
OF THIS.

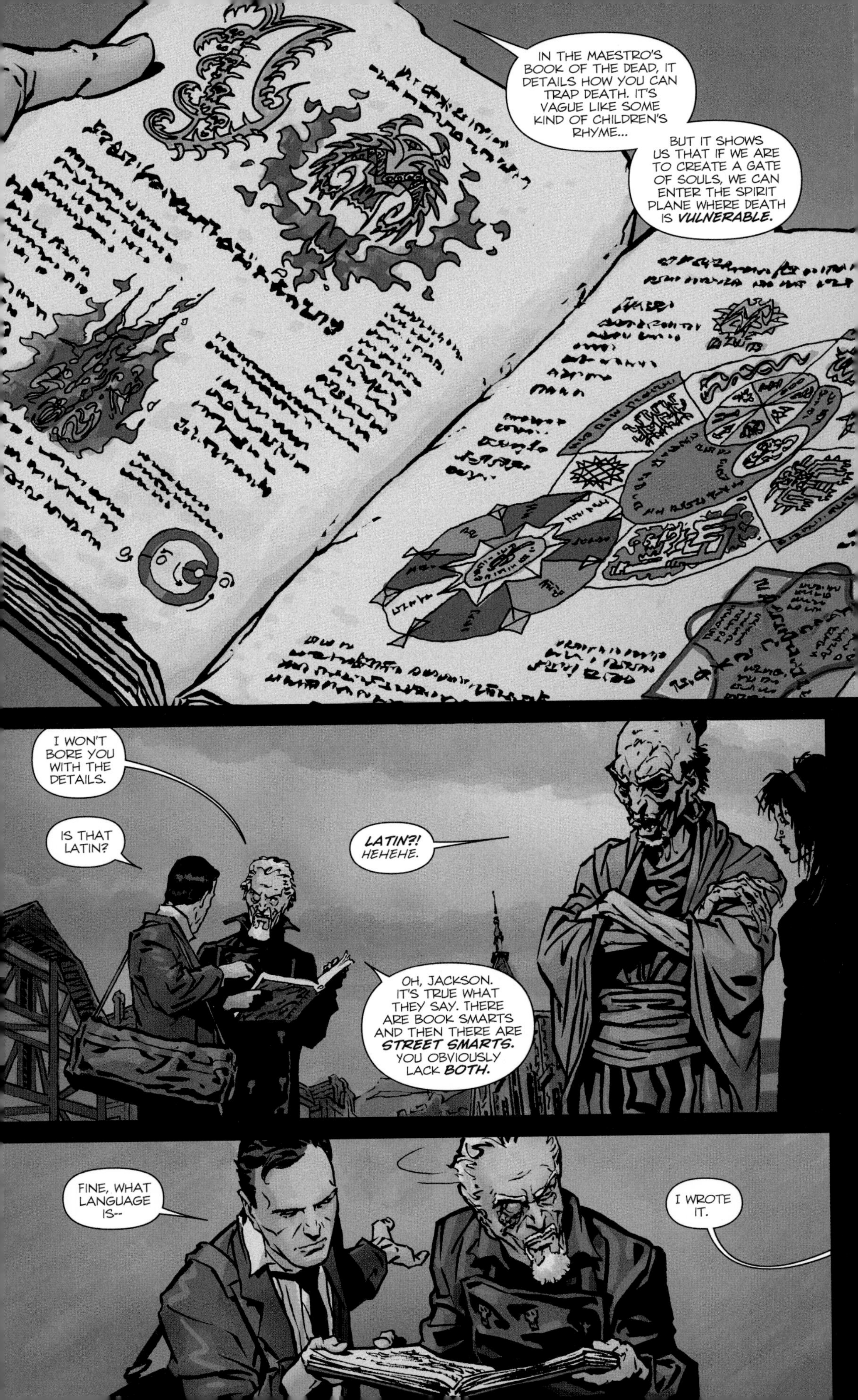
IN THE MAESTRO'S BOOK OF THE DEAD, IT DETAILS HOW YOU CAN TRAP DEATH. IT'S VAGUE LIKE SOME KIND OF CHILDREN'S RHYME...
BUT IT SHOWS US THAT IF WE ARE TO CREATE A GATE OF SOULS, WE CAN ENTER THE SPIRIT PLANE WHERE DEATH IS **VULNERABLE.**
I WON'T BORE YOU WITH THE DETAILS.
IS THAT LATIN?
LATIN?! HEHEHE.
OH, JACKSON. IT'S TRUE WHAT THEY SAY. THERE ARE BOOK SMARTS AND THEN THERE ARE **STREET SMARTS.** YOU OBVIOUSLY LACK **BOTH.**
FINE, WHAT LANGUAGE IS--
I WROTE IT.

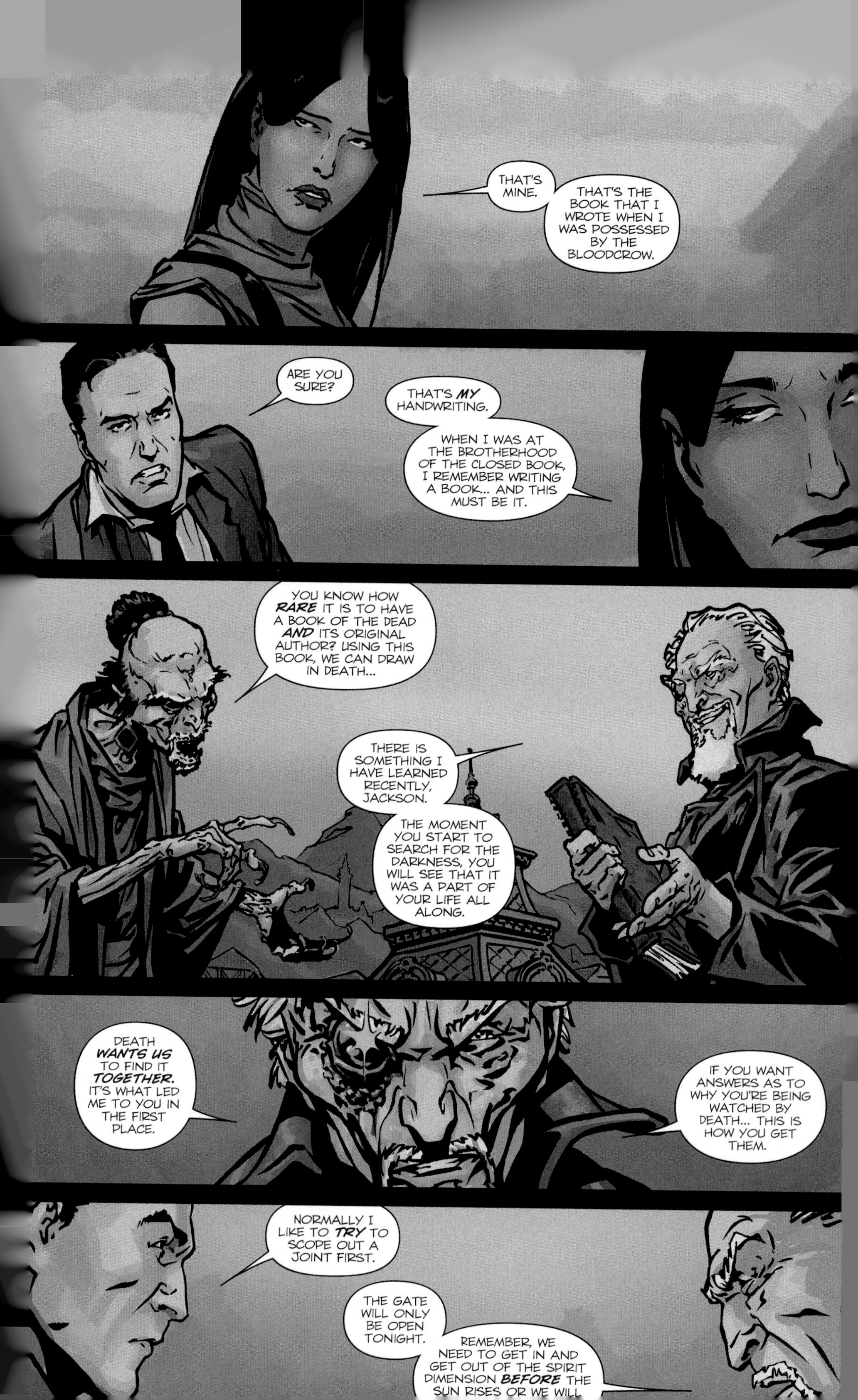
THAT'S MINE.
THAT'S THE BOOK THAT I WROTE WHEN I WAS POSSESSED BY THE BLOODCROW.
ARE YOU SURE?
THAT'S *MY* HANDWRITING.
WHEN I WAS AT THE BROTHERHOOD OF THE CLOSED BOOK, I REMEMBER WRITING A BOOK... AND THIS MUST BE IT.
YOU KNOW HOW *RARE* IT IS TO HAVE A BOOK OF THE DEAD *AND* ITS ORIGINAL AUTHOR? USING THIS BOOK, WE CAN DRAW IN DEATH...
THERE IS SOMETHING I HAVE LEARNED RECENTLY, JACKSON.
THE MOMENT YOU START TO SEARCH FOR THE DARKNESS, YOU WILL SEE THAT IT WAS A PART OF YOUR LIFE ALL ALONG.
DEATH *WANTS US* TO FIND IT *TOGETHER.* IT'S WHAT LED ME TO YOU IN THE FIRST PLACE.
IF YOU WANT ANSWERS AS TO WHY YOU'RE BEING WATCHED BY DEATH... THIS IS HOW YOU GET THEM.
NORMALLY I LIKE TO *TRY* TO SCOPE OUT A JOINT FIRST.
THE GATE WILL ONLY BE OPEN TONIGHT.
REMEMBER, WE NEED TO GET IN AND GET OUT OF THE SPIRIT DIMENSION *BEFORE* THE SUN RISES OR WE WILL

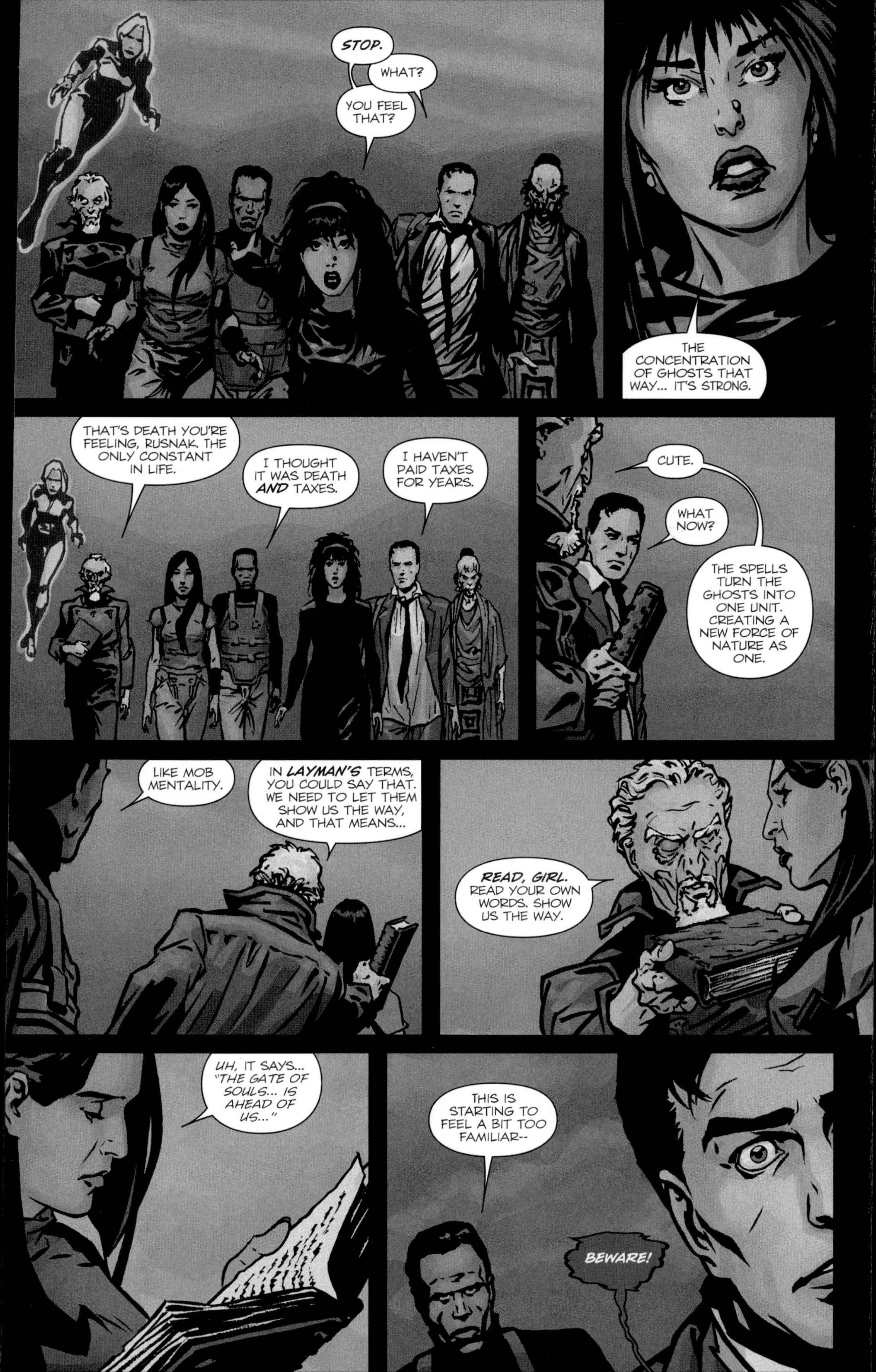
STOP.
WHAT?
YOU FEEL THAT?
THE CONCENTRATION OF GHOSTS THAT WAY... IT'S STRONG.
THAT'S DEATH YOU'RE FEELING, RUSNAK. THE ONLY CONSTANT IN LIFE.
I THOUGHT IT WAS DEATH AND TAXES.
I HAVEN'T PAID TAXES FOR YEARS.
CUTE.
WHAT NOW?
THE SPELLS TURN THE GHOSTS INTO ONE UNIT. CREATING A NEW FORCE OF NATURE AS ONE.
LIKE MOB MENTALITY.
IN LAYMAN'S TERMS, YOU COULD SAY THAT. WE NEED TO LET THEM SHOW US THE WAY, AND THAT MEANS...
READ, GIRL. READ YOUR OWN WORDS. SHOW US THE WAY.
UH, IT SAYS... "THE GATE OF SOULS... IS AHEAD OF US..."
THIS IS STARTING TO FEEL A BIT TOO FAMILIAR--
BEWARE!

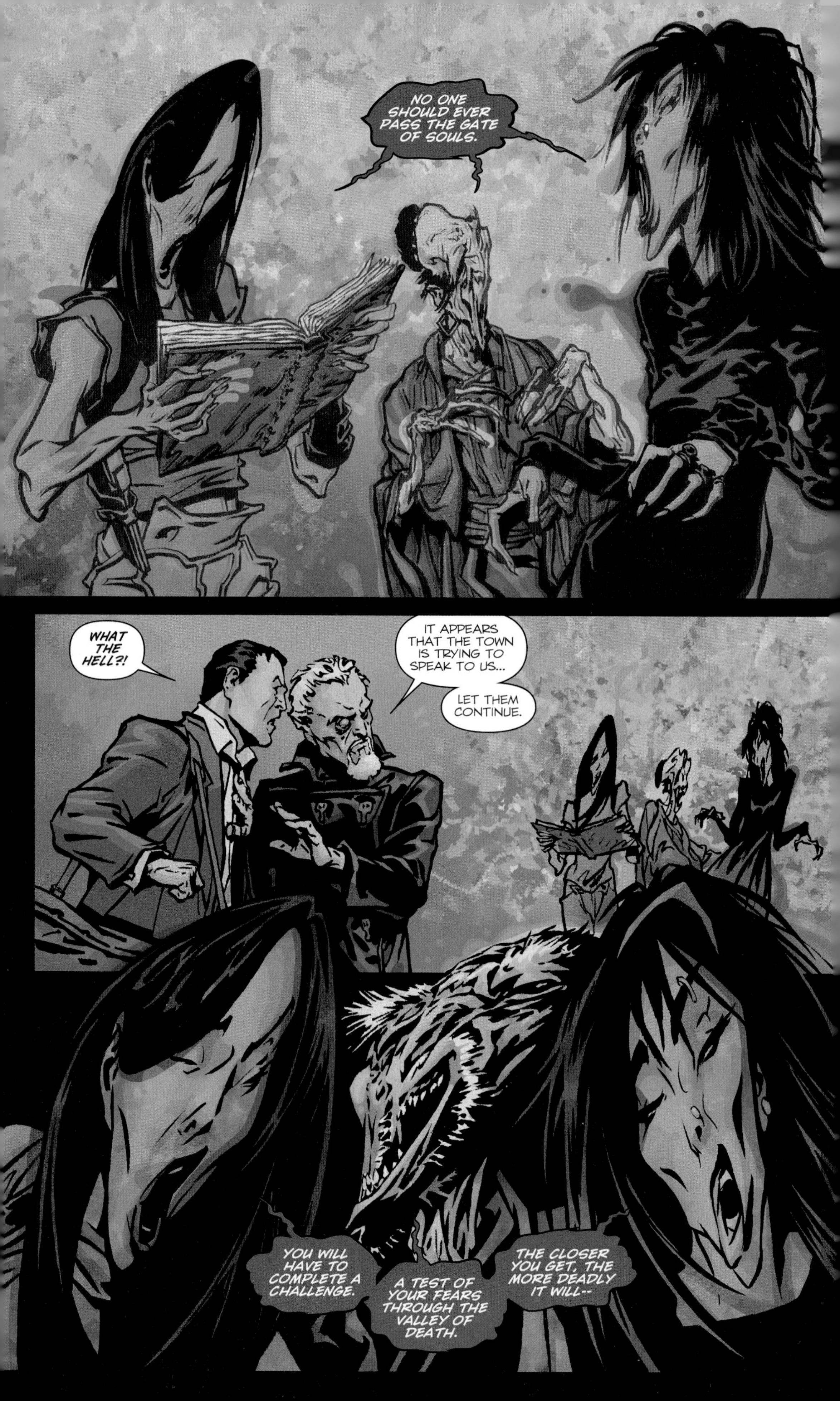
NO ONE SHOULD EVER PASS THE GATE OF SOULS.
WHAT THE HELL?!
IT APPEARS THAT THE TOWN IS TRYING TO SPEAK TO US...
LET THEM CONTINUE.
YOU WILL HAVE TO COMPLETE A CHALLENGE.
A TEST OF YOUR FEARS THROUGH THE VALLEY OF DEATH.
THE CLOSER YOU GET, THE MORE DEADLY IT WILL--

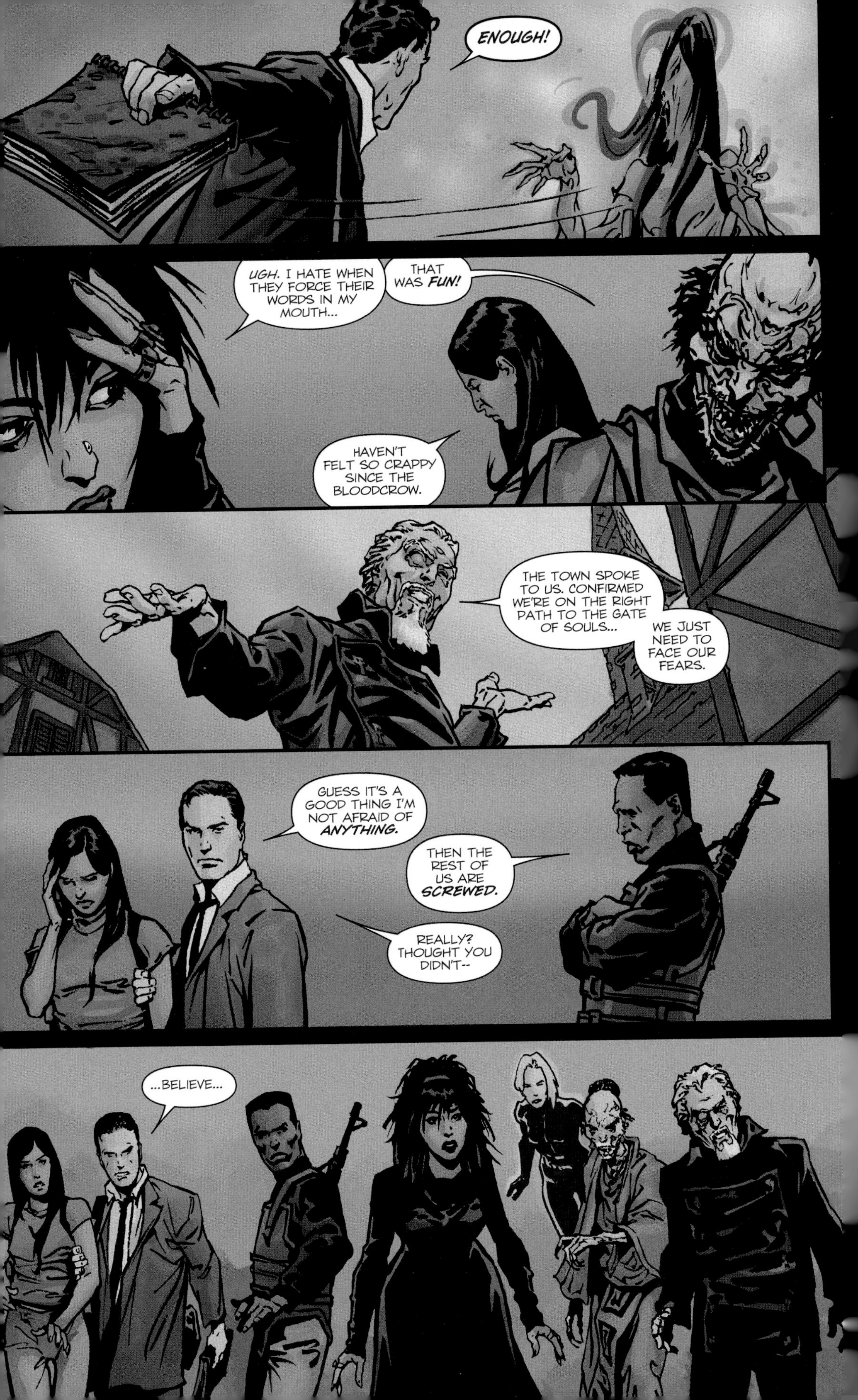
ENOUGH!
UGH. I HATE WHEN THEY FORCE THEIR WORDS IN MY MOUTH...
THAT WAS FUN!
HAVEN'T FELT SO CRAPPY SINCE THE BLOODCROW.
THE TOWN SPOKE TO US. CONFIRMED WE'RE ON THE RIGHT PATH TO THE GATE OF SOULS...
WE JUST NEED TO FACE OUR FEARS.
GUESS IT'S A GOOD THING I'M NOT AFRAID OF ANYTHING.
THEN THE REST OF US ARE SCREWED.
REALLY? THOUGHT YOU DIDN'T--
...BELIEVE...

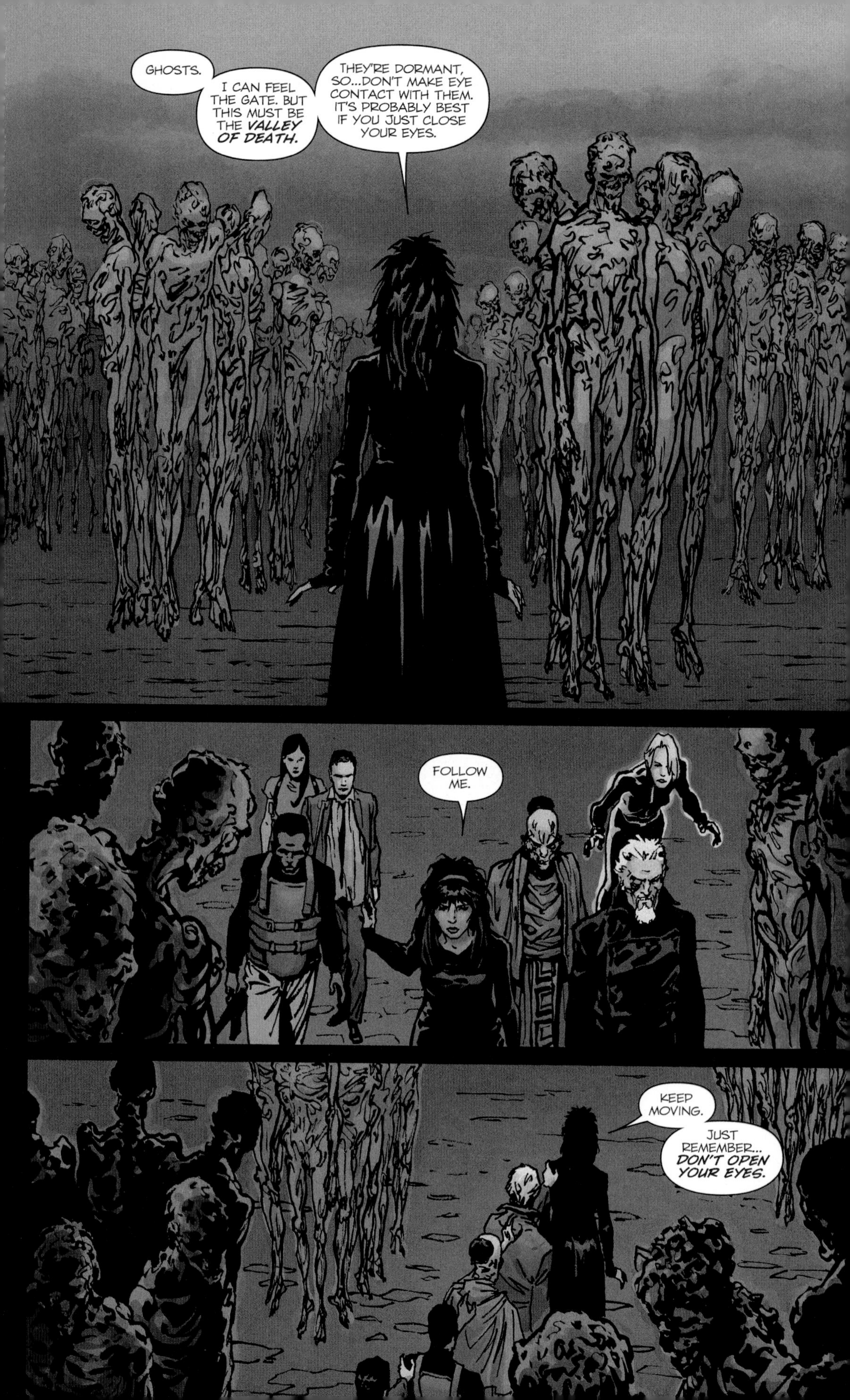
GHOSTS.
I CAN FEEL THE GATE. BUT THIS MUST BE THE VALLEY OF DEATH.
THEY'RE DORMANT, SO...DON'T MAKE EYE CONTACT WITH THEM. IT'S PROBABLY BEST IF YOU JUST CLOSE YOUR EYES.
FOLLOW ME.
KEEP MOVING.
JUST REMEMBER... DON'T OPEN YOUR EYES.

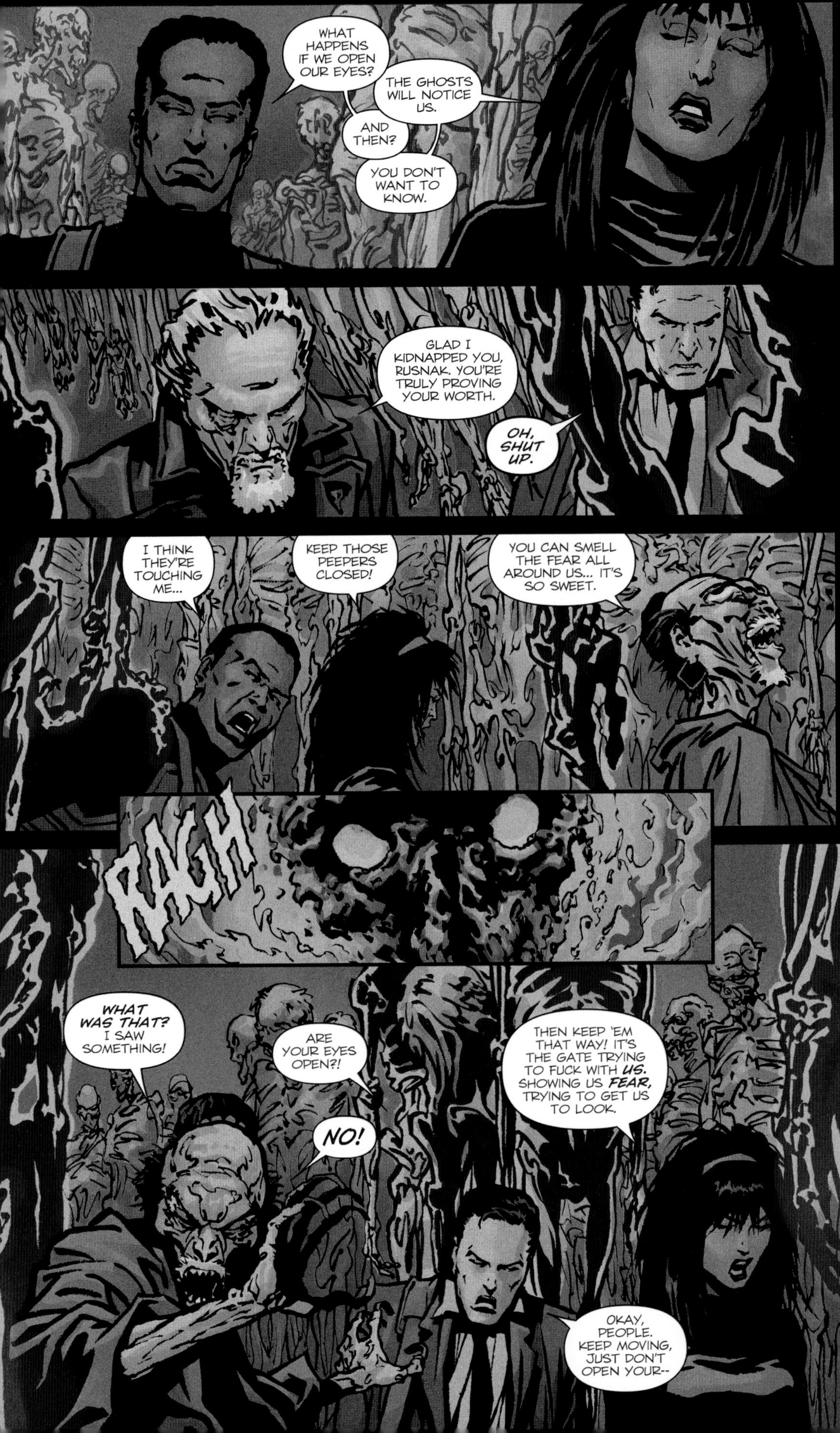
WHAT HAPPENS IF WE OPEN OUR EYES?
THE GHOSTS WILL NOTICE US.
AND THEN?
YOU DON'T WANT TO KNOW.
GLAD I KIDNAPPED YOU, RUSNAK. YOU'RE TRULY PROVING YOUR WORTH.
OH, SHUT UP.
I THINK THEY'RE TOUCHING ME...
KEEP THOSE PEEPERS CLOSED!
YOU CAN SMELL THE FEAR ALL AROUND US... IT'S SO SWEET.
RAGH
WHAT WAS THAT? I SAW SOMETHING!
ARE YOUR EYES OPEN?!
NO!
THEN KEEP 'EM THAT WAY! IT'S THE GATE TRYING TO FUCK WITH US. SHOWING US FEAR, TRYING TO GET US TO LOOK.
OKAY, PEOPLE. KEEP MOVING, JUST DON'T OPEN YOUR--

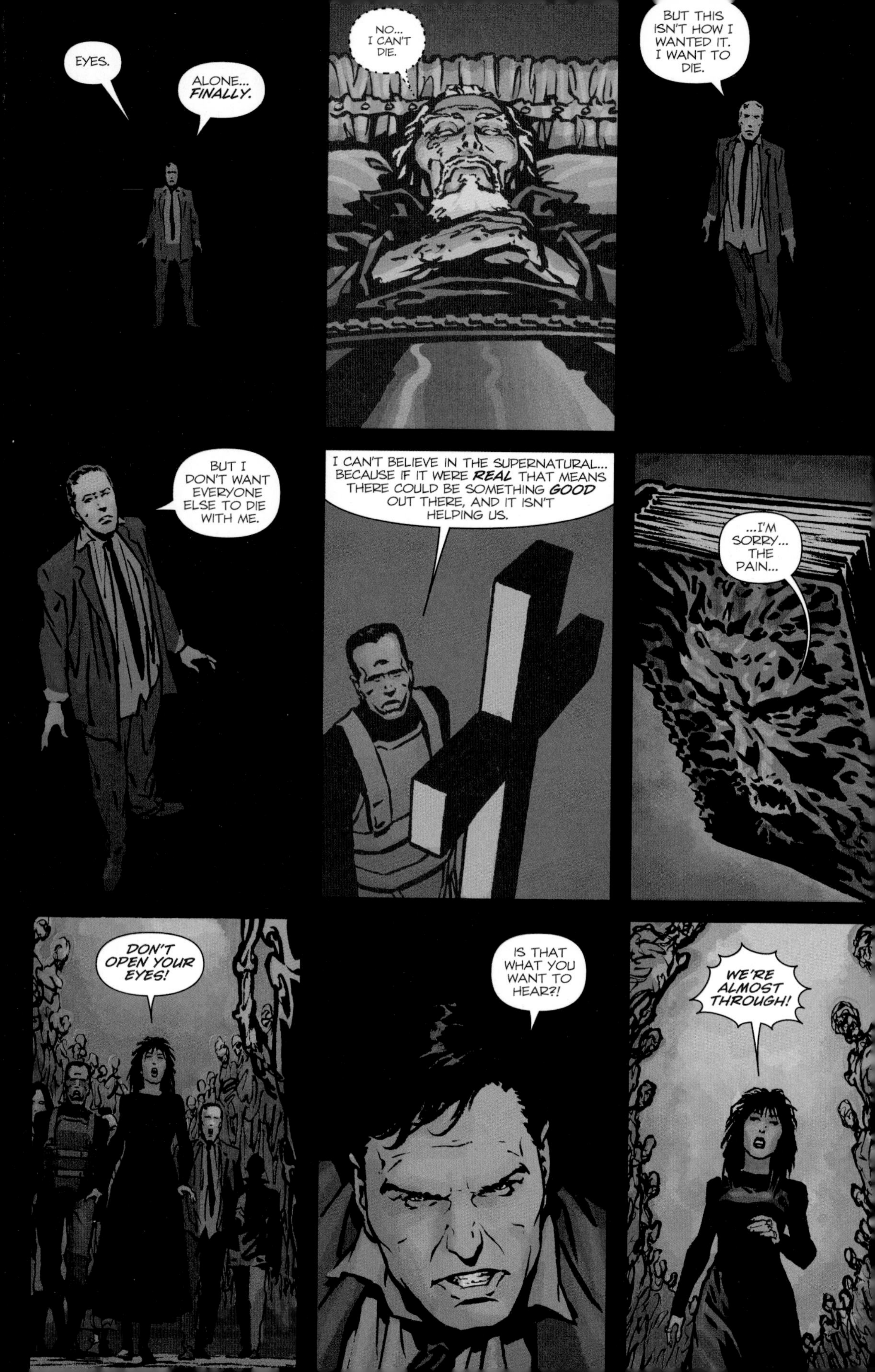

EYES.
ALONE... *FINALLY.*
NO... I CAN'T DIE.
BUT THIS ISN'T HOW I WANTED IT. I WANT TO DIE.
BUT I DON'T WANT EVERYONE ELSE TO DIE WITH ME.
I CAN'T BELIEVE IN THE SUPERNATURAL... BECAUSE IF IT WERE *REAL* THAT MEANS THERE COULD BE SOMETHING *GOOD* OUT THERE, AND IT ISN'T HELPING US.
...I'M SORRY... THE PAIN...
DON'T OPEN YOUR EYES!
IS THAT WHAT YOU WANT TO HEAR?!
WE'RE ALMOST THROUGH!

WHAT IF I'M JUST LIKE THOSE RED GHOSTS... NOT REALLY IN CONTROL?

NONE OF IT IS REAL. JUST KEEP MOVING!

NO... I'M NOTHING LIKE HER. MY GRANDMOTHER WAS A MONSTER.

I'M... AFRAID... THAT BY BEING AROUND ME...

HELP ME. TELL HIM I LOVED HIM. HATE. LOVE. WHERE AM I? IS THIS HELL? WHY DID I DIE? CAN YOU HEAR ME? TELL HIM I LOVED HIM. HATE. LOVE. WHERE AM I? IS THIS HELL? WHY DID I DIE? CAN YOU HEAR ME? HELP ME. TELL HIM I LOVED HIM. HATE. LOVE. WHERE AM I? IS THIS HELL? WHY DID I DIE? CAN YOU HEAR ME? HELP ME. TELL HIM I LOVED HIM. HATE. LOVE. WHERE AM I? IS THIS HELL? WHY DID I DIE? CAN YOU HEAR ME? HELP ME. TELL

I CAN HEAR ALL THE DEAD IN THE WORLD! GO AWAY!

HATE

MY FRIENDS WILL DIE.

NO NO NO... I CAN'T... I CAN'T... PLEASE...

I'M AFRAID!

STOP!

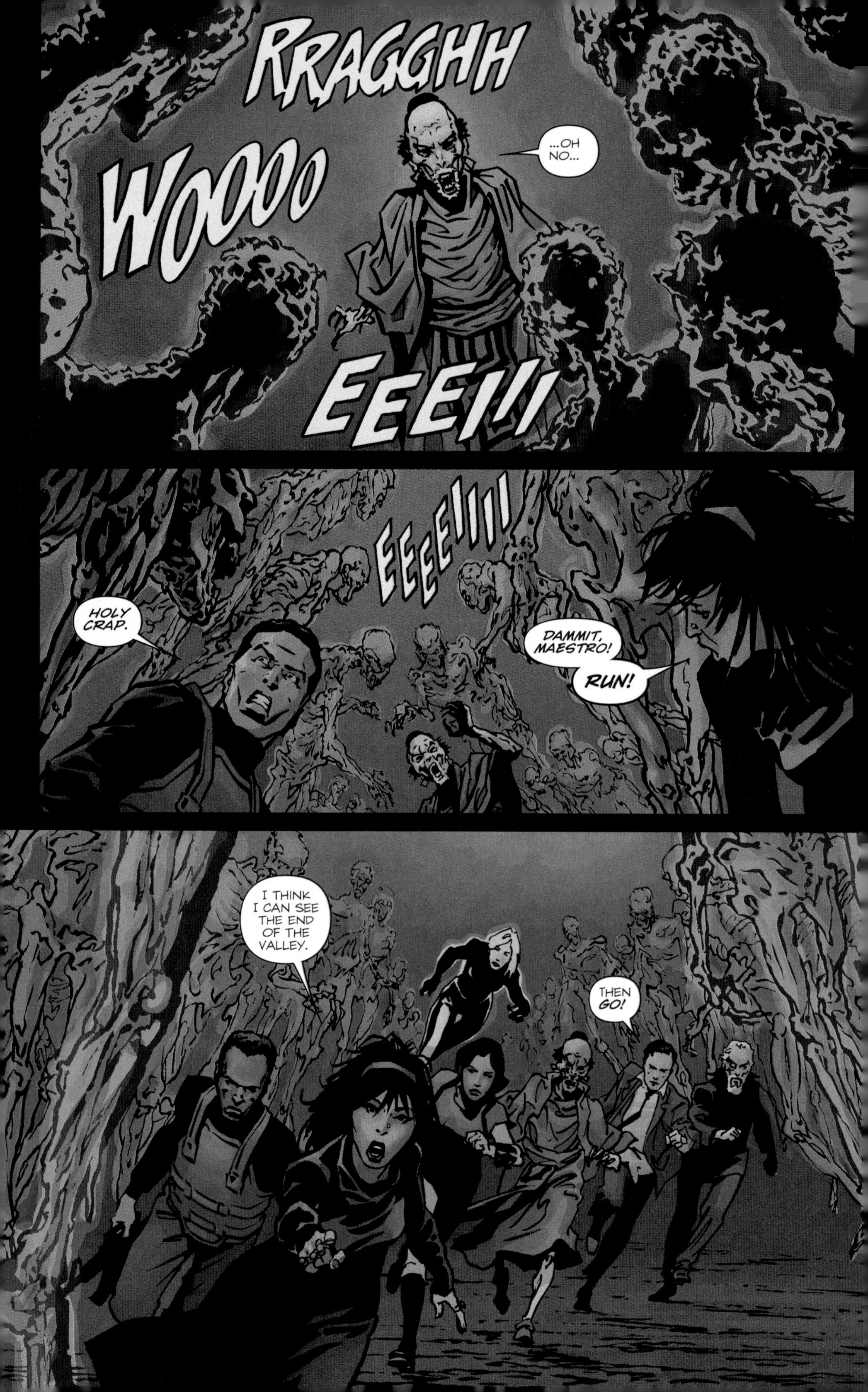
RRAGGHH
WOOOO
...OH NO...
EEEI!I
EEEEI!!!
HOLY CRAP.
DAMMIT, MAESTRO!
RUN!
I THINK I CAN SEE THE END OF THE VALLEY.
THEN GO!

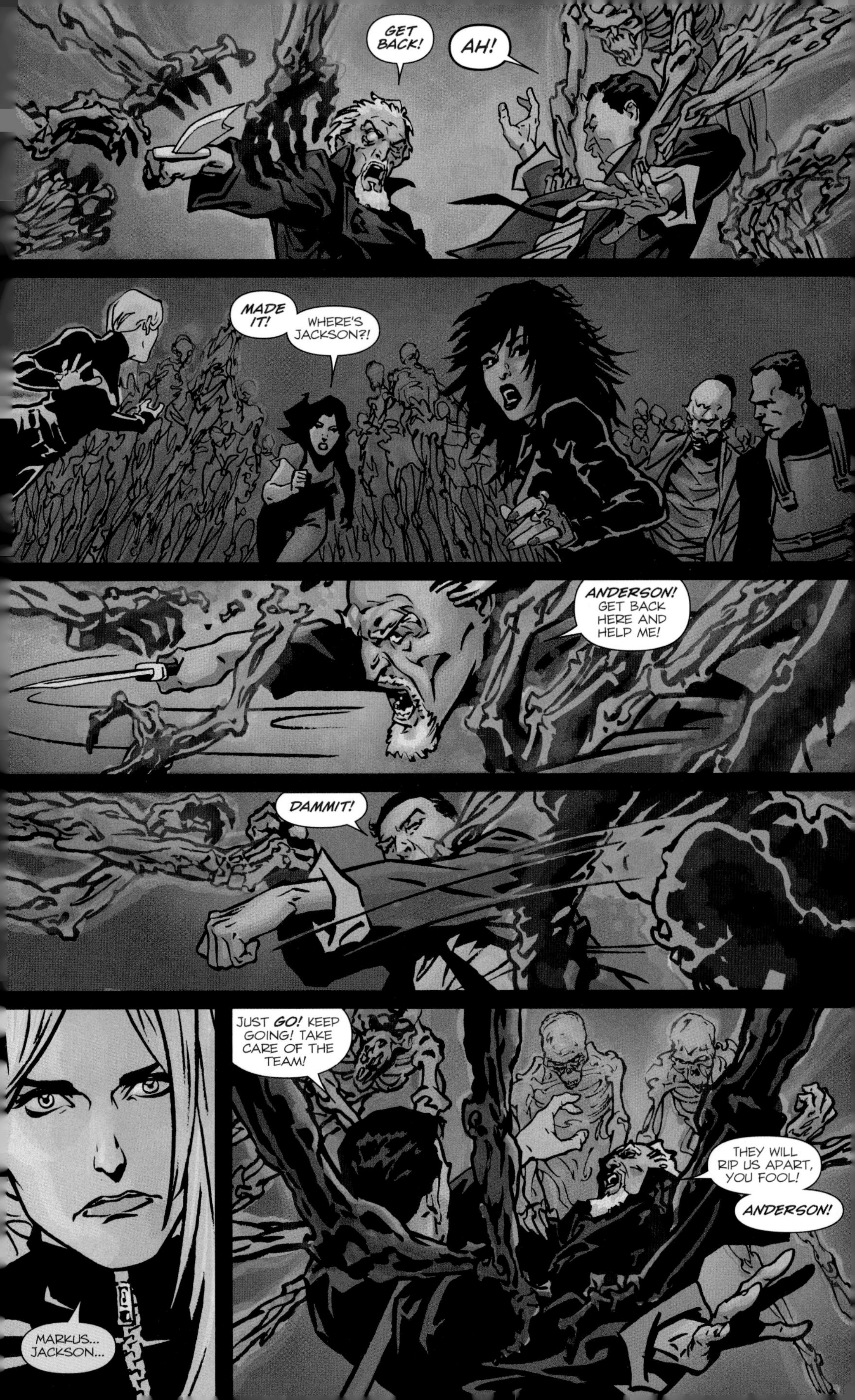
GET BACK!
AH!
MADE IT!
WHERE'S JACKSON?!
ANDERSON! GET BACK HERE AND HELP ME!
DAMMIT!
JUST GO! KEEP GOING! TAKE CARE OF THE TEAM!
THEY WILL RIP US APART, YOU FOOL!
ANDERSON!
MARKUS... JACKSON...

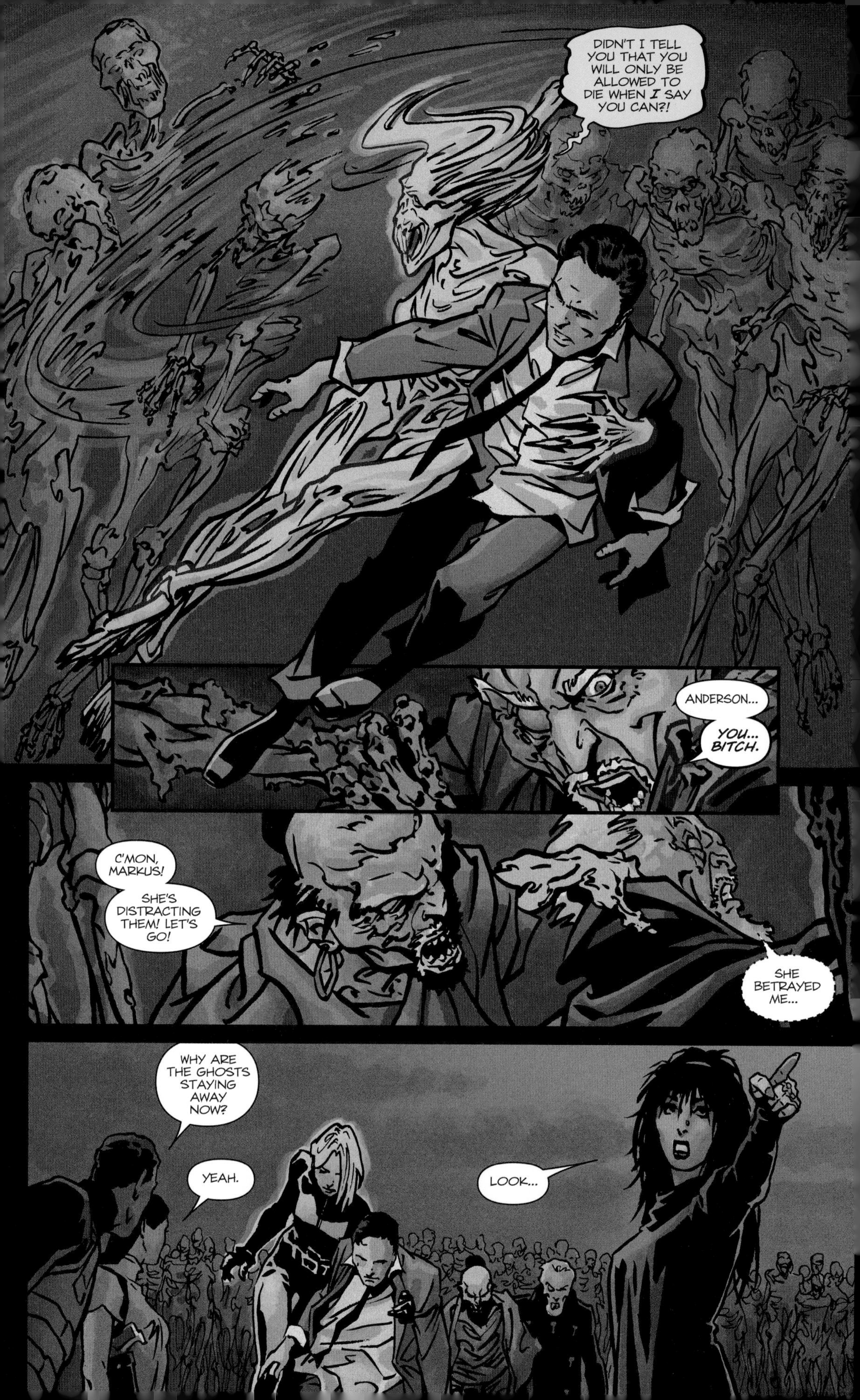
DIDN'T I TELL YOU THAT YOU WILL ONLY BE ALLOWED TO DIE WHEN I SAY YOU CAN?!
ANDERSON...
YOU... BITCH.
C'MON, MARKUS!
SHE'S DISTRACTING THEM! LET'S GO!
SHE BETRAYED ME...
WHY ARE THE GHOSTS STAYING AWAY NOW?
YEAH.
LOOK...

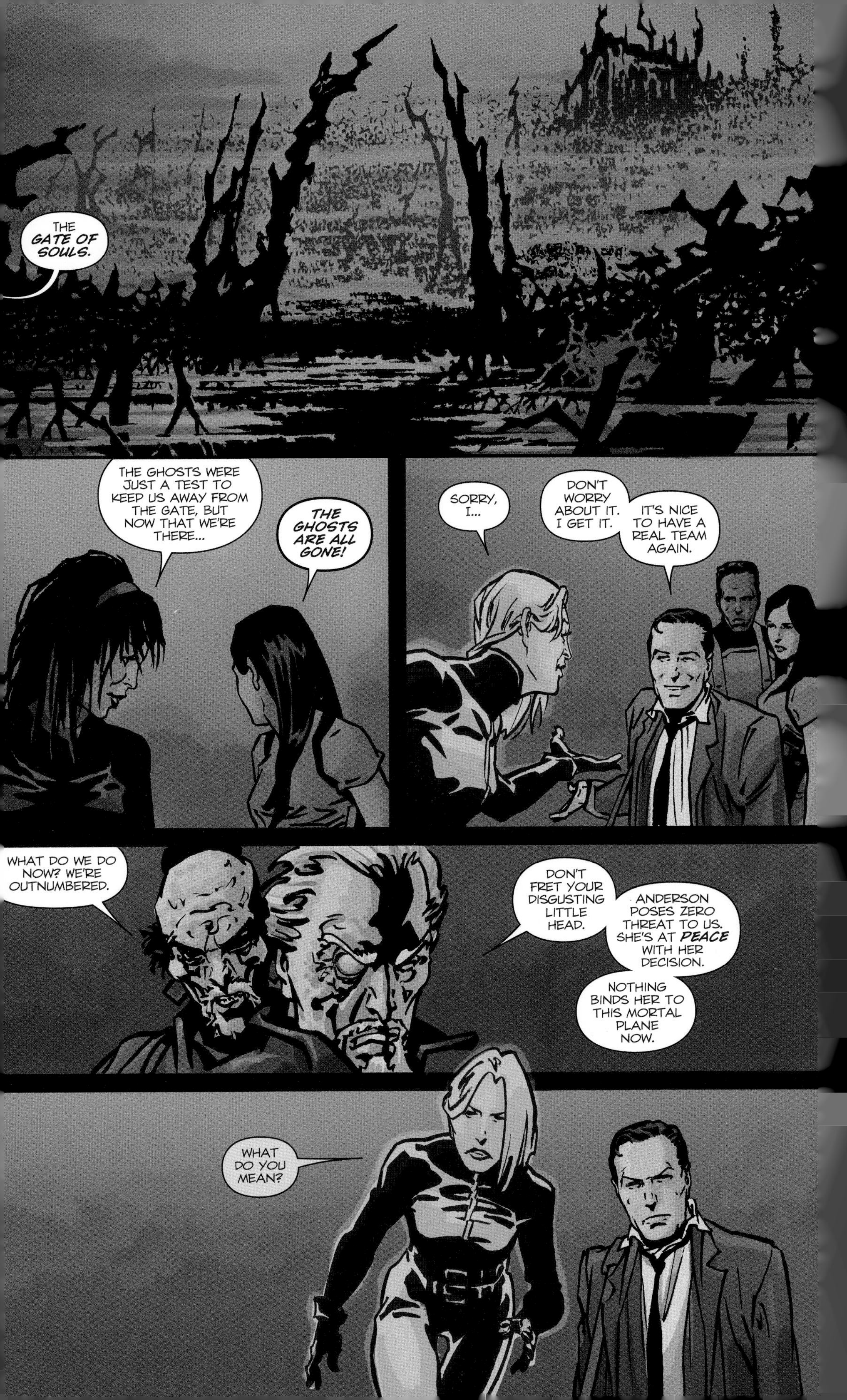
THE GATE OF SOULS.
THE GHOSTS WERE JUST A TEST TO KEEP US AWAY FROM THE GATE, BUT NOW THAT WE'RE THERE...
THE GHOSTS ARE ALL GONE!
SORRY, I...
DON'T WORRY ABOUT IT. I GET IT.
IT'S NICE TO HAVE A REAL TEAM AGAIN.
WHAT DO WE DO NOW? WE'RE OUTNUMBERED.
DON'T FRET YOUR DISGUSTING LITTLE HEAD.
ANDERSON POSES ZERO THREAT TO US. SHE'S AT PEACE WITH HER DECISION.
NOTHING BINDS HER TO THIS MORTAL PLANE NOW.
WHAT DO YOU MEAN?

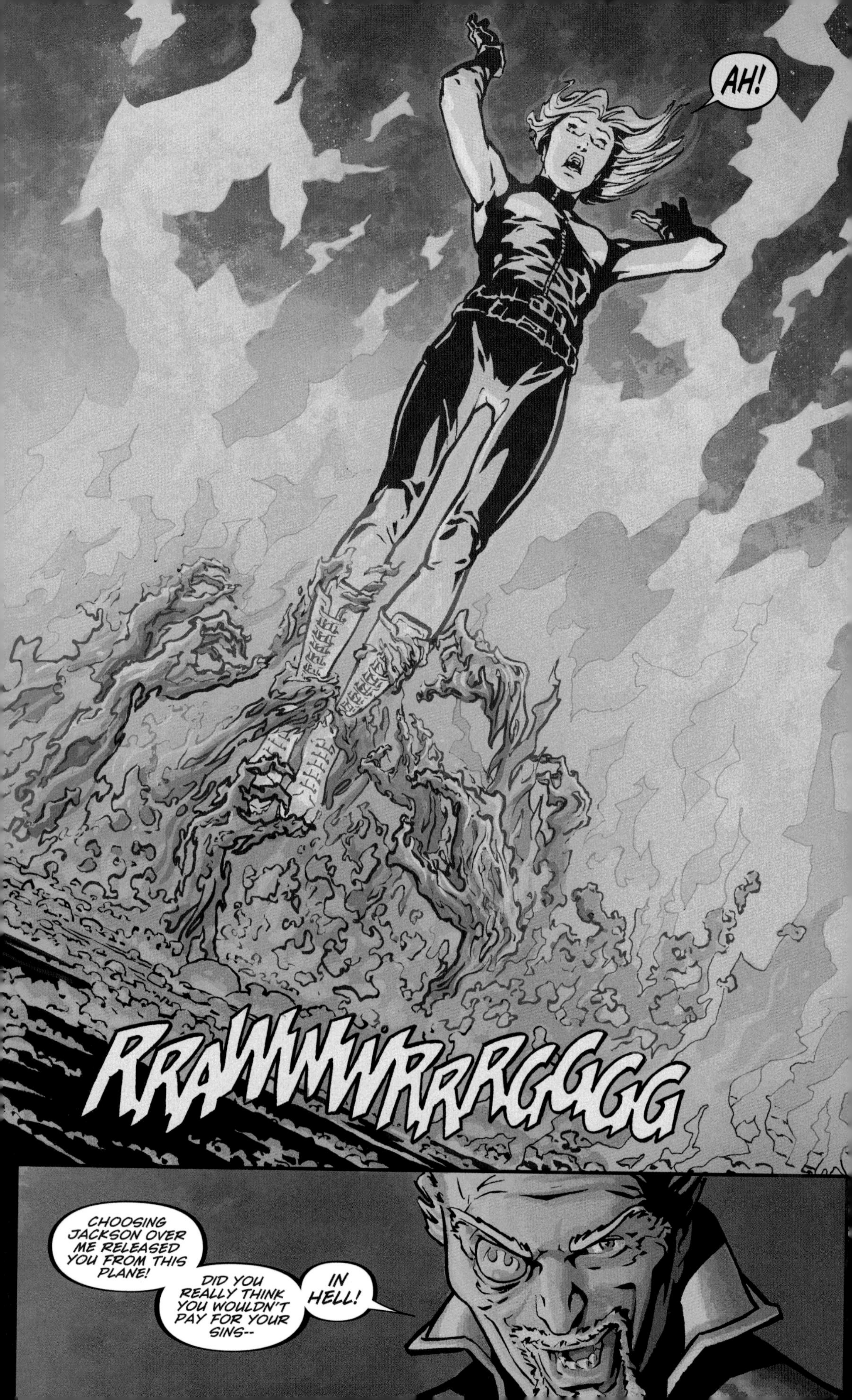
AH!
RRAWWWRRRGGGG
CHOOSING JACKSON OVER ME RELEASED YOU FROM THIS PLANE!
DID YOU REALLY THINK YOU WOULDN'T PAY FOR YOUR SINS--
IN HELL!

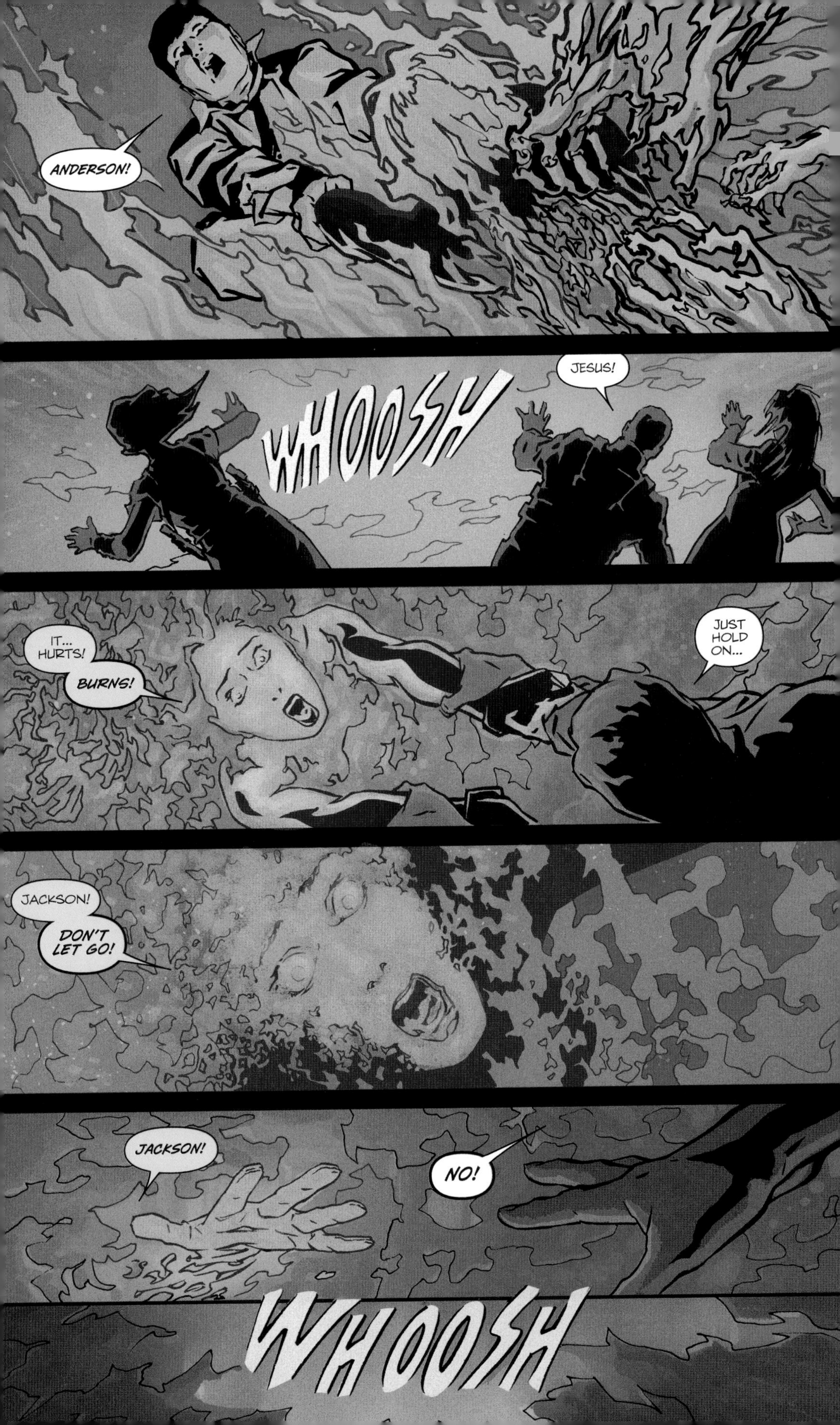
ANDERSON!
WHOOSH
JESUS!
IT... HURTS!
BURNS!
JUST HOLD ON...
JACKSON!
DON'T LET GO!
JACKSON!
NO!
WHOOSH

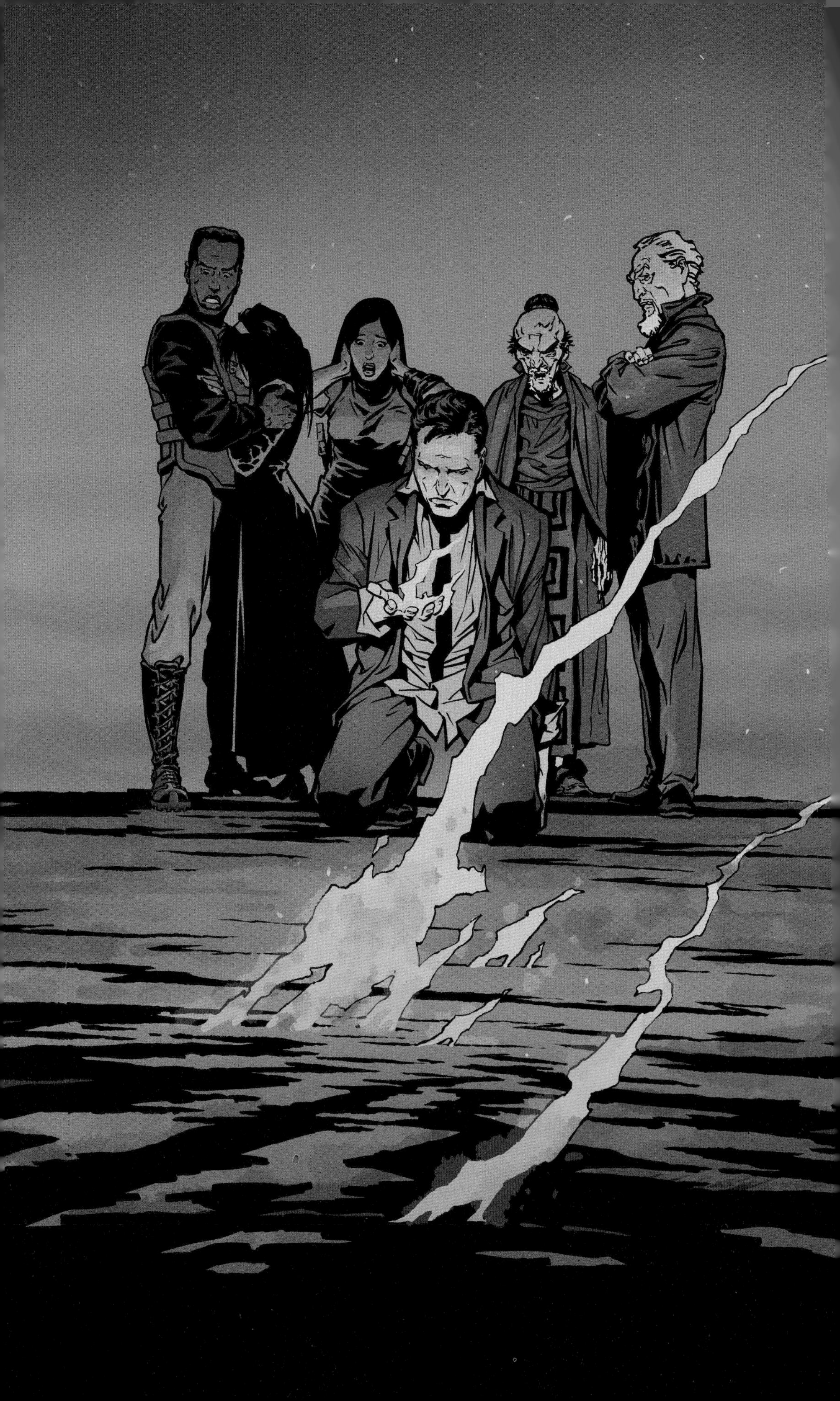

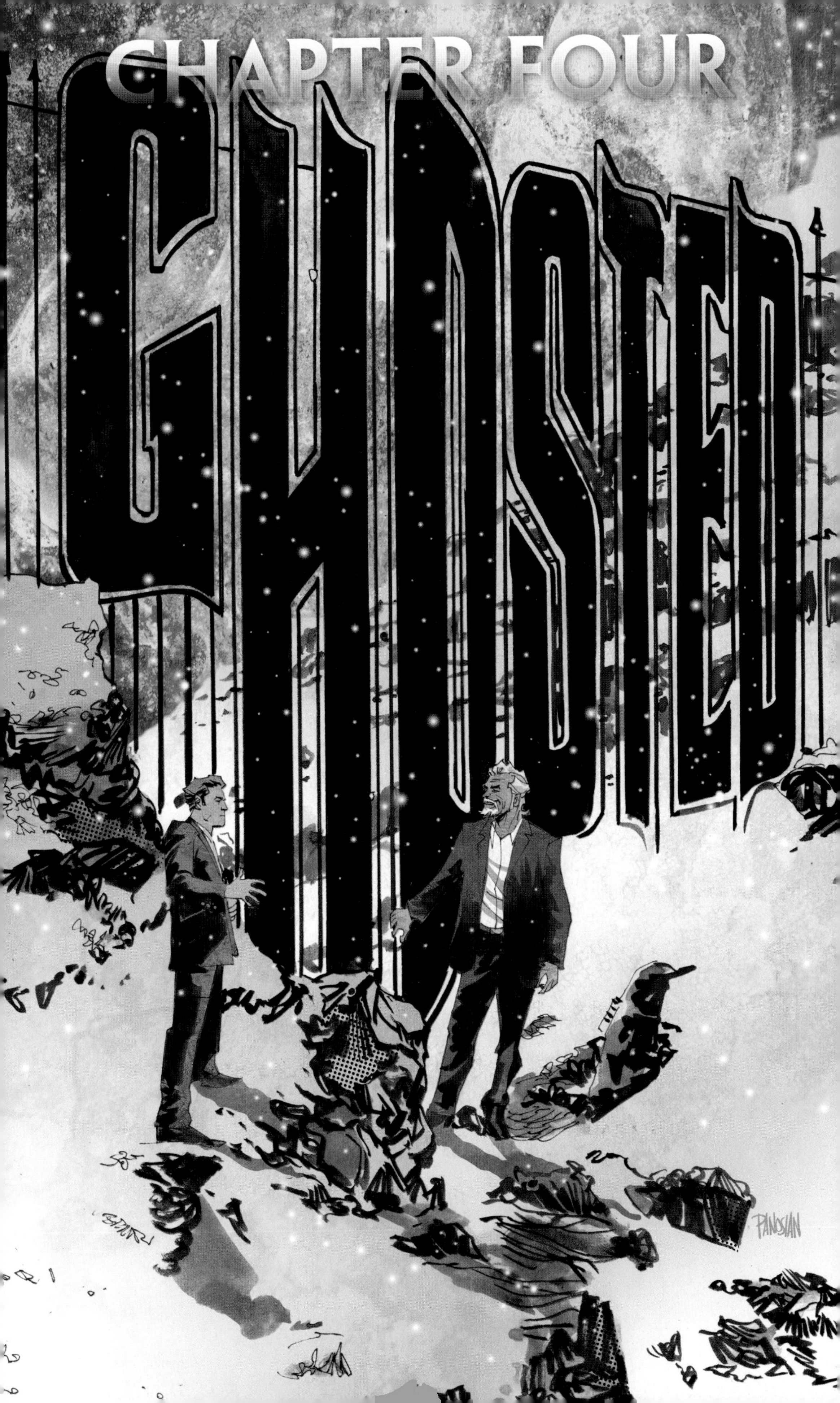
CHAPTER FOUR
GHOSTED
PANOSIAN

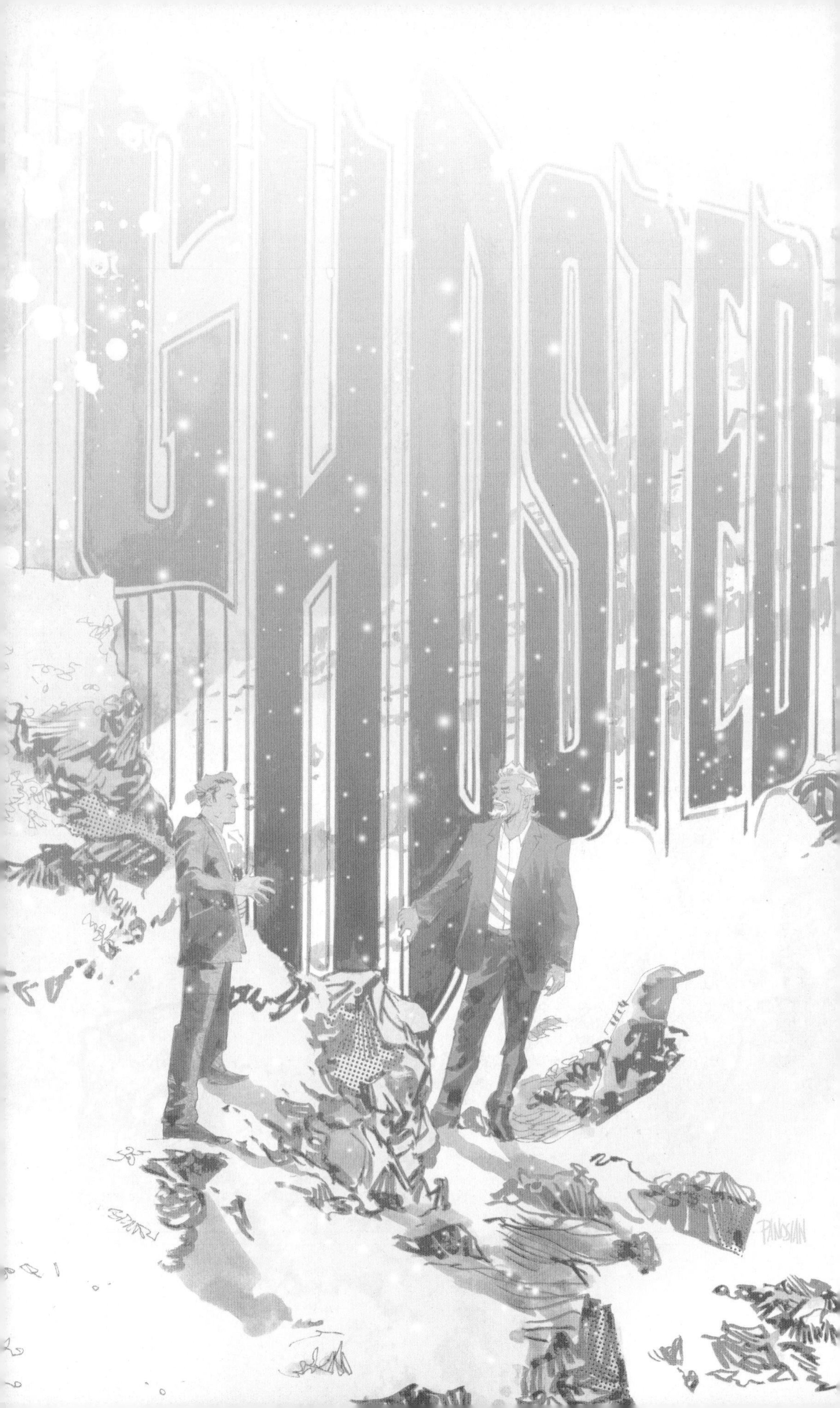
GHOSTED
PANOSIAN

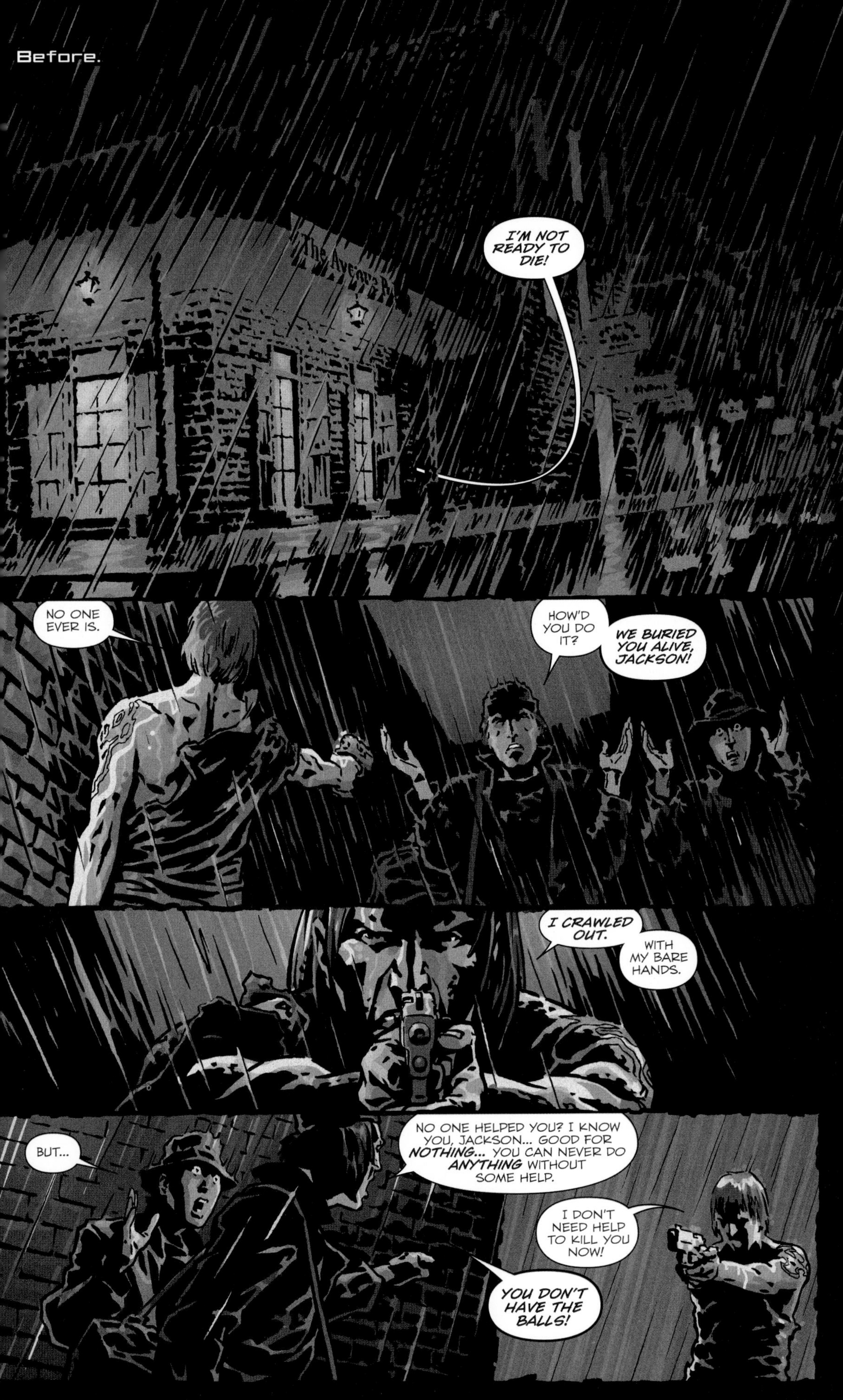
Before.
I'M NOT READY TO DIE!
NO ONE EVER IS.
HOW'D YOU DO IT?
WE BURIED YOU ALIVE, JACKSON!
I CRAWLED OUT.
WITH MY BARE HANDS.
BUT...
NO ONE HELPED YOU? I KNOW YOU, JACKSON... GOOD FOR NOTHING... YOU CAN NEVER DO ANYTHING WITHOUT SOME HELP.
I DON'T NEED HELP TO KILL YOU NOW!
YOU DON'T HAVE THE BALLS!

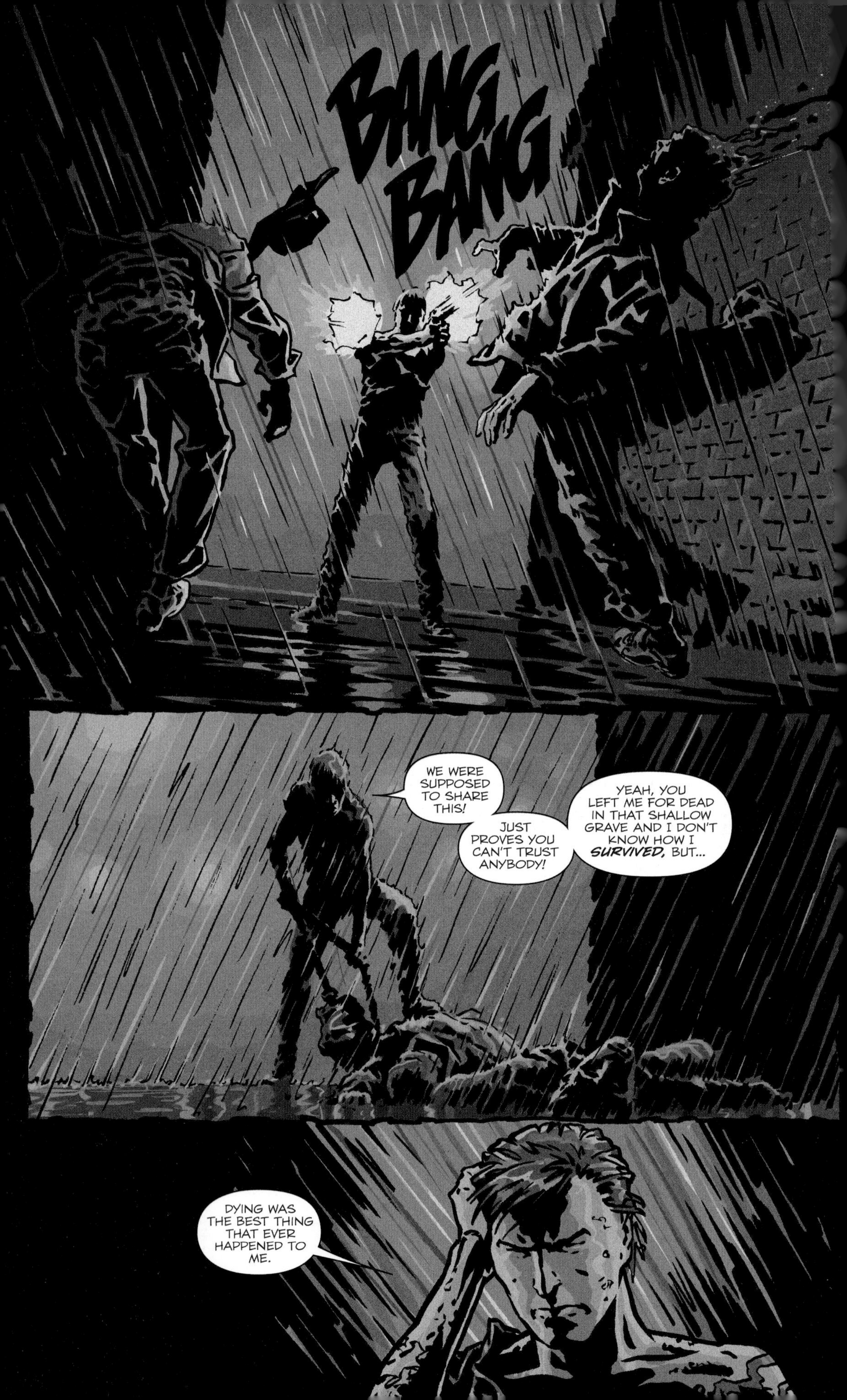
BANG BANG
WE WERE SUPPOSED TO SHARE THIS!
JUST PROVES YOU CAN'T TRUST ANYBODY!
YEAH, YOU LEFT ME FOR DEAD IN THAT SHALLOW GRAVE AND I DON'T KNOW HOW I SURVIVED, BUT...
DYING WAS THE BEST THING THAT EVER HAPPENED TO ME.

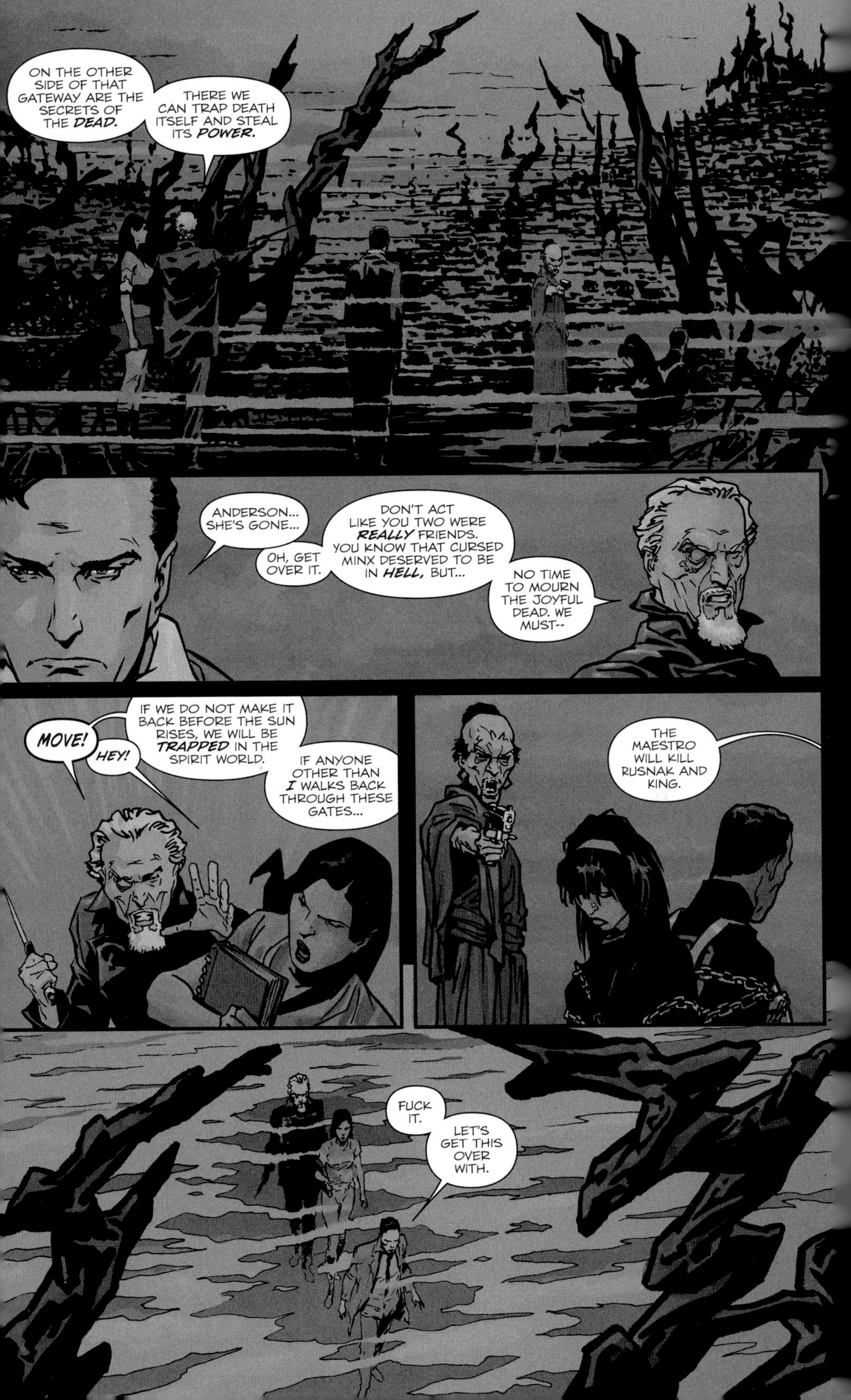

ON THE OTHER SIDE OF THAT GATEWAY ARE THE SECRETS OF THE *DEAD.*
THERE WE CAN TRAP DEATH ITSELF AND STEAL ITS *POWER.*
ANDERSON... SHE'S GONE...
OH, GET OVER IT.
DON'T ACT LIKE YOU TWO WERE *REALLY* FRIENDS. YOU KNOW THAT CURSED MINX DESERVED TO BE IN *HELL,* BUT...
NO TIME TO MOURN THE JOYFUL DEAD. WE MUST--
MOVE!
HEY!
IF WE DO NOT MAKE IT BACK BEFORE THE SUN RISES, WE WILL BE *TRAPPED* IN THE SPIRIT WORLD.
IF ANYONE OTHER THAN *I* WALKS BACK THROUGH THESE GATES...
THE MAESTRO WILL KILL RUSNAK AND KING.
FUCK IT.
LET'S GET THIS OVER WITH.

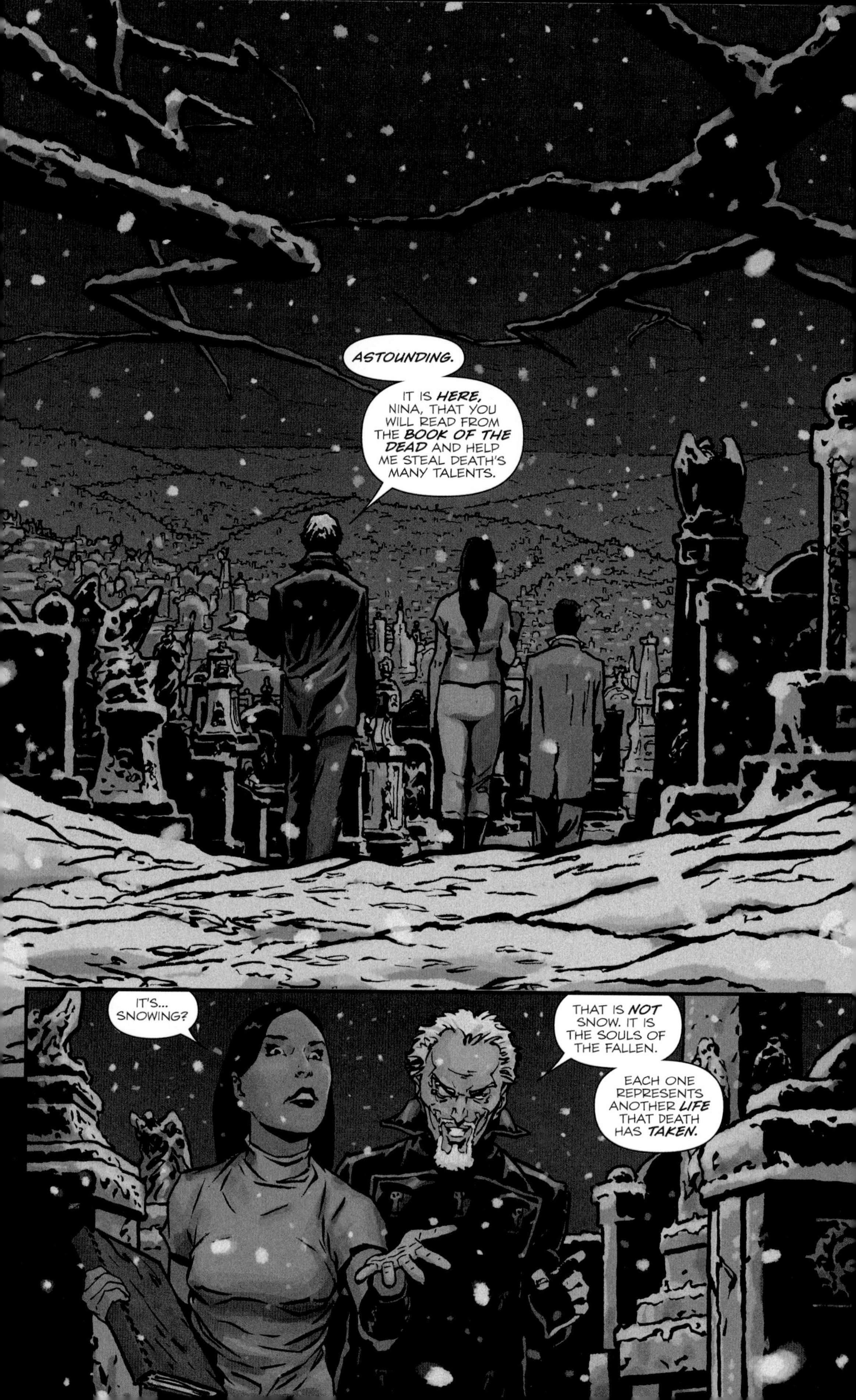
ASTOUNDING.
IT IS HERE, NINA, THAT YOU WILL READ FROM THE BOOK OF THE DEAD AND HELP ME STEAL DEATH'S MANY TALENTS.
IT'S... SNOWING?
THAT IS NOT SNOW. IT IS THE SOULS OF THE FALLEN.
EACH ONE REPRESENTS ANOTHER LIFE THAT DEATH HAS TAKEN.

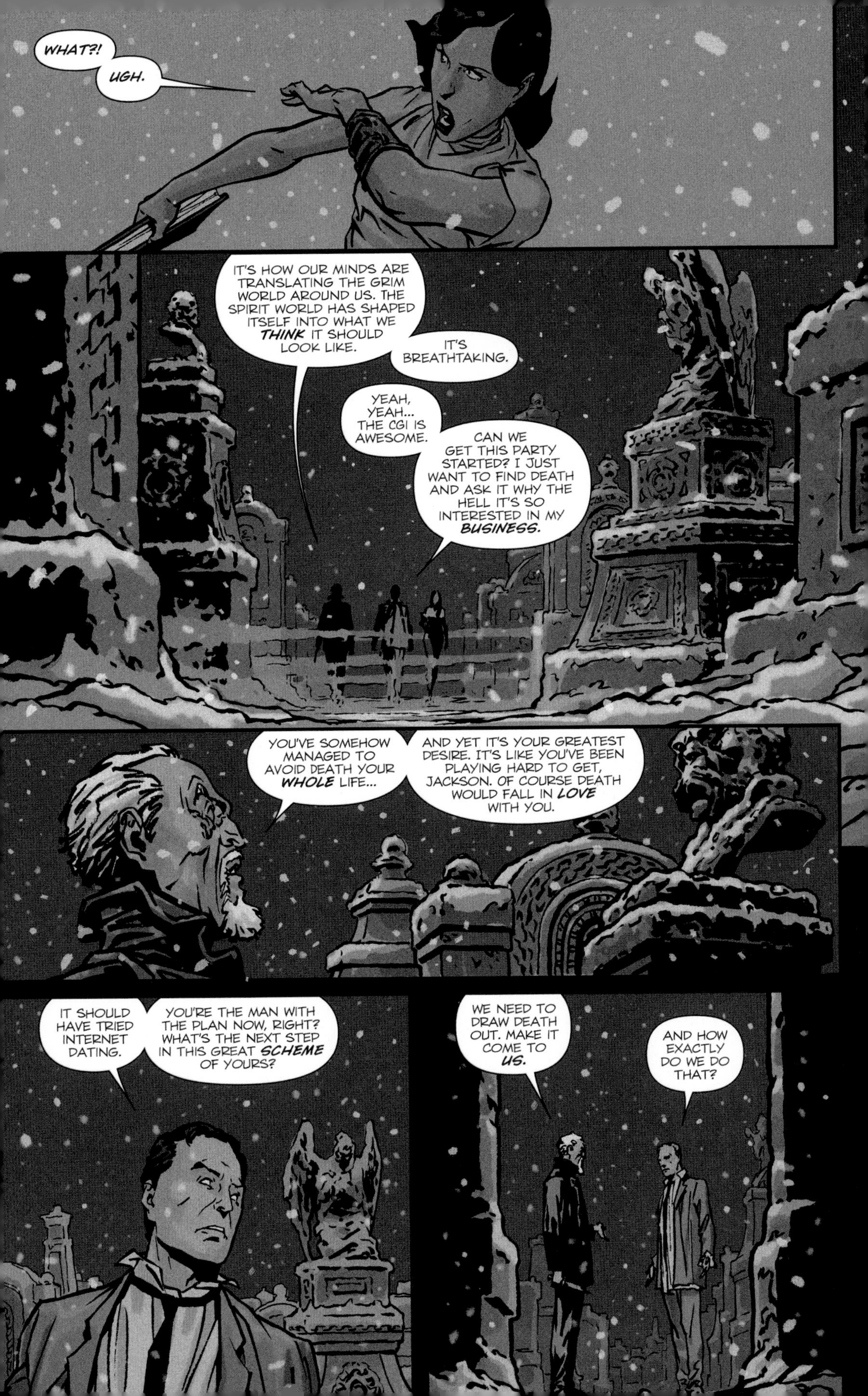
WHAT?!
UGH.
IT'S HOW OUR MINDS ARE TRANSLATING THE GRIM WORLD AROUND US. THE SPIRIT WORLD HAS SHAPED ITSELF INTO WHAT WE THINK IT SHOULD LOOK LIKE.
IT'S BREATHTAKING.
YEAH, YEAH... THE CGI IS AWESOME.
CAN WE GET THIS PARTY STARTED? I JUST WANT TO FIND DEATH AND ASK IT WHY THE HELL IT'S SO INTERESTED IN MY BUSINESS.
YOU'VE SOMEHOW MANAGED TO AVOID DEATH YOUR WHOLE LIFE...
AND YET IT'S YOUR GREATEST DESIRE. IT'S LIKE YOU'VE BEEN PLAYING HARD TO GET, JACKSON. OF COURSE DEATH WOULD FALL IN LOVE WITH YOU.
IT SHOULD HAVE TRIED INTERNET DATING.
YOU'RE THE MAN WITH THE PLAN NOW, RIGHT? WHAT'S THE NEXT STEP IN THIS GREAT SCHEME OF YOURS?
WE NEED TO DRAW DEATH OUT. MAKE IT COME TO US.
AND HOW EXACTLY DO WE DO THAT?

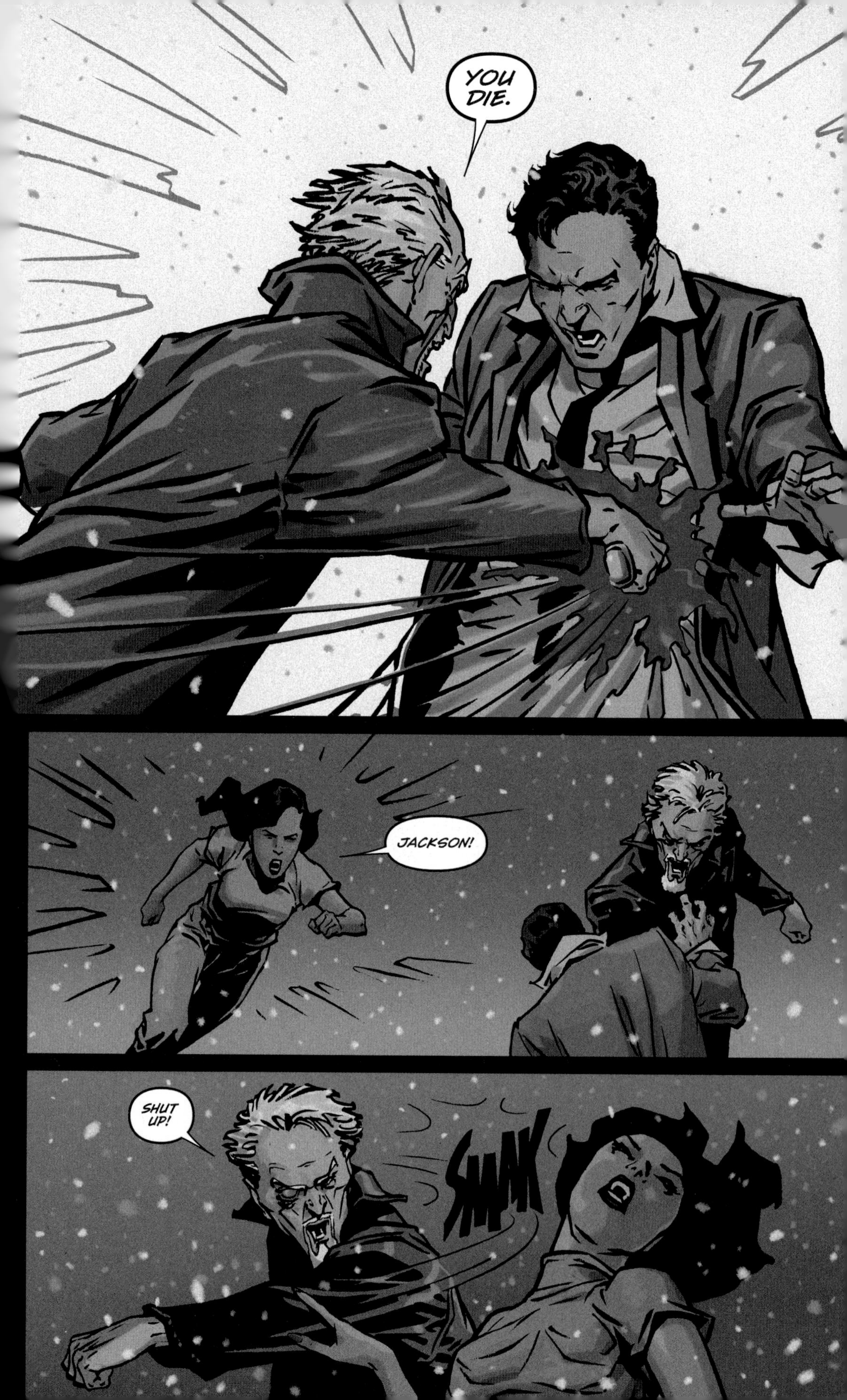
YOU DIE.
JACKSON!
SHUT UP!
SMAK

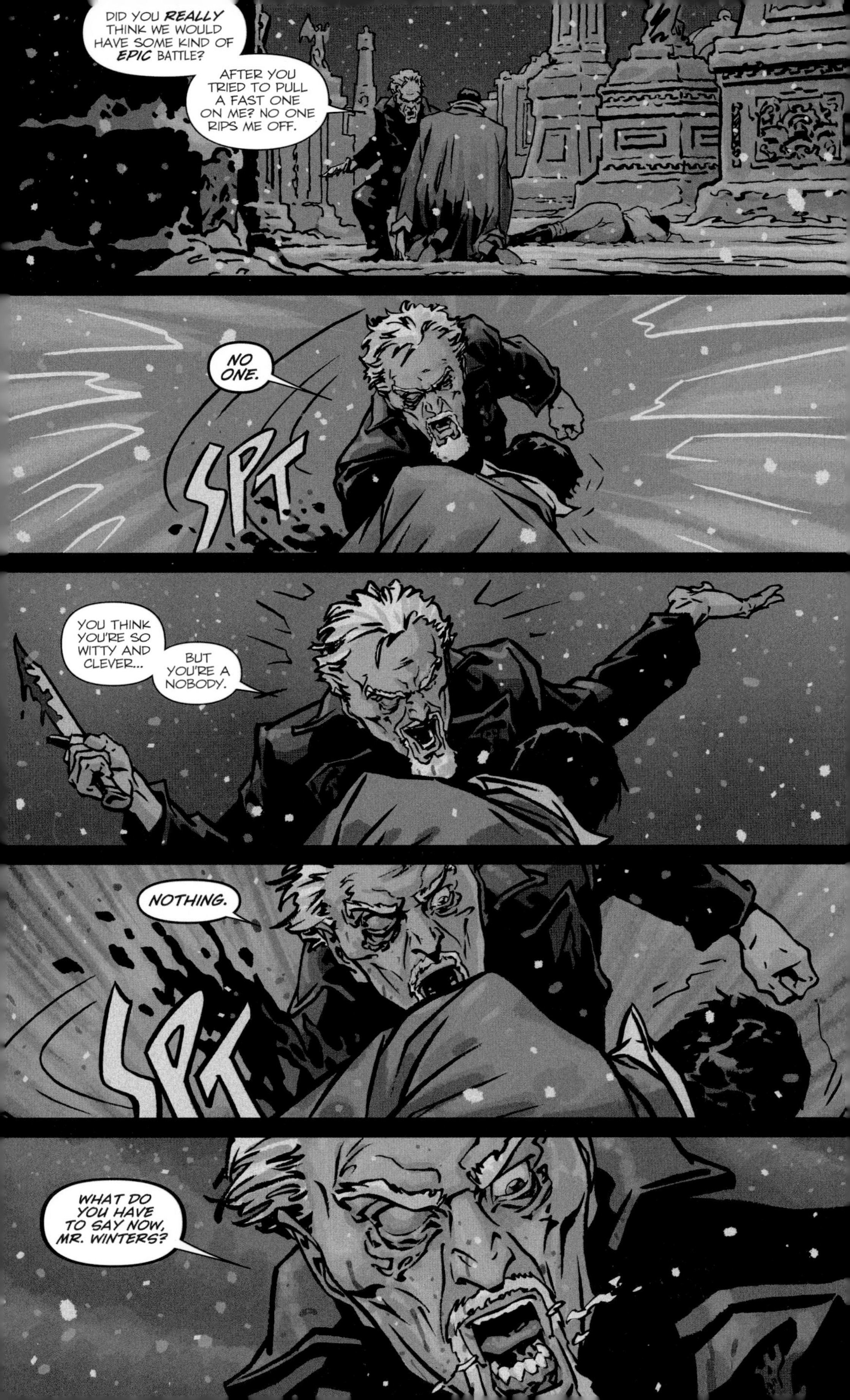
DID YOU REALLY THINK WE WOULD HAVE SOME KIND OF EPIC BATTLE?
AFTER YOU TRIED TO PULL A FAST ONE ON ME? NO ONE RIPS ME OFF.
NO ONE.
SPT
YOU THINK YOU'RE SO WITTY AND CLEVER...
BUT YOU'RE A NOBODY.
NOTHING.
SPT
WHAT DO YOU HAVE TO SAY NOW, MR. WINTERS?

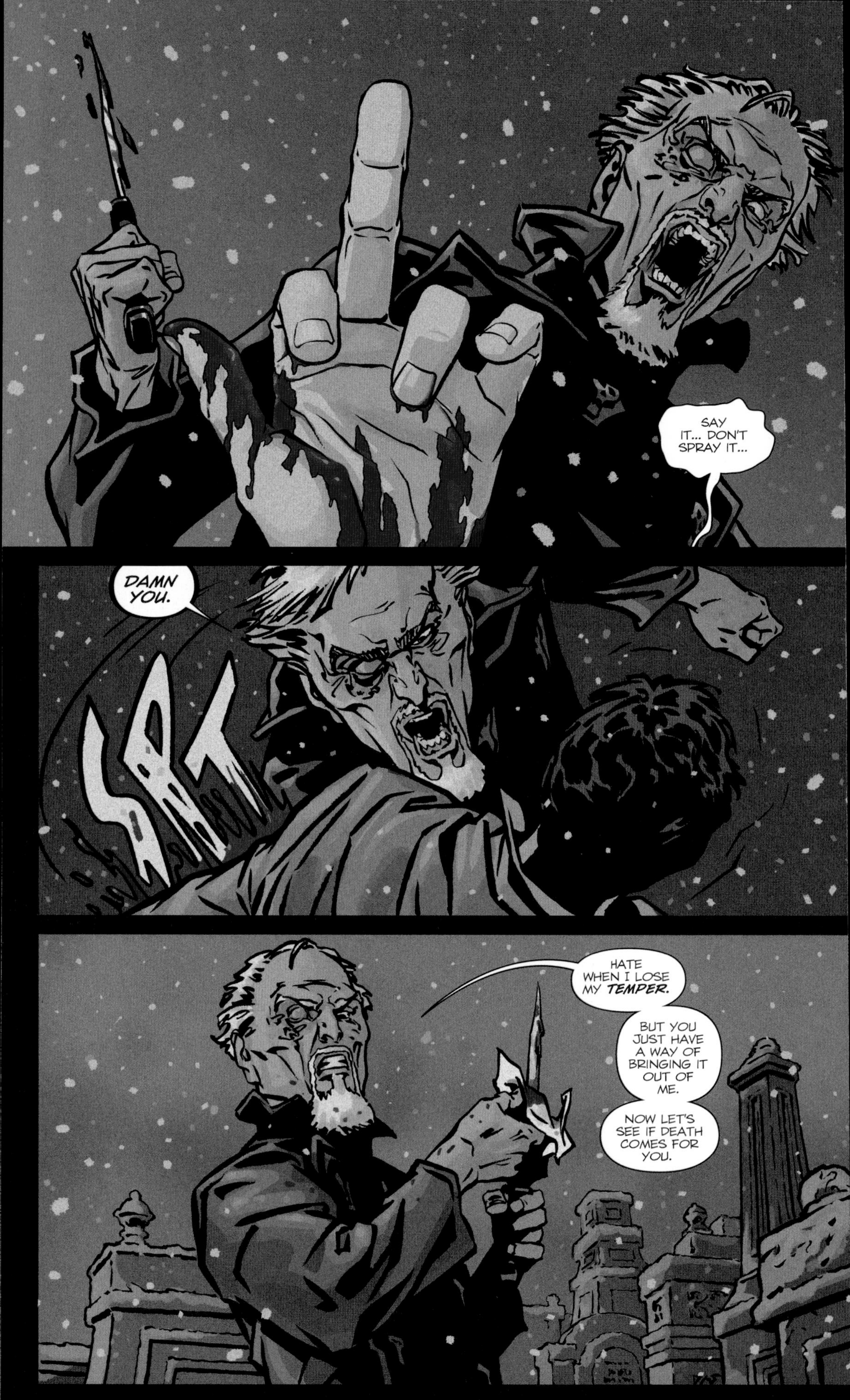
SAY IT... DON'T SPRAY IT...
DAMN YOU.
HATE WHEN I LOSE MY *TEMPER.*
BUT YOU JUST HAVE A WAY OF BRINGING IT OUT OF ME.
NOW LET'S SEE IF DEATH COMES FOR YOU.

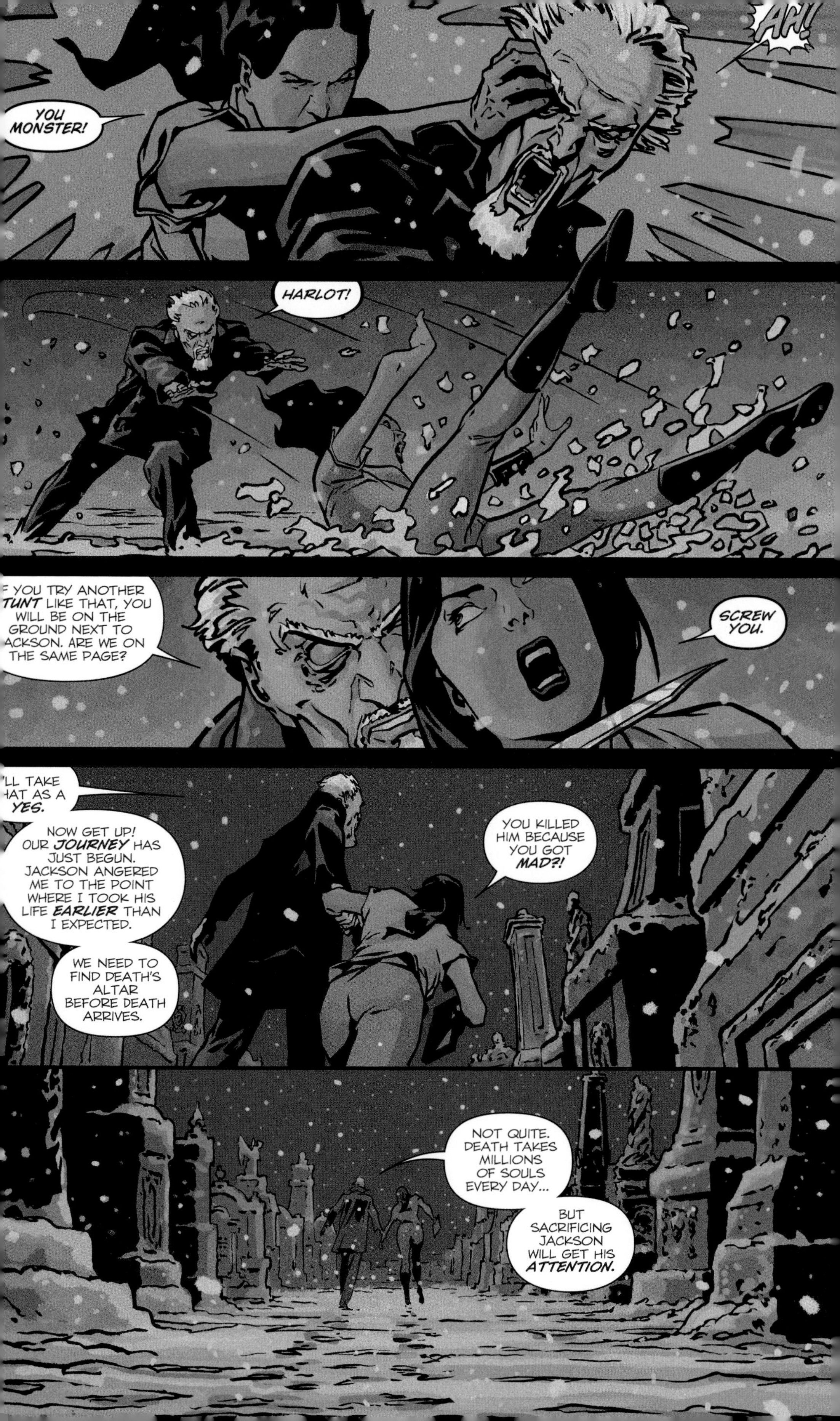
AH!
YOU MONSTER!
HARLOT!
F YOU TRY ANOTHER TUNT LIKE THAT, YOU WILL BE ON THE GROUND NEXT TO ACKSON. ARE WE ON THE SAME PAGE?
SCREW YOU.
'LL TAKE HAT AS A YES.
NOW GET UP! OUR JOURNEY HAS JUST BEGUN. JACKSON ANGERED ME TO THE POINT WHERE I TOOK HIS LIFE EARLIER THAN I EXPECTED.
WE NEED TO FIND DEATH'S ALTAR BEFORE DEATH ARRIVES.
YOU KILLED HIM BECAUSE YOU GOT MAD?!
NOT QUITE. DEATH TAKES MILLIONS OF SOULS EVERY DAY...
BUT SACRIFICING JACKSON WILL GET HIS ATTENTION.

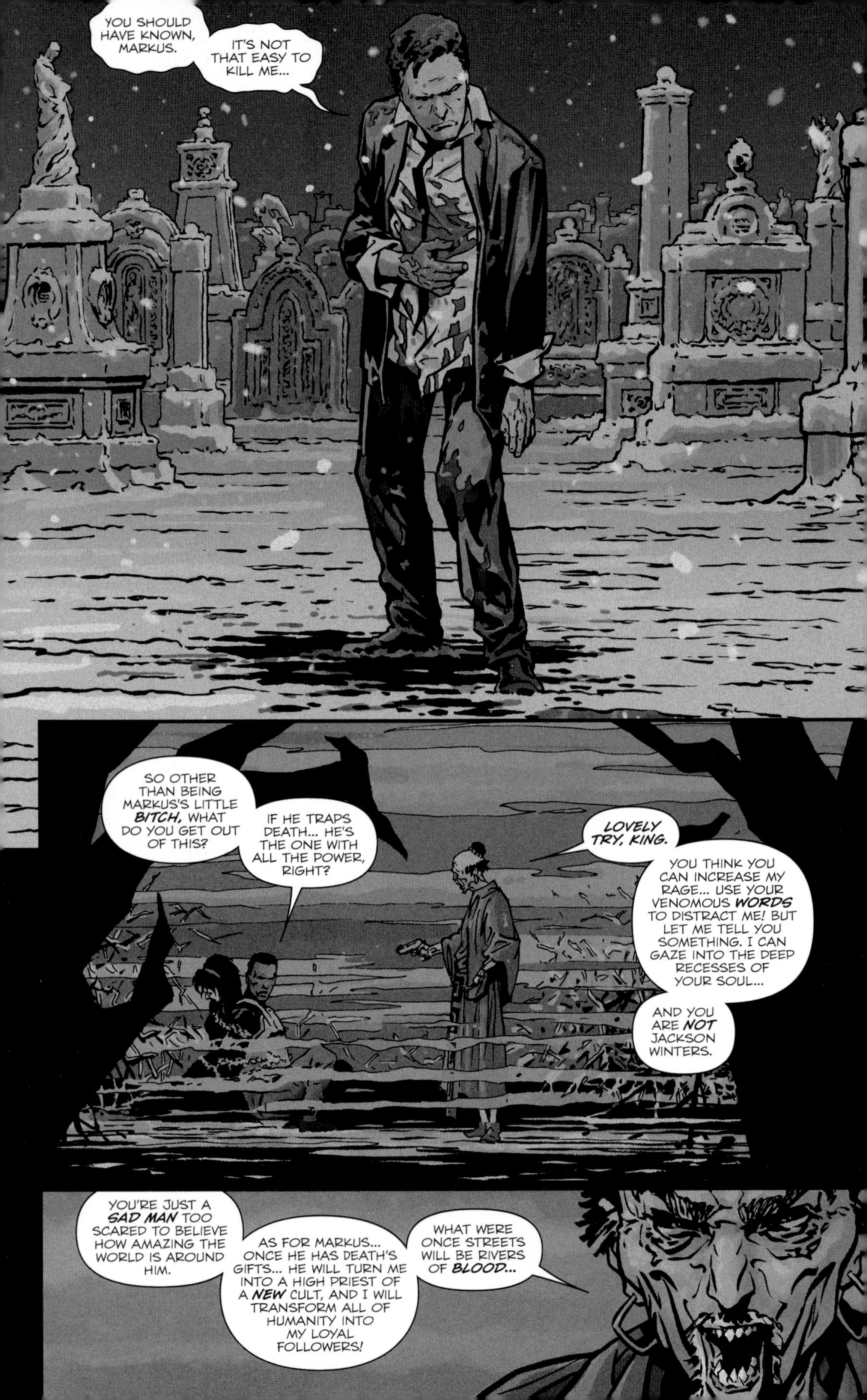

YOU SHOULD HAVE KNOWN, MARKUS.
IT'S NOT THAT EASY TO KILL ME...
SO OTHER THAN BEING MARKUS'S LITTLE BITCH, WHAT DO YOU GET OUT OF THIS?
IF HE TRAPS DEATH... HE'S THE ONE WITH ALL THE POWER, RIGHT?
LOVELY TRY, KING.
YOU THINK YOU CAN INCREASE MY RAGE... USE YOUR VENOMOUS WORDS TO DISTRACT ME! BUT LET ME TELL YOU SOMETHING. I CAN GAZE INTO THE DEEP RECESSES OF YOUR SOUL...
AND YOU ARE NOT JACKSON WINTERS.
YOU'RE JUST A SAD MAN TOO SCARED TO BELIEVE HOW AMAZING THE WORLD IS AROUND HIM.
AS FOR MARKUS... ONCE HE HAS DEATH'S GIFTS... HE WILL TURN ME INTO A HIGH PRIEST OF A NEW CULT, AND I WILL TRANSFORM ALL OF HUMANITY INTO MY LOYAL FOLLOWERS!
WHAT WERE ONCE STREETS WILL BE RIVERS OF BLOOD...

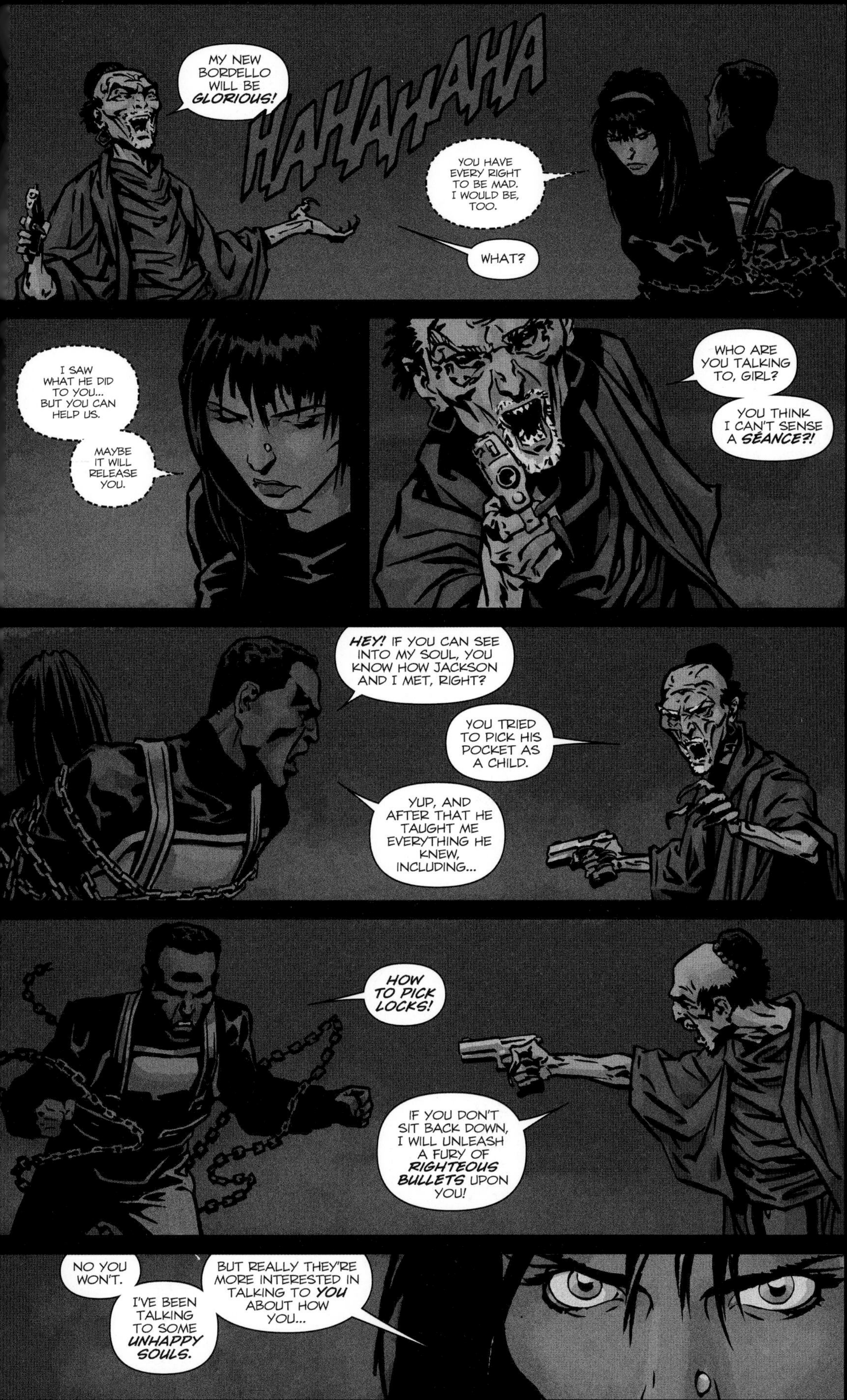
MY NEW BORDELLO WILL BE **GLORIOUS!**
HAHAHAHA
YOU HAVE EVERY RIGHT TO BE MAD. I WOULD BE, TOO.
WHAT?
I SAW WHAT HE DID TO YOU... BUT YOU CAN HELP US.
MAYBE IT WILL RELEASE YOU.
WHO ARE YOU TALKING TO, GIRL?
YOU THINK I CAN'T SENSE A **SÉANCE?!**
HEY! IF YOU CAN SEE INTO MY SOUL, YOU KNOW HOW JACKSON AND I MET, RIGHT?
YOU TRIED TO PICK HIS POCKET AS A CHILD.
YUP, AND AFTER THAT HE TAUGHT ME EVERYTHING HE KNEW, INCLUDING...
HOW TO PICK LOCKS!
IF YOU DON'T SIT BACK DOWN, I WILL UNLEASH A FURY OF **RIGHTEOUS BULLETS** UPON YOU!
NO YOU WON'T.
I'VE BEEN TALKING TO SOME **UNHAPPY SOULS.**
BUT REALLY THEY'RE MORE INTERESTED IN TALKING TO **YOU** ABOUT HOW YOU...

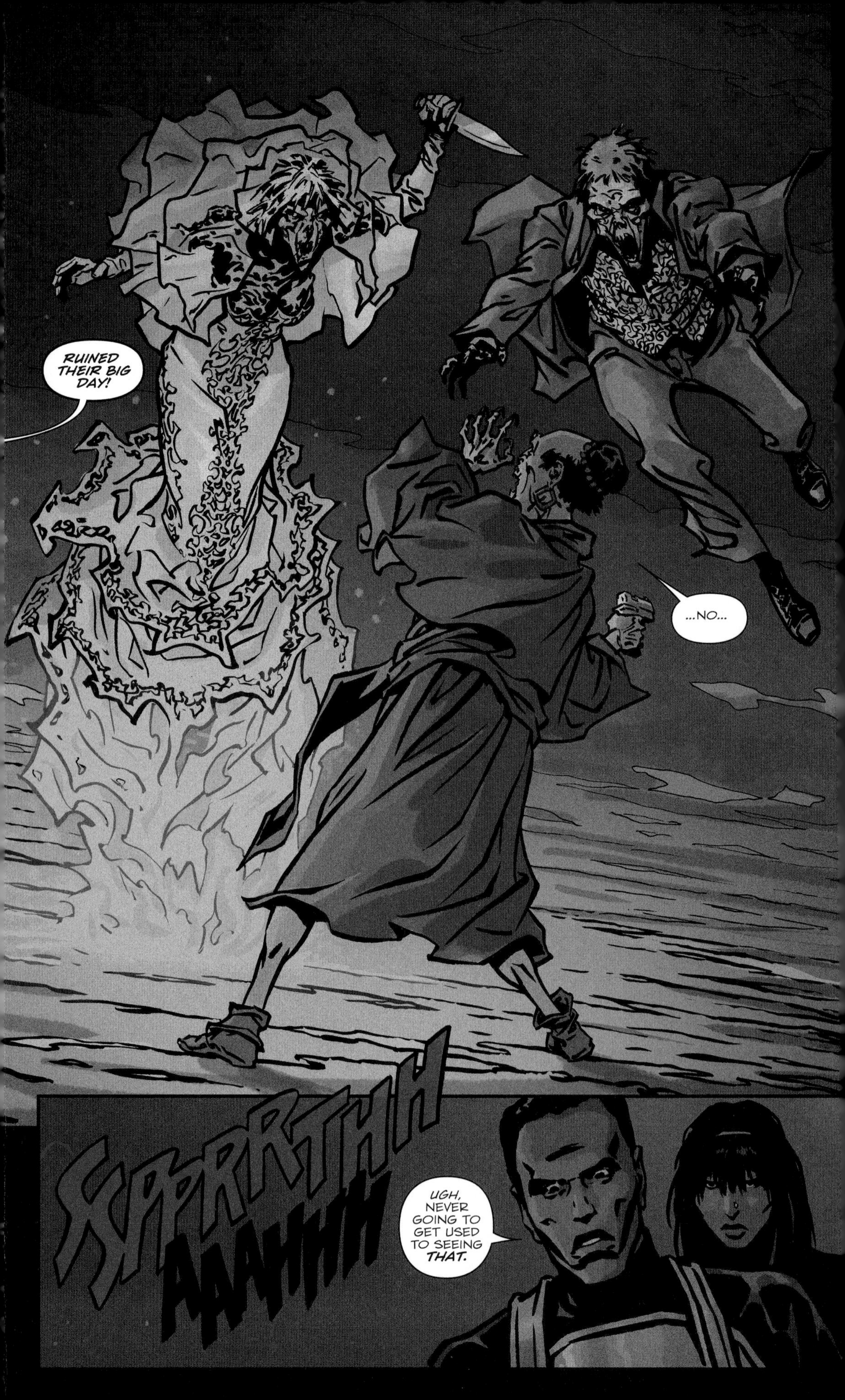
RUINED THEIR BIG DAY!
...NO...
SPRRTHH
AAAHHH
UGH, NEVER GOING TO GET USED TO SEEING *THAT.*

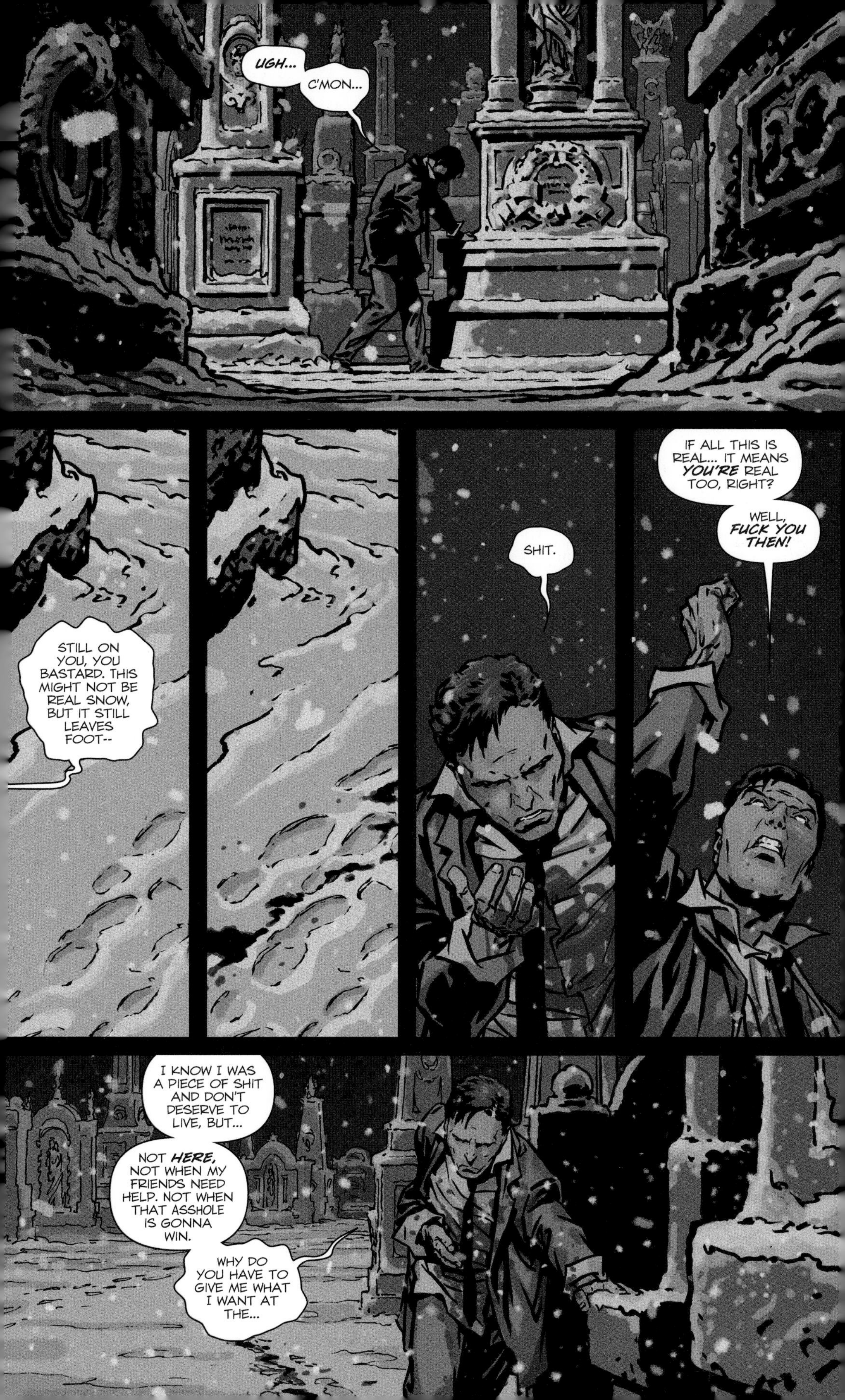
UGH...
C'MON...
STILL ON YOU, YOU BASTARD. THIS MIGHT NOT BE REAL SNOW, BUT IT STILL LEAVES FOOT--
SHIT.
IF ALL THIS IS REAL... IT MEANS YOU'RE REAL TOO, RIGHT?
WELL, FUCK YOU THEN!
I KNOW I WAS A PIECE OF SHIT AND DON'T DESERVE TO LIVE, BUT...
NOT HERE, NOT WHEN MY FRIENDS NEED HELP. NOT WHEN THAT ASSHOLE IS GONNA WIN.
WHY DO YOU HAVE TO GIVE ME WHAT I WANT AT THE...

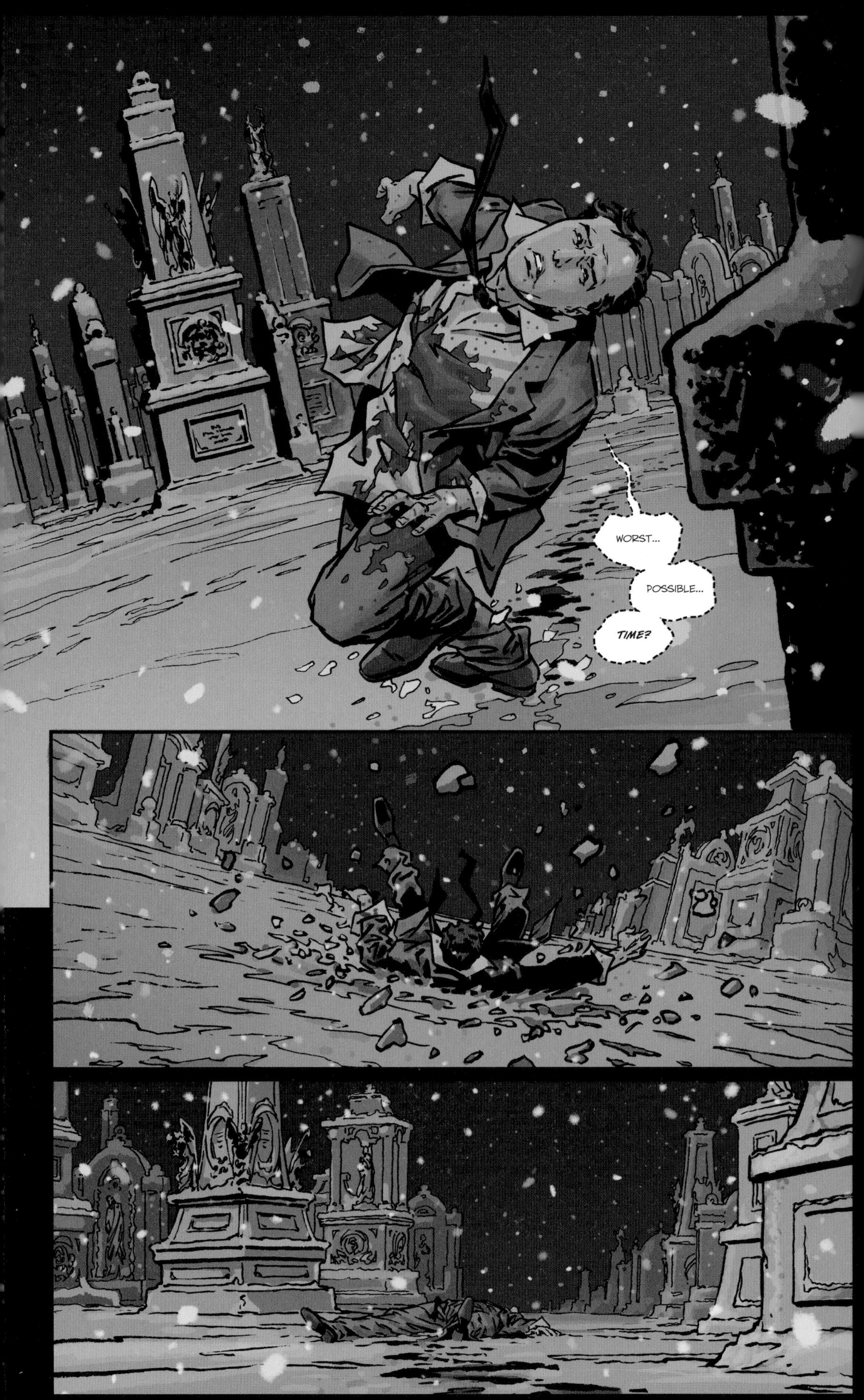
WORST...
POSSIBLE...
TIME?

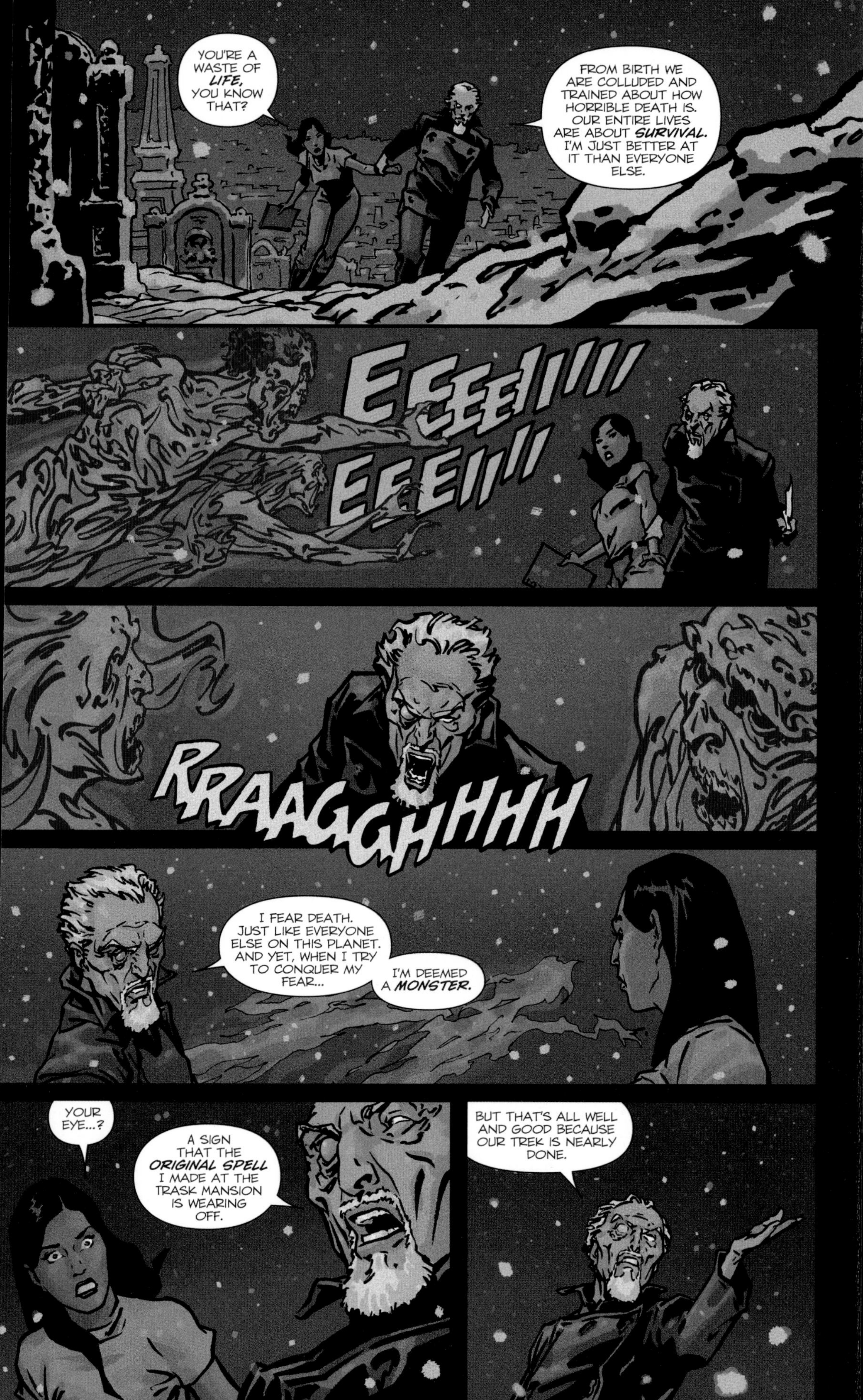
YOU'RE A WASTE OF LIFE, YOU KNOW THAT?
FROM BIRTH WE ARE COLLUDED AND TRAINED ABOUT HOW HORRIBLE DEATH IS. OUR ENTIRE LIVES ARE ABOUT SURVIVAL. I'M JUST BETTER AT IT THAN EVERYONE ELSE.
EEEEIIIII
EEEIIII
RRAAGGHHHH
I FEAR DEATH. JUST LIKE EVERYONE ELSE ON THIS PLANET. AND YET, WHEN I TRY TO CONQUER MY FEAR...
I'M DEEMED A MONSTER.
YOUR EYE...?
A SIGN THAT THE ORIGINAL SPELL I MADE AT THE TRASK MANSION IS WEARING OFF.
BUT THAT'S ALL WELL AND GOOD BECAUSE OUR TREK IS NEARLY DONE.

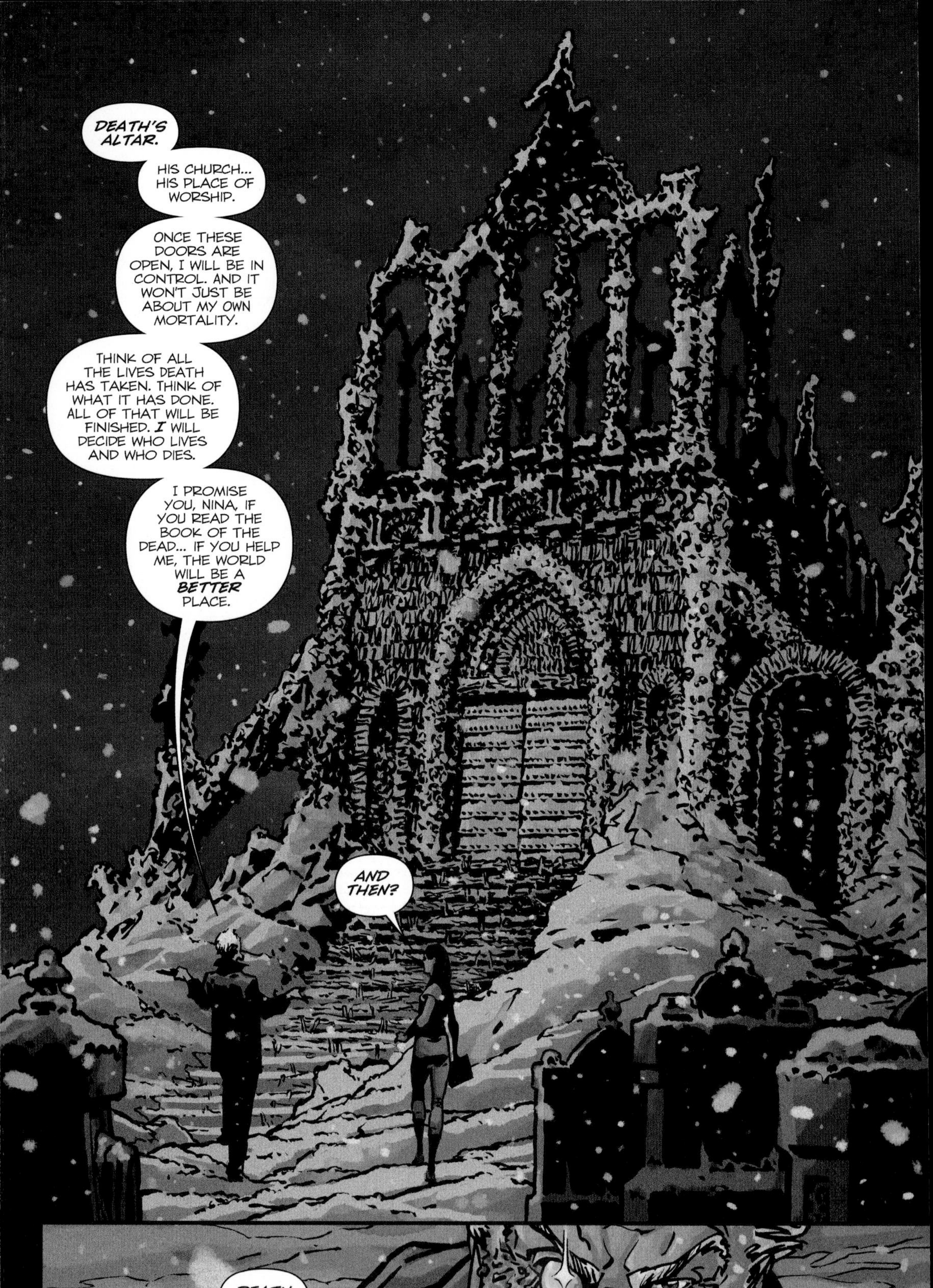
DEATH'S ALTAR.
HIS CHURCH... HIS PLACE OF WORSHIP.
ONCE THESE DOORS ARE OPEN, I WILL BE IN CONTROL. AND IT WON'T JUST BE ABOUT MY OWN MORTALITY.
THINK OF ALL THE LIVES DEATH HAS TAKEN. THINK OF WHAT IT HAS DONE. ALL OF THAT WILL BE FINISHED. I WILL DECIDE WHO LIVES AND WHO DIES.
I PROMISE YOU, NINA, IF YOU READ THE BOOK OF THE DEAD... IF YOU HELP ME, THE WORLD WILL BE A BETTER PLACE.
AND THEN?

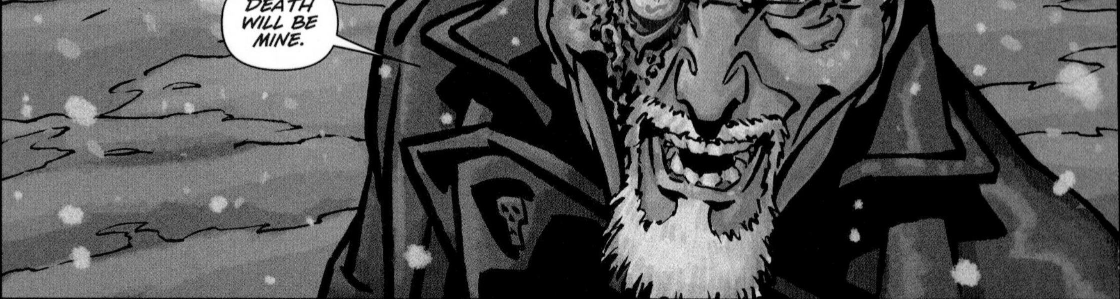
DEATH WILL BE MINE.

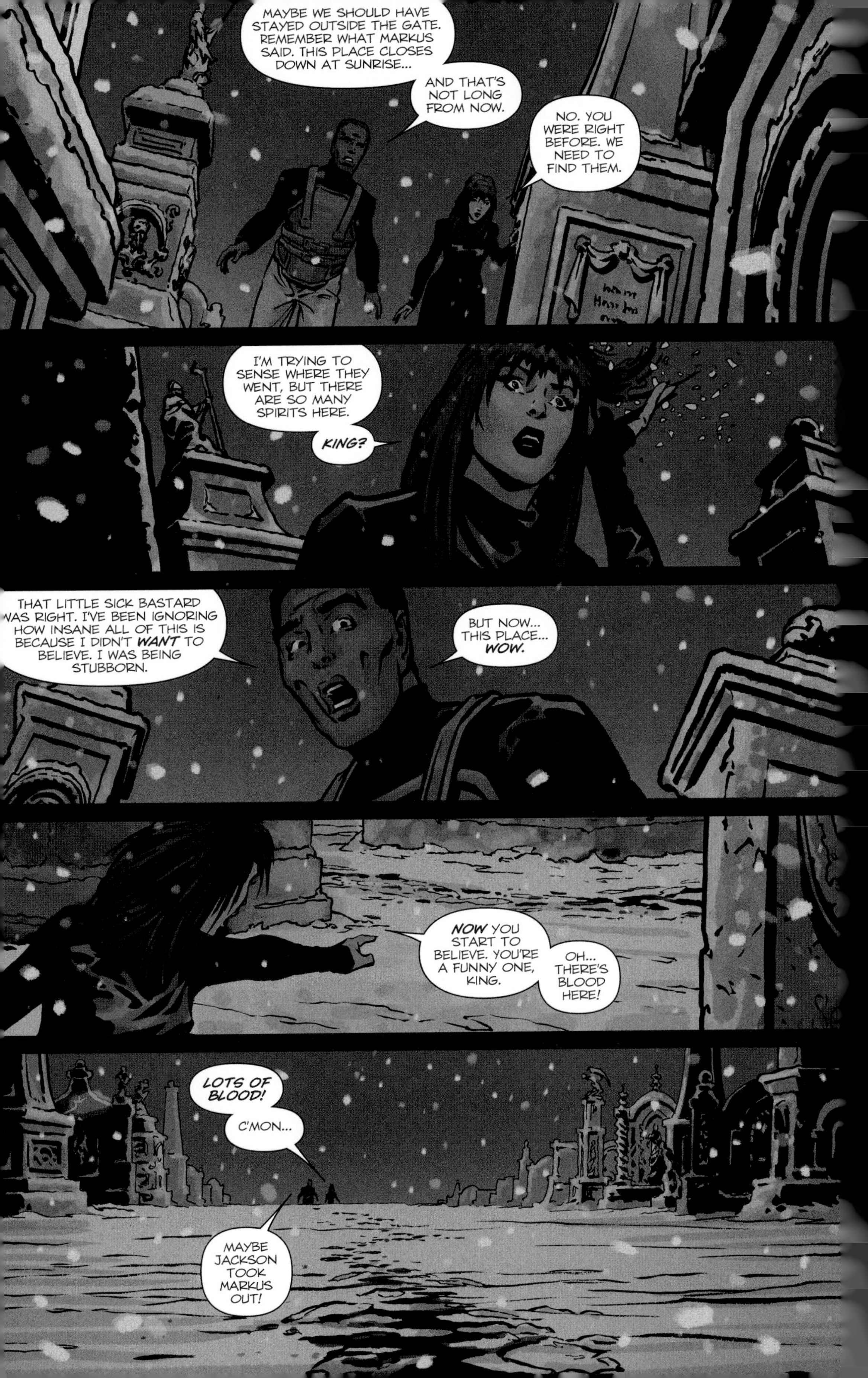
MAYBE WE SHOULD HAVE STAYED OUTSIDE THE GATE. REMEMBER WHAT MARKUS SAID. THIS PLACE CLOSES DOWN AT SUNRISE...
AND THAT'S NOT LONG FROM NOW.
NO. YOU WERE RIGHT BEFORE. WE NEED TO FIND THEM.
I'M TRYING TO SENSE WHERE THEY WENT, BUT THERE ARE SO MANY SPIRITS HERE.
KING?
THAT LITTLE SICK BASTARD WAS RIGHT. I'VE BEEN IGNORING HOW INSANE ALL OF THIS IS BECAUSE I DIDN'T WANT TO BELIEVE. I WAS BEING STUBBORN.
BUT NOW... THIS PLACE... WOW.
NOW YOU START TO BELIEVE. YOU'RE A FUNNY ONE, KING.
OH... THERE'S BLOOD HERE!
LOTS OF BLOOD!
C'MON...
MAYBE JACKSON TOOK MARKUS OUT!

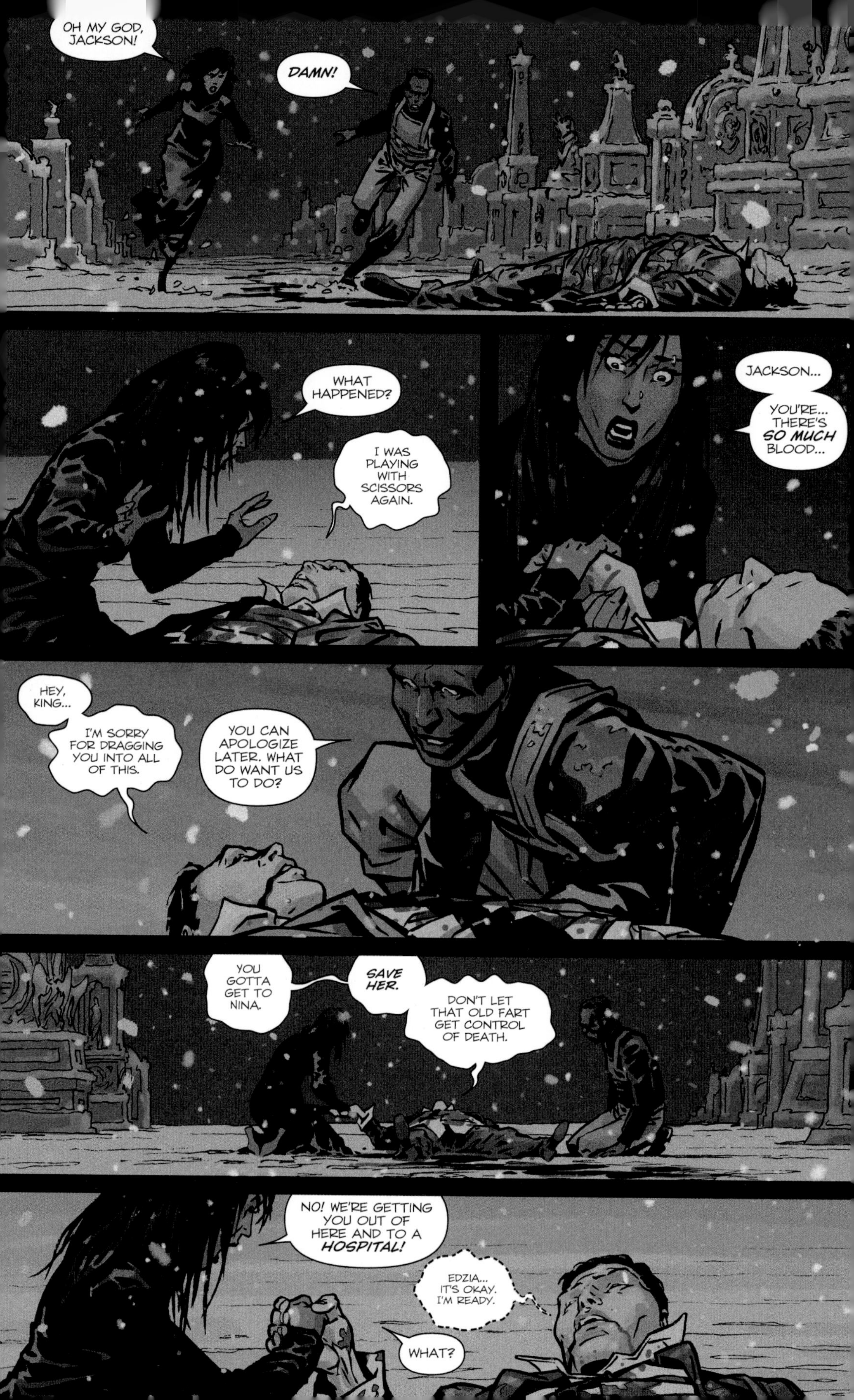
OH MY GOD, JACKSON!
DAMN!
WHAT HAPPENED?
I WAS PLAYING WITH SCISSORS AGAIN.
JACKSON...
YOU'RE... THERE'S SO MUCH BLOOD...
HEY, KING...
I'M SORRY FOR DRAGGING YOU INTO ALL OF THIS.
YOU CAN APOLOGIZE LATER. WHAT DO WANT US TO DO?
YOU GOTTA GET TO NINA.
SAVE HER.
DON'T LET THAT OLD FART GET CONTROL OF DEATH.
NO! WE'RE GETTING YOU OUT OF HERE AND TO A HOSPITAL!
EDZIA... IT'S OKAY. I'M READY.
WHAT?

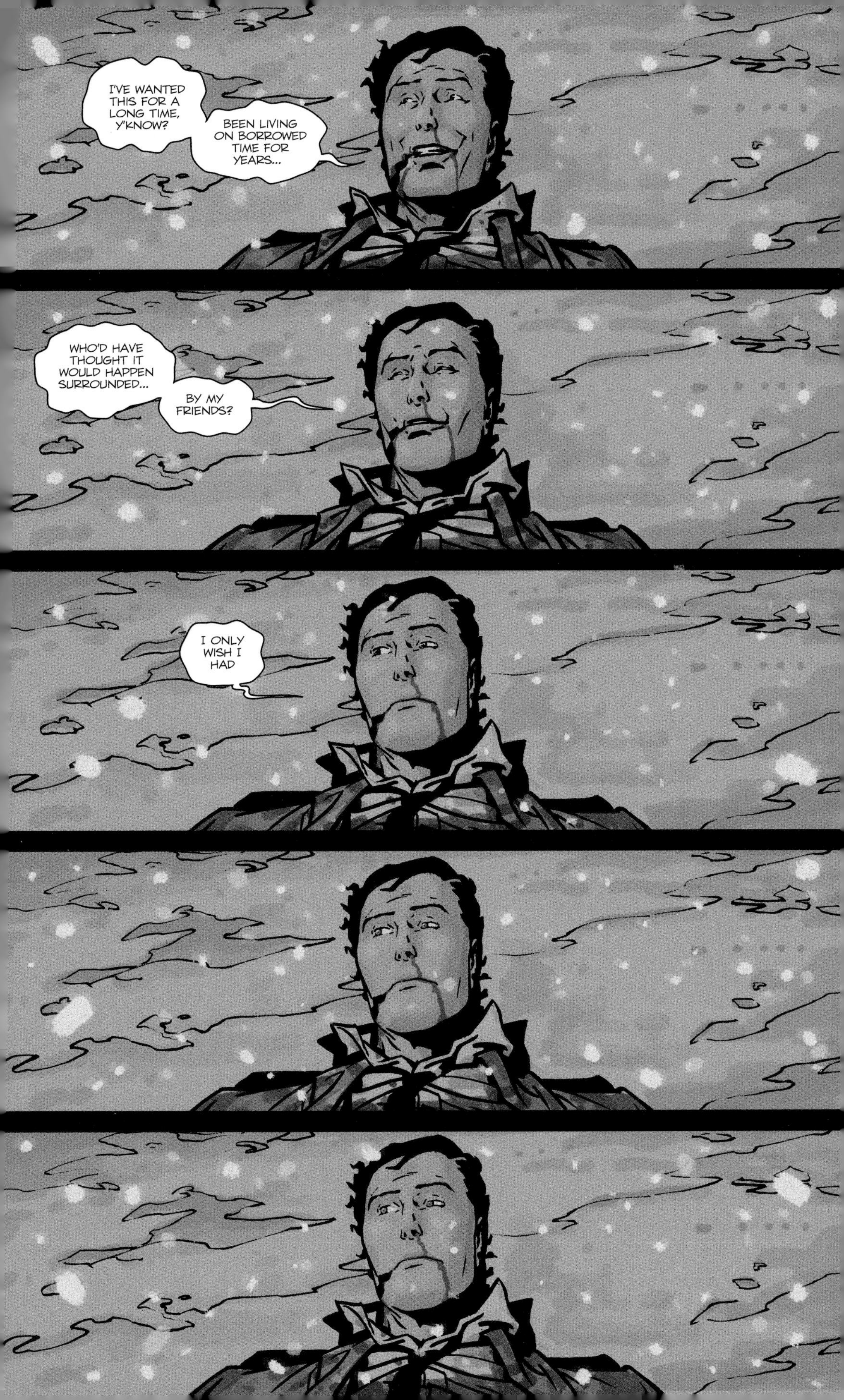
I'VE WANTED THIS FOR A LONG TIME, Y'KNOW?
BEEN LIVING ON BORROWED TIME FOR YEARS...
WHO'D HAVE THOUGHT IT WOULD HAPPEN SURROUNDED...
BY MY FRIENDS?
I ONLY WISH I HAD

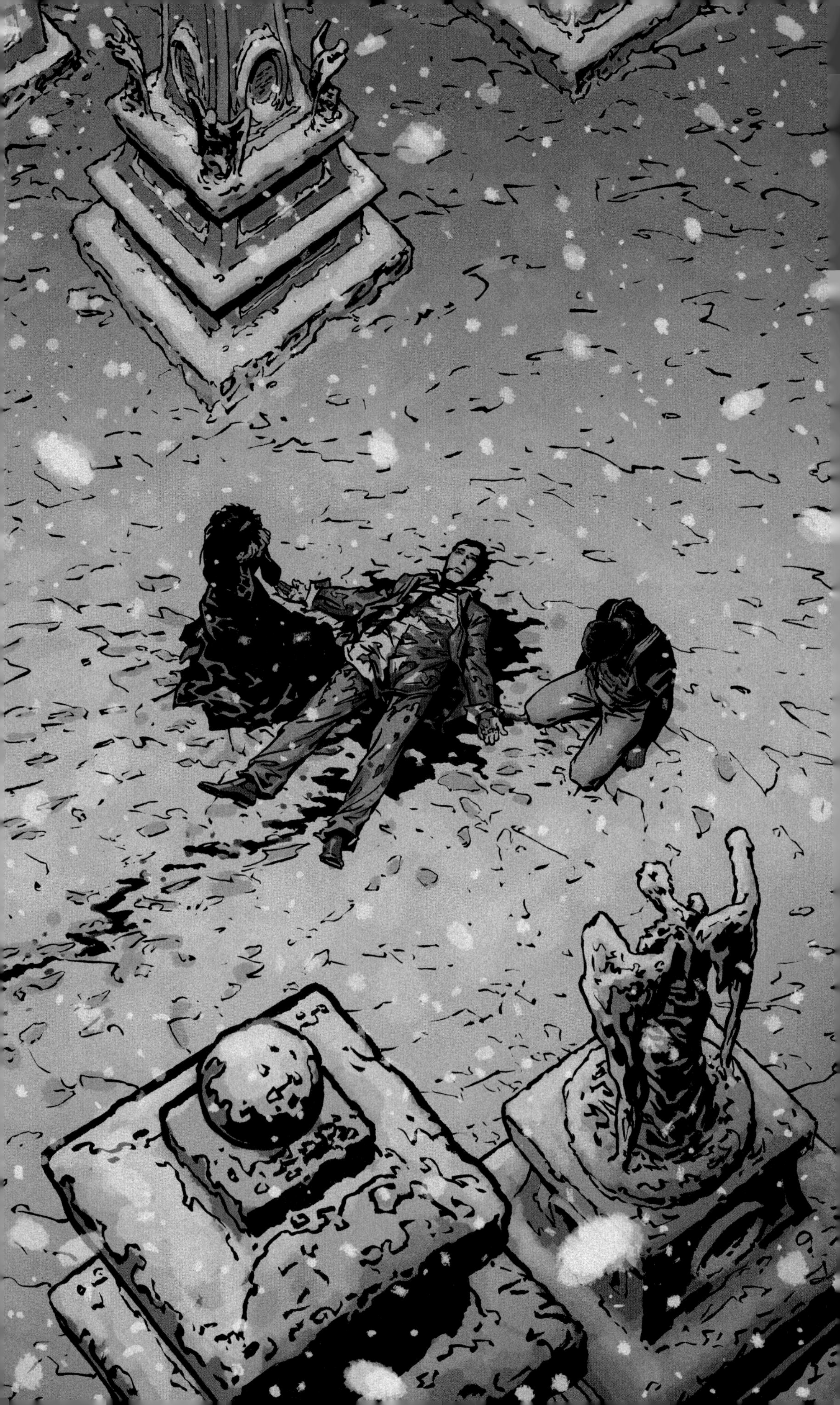

CHAPTER FIVE

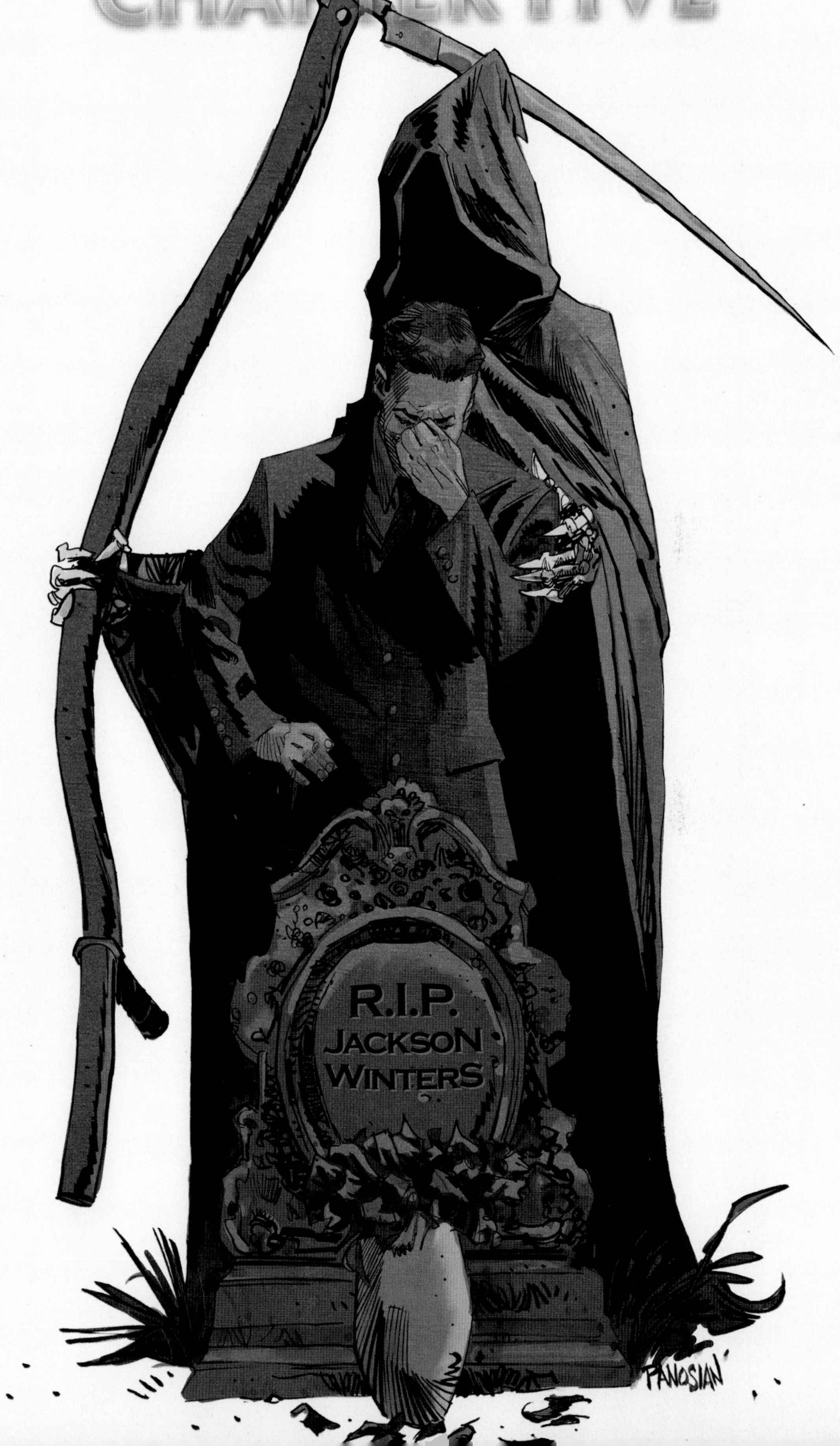
R.I.P.
JACKSON
WINTERS
PANOSIAN

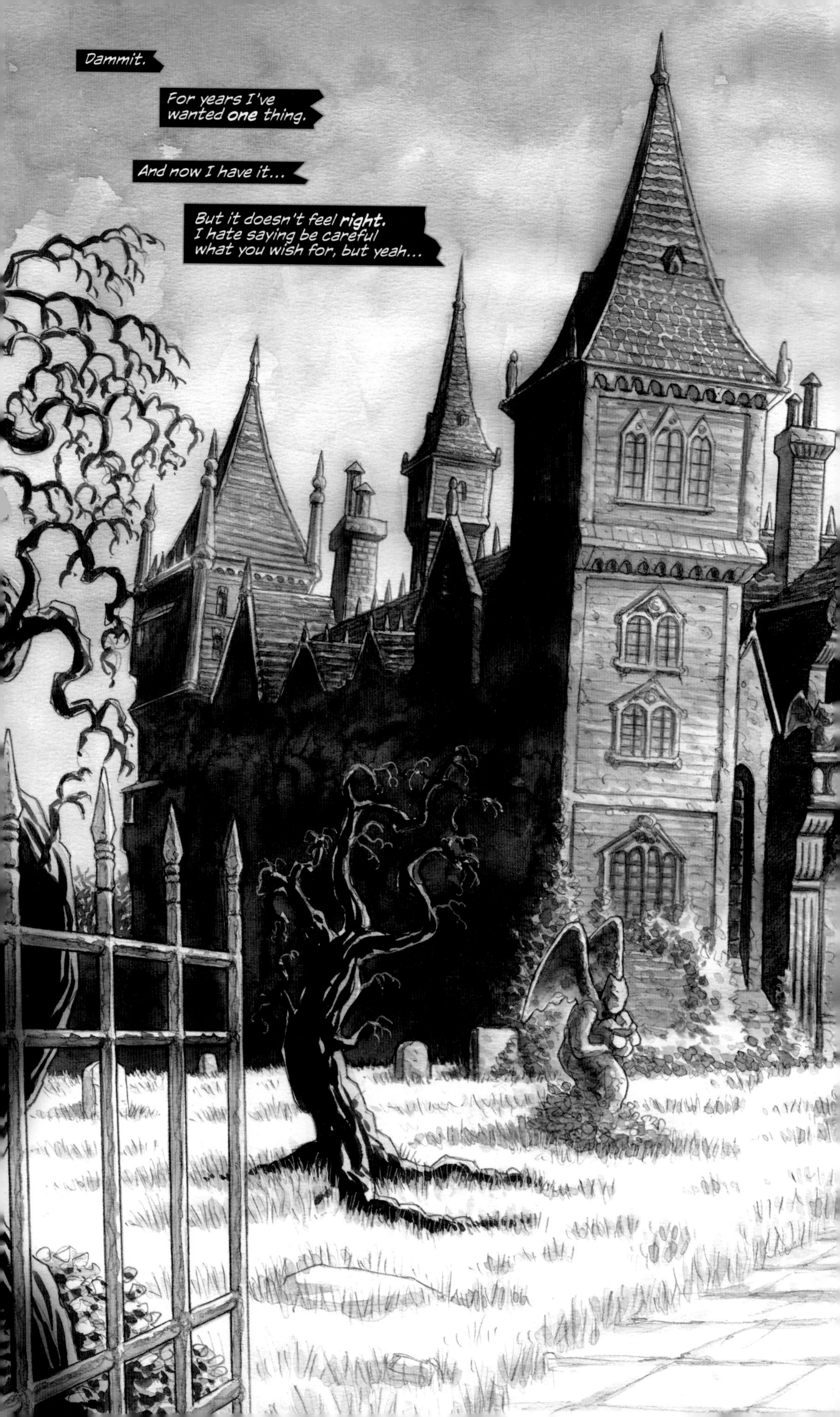
Dammit.
For years I've wanted **one** thing.
And now I have it...
But it doesn't feel **right.** I hate saying be careful what you wish for, but yeah...

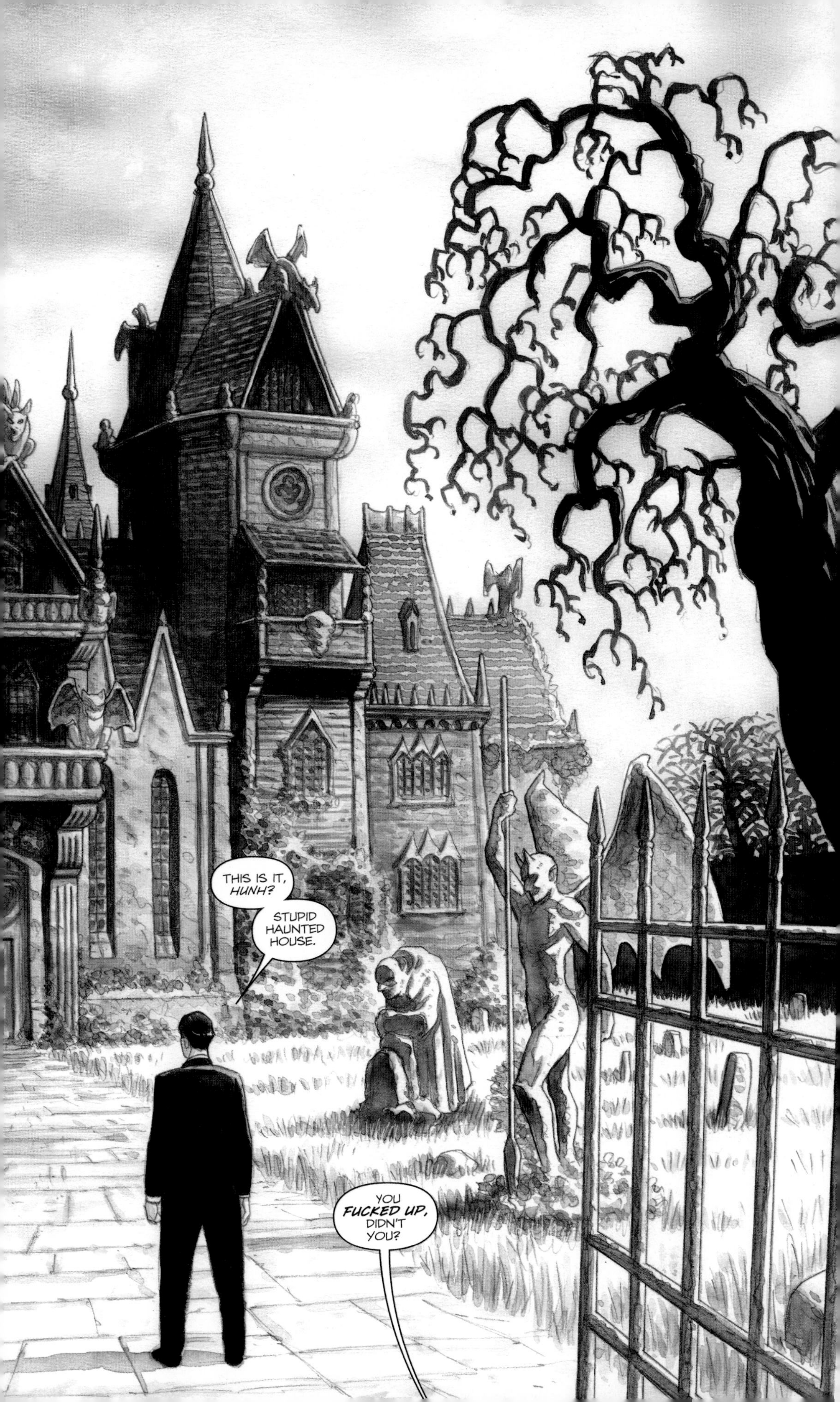
THIS IS IT, *HUNH?*
STUPID HAUNTED HOUSE.
YOU **FUCKED UP,** DIDN'T YOU?

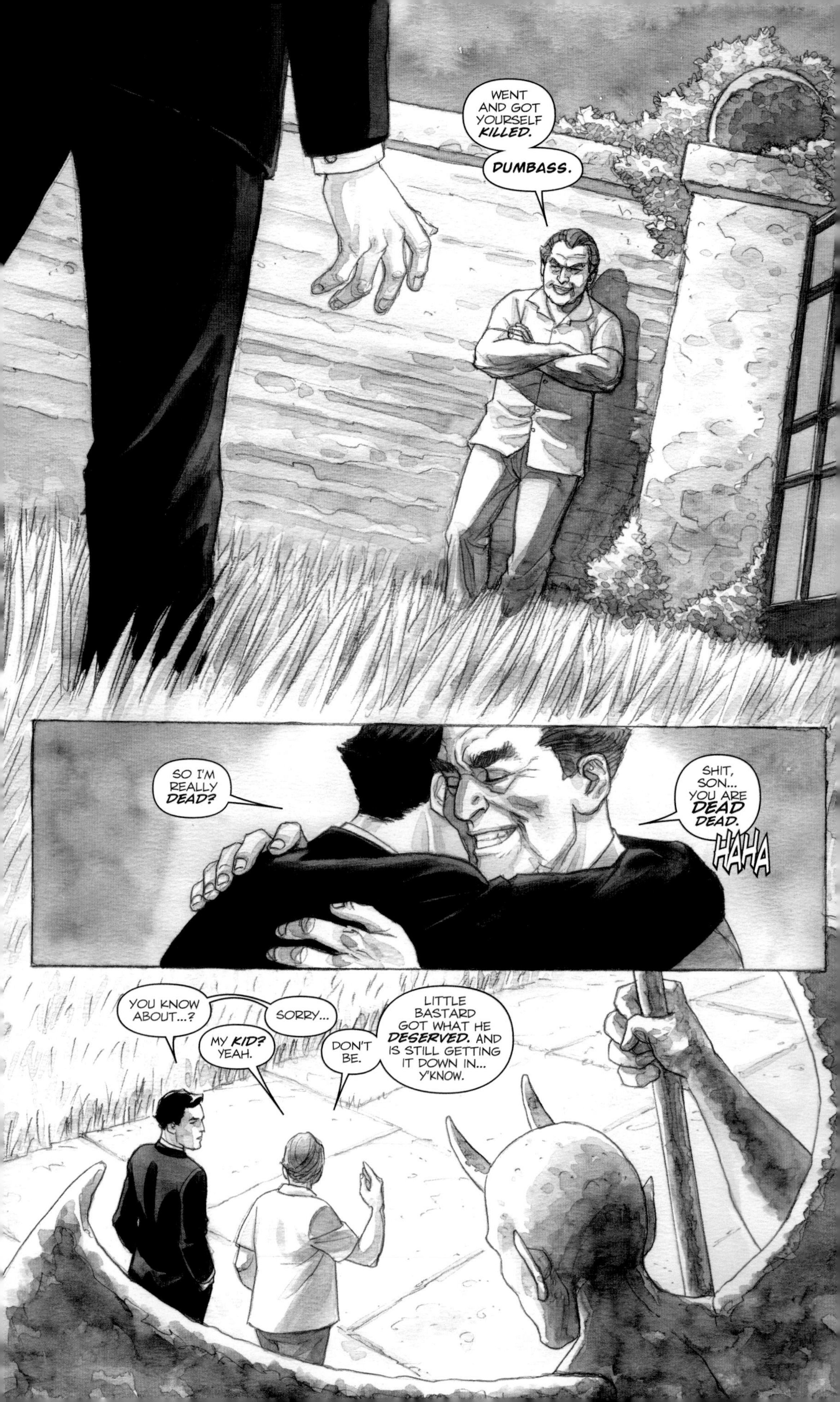
WENT AND GOT YOURSELF KILLED.
DUMBASS.
SO I'M REALLY DEAD?
SHIT, SON... YOU ARE DEAD DEAD.
HAHA
YOU KNOW ABOUT...?
SORRY...
MY KID? YEAH.
DON'T BE.
LITTLE BASTARD GOT WHAT HE DESERVED. AND IS STILL GETTING IT DOWN IN... Y'KNOW.

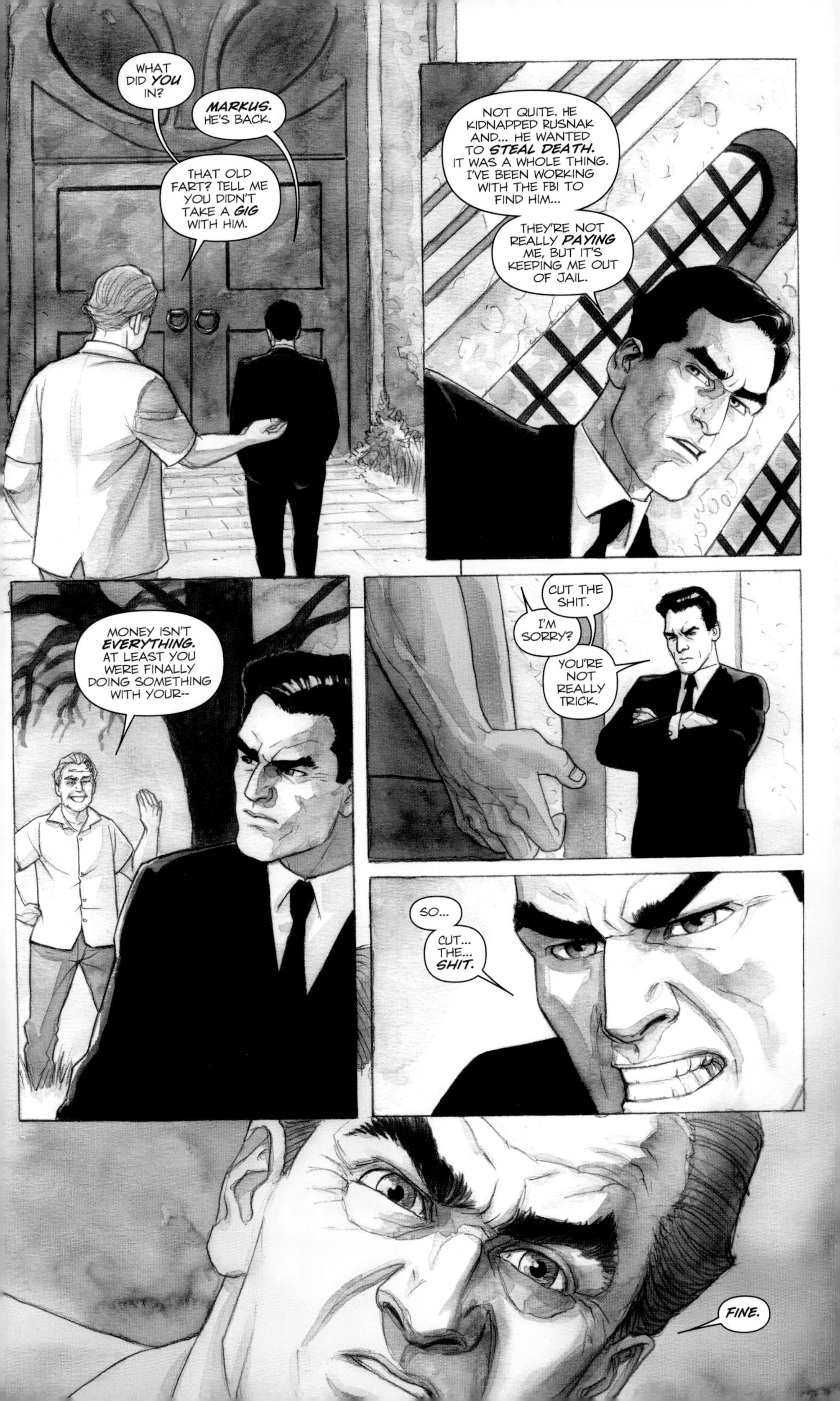
WHAT DID YOU IN?
MARKUS. HE'S BACK.
THAT OLD FART? TELL ME YOU DIDN'T TAKE A GIG WITH HIM.
NOT QUITE. HE KIDNAPPED RUSNAK AND... HE WANTED TO STEAL DEATH. IT WAS A WHOLE THING. I'VE BEEN WORKING WITH THE FBI TO FIND HIM...
THEY'RE NOT REALLY PAYING ME, BUT IT'S KEEPING ME OUT OF JAIL.
MONEY ISN'T EVERYTHING. AT LEAST YOU WERE FINALLY DOING SOMETHING WITH YOUR--
CUT THE SHIT.
I'M SORRY?
YOU'RE NOT REALLY TRICK.
SO...
CUT... THE... SHIT.
FINE.

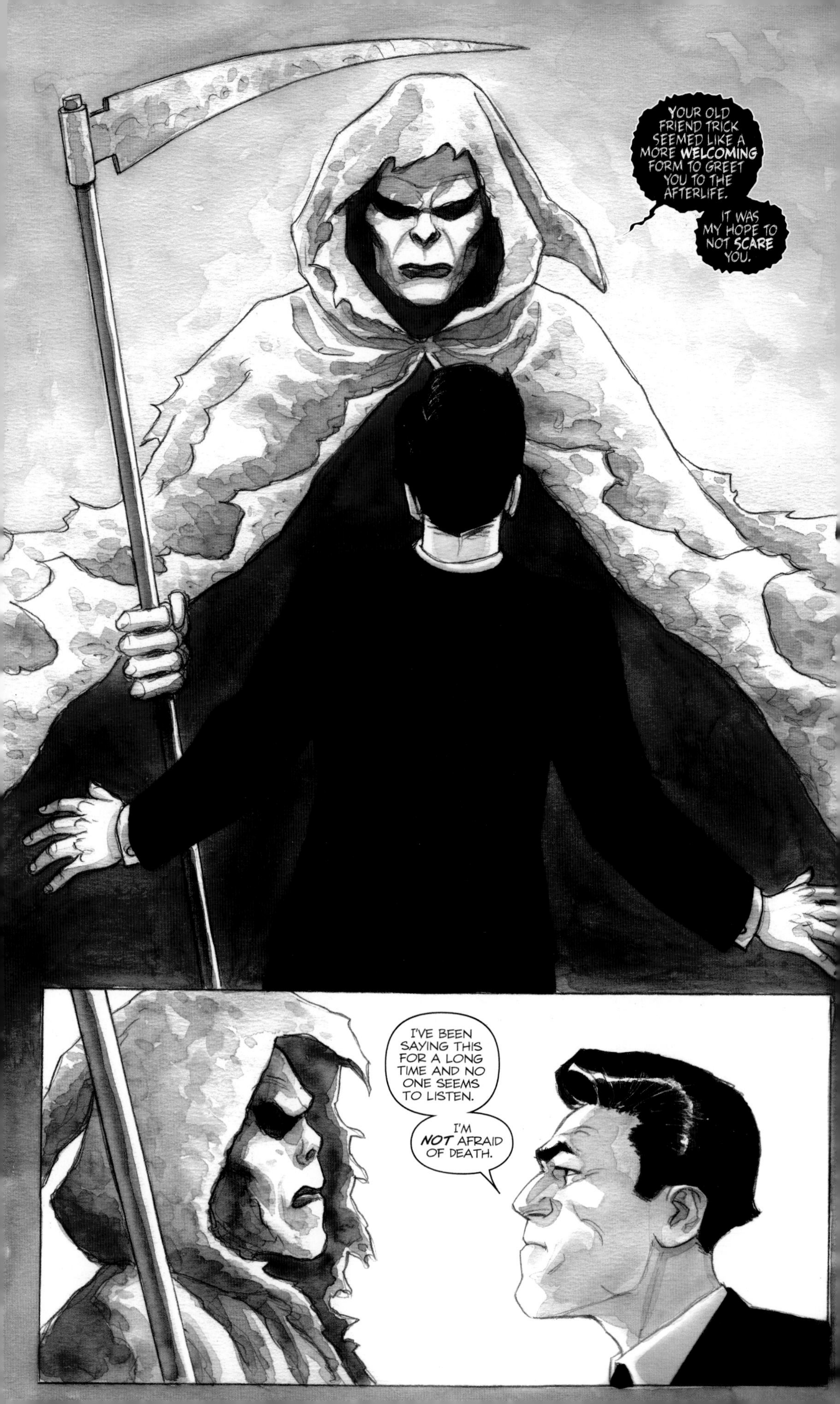
YOUR OLD FRIEND TRICK SEEMED LIKE A MORE WELCOMING FORM TO GREET YOU TO THE AFTERLIFE.
IT WAS MY HOPE TO NOT SCARE YOU.
I'VE BEEN SAYING THIS FOR A LONG TIME AND NO ONE SEEMS TO LISTEN.
I'M NOT AFRAID OF DEATH.

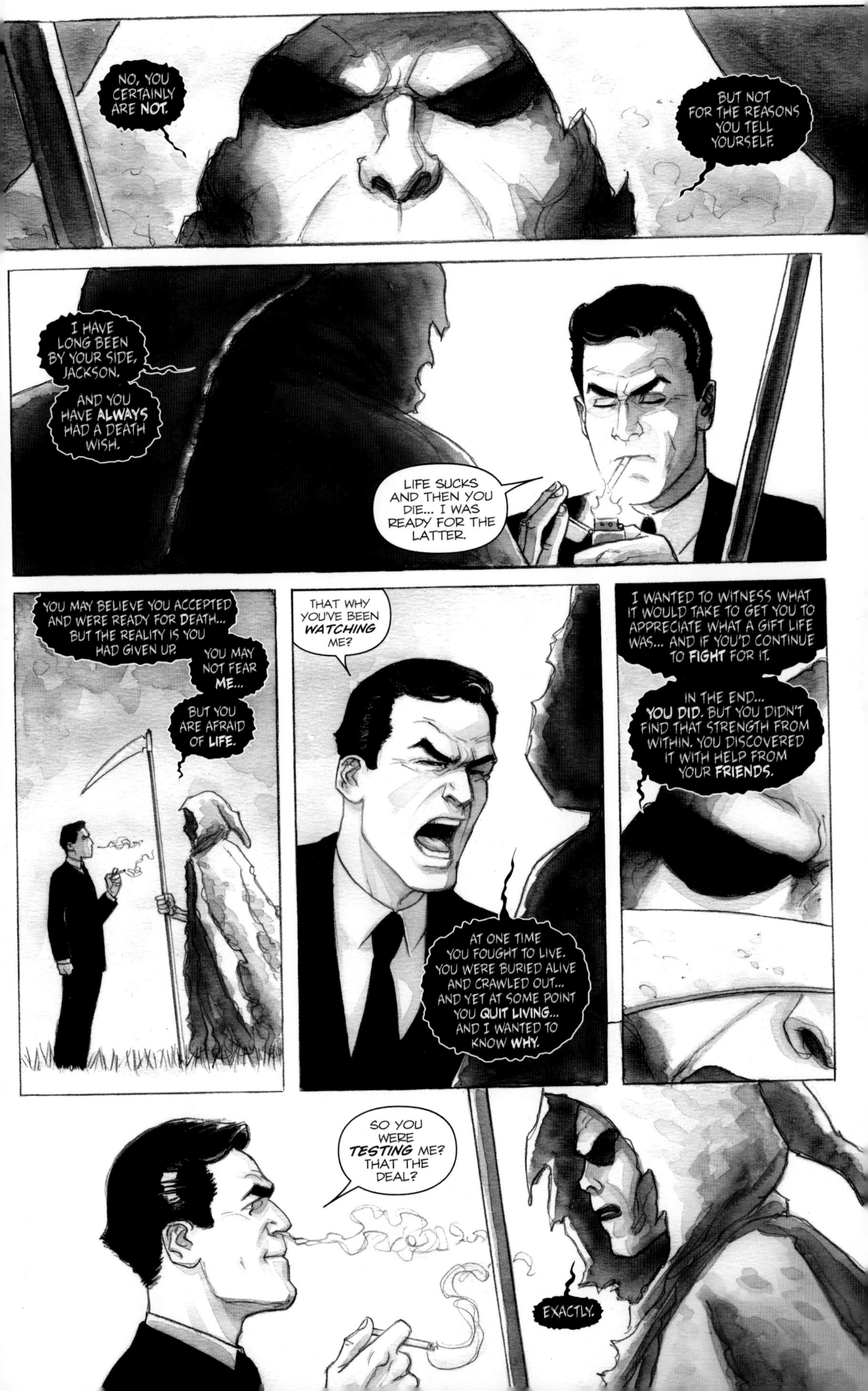

NO, YOU CERTAINLY ARE NOT.
BUT NOT FOR THE REASONS YOU TELL YOURSELF.
I HAVE LONG BEEN BY YOUR SIDE, JACKSON.
AND YOU HAVE ALWAYS HAD A DEATH WISH.
LIFE SUCKS AND THEN YOU DIE... I WAS READY FOR THE LATTER.
YOU MAY BELIEVE YOU ACCEPTED AND WERE READY FOR DEATH... BUT THE REALITY IS YOU HAD GIVEN UP.
YOU MAY NOT FEAR ME...
BUT YOU ARE AFRAID OF LIFE.
THAT WHY YOU'VE BEEN WATCHING ME?
AT ONE TIME YOU FOUGHT TO LIVE. YOU WERE BURIED ALIVE AND CRAWLED OUT... AND YET AT SOME POINT YOU QUIT LIVING... AND I WANTED TO KNOW WHY.
I WANTED TO WITNESS WHAT IT WOULD TAKE TO GET YOU TO APPRECIATE WHAT A GIFT LIFE WAS... AND IF YOU'D CONTINUE TO FIGHT FOR IT.
IN THE END... YOU DID. BUT YOU DIDN'T FIND THAT STRENGTH FROM WITHIN. YOU DISCOVERED IT WITH HELP FROM YOUR FRIENDS.
SO YOU WERE TESTING ME? THAT THE DEAL?
EXACTLY.

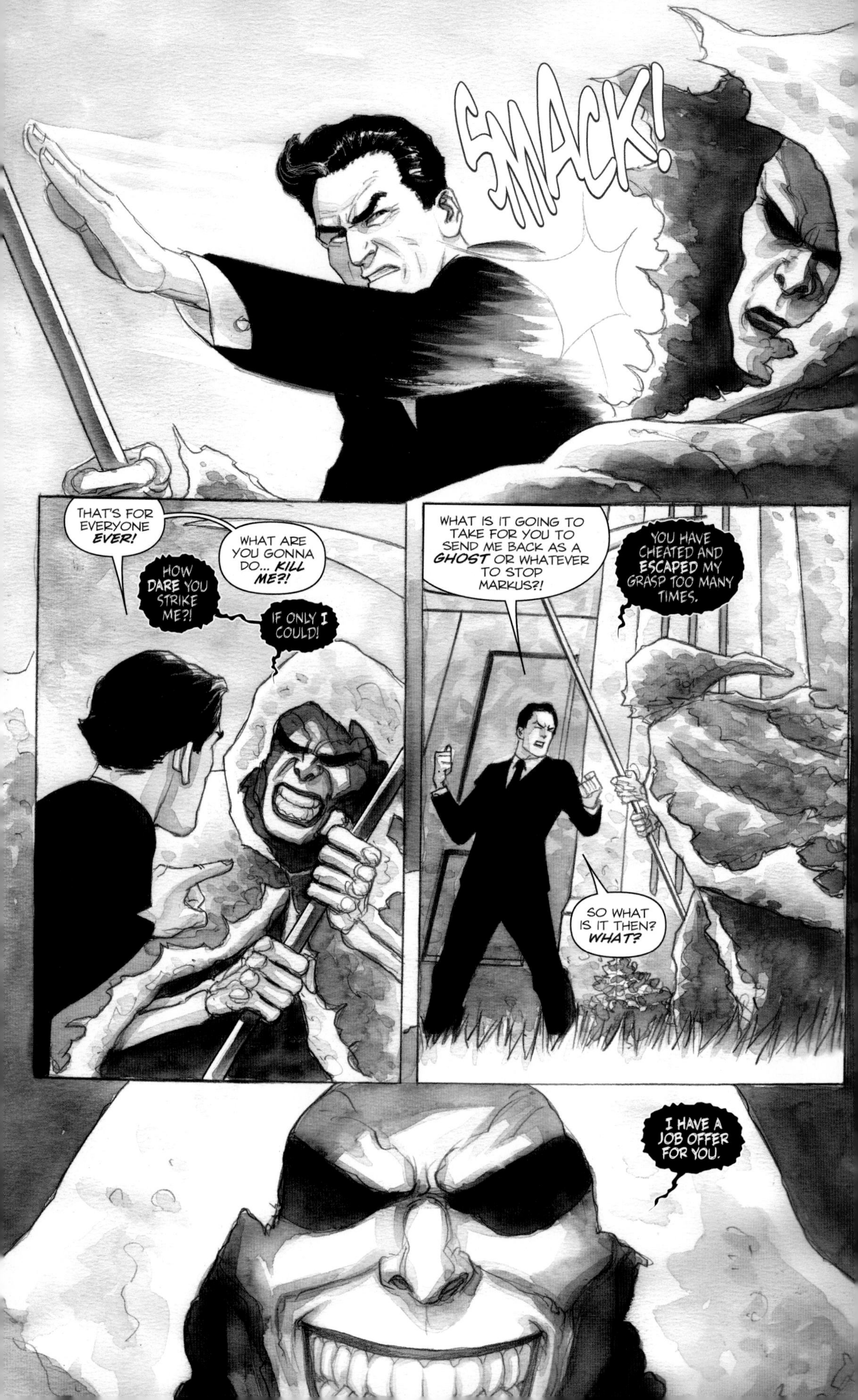
SMACK!
THAT'S FOR EVERYONE EVER!
HOW DARE YOU STRIKE ME?!
WHAT ARE YOU GONNA DO... KILL ME?!
IF ONLY I COULD!
WHAT IS IT GOING TO TAKE FOR YOU TO SEND ME BACK AS A GHOST OR WHATEVER TO STOP MARKUS?!
YOU HAVE CHEATED AND ESCAPED MY GRASP TOO MANY TIMES.
SO WHAT IS IT THEN? WHAT?
I HAVE A JOB OFFER FOR YOU.

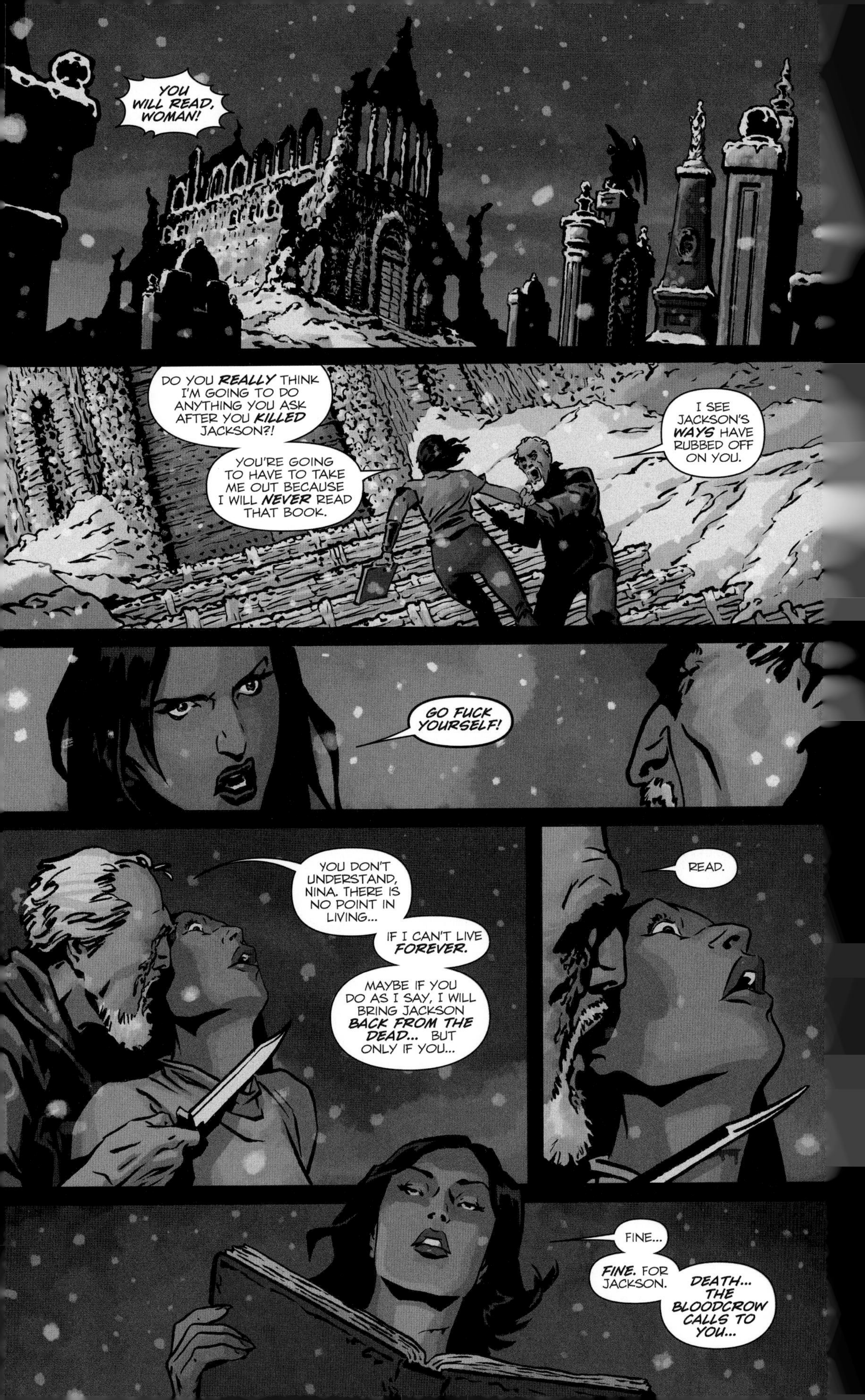
YOU WILL READ, WOMAN!
DO YOU REALLY THINK I'M GOING TO DO ANYTHING YOU ASK AFTER YOU KILLED JACKSON?!
YOU'RE GOING TO HAVE TO TAKE ME OUT BECAUSE I WILL NEVER READ THAT BOOK.
I SEE JACKSON'S WAYS HAVE RUBBED OFF ON YOU.
GO FUCK YOURSELF!
YOU DON'T UNDERSTAND, NINA. THERE IS NO POINT IN LIVING...
IF I CAN'T LIVE FOREVER.
MAYBE IF YOU DO AS I SAY, I WILL BRING JACKSON BACK FROM THE DEAD... BUT ONLY IF YOU...
READ.
FINE...
FINE. FOR JACKSON.
DEATH... THE BLOODCROW CALLS TO YOU...

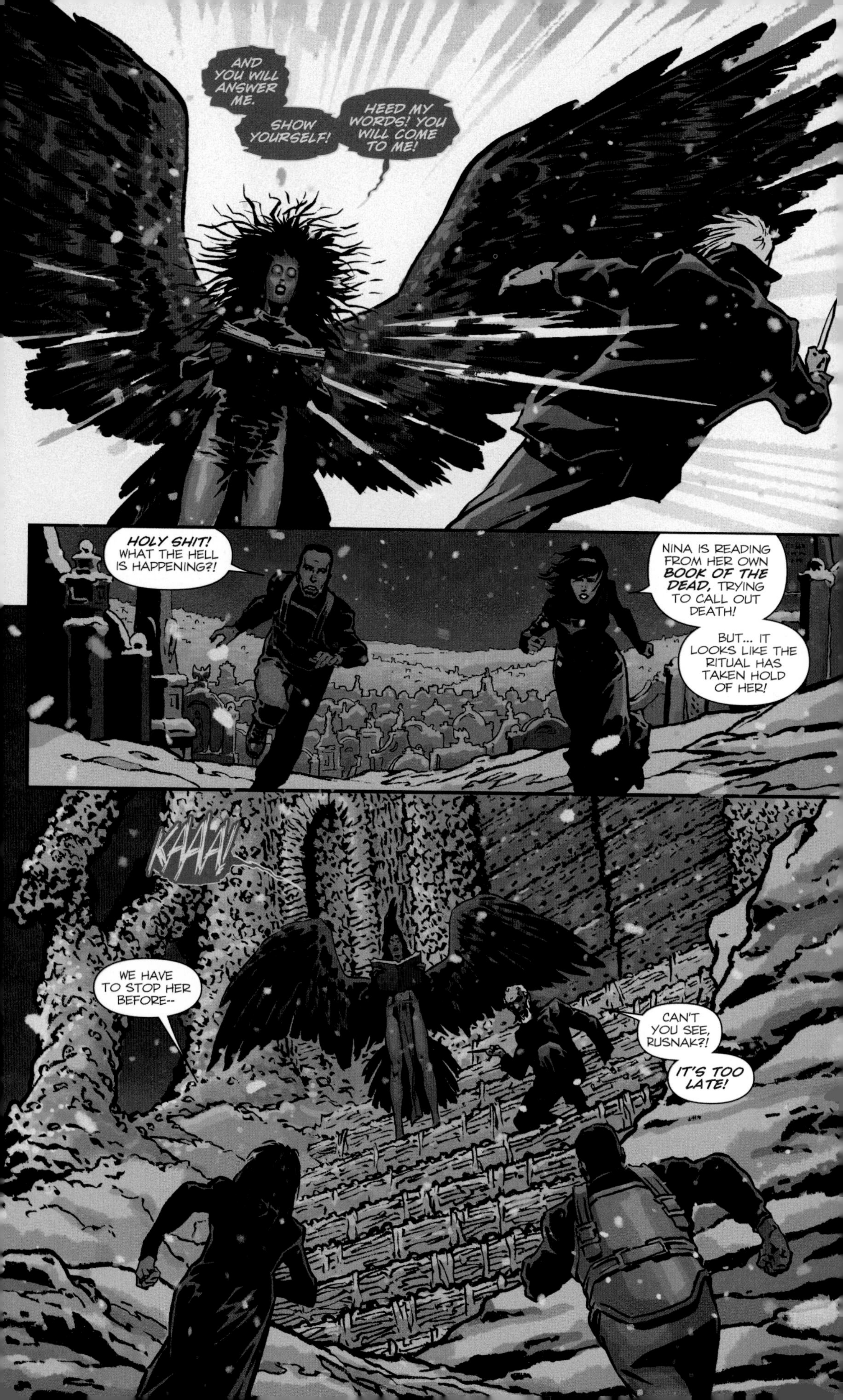
AND YOU WILL ANSWER ME.
SHOW YOURSELF!
HEED MY WORDS! YOU WILL COME TO ME!
HOLY SHIT! WHAT THE HELL IS HAPPENING?!
NINA IS READING FROM HER OWN BOOK OF THE DEAD, TRYING TO CALL OUT DEATH!
BUT... IT LOOKS LIKE THE RITUAL HAS TAKEN HOLD OF HER!
KAAAA!
WE HAVE TO STOP HER BEFORE--
CAN'T YOU SEE, RUSNAK?!
IT'S TOO LATE!

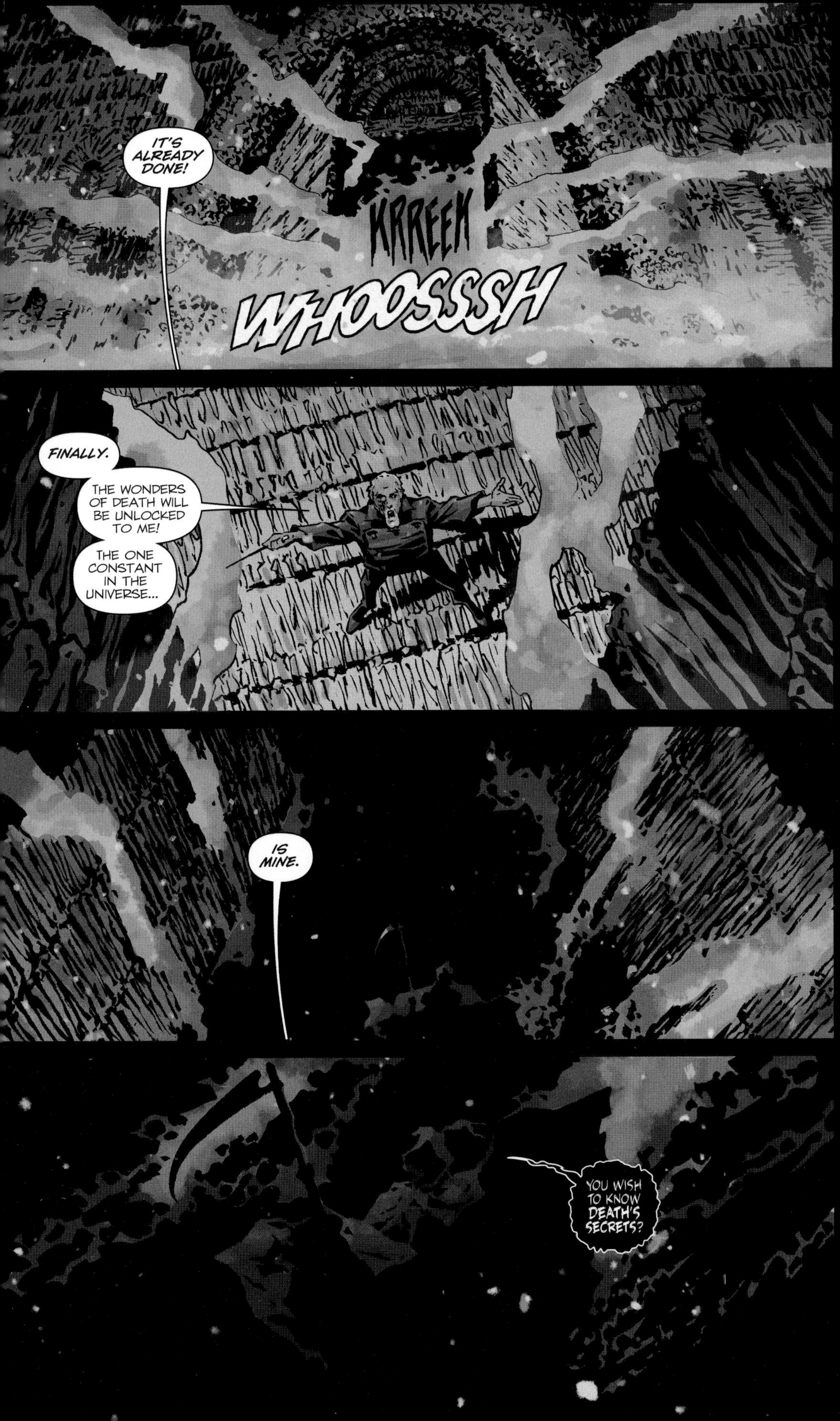
IT'S ALREADY DONE!
KRREEK
WHOOSSSH
FINALLY.
THE WONDERS OF DEATH WILL BE UNLOCKED TO ME!
THE ONE CONSTANT IN THE UNIVERSE...
IS MINE.
YOU WISH TO KNOW DEATH'S SECRETS?

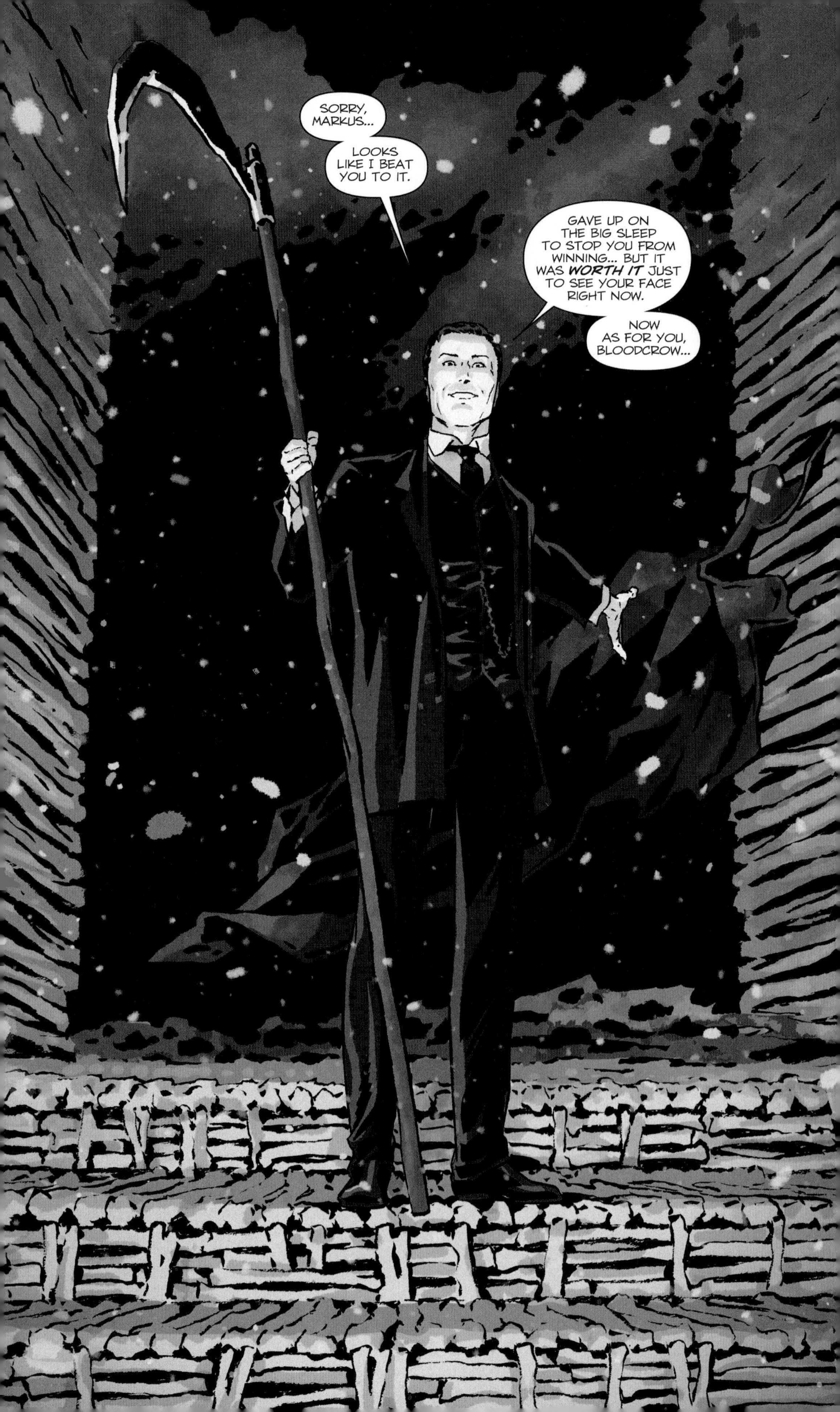
SORRY, MARKUS...
LOOKS LIKE I BEAT YOU TO IT.
GAVE UP ON THE BIG SLEEP TO STOP YOU FROM WINNING... BUT IT WAS WORTH IT JUST TO SEE YOUR FACE RIGHT NOW.
NOW AS FOR YOU, BLOODCROW...

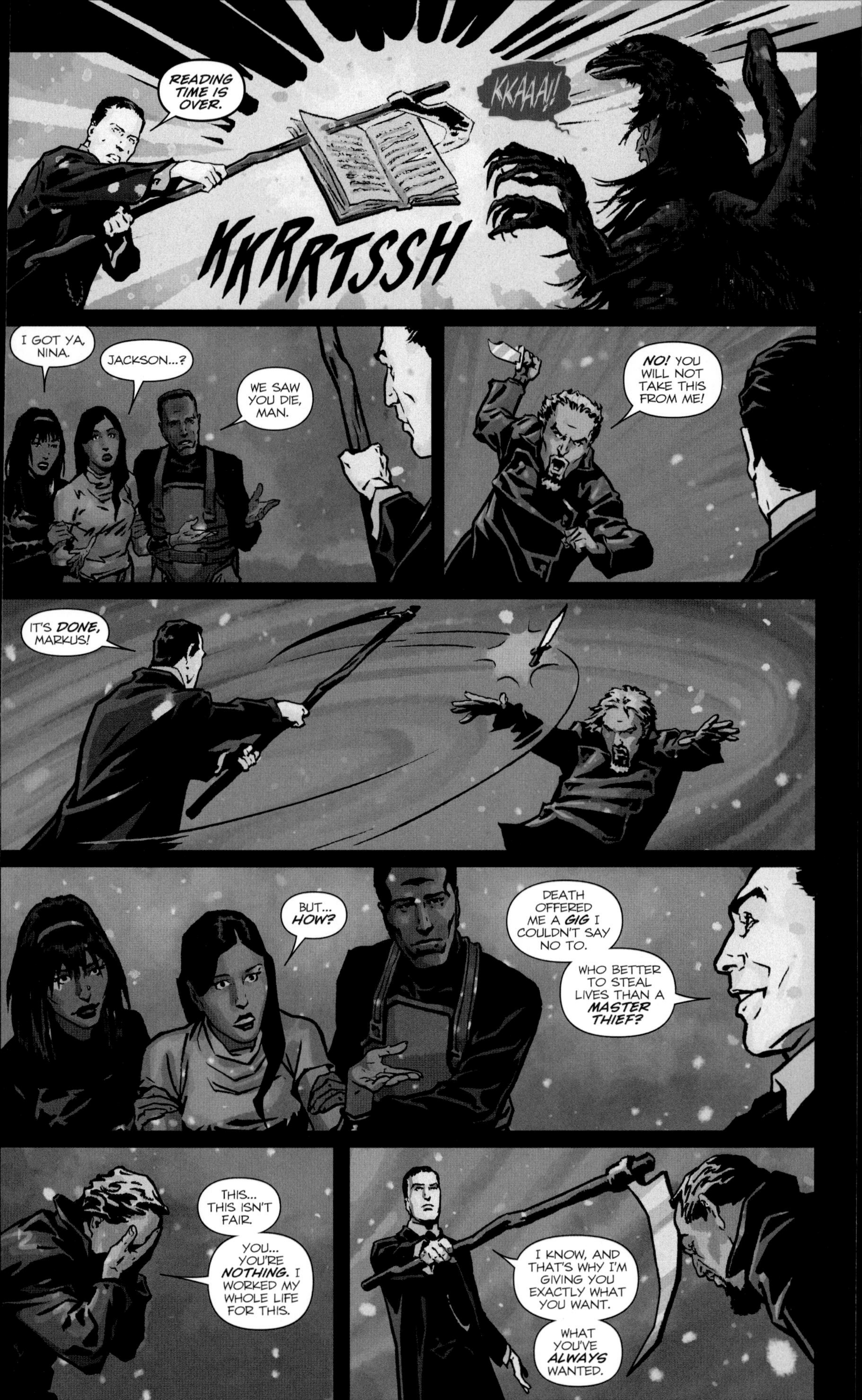
READING TIME IS OVER.
KKAAA!!
KKRRTSSH
I GOT YA, NINA.
JACKSON...?
WE SAW YOU DIE, MAN.
NO! YOU WILL NOT TAKE THIS FROM ME!
IT'S DONE, MARKUS!
BUT... HOW?
DEATH OFFERED ME A GIG I COULDN'T SAY NO TO.
WHO BETTER TO STEAL LIVES THAN A MASTER THIEF?
THIS... THIS ISN'T FAIR.
YOU... YOU'RE NOTHING. I WORKED MY WHOLE LIFE FOR THIS.
I KNOW, AND THAT'S WHY I'M GIVING YOU EXACTLY WHAT YOU WANT.
WHAT YOU'VE ALWAYS WANTED.

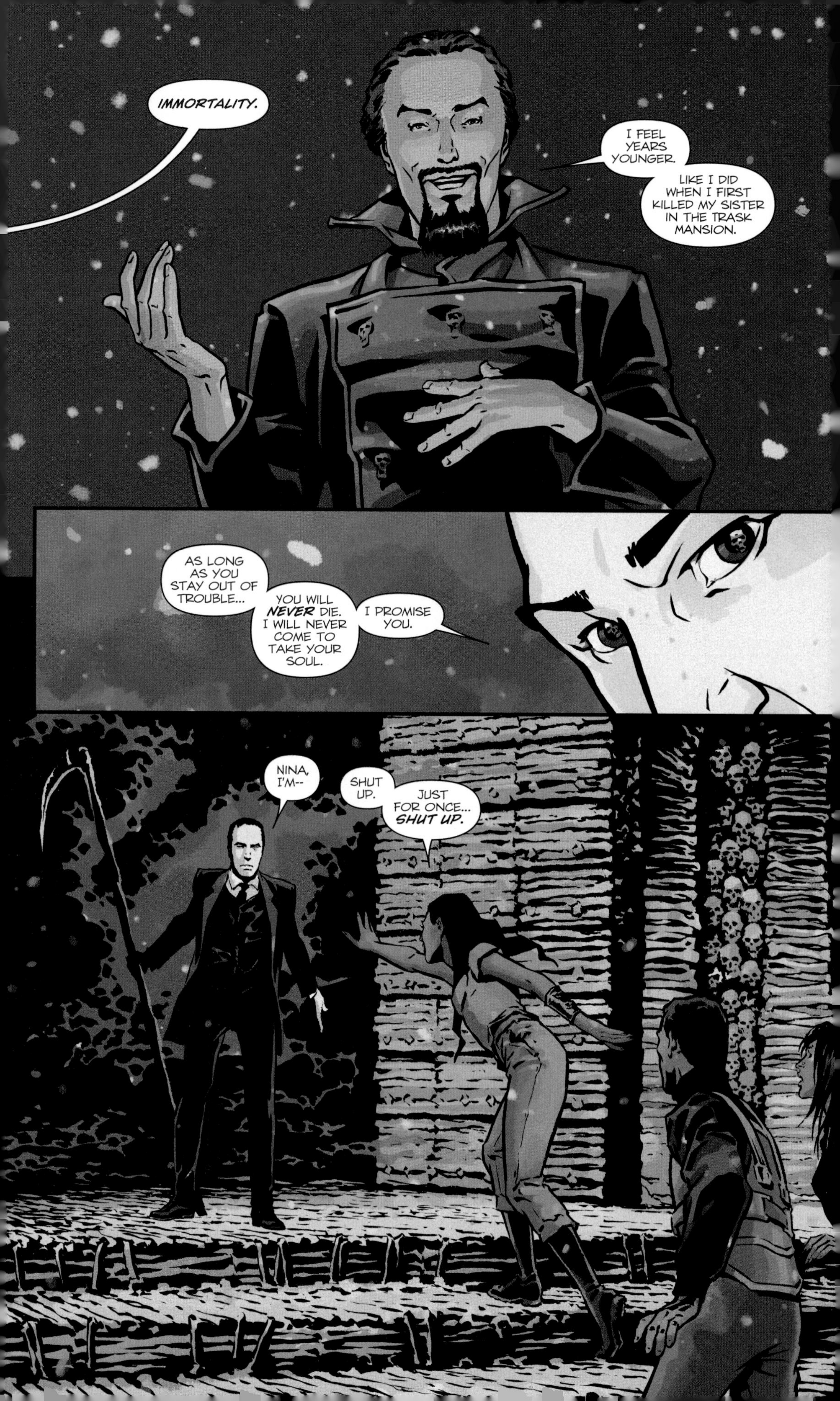
IMMORTALITY.
I FEEL YEARS YOUNGER.
LIKE I DID WHEN I FIRST KILLED MY SISTER IN THE TRASK MANSION.
AS LONG AS YOU STAY OUT OF TROUBLE...
YOU WILL NEVER DIE. I WILL NEVER COME TO TAKE YOUR SOUL.
I PROMISE YOU.
NINA, I'M--
SHUT UP.
JUST FOR ONCE... SHUT UP.

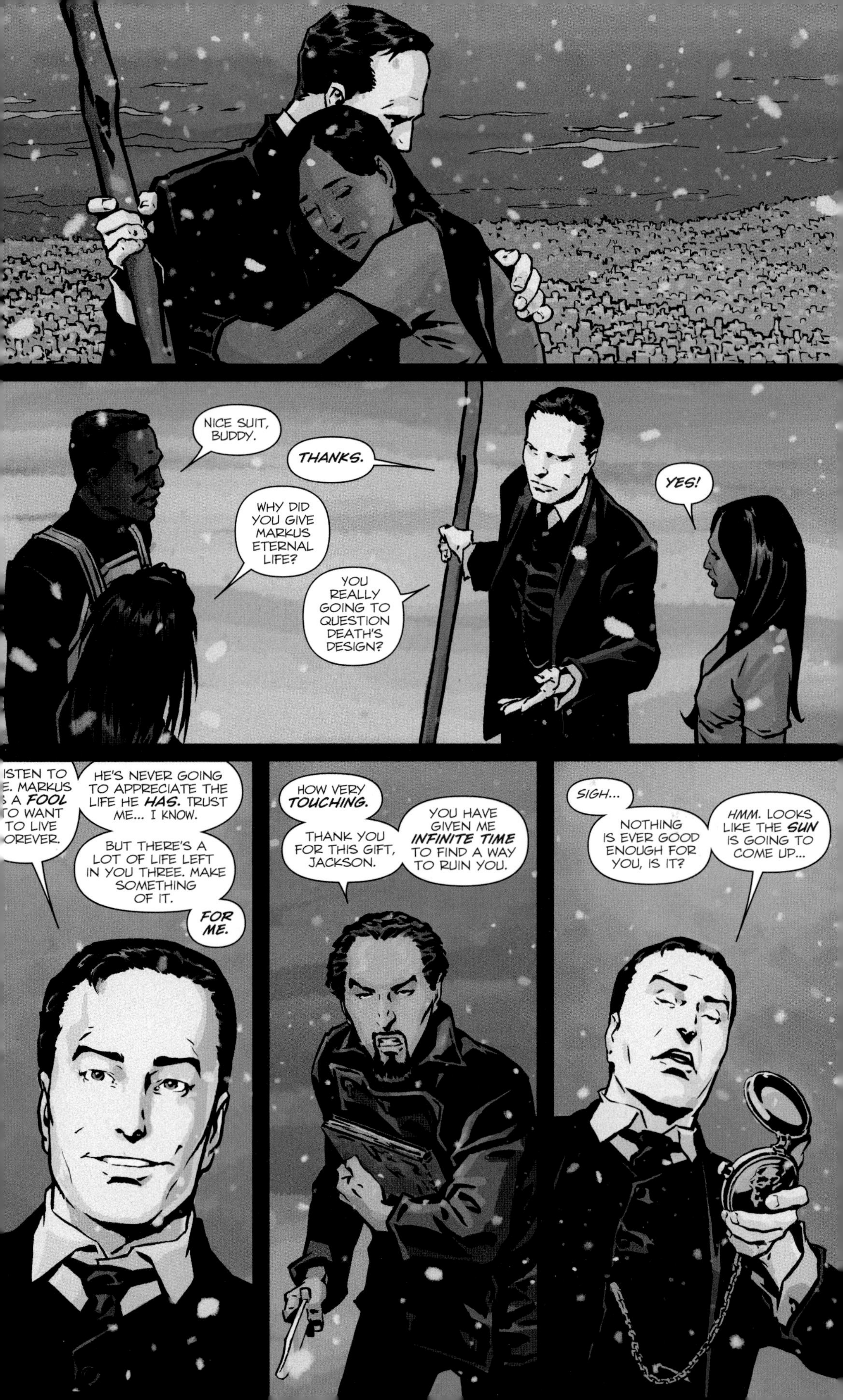

NICE SUIT, BUDDY.
THANKS.
YES!
WHY DID YOU GIVE MARKUS ETERNAL LIFE?
YOU REALLY GOING TO QUESTION DEATH'S DESIGN?
ISTEN TO E. MARKUS S A FOOL TO WANT TO LIVE OREVER.
HE'S NEVER GOING TO APPRECIATE THE LIFE HE HAS. TRUST ME... I KNOW.
BUT THERE'S A LOT OF LIFE LEFT IN YOU THREE. MAKE SOMETHING OF IT.
FOR ME.
HOW VERY TOUCHING.
THANK YOU FOR THIS GIFT, JACKSON.
YOU HAVE GIVEN ME INFINITE TIME TO FIND A WAY TO RUIN YOU.
SIGH...
NOTHING IS EVER GOOD ENOUGH FOR YOU, IS IT?
HMM. LOOKS LIKE THE SUN IS GOING TO COME UP...

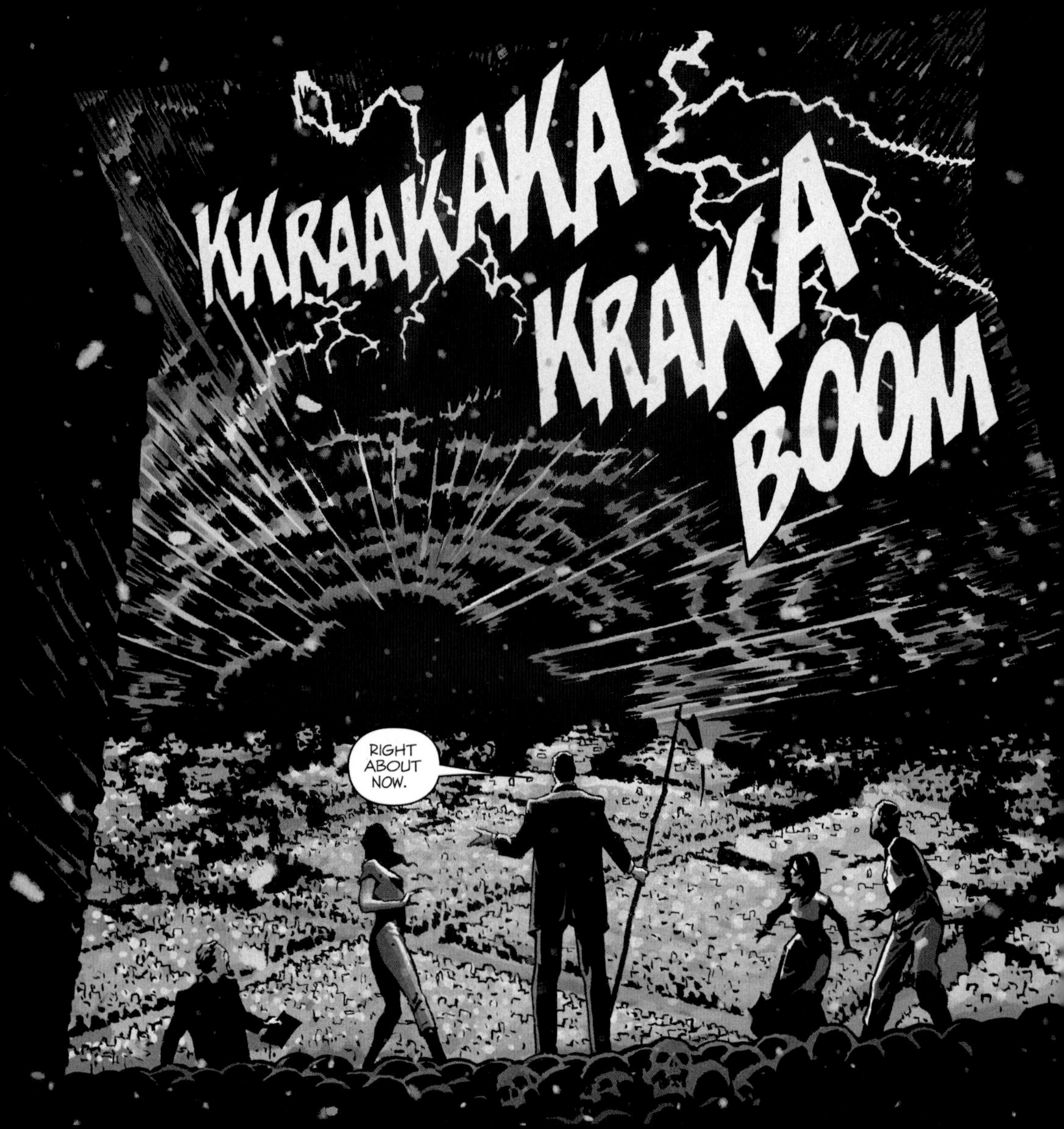
KKRAAKAKA KRAKA BOOM
RIGHT ABOUT NOW.
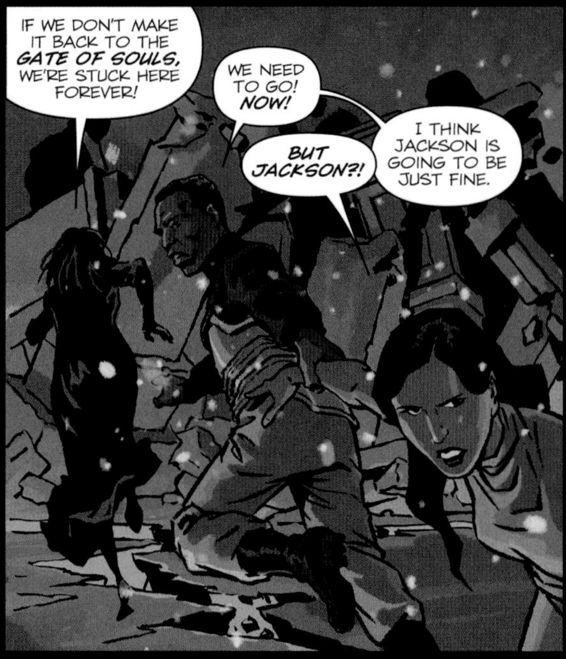
IF WE DON'T MAKE IT BACK TO THE GATE OF SOULS, WE'RE STUCK HERE FOREVER!
WE NEED TO GO! NOW!
BUT JACKSON?!
I THINK JACKSON IS GOING TO BE JUST FINE.
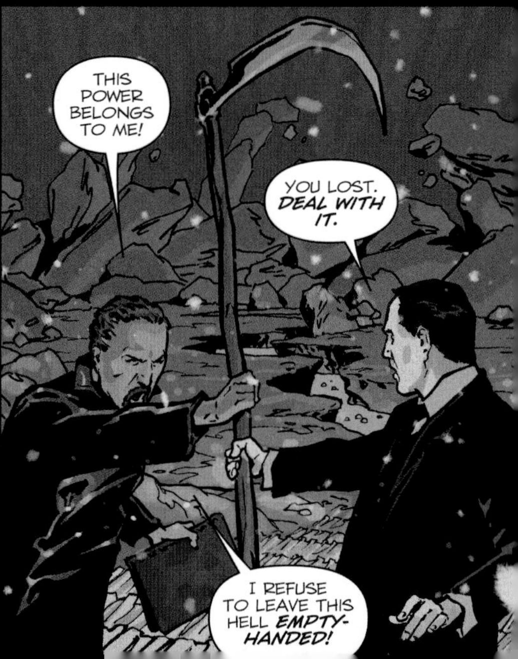
THIS POWER BELONGS TO ME!
YOU LOST. DEAL WITH IT.
I REFUSE TO LEAVE THIS HELL EMPTY-HANDED!

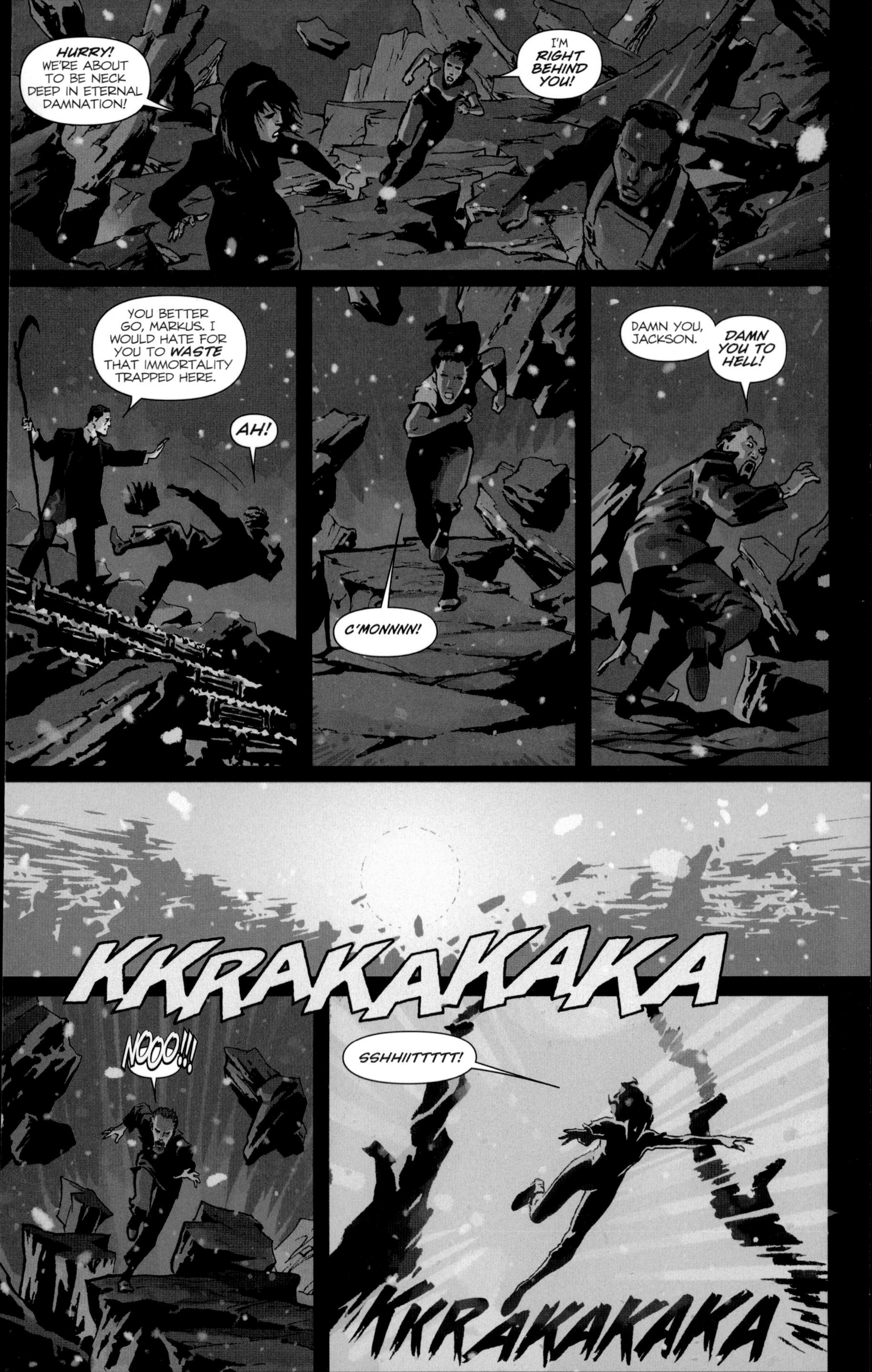
HURRY! WE'RE ABOUT TO BE NECK DEEP IN ETERNAL DAMNATION!
I'M RIGHT BEHIND YOU!
YOU BETTER GO, MARKUS. I WOULD HATE FOR YOU TO WASTE THAT IMMORTALITY TRAPPED HERE.
AH!
C'MONNNN!
DAMN YOU, JACKSON.
DAMN YOU TO HELL!
KKRAKAKAKA
NOOO!!!
SSHHIITTTTTT!
KKRAKAKAKA

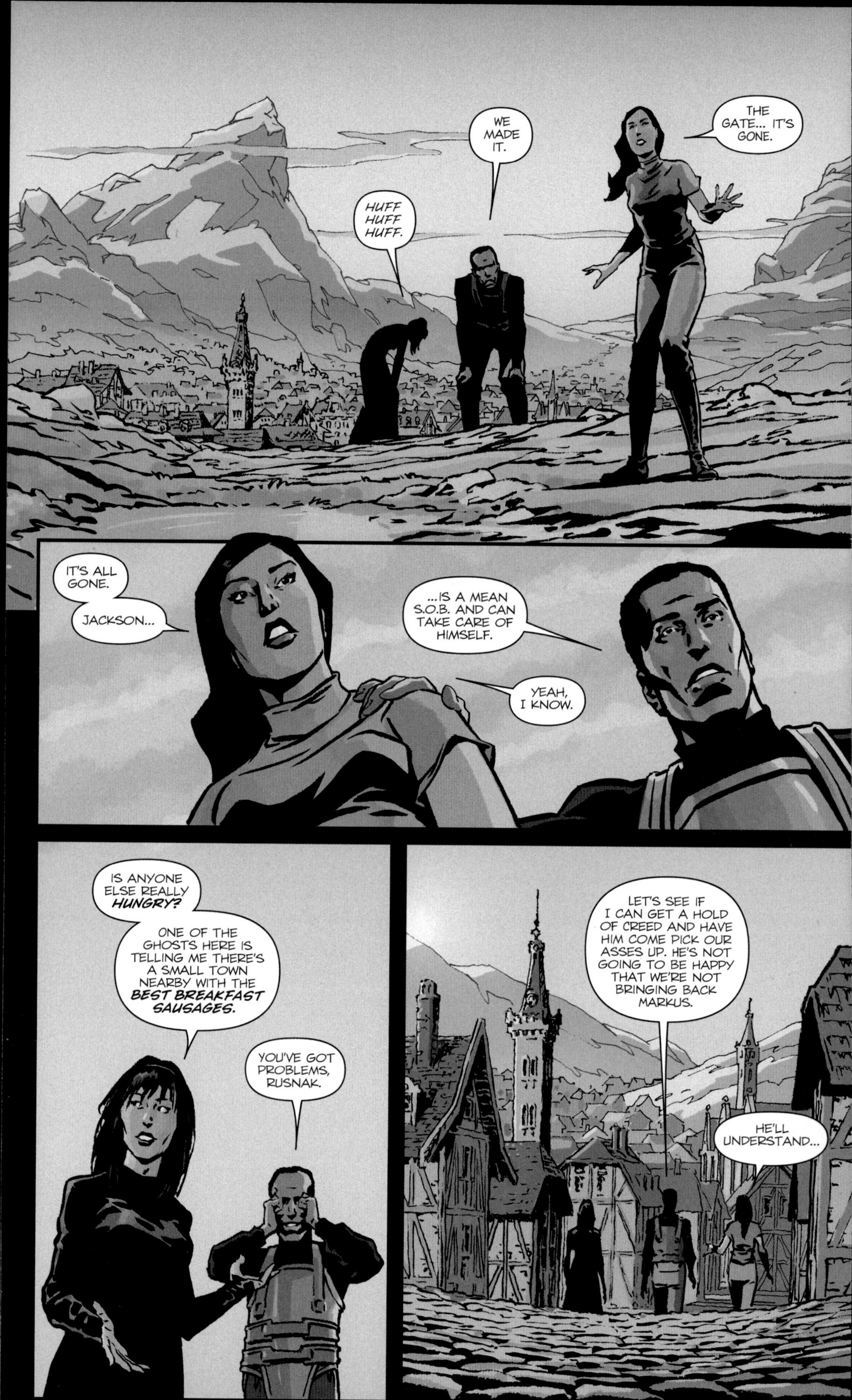
HUFF HUFF HUFF.
WE MADE IT.
THE GATE... IT'S GONE.
IT'S ALL GONE.
JACKSON...
...IS A MEAN S.O.B. AND CAN TAKE CARE OF HIMSELF.
YEAH, I KNOW.
IS ANYONE ELSE REALLY HUNGRY?
ONE OF THE GHOSTS HERE IS TELLING ME THERE'S A SMALL TOWN NEARBY WITH THE BEST BREAKFAST SAUSAGES.
YOU'VE GOT PROBLEMS, RUSNAK.
LET'S SEE IF I CAN GET A HOLD OF CREED AND HAVE HIM COME PICK OUR ASSES UP. HE'S NOT GOING TO BE HAPPY THAT WE'RE NOT BRINGING BACK MARKUS.
HE'LL UNDERSTAND...

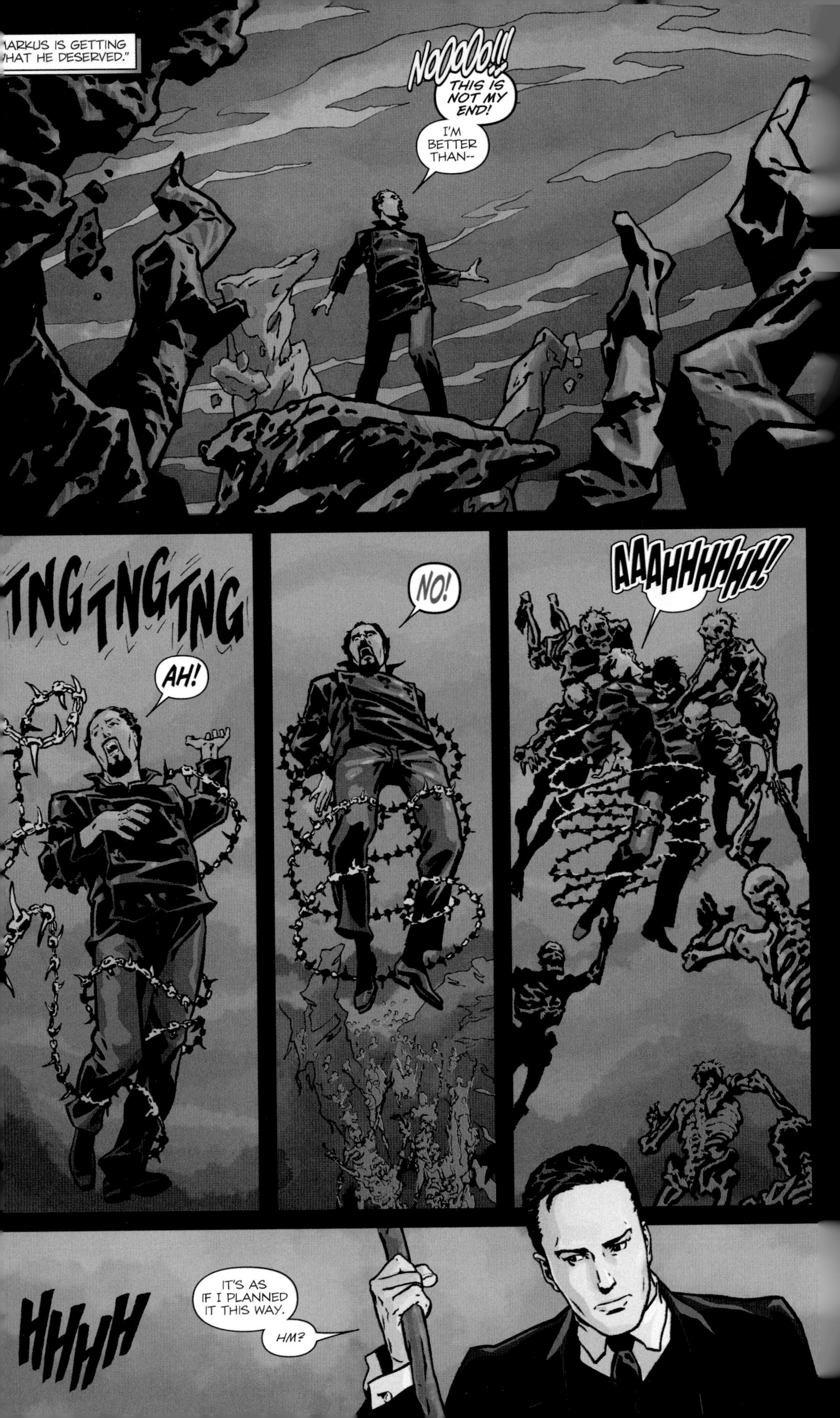

MARKUS IS GETTING WHAT HE DESERVED."
NOOOOO!!!
THIS IS NOT MY END!
I'M BETTER THAN--
TNG TNG TNG
AH!
NO!
AAAHHHHHH!
HHHH
IT'S AS IF I PLANNED IT THIS WAY.
HM?

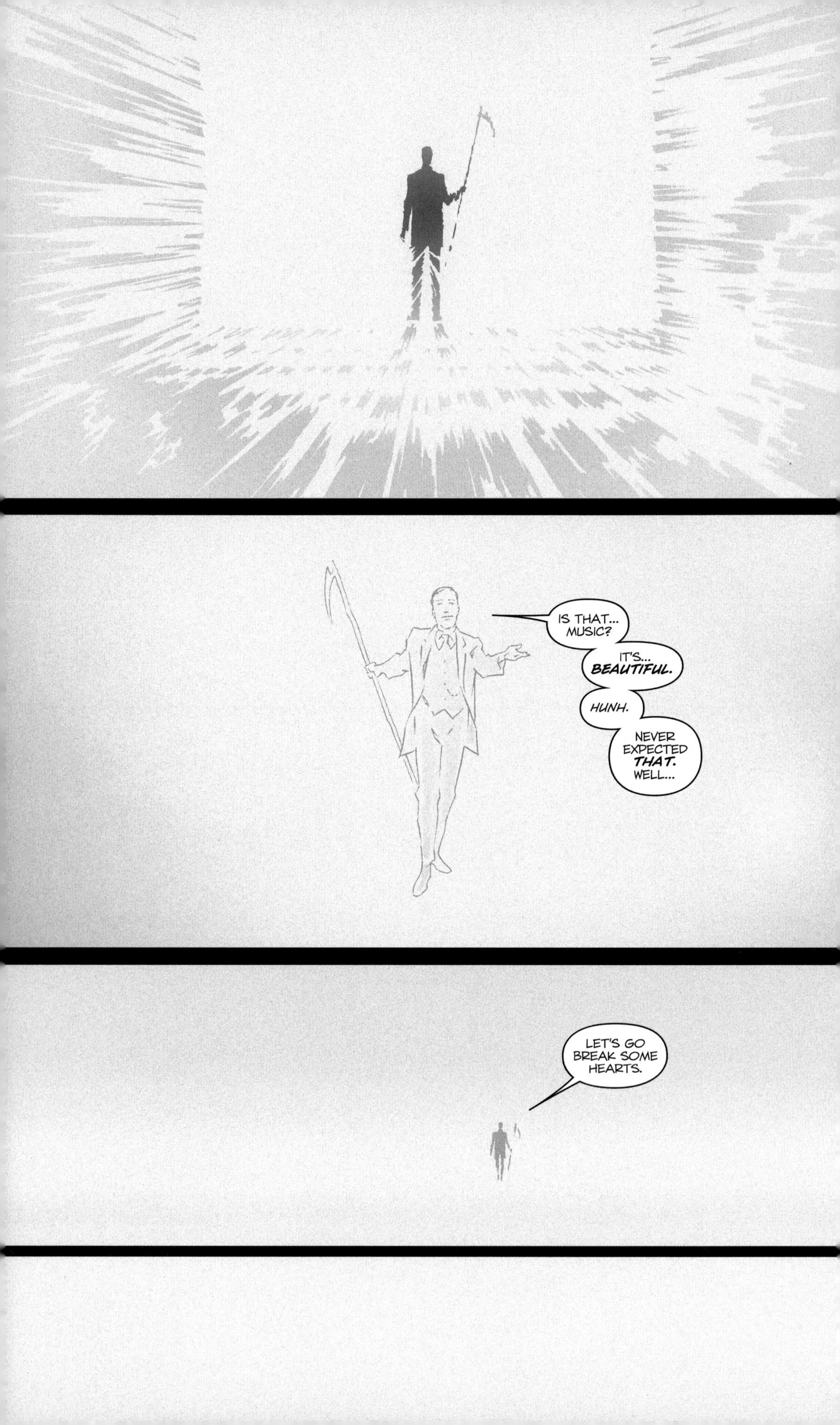
IS THAT... MUSIC?
IT'S... BEAUTIFUL.
HUNH.
NEVER EXPECTED THAT. WELL...
LET'S GO BREAK SOME HEARTS.

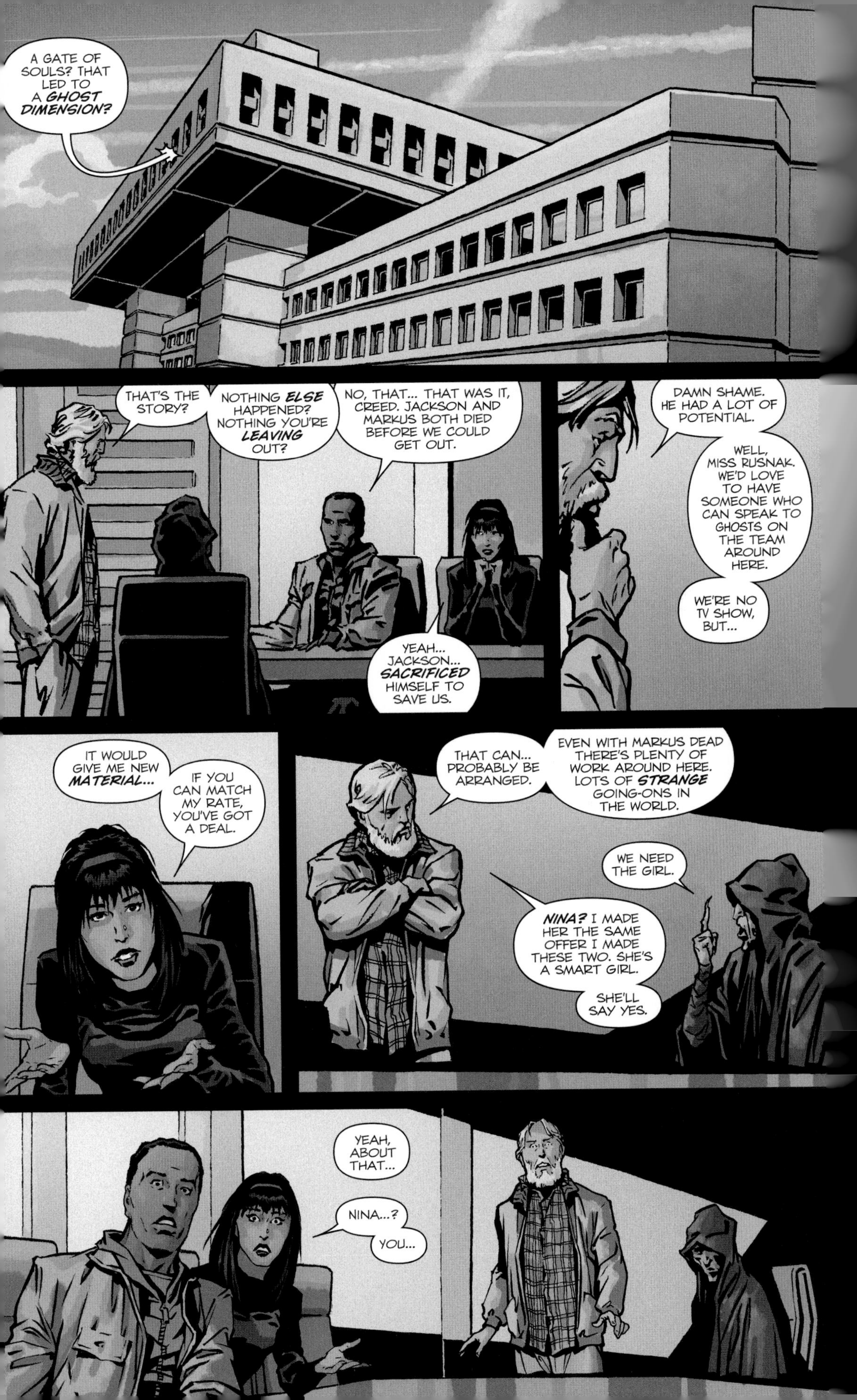
A GATE OF SOULS? THAT LED TO A GHOST DIMENSION?
THAT'S THE STORY?
NOTHING ELSE HAPPENED? NOTHING YOU'RE LEAVING OUT?
NO, THAT... THAT WAS IT, CREED. JACKSON AND MARKUS BOTH DIED BEFORE WE COULD GET OUT.
YEAH... JACKSON... SACRIFICED HIMSELF TO SAVE US.
DAMN SHAME. HE HAD A LOT OF POTENTIAL.
WELL, MISS RUSNAK. WE'D LOVE TO HAVE SOMEONE WHO CAN SPEAK TO GHOSTS ON THE TEAM AROUND HERE.
WE'RE NO TV SHOW, BUT...
IT WOULD GIVE ME NEW MATERIAL...
IF YOU CAN MATCH MY RATE, YOU'VE GOT A DEAL.
THAT CAN... PROBABLY BE ARRANGED.
EVEN WITH MARKUS DEAD THERE'S PLENTY OF WORK AROUND HERE. LOTS OF STRANGE GOING-ONS IN THE WORLD.
WE NEED THE GIRL.
NINA? I MADE HER THE SAME OFFER I MADE THESE TWO. SHE'S A SMART GIRL.
SHE'LL SAY YES.
YEAH, ABOUT THAT...
NINA...?
YOU...

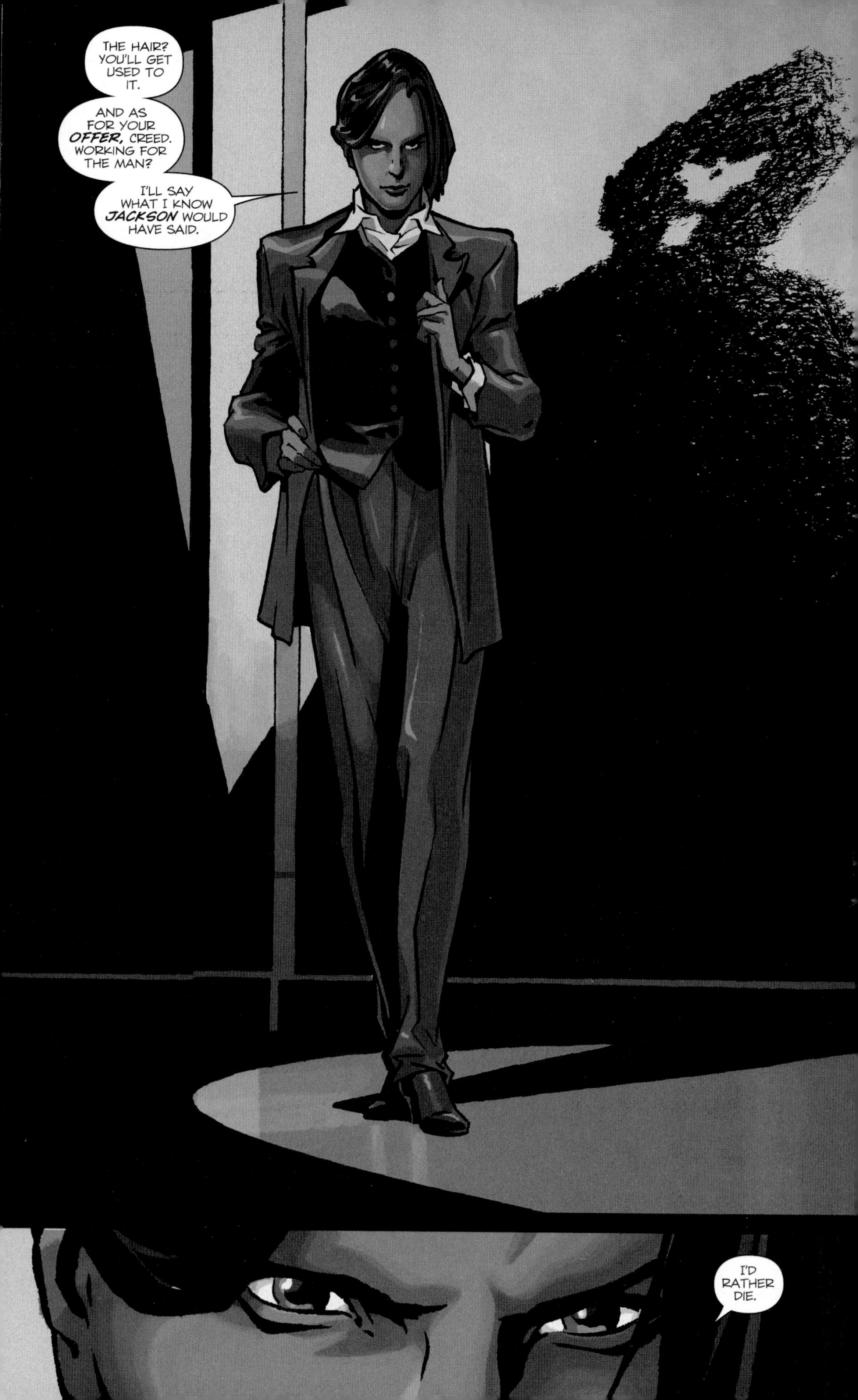
THE HAIR? YOU'LL GET USED TO IT.
AND AS FOR YOUR OFFER, CREED. WORKING FOR THE MAN?
I'LL SAY WHAT I KNOW JACKSON WOULD HAVE SAID.
I'D RATHER DIE.